Dear Reader:

Quilting is a magic art form, one with a long tradition in my family. I remember my grandmother, on winter evenings before the fire, taking pieces of cloth from her scrap bag and carefully cutting them into geometric shapes. As she worked, she would tell stories about the fragments of material, the dress or skirt made of it, who wore it and when. Then there was the "friendship" quilt that belonged to my mother. She would take it down sometimes for me to look at, and talk about her friends who had embroidered their names in the squares of silk, satin, and velvet before she left home to be married. After my own marriage, I heard the tale of how my husband's grandmother met her true love when the "cat on the quilting frame" tradition foretold that he would appear.

Stories and quilts seem to go together. Every quilt stitched over the years represents not only warm covers lovingly constructed, but also bits and pieces of the lives of women.

From this central idea comes *The Quilting Circle,* a collection of stories created around a special quilt and its extraordinary effect on the lives of the four women who are touched by it. I present this collection with great pride and pleasure, and also my warmest wish that its magic may become a small piece of your life.

Happy endings always,

Jennifer Blake

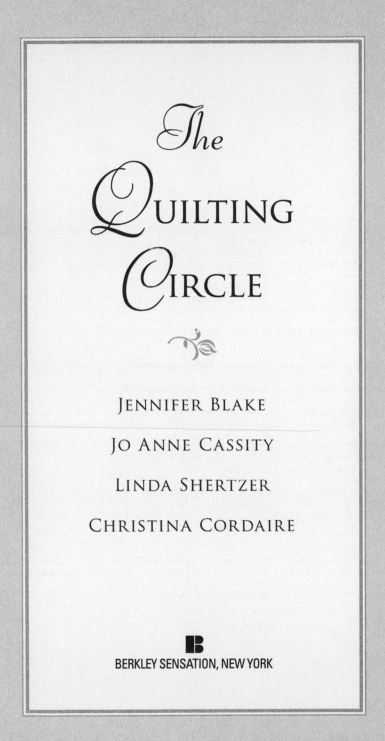

The
Quilting
Circle

Jennifer Blake

Jo Anne Cassity

Linda Shertzer

Christina Cordaire

BERKLEY SENSATION, NEW YORK

THE BERKLEY PUBLISHING GROUP
Published by the Penguin Group
Penguin Group (USA) Inc.
375 Hudson Street, New York, New York 10014, USA
Penguin Group (Canada), 90 Eglinton Avenue East, Suite 700, Toronto, Ontario M4P 2Y3, Canada
(a division of Pearson Penguin Canada Inc.)
Penguin Books Ltd., 80 Strand, London WC2R 0RL, England
Penguin Group Ireland, 25 St. Stephen's Green, Dublin 2, Ireland (a division of Penguin Books Ltd.)
Penguin Group (Australia), 250 Camberwell Road, Camberwell, Victoria 3124, Australia
(a division of Pearson Australia Group Pty. Ltd.)
Penguin Books India Pvt. Ltd., 11 Community Centre, Panchsheel Park, New Delhi—110 017, India
Penguin Group (NZ), 67 Apollo Drive, Rosedale, North Shore 0632, New Zealand
(a division of Pearson New Zealand Ltd.)
Penguin Books (South Africa) (Pty.) Ltd., 24 Sturdee Avenue, Rosebank, Johannesburg 2196,
South Africa

Penguin Books Ltd., Registered Offices: 80 Strand, London WC2R 0RL, England

This is a work of fiction. Names, characters, places, and incidents either are the product of the author's imagination or are used fictitiously, and any resemblance to actual persons, living or dead, business establishments, events, or locales is entirely coincidental. The publisher does not have any control over and does not assume any responsibility for author or third-party websites or their content.

PRINTING HISTORY
Berkley mass market edition / September 1996
Berkley Sensation trade paperback edition / April 2010

Berkley Sensation trade paperback ISBN: 978-0-425-23088-6

PRINTED IN THE UNITED STATES OF AMERICA

10   9   8   7   6   5   4   3   2   1

Contents

Pieces of Dreams

JENNIFER BLAKE

ONE

Amelia Bennington glanced up from her stitching as the steam whistle of the *J. B. Cates* blasted one last time from the landing at the end of Main Street. The steamboat was leaving, finished with the stop for Good Hope on its regular run from New Orleans to St. Louis and beyond. It had made a fairly long halt this evening. There must have been a team of Missouri mules to be loaded, or maybe a passenger to be put off.

None of the other young women sitting around the quilting frame suspended from the ceiling by grass ropes was paying the least attention to the boat. As Melly looked around at her friends in the glow of the lamplight and listened to their low, laughing voices, she felt the sudden rise of emotion. They were all so dear. She wanted to remember this evening for the rest of her life, every last detail: the steamboat's musical warning, the bumbling of moths and gnats about the hot lamp globes, the smell of the fresh-made lemonade served by Aunt

Dora to ward off the late August heat, the scents of thyme and basil and roses wafting from the front garden through the open windows.

Soon it would all change. She would become Caleb's wife, and nothing would ever be the same again.

The waves of her thick, dark hair caught the lamplight as she allowed her gaze to rest on each of the four friends who had been such a large part of her life, the four who would be her bridesmaids. Green-eyed Esther Montgomery, with her strong face softened by incredibly long lashes and her forthright, common-sense views on everything from female suffrage to the best way to make wax posies. Lydia McDougall, tall, auburned-haired, with her tendency toward the dramatic, her warm temper, and her warmer heart. Barbara Zane of the doll-like china-blue eyes and ash-brown curls, known to all as Biddy because she was as petite and aggressive as a bantam chick. And Sarah Franks, Melly's second cousin, statuesque as a goddess, with silvery-blond hair and deep blue eyes, always doing for others, especially her father and three brothers. Of all the friends she had known since childhood, these four were truly special.

It had been a blessing to be near them over the past few years, Melly thought, sharing their problems and heartaches as they had shared hers. Three near spinsters and a widow, they were all over twenty and without husbands, a fact that had made them unusually close.

It was the natural order of things that they would marry, change, grow apart; Melly knew that. She was anxious to be wed, to go with Caleb to the farm he was building for the two of them outside town, of course she was. But at the same time, she could not help feeling a little blue, and even a tiny bit fearful.

Leaving her needle standing upright in the thickness created by two layers of cloth on either side of fluffy cotton batting, she smoothed slender fingers over the silken surface of the quilt top on which they were all working. There was so much love, so many hopes and dreams sewn into it.

The center square was in a starburst design that she herself had pieced over the winter and spring just past. Put together with the scraps left from her wedding gown of pearl-colored Oriental silk, it also incorporated pieces of silk and satin in various shades of blue remaining from the dresses made for her bridesmaids. In the center of the starburst was a Greek cross with four arms of equal length. Across the center Melly had used gold thread and looping Spencerian script to embroider her wedding date: *September 10, 1843*. Her initials had been inscribed in the arm above it, with Caleb's in the one below. The squares set around this focal point, in a star design with a diagonal cross, had been pieced from the silk and satin dress scraps by Melly's Aunt Dora, the woman who had raised her after the steamboat accident that killed her parents. Then each of the four corner squares had been done by a bridesmaid, and featured diagonal bars embroidered with their names and a small sentiment or token of remembrance.

Though they all called it a Friendship Quilt among themselves, it was far more to Melly. Wedding present, housewarming gift, treasured keepsake, it was a shimmering work of art and a lovely reminder of her friends and everything they had meant to each other. More than that, it was a symbol of everything that she would soon become.

Two weeks from this very night, she would walk down the aisle of the church in her gown of rich, flowing silk. Afterward, she would drive away with Caleb. In the house he was building for her with sweat and the toil of loving hands, the two of them would truly become man and wife.

How strange to think that it would be upon her in just a matter of days. The waiting of their three-year engagement had been so long it sometimes seemed it would never end.

"Melly's daydreaming again, girls." Esther Montgomery, seated at the lower right corner of the frame, made the accusation with a quick glance from her soft green eyes. "Just look at her blush. Two guesses what's on her mind!"

"Nothing of the kind!" Melly said in laughing indignation, though she could not help the now even darker flush that invaded the creamy skin of her face.

What would it be like, really, to be a wife? What would she and Caleb say to each other, what would they do, once they were alone together? How would they find their way past the embarrassment of undressing and getting into bed?

Yes, and what precisely would happen then?

Melly thought she had a glimmering from the few comments she had overheard between Aunt Dora and her bosom cronies. It seemed all too likely that this physical union would be awkward. Yet from it would come the mingling of their two souls, hers and Caleb's, as well as the birth of their children. Caleb was a good man, levelheaded, kind, gentle; she would have to trust that his love and her own common sense would see her through the ordeal.

"And why shouldn't she be thinking about it?" Sarah Franks asked with her usual protective instinct. "Caleb Wells is handsome enough to make anybody's heart beat faster."

"As if she would dwell on such a thing!" Biddy, used to making herself heard above the hubbub of a one-room school as a teacher, had no trouble speaking over the other girl's voice. "Melly's more likely contemplating how to decorate her new parlor."

Esther made a disparaging noise, but Melly seized on the suggestion. "That's exactly what I was doing, thinking how nice it would be to display our quilt for visitors to see. I could fold it over a bench—or maybe hang it like a tapestry if I can persuade Caleb to make some kind of support for it."

"If?" Sarah said with lifted brows. "You know Caleb would cut off his arm and hand it to you if he thought you wanted it."

"Oh, Sarah, don't be disgusting," Biddy said.

"Well, he would!"

"Sarah's right," Lydia McDougall joined in with a nod that made her auburn curls dance. "Do you recall the time Caleb took off his coat and laid it across the mud so Melly wouldn't get her new shoes muddy? That was years ago, when she was hardly more than twelve or thirteen."

"I thought that was Conrad," Esther said, referring to the twin brother of Melly's fiancé.

"I'll have to say it sounds the kind of thing Conrad would do," Sarah Franks said with a thoughtful look in her eyes. "He did have a flair about him."

"Still does, I'd say," Esther agreed. "Just look at the way he sent the silk for Melly's wedding dress. Amazing to think that he picked out such lovely stuff in far-off Cathay and sent it all the way across the sea."

"It would have been more to the point if he had brought it himself," Biddy said. "And come to his brother's wedding."

"A sea captain in the China tea trade can't do just what he wants, Biddy," Sarah said in tones of quiet reason.

"Anyway," Lydia said, "I know Caleb gave Melly his piece of apple pie at the last church homecoming because I saw him."

"Yes, and he gave her his hat to use for a fan last Sunday when it was so hot we were all about to swoon."

"I forgot my fan," Melly said. "And Caleb said he didn't care for the apple pie."

Sarah laughed. "Well, that was a bold-faced lie, because I saw your aunt Dora put a piece big enough for two men on his plate not ten minutes before."

"No wonder he was so generous, then!" Lydia's golden brown eyes sparkled as she spoke.

"Anybody who works as hard as Caleb needs a lot of nourishment," Sarah said. "It was still good of him to give up a treat for Melly."

Esther waved her needle in Sarah's direction. "You ask me, he works too hard. He used to be a lot of fun, back before Conrad went off to sea. Now he's turning into a drudge without two words to say for himself."

"Don't you think that's natural?" Melly looked across the quilt with an earnest smile in her dark eyes. "Caleb has a lot on his mind with the farm, the new house, and the responsibilities ahead of him."

"All I'm saying is, you'd think he'd act happier about the whole thing."

Melly had to agree that Caleb had been rather solemn of late. Still, he had always been known as the steadfast, dependable twin; that was his strength. She said, "He's happy in his own way. I'm sure of it. He's just quieter about it than . . . well, than Conrad used to be."

"Who wants cookies with the next round of lemonade?"

That cheerful call came from the doorway leading from the back of the house into the front parlor where they were working. It was Aunt Dora, bustling in with a platter of gingersnaps in one hand and a new pitcher of frothy lemonade in the other. Her gray-streaked blond hair curled in wiry tendrils from the bun on top of her head, and her round face was flushed from the heat of the outdoor kitchen where she had been baking in the relative cool of the evening. She set her burdens down on a side table and wiped her hands on her apron, then began to refill glasses.

"Did I hear somebody mention Conrad? Mercy me, but that boy was a scamp! Enough to give trouble a bad name, he was, but such a charmer that a body really hadn't the heart to scold. I recall the time he put a bucket of water up the apple tree outside my window so Mr. Prine got a regular drenching when he came prowling around on Saturday night. Dampened the man's ardor for a good two weeks!"

Mr. Seymour Prine was a longtime resident at the boardinghouse run by Melly's aunt. He was also a suitor of many years' standing. But as the Widow Bennington had a fierce dislike of the indulgence in strong liquor, while Mr. Seymour got drunk every Saturday night, the pair seemed destined to remain apart. It was a shame, really. Mr. Prine was as quiet and pleasant-spoken a gentleman as anyone could expect from Monday through Friday: neat and clean in his habits, with upright posture and a fine head of silver hair, highly respected as a teller at the bank just down Main Street. But on Saturday night he wended his way to the riverfront saloons. There he had a few, then a few more. By midnight he was back at the boardinghouse outside Aunt Dora's window, where he stood with his hat held over his heart while he spouted stanza after endless stanza of *The Rubáiyát of Omar Khayyám*—with special emphasis on those concerned with wine and amorous dalliance. Aunt Dora was scandalized, or pretended to be.

"Poor Mr. Prine," Sarah said.

"Poor Mr. Prine, my eye!" Aunt Dora set a fist on her ample hip. "The idiotic man just stood there dripping and moaning about drowning his glory in a shallow cup!"

Esther winked at Melly as she joined Sarah in teasing the other woman. "But only think how faithful he's been."

"Yes, and think of how convenient it is that his bed and his ladylove are in the same place."

A wicked smile tilted Esther's wide, mobile mouth. "Dear me, Aunt Dora, you don't mean—"

"I do not," the older woman fumed, her blue eyes snapping,

"which is a fact you know very well, Miss Priss! It will be a cold day in Hades before that whiskey-soaked gallant winds up in my bed. The very idea! I've a good mind to take my gingersnaps straight back to the kitchen."

"No, no, don't do that, dear Aunt Dora," Lydia cried. "You know she didn't mean anything."

"What Lydia is trying to say," Melly interpreted with a laugh, "is that she's starving, as usual. I'm sure everyone will be nice as you please in return for a cookie."

"Well, that's all and good, but it's a man she should be trying to please, along with all the rest of you."

"Like you?" Esther inquired, all innocence as she met the older woman's gaze.

"I had a man once, God rest his soul, and don't need another one."

"Nor I," Biddy said in near inaudible tones.

There was a brief and sympathetic silence. They were all well aware that Biddy's young husband had been struck by lightning as he plowed in the field only months after they were wed. That had been over two years ago, but she still wore black.

Then there was Sarah. Though she never spoke of it, and did not now, she had also lost her man. She and a young carpenter named Theodore Frazier had been engaged a few years back, but Theo had stepped on a nail while repairing a barn and died, agonizingly, of lockjaw. Since then, Sarah had devoted herself to her father and brothers, and to nurturing her roses and herbs and her flock of chickens.

"Yes, well," Aunt Dora said, clearing her throat. "You're all still young and prime for loving, regardless, and there's no reason you shouldn't find it like Melly here." Her eyes took on a sudden brightness. Abruptly she turned and set down her pitcher. "Hold on, now. You've just put me in mind of a way to maybe help things along.

I'll be right back!" Her skirts jerked and swayed as she hustled off in the direction of the kitchen.

The young women looked at each other, mystified and a little wary. Melly pushed her chair back from the quilting frame and rose to fetch the cookie platter. "I don't know what Aunt Dora's up to," she said as she began to pass them around, "but we can't let good gingersnaps go to waste while we find out, now can we?"

She was back in her chair, brushing cookie crumbs from her mouth while leaning carefully away from the quilt top, when her aunt returned. As she saw the kitten in the older woman's arms, her brows lifted. Aunt Dora paid no attention.

"All right, ladies, gather close around the quilt now, and push all the needles through and underneath out of the way," the older woman called with a wave of her free hand. "What we're going to try is a tradition handed down from my grannie, one that maybe came from the old country in years gone by. The saying goes that if you drop a cat onto the quilt frame at a quilting bee, then the girl it runs to will be the next to marry. Yes, and the first man through the door will be her groom."

"But that's not a cat, only one of Vanilla's kittens," Melly protested.

"Looks mighty like a cat to me," Aunt Dora said, holding the mewling kitten up to her face and rubbing noses affectionately. "Besides, a big one like Vanilla might claw the silk, and we can't have that. Now, ladies, are you ready?"

Esther tilted her head. "What if the first man through the door should be Mr. Prine?"

"Then I pity the bride," Aunt Dora said shortly. "Enough sass. Here we go!"

Stepping to the frame on the side opposite Melly, she held the kitten above the center of the half-finished quilt, letting it dangle bonelessly for a few seconds. Then she dropped it.

The small cat landed spraddle-legged, looking startled and annoyed as the quilt bounced and sagged in the middle. Gathering itself with immense dignity, it patted the starburst under it, then took a tentative step.

"Call to it, girls," Aunt Dora directed. "Come on, now. You have to do your part if you want it to be a fair trial."

"Here, kitty, kitty," Sarah said, obliging as always.

"Over here, cat," Esther said, trying not to laugh.

Biddy eyed it askance. "Don't let that creature come near me, or I'll start to sneeze and won't quit till doomsday."

"Sweet little kitty," Lydia crooned with a grin and a competitive glance at the others. "Come here, darling bitty kitty. Over here. Come to Lydia."

The cat sat down and started to lick a paw.

A gust of giggles and half-smothered jeers greeted the performance. Melly looked toward her aunt, humor flashing bright in the black-eyed-Susan brown of her eyes. She made no effort to coax the kitten herself, of course, since she knew perfectly well when she would be married, and to whom. "Now what?"

"Call it again," Aunt Dora urged the others as she placed her fists on her hips. Her frown was earnest, as if she actually expected the kitten to reveal the future happiness of at least one of their number.

They did as suggested, except for Biddy, who made shooing motions in the direction of the others with her small hands. The kitten looked up from its ablutions and pricked its ears, but made no move to leave its seat.

"Oh, dear," Lydia moaned in mock dismay. "Does this mean we're all hopeless?"

"Don't be ridiculous," Melly said bracingly. "It's my belief you're all trying to avoid your fate. Call him as if you mean it!"

At the sound of Melly's voice, the kitten blinked and turned its head in her direction. Then, as if executing a tiresome duty, the small animal rose and glided into a dainty walk, picking its way over silk and satin and the gold featherstitching that outlined the connecting seams of the squares. At once, the bridesmaids renewed their giggling, cajoling efforts.

The kitten paid no attention. It did not hesitate, but made its way straight to Melly. Dropping into a crouch in front of her, it launched into a graceful leap. As she caught it in her arms, it climbed up to snuggle into the tender curve of her neck. Immediately it began to purr.

"Hey! No fair!" Lydia cried.

Biddy made a sound of mild disgust. "What can you expect? The silly thing belongs to Melly, after all."

"She is definitely going to be married, you'll have to give the cat that much," Sarah pointed out on a throaty chuckle.

At that moment, the front door swung open. The young women turned as one to see who had arrived. Their lively chatter died away into sudden, breathless silence.

The man who stepped into the room was tall and broad and bronzed, with hair so bleached by the sun that it had the color and sheen of spun gold. Standing relaxed and foursquare in the doorway, he appeared as sure of his welcome as a conquering Caesar. As he saw the women staring at him, his blue eyes took on a brilliant sheen of merriment while a slow grin curved his mouth.

"Caleb!" Melly cried. Driven by amazement over the opportune arrival, she lowered the kitten to the quilt, pushed back her chair, and sprang up. Then, laughing, she ran to fling herself into her fiancé's arms.

A soft grunt of surprise left him as he caught her against his chest. An instant later, his blue gaze turned smoky with the rise of desire. His firm lips parted for a quiet oath, then he lowered his head and touched his mouth to hers.

It was like stepping into a whirlwind, a spinning fury of the senses. Melly's lips tingled, heating with the contact. Her heart seemed to stop. She felt buffeted, storm-tossed, lost in a delirium of sheer, pulsating magic. Dimly she was aware of the parlor, her aunt, her friends, but they did not seem to matter. All that had being or reason was the warm, hard arms around her and the sweet, tender taste of the man who held her so close to his heart.

"Melly!"

That voice. Her name, resounding in heavy syllables that held accusation, disbelief, disapproval. And pain.

It was the last that reached her. The pain.

She pushed free, stepped back, though she had to hold to the arms of the man she had just greeted for balance. Turning her head slowly, she stared at the person who had called to her, the man who now moved from behind the first to enter and then stopped at his side.

It was like seeing double. There were two of them, two men of devastating power and appearance, two men dangerously alike.

And the second, the latecomer, was Caleb, her future husband.

Melly's heart sank, shivering inside her, as she saw what she had done. The first man through the door had been Conrad. The second had called her name.

She had kissed the wrong brother.

Two

"I'm sorry," Conrad said in husky tones as he gazed down at Melly. "I-I didn't mean, that is, I just—" He stopped and took a deep breath to prevent himself from stammering like a schoolboy. "It was the surprise."

The apology was a sham, and Conrad knew it. He had taken shameless advantage, though he didn't regret it for a minute. He wasn't a man to turn down a taste of heaven when it came his way.

And it had been heavenly. He would never forget the intoxicating taste of Melly's lips, that fresh and tender assault on his senses. Not if he lived to be a hundred.

He hadn't seen it coming—how could he have? For a single instant he had thought it was just plain surprise that caused him to react with such stunning intensity. But that wasn't it at all.

Melly, that was what had shook him, left him wanting more. Melly herself—the rich welcome and joy in her eyes as she came toward him, the entrancing shape of her face, the slender curves of her body pressing against his in a fit so right, so perfect, it was as if he had been born to hold her. She had stolen his breath and his common sense, knocked his notions of proper behavior for a loop. For a single instant she had made him forget who she was, who he was—had made him forget that he was not his brother.

He had kissed Melly, his twin's promised wife. God, how stupid could he be?

Caleb, he saw, was mad as hell, and who could blame him? If Melly belonged to him and he had seen Caleb kissing her, he would be ready to wear the mark of Cain right square in the middle of his forehead.

That was, of course, one of the major curses of being a twin. It was too easy to put himself in his brother's place. Far too easy.

"Come in here, you rapscallion!" Aunt Dora cried, stepping forward to envelop him in a quick, well-padded hug. "Have a seat, both you boys. Have a cookie while I bring two more glasses. Mercy above, Conrad, if it's not just like you to drop in out of the blue!"

"Not quite," he offered with a grin. "I only stepped off the steamer like anybody else."

"Which is still enough to give a body heart palpitations when we thought you were on the other side of the world. You might have let us know you were coming! Though I expect we should have guessed you'd not let Caleb marry without you."

"So you should have," he said promptly, his gaze bright.

"Cheeky as always, Conrad. But maybe we should be calling you *Captain* Conrad now?"

He shook his head and tried to look doleful. "Not when you'll probably have me swabbing the deck before the night's done."

"When did I ever do such a thing?" Aunt Dora demanded, setting her fists on her hips in mock irritation.

"Often!"

The older woman laughed. "Maybe so, but I'll let you off

tonight, seeing as how you're the prodigal. But mind you, I make no promises about tomorrow."

Conrad was grateful for the teasing welcome masked as scolding. It was exactly what was needed to ease the strained atmosphere and return things to normal. More than that, it made him feel as if he had come home.

As the older woman trundled off in the direction of the kitchen, Melly reached to take Caleb's hand and give him a swift peck on the cheek that made his stodgy brother blush scarlet. Falling back on her role as hostess then, she directed Caleb to draw up the single chair that sat against the near wall. As that was being done, she turned back to Conrad.

"You remember everyone, don't you?" she said with careful politeness. "That's Lydia there on the end, of course. Her father owns McDougall's Mercantile. And my cousin Sarah, seated there next to her?"

He smiled, responding easily to the greetings as Melly continued quickly around the sewing circle. He was glad of the reminders. The ladies had changed out of all recognition since he'd left Good Hope. Except for Melly.

The introductions done, Melly resumed her seat and drew Caleb down next to her. Conrad, left to fend for himself, dragged a chair closer to the group of females, though not quite near enough to be a part of it. That was always the way it had been for him, or so it seemed—outside the charmed circle.

"Well, I have to say Melly's mistake seems perfectly natural to me," tall, blond Sarah Franks declared as she looked with raised brows from him to his brother. "I think I might have trouble telling the two of them apart if we met on the street tomorrow."

"Maybe," tall, auburn-haired Lydia McDougall said with a sly and laughing glance at her friend, "but Melly never kisses Caleb hello like that."

Now that was interesting, Conrad thought, his gaze on Mel-ly's flaming face. Why? he wondered. No cooperation? But the answer ceased to matter as he caught the fleeting glance she flung in his direction. That look reproached him, castigated him for his presumption—and sent a shaft of pure yearning winging through him.

"Yes, and maybe it's just that we've never seen her do it," Esther Montgomery said.

Conrad didn't care for that idea, didn't care for it at all.

"She used to be able to tell Caleb and Conrad apart with a single glance, the one person in the whole town who could," the little one, Biddy, commented. "Seems she had better start practic-ing that trick again."

They were all looking at him and his brother now. Conrad shifted uncomfortably, feeling the tips of his ears grow hot. At the same time, he knew that Biddy was right. Melly had usually been able to recognize him on sight back in the old days. He could fool her sometimes, if he tried hard enough, but not often.

Aunt Dora came scurrying in again. Taking charge without effort, she steered the conversation into safer channels, demanding to know where he had been and all the things he had done in the long years he had been gone. Conrad obliged with a version that was considerably more colorful than the reality in some cases, con-siderably less in others. Mustn't disappoint the ladies, he knew, but heaven forbid that he should shock them.

Even as he spoke, however, his mind was busy elsewhere. Melly had been—what?—all of thirteen when he left? He remembered her as a princess in pigtails, one of those girls who never seemed to go through an awkward stage. Smart, sweet, tenderhearted, though she had her temper, maybe from being a little spoiled after what she'd gone through in the steamboat explosion, being thrown into the water and half drowned, losing her parents. She had ruled the play yard with a high hand, ordering all the boys around like so many hired hands. He had not been among them, of course, being nearly ten years older, but he had enjoyed watching her antics and always felt a warm spot for her in his heart.

All the signs had pointed toward Melly being a beauty one day, but he hadn't been able to stick around to see it. The sea had called to him—or so he had thought. Mostly he had just needed to get away from his old man and Good Hope, Missouri, to see the world, be on his own, make something of himself.

Conrad hadn't gotten along with his father at all. His greatest failing, he sometimes thought, was that he wasn't Caleb. Caleb had been the good twin, a fine son, steady, hardworking, obedient, good with animals, especially horses. In short, he had been everything that Conrad was not.

Conrad had cordially disliked anything that ate grain back then, still did if the truth were known. Since his father owned a livery stable and acted as the town blacksmith, that had been the ultimate sin.

The old man had expected his sons, both of them, to follow in his footsteps. Caleb had seemed content for it to be so; Conrad couldn't stomach it. The punishment for that rebellion had been unremitting. He had escaped it finally by stowing away on a river steamer heading down to New Orleans. There he had found a ship that agreed to take him on as a seaman.

And the sea had embraced him with its siren arms and treated him well. He had learned a lot about himself from it, had grown up with it. Over the years, the roving, deep-sea life had taken a strong hold on him, one almost impossible to break, even for a visit home.

He had managed to pull away this time because he felt the tug of something stronger, some need he didn't fully understand but had been forced to heed.

It had begun when news of Caleb's engagement to Melly had reached him, by means of a water-stained letter left waiting in a letter box in a distant port until he picked it up. Not long afterward, he had come across the bolt of pearl-colored silk in a tiny shop in Hong Kong. He had held the heavy, fluid material in his hands, captivated by its smooth texture. In that instant, he had seen Melly's face, seen her with his twin who had looked so much like himself, might even have been himself. The silk had been bought and shipped as a wedding present, but the damage had been done.

Nights without end, he had stayed awake in his bunk, thinking of Good Hope, of the simple life in the little river town, of Caleb and Melly and all the good, decent people he had known as he was growing up. Mr. McDougall at the mercantile who handed out licorice whips when he wasn't drinking. The fire-and-brimstone preacher who harried his flock like a sheepdog, keeping the strays in line. Gandy Jack, down at the riverfront saloon just across from the livery, who used to give him two bits now and then for sweeping out the place. And especially Melly's Aunt Dora, who, with no children of her own, had taken pleasure in feeding half-grown boys who were always starving.

His restlessness had ended when he'd decided to start homeward. His ship, the *Queen of the Sea,* had needed to go into dry dock to have the barnacles scraped off her bottom anyway; a ship needed to be clean to compete in the China trade, where every ounce of extra weight meant slower time and therefore less money for the captain. He had left his ship in Baltimore while he continued on to Good Hope by steamer.

Now he was here, and Melly had kissed him. Funny, but it had not seemed like a mistake. Rather, it had felt like a homecoming.

Melly could not stop staring at Conrad. He looked so familiar: the broad forehead and thick, gold-dusted brows, the straight line of his nose, the rugged planes of his face. She knew precisely the way his hair grew in a wheat-straw whorl of a cowlick on the back of his head, and the angle where the strong column of his neck merged with his wide shoulders. He was so very like Caleb.

Yet he was also different. His eyes were a more brilliant blue, his hair bleached a shade lighter by an equatorial sun; his skin carried a darker golden-oak glaze. The way his firm lips shifted into a smile was not the same, nor were the lines that bracketed his eyes. He had seen more, done more, felt more, and the experiences had etched themselves into his features in ways that baffled and intrigued her.

Caleb's fingers tightened on Melly's hand where he still held it. She glanced at him and saw what appeared to be a warning in his eyes. She gave him a reassuring smile. An instant later, her gaze dropped to his mouth, and she remembered the kiss he had given her two evenings ago as he said good night. It had been brief, circumspect, pleasant. The contours of his mouth had been smooth and gentle. But her heart had not tripped into a hammer beat, her head had not spun, or her body shivered as if with fever.

"What's this?"

It was Conrad who spoke from the other side of the quilt, leaning toward one corner where Lydia had been making arabesques of stitching around the square she had inscribed. With a long, brown finger, he touched the small motif embroidered there.

"It's a ship, of course!" Lydia answered with mock indignation. "Can't you tell?"

"Indeed I can, but it seems a bit unusual." His smiling glance held inquiry.

Lydia gave a small shrug, even as she sent a quick look at Melly. "It's to remember the times when Melly and I used to fancy ourselves taking a steamer down the Mississippi to New Orleans, then sailing away, maybe living in places with strange, foreign names like Tahiti."

"I've been there," he said softly.

"Oh, I know—we both knew, because you wrote about it to Caleb. Which is what brought it on, I expect." Lydia's lips curved in a faint, disconsolate smile. "It was just silly make-believe to pass the time. Of course we outgrew it."

"Too bad," he said, and looked straight at Melly.

She wanted to look away, to deny that she had ever thought of him while he was gone, that she had ever indulged in make-believe.

It was impossible.

She wasn't quite that good at pretending.

THREE

The trees that shaded Good Hope's Main Street made islands of coolness on either side of its arrow-straight length, stretching from the church at one end to the riverboat landing at the other. Great oaks and elms, they had been left standing when the town was laid out soon after being established by French trappers and traders. The searing heat of the last two days had made their leaves droop, sucking the moisture from them so they rustled in the warm wind.

It was not a particularly good evening for a box social at the church. But that didn't matter much, since it was also too hot for anything else.

The basket Melly carried was heavy. A large part of the weight was Aunt Dora's fault; she had kept offering additions, such as a jar of pickled peaches to go with the pound cake and yeast rolls that accompanied Melly's fried chicken and potato salad. But Melly had added things as well, as if she intended to feed two men instead of one.

The very idea was silly beyond words, of course. Conrad was perfectly capable of finding another young woman to feed him. In any case, she wasn't sure her future husband would be there tonight, much less his brother.

Across the street, Biddy and Lydia emerged from the mercantile and started toward the church. They waved and called, then began to pick their way across the dusty street to join her. Like her, each had a basket on her arm. Lydia's, done in bronze straw, was a nice match for the flamboyance of her iridescent bronze-green twill. Biddy's basket, like her widow's clothing, was perfectly simple, being of woven white oak covered by a black-and-white-checked cloth.

"Your mother and father aren't coming?" Melly said to Lydia as the two women gained the sidewalk.

"Mother will be along as soon as she decides what to wear. Daddy isn't feeling well this evening, so he won't be able to make it."

Melly made sympathetic noises, though she was not at all surprised. It was understood that any excuse of ill health on the part of Mr. McDougall was to be taken as an indication that he had been drinking. As for Lydia's mother, that fading, dithery lady was always late, being congenitally unable to make up her mind until the last possible second. Though the polite fiction was that the older couple ran the mercantile store that bore the McDougall name, it was Lydia who kept the place going.

"Where's Caleb?" Biddy asked, glancing toward the boarding-house then back down the street behind them in the direction of the livery stable.

"I'm not too sure he's going to make it, either," Melly said with a wry grimace.

"I thought I saw him heading out early this morning in a wagon."

Melly nodded. "He drove out to the Bedgood estate sale. He said he might run late, especially if they parcel out the house furnishings before they get to the tools and animals."

"You should have gone with him," Lydia put in from Melly's other side.

"I did suggest it," Melly answered with an unhappy shrug. "But Caleb thought it might cause talk if we were caught on the road together after dark."

"Yes, I suppose," Lydia answered.

Biddy did not look convinced, nor was Melly herself. It was sweet of Caleb to be concerned for her good name, but she would have enjoyed the outing, not to mention the opportunity to find things she would need to set up housekeeping.

It might also have been more flattering if her bridegroom had been less insistent on avoiding gossip. He was supposed to be anxious to be alone with her, wasn't he?

No, she told herself, she must not think that way. It was not that Caleb did not want her with him. He just always knew the right thing to do and did it no matter the cost to himself.

Melly gazed down the street toward the river. She could see the front of the livery stable at its end, near the landing, with the house just this side of it where Caleb and Conrad had been brought up. There was no sign of Caleb's wagon, no movement anywhere in the vicinity if you didn't count the hound scratching its fleas near the stable door.

Nor was there any sign of Conrad.

On the other side of the street, a couple of men sat shooting the bull, balancing on straight chairs that were rocked back against the wall of the steamboat office. Just back this way, the milliner, Miss Tate, was pulling down the blinds on the front windows of her shop next door to the mercantile. Farther along, past the turning for Hickory Street, the elderly doctor came out of the frame building that served as his office, hospital, and home. He waited until his wife joined him, then escorted her in the direction of the church with a hand in the middle of her wide back. As the two passed, they called a pleasant good evening across the street.

The three young women returned the greeting, then turned by common consent and followed along after the older couple.

The church that marked the opposite end of Main Street was of white clapboard with windows of stained glass and a steeple surmounted by a lightning rod. The young bachelor preacher, who had taken the place of their previous pastor back in the spring, stood greeting his parishioners on the steps. He could not be considered particularly handsome, having craggy features and the stooped shoulders of a scholar, but was so kind and possessed such dry, self-deprecating humor that he was universally well liked. Some of the congregation would have preferred more fire and brimstone in his sermons, but Melly enjoyed his erudite expositions on good and evil followed by polite benedictions.

As they paused near the steps to allow elderly Mrs. Pollack, who had a crooked back, to mount slowly ahead of them, Lydia leaned to whisper, "Did you know Esther has been walking out with the reverend?"

Melly gave a quick nod. "I saw them strolling along the river levee last Sunday afternoon. Isn't it lovely?"

"Oh, do you think so?"

"Don't you? It was what I was hoping for when she started teaching Sunday school after her mother died. She would make a grand pastor's wife."

"Well, she adores children," Biddy said, frowning, "but don't you think she's had enough drabness in her life?"

Melly bit the inside of her bottom lip as she considered that point. It was true that Esther had never had much fun. Her father had stepped out for a mug of beer when she was a child and had never come back. Her mother had taken to her bed, becoming an invalid. Esther had cared for the older woman for years while her youth slipped away.

"Yes, but Esther is firm in her faith," Melly said. "She's really a good person, much better than I am."

"Oh, don't say that!" Lydia exclaimed. "We all know you're as good as gold."

"No, I'm only saying I don't believe it would be a sacrifice for her to marry the Reverend Milken if she loved him."

"But she might marry him just to have somebody—or else to keep from hurting his feelings," Biddy said with a shake of her head.

Melly saw what she meant. Neither the need for companionship nor compassion seemed likely to lead to a happy wedded life. It seemed some stronger emotion was necessary to make marriage worth the risk, some greater heat required to fuse a lasting union.

"Ladies," the Reverend Milken said politely as they climbed the steps. "I see Miss Esther and Miss Sarah aren't with you. I trust they will be along presently?"

"Oh, I'm sure of it," Melly said, carefully avoiding looking at Lydia or Biddy. "You needn't worry."

"I wasn't worried; it's only that the five of you have been so much together of late that I never see one with out looking around for the others."

Melly felt her lips twitch as she suppressed a smile over the reverend's grave demeanor. "Indeed we have, with all the preparations for the wedding." She leaned a little closer, adding in low tones, "But if you'd like a little time alone with Esther, you might remember her basket has an apple-green bow."

"Does it truly?" he murmured with a twinkle in his eyes. "I'll bear that in mind."

Melly and the others moved on into the church, where they

were joined shortly by Esther and Sarah, carrying baskets. The five of them circled the church's meeting room, with its gay paper decorations and its table piled high with baskets, exchanging greetings and stopping now and then to talk. There were any number of questions about Caleb's whereabouts, of course; everyone had watched their courtship and was looking forward to attending their wedding. Unwilling to keep constantly explaining and making excuses, Melly only smiled and said she expected him to be along eventually.

Conrad's activities in the last day or two were also a subject of interest; somehow they all seemed to think Melly must know the latest. Actually she had barely seen him, and was happy to learn of his various visits to old friends and neighbors.

The purpose of the box social was to bring in the money for new hymnals. The baskets brought by the unmarried ladies would be put up for bids. The gentleman who was top bidder for each would be privileged to eat its contents, in company with the lady who had prepared them. It would be a blind auction; no names would be announced. A large part of the fun was watching the shenanigans as some of the young men tried to gain inside information about the offerings of the prettiest belles. The ladies, of course, were not above swapping baskets and trims with their friends to add to the confusion.

Melly had not bothered with such elaborate precautions. The unattached men in town, she figured, would most likely leave her basket for Caleb's bid out of common courtesy. If he did not appear in time, she would simply take her chances, as it was for a good cause.

The oldest of the deacons, a bent fellow with a white beard that hung halfway down his chest, wielded the auction hammer. Melly and the other girls smiled at their excitement as they waited to see what their fate would be.

Esther's basket was among the first to be presented. She turned pink with pleasure as the reverend placed the winning bid. There was much good-natured kidding from all sides, which he and Esther took in good part, as he picked up his prize and came to claim his lady.

Biddy's basket went next, claimed by the bashful young giant who worked as printer's devil at the newspaper office. She seemed pleased enough as she went off with him.

Mr. Seymour Prine, to no one's surprise, carried off Aunt Dora's basket and meekly presented himself to his vexed partner. A few moments later, Sarah's basket was bought by Sheriff Telford, a tall, dark-haired man with wide shoulders and a swagger in his walk.

One by one, then, the baskets of the young unmarried women vanished from the table where they were on display. There were still several left, however, Lydia's among them, when Melly's basket was brought forward.

She looked around one last time for Caleb, but there was no sign of him. Nor had Conrad put in an appearance. From the advantage of her greater height, Lydia peered over the crowd as well, then grimaced and shrugged. Melly gave a resigned sigh.

The elderly deacon made a show of staggering about with her basket, joking about its weight. Melly flushed, but joined in the general laughter. Bids were slow in getting started, however, as people glanced around for some sign of her intended. Finally the sheriff's deputy, Leamon Stotts, a nervous, gangling man with a thatch of red hair and only a vague acquaintance with soap and water, yelled out, "Five dollars!"

Lydia giggled behind her hand. Melly gave her a quelling look in spite of her dismay.

"A hundred dollars!"

That firm call came from the back of the room. A murmur spread around the crowd. Five dollars was a fair sum for a basket, ten was generous indeed, and twenty was wildly extravagant. People craned their necks to see who was crazy enough to throw away so much hard-earned gold on a supper.

The deacon also squinted in the direction of the bidder. Abruptly he gave a crack of laughter and brought his hammer down with a solid thump. "Sold!"

"Oh, it was Caleb!" Lydia said, standing on tiptoe to catch sight of the winner. "What a sneak, hiding away like that to make you think he wasn't coming. You'll have to make him pay for that."

"I think he already has," Melly said dryly as she began to move forward.

She saw his golden head as he threaded through the crowd to collect his prize. He moved with such confidence, exchanging greetings, shaking the offered hand here and there, fending off the comments that came his way with laughing ease. An odd feeling shivered down the back of her neck. She slowed her footsteps as suspicion brushed her.

A hundred dollars. And Caleb had been hoarding every penny to buy farm equipment and livestock.

Then he was stepping up, taking her basket, pretending to need both hands to heft it. He exchanged another quip or two with the men gathered around before turning in her direction. His stride was free, his gaze a bright, rich blue, his smile brilliant as he gazed into her eyes.

"Well, love," he said as he stopped before her and offered his arm, "and where shall we go to enjoy our feast?"

Conrad.

She had not the smallest doubt. It was not Caleb, but his brother. Why was he pretending?

She opened her mouth to accuse him, then closed it. It was possible Caleb had sent him. It could also be, she mused, that he meant to save her face, to prevent people from knowing that his brother had failed her. Or it could be that he felt sorry for her and thought she might prefer sharing her basket with him than with Leamon Stotts. In the last, at least, he was perfectly right.

But if he was trying to fool her, then he deserved to have the tables turned on him. Didn't he?

FOUR

The town park was a tree-shaded space sweeping in a wide apron from the cemetery behind the church to the river. At its center was a pavilion where the local brass band played on Sunday afternoons. Radiating from this central point were walks set with rustic benches. During the long days of summer, the older men gathered in the park to play checkers and pitch horseshoes. Elderly matrons came to crochet and gossip, while young mothers spread picnics under the trees and watched their babies nap as older children bowled hoops or used the fallen acorn shells as cups for tea parties.

For the box social, a long line of tables knocked together from scrap lumber had been set up behind the church. It was there that the married ladies spread the food they had brought in their baskets. Most of the unmarried couples joined them, for the sake of both convenience and propriety.

Caleb would have headed at once for those long, crowded tables, with their chattering and neighborly congregation of folks. Conrad had other ideas.

Melly gave him a quick glance of surprise as he led her off down the path of packed sand that wended deeper into the park, but raised no objection. So far, so good, he thought.

Or was it? Could it be his brother was not always as circumspect as might have been expected? Conrad frowned as he considered that possibility.

The sun had set, and the blue twilight of evening was deepening, the shadows under the trees growing thicker. Faint smells of dust and smoke and food drifted on the air, along with a hint of dankness from the river. The sounds of voices and laughter faded behind them as they strolled.

"So," Melly said, releasing his arm and snatching a leaf from a tree branch hanging low over the trail. "Did you have a profitable trip?"

"Trip?"

The smile that she slanted him had a vivid gleam. "To the estate sale, of course. Did you find what you wanted?"

Conrad thought quickly of how a fiancé might answer. "One or two things. It would have been much better if you could have come with me."

"Oh?" She gave him a wide-eyed look as she shredded her leaf, dropping the pieces.

"You might have found something for the house—besides which, it would have been a pleasant outing for the two of us. But I suppose you had other things to do, cooking and so forth."

"If the sale had run late, we might have been caught on the road by darkness."

He gave her a long, slow smile as he reached to take her hand. "Would that have been so bad?"

"I—possibly not," she said in low tones as she veiled her gaze with her thick, dark lashes, "but only think what people would have said."

"Why should I do that," he said, his own voice husky, "when it makes not a particle of difference?"

He could have sworn her fingers trembled in his for an instant. Could she be as affected as he was by the mental picture of what might have taken place between them during the homeward drive in the dark? He hoped not, since he was supposed to be Caleb.

Abruptly she snatched her hand away. "Caleb Wells! What has come over you?"

"You," he said, allowing the warmth inside him to surface as he smiled down at her. "Is that so strange?"

"Downright astonishing, I would say."

Her stringent tone made him think he might have overplayed his hand—or rather Caleb's. A wry smile curved his mouth as he attempted to bottle his ardor. "It's been a long engagement, love."

"Yes," she agreed. "But it was you who refused to think of marriage until you had bought and paid for land and could build a proper home."

"Did I say that? I must have been an idiot."

She gave him another slanting glance. "I'll admit I thought so. Even if you didn't want to live with your father, Aunt Dora would have loved having you around. Of course, I understand that you want to be able to provide for me, but we could have been together so much sooner."

He reached for her hand again and tightened his grip to draw her closer against his side. "Has the waiting been so bad, then? As terrible as for me?"

"You—you've found it hard?" she said with a slight catch in her voice as the curve of her breast brushed his arm.

St. Elmo's fire seemed to dance along his body every time she touched him. His voice tight, he said, "You've no idea."

She pressed more fully against him and rested her head an instant against his shoulder as she spoke in a low, sultry murmur.

"It won't be long now until the wedding. We will be together then—alone in the dark."

"Melly—" The single word was strangled as forbidden images sprang full blown into his mind.

Melly with her hair down, swirling around her in a silken curtain as she came toward him where he waited in the bed. The look of love and sweet anticipation in her face as he drew her nightgown away to reveal lovely, tender curves. The moment when their bodies were joined, and she was his inescapably, eternally.

Not his. Never his.

Caleb's. His brother's bride. Conrad dragged air into his cramped, aching lungs.

"Caleb?"

She was on to him. He knew it with sudden and positive instinct.

Or was it the faint quiver of laughter he felt where her chest still pressed his arm? The hint of diabolical teasing that laced her use of his brother's name? Or maybe just the simple fact that he recalled, belatedly, how Melly had once been able to tell him and his brother apart when no one else could manage it?

The witch. The conniving, enticing little witch!

"Darling," he whispered as he leaned over to set the heavy basket on the path. Straightening again, he snaked a hard arm around her narrow waist. With smooth and easy strength, he swung her into the shadows under the low-hanging limbs of an ancient oak and pressed her back to its trunk.

"Caleb!" she gasped as he moved in so close her swinging skirts piled against his booted feet.

He chuckled deep in his throat as he cupped her face in his free hand. "My sweetest love, why should we torture ourselves? There's no need at all to wait. . . ."

On the last word, he lowered his head and took her mouth in

a searing kiss. At the same time, he trailed his fingers down the curve of her neck and over her collarbone to cup the gentle globe of her breast.

For an endless, aching moment, Melly was completely still, stunned into immobility by the onslaught of sensations that whipped through her at gale force. A rippling of purest pleasure ran along her nerves, tightening them as it went. She had the insane need to cling forever to the man who held her. Then his tongue touched hers, retreated, plunged boldly deeper.

Caleb had never done such a thing, not in quite that way. She had never felt this warm presentiment of what physical union might be like, never known such an abrupt and reckless rush of her entire being toward heated fulfillment. She wanted to feel the power of his male strength against her, inside her. She needed to have him teach her the power and mystery of love between a man and woman so she would not fear it.

Want. Need. Such foreign words to her. Until this moment.

She stiffened on a sharp gasp. Spreading the fingers of her hands, which were trapped between them, she shoved him away, dragged her mouth free. She shuddered, then breathed deep once, twice. Her voice low and not quite steady, she said, "Conrad Wells, what do you think you're doing?"

He laughed, a rich yet strained sound that she felt in his chest against the palms of her hands as he caught and held them against him. "Playing along. Isn't that what you wanted?"

"No! I never expected—" She stopped and drew a quick breath before she brought out the thought upper-most in her mind. "Your brother would never have tried such a thing!"

"Wouldn't he? Poor Caleb. Or maybe I should say poor Melly."

Anger boiled up inside her in a red-hot tide. Without conscious thought, she jerked loose and lashed at him with the flat of her hand.

The slap never landed. He caught her wrist and forced it down. And the humor disappeared from his face as if it had never been there. He stared at her while a muscle corded in his jaw and the blue of his eyes went dark as night there in the gathering shadows.

Her fingers turned numb from his grip. She could feel his anger, and something more, beating around her like storm waves. She lifted her chin and tightened the corners of her mouth to prevent them from quivering.

His gold-tipped lashes flickered. All expression was wiped from his face. Opening his fingers in abrupt, complete release, he stepped back, well away from her. "I apologize—something that looks fair to becoming a habit. I meant only to pay you back for stringing me along. I may have gone too far."

"Indeed you did," she said, dropping her gaze to her wrist as she rubbed it to restore the circulation. The blame was not all his, however, and she knew it. "I suppose I shouldn't have led you down the garden path—or the park path, in this case."

He tipped his head. "Here I was, thinking I was the one doing the leading."

A brief smile touched her lips. "You were so sure you had me fooled. I wanted to discover just how far . . . that is . . ." She trailed off as she realized where the thought was leading her.

"Unfortunately you found out that I'm not so noble as Caleb. My impulses sometimes lead me to do things I regret; I'm not called the wicked twin for nothing. But if I promise it won't happen again, will you still let me share your supper?"

The quiet words were a release. She breathed easier as the tension between them faded. "Certainly. I-I expect Caleb asked you to see after me if he didn't make it back. It was kind of you to go to the trouble."

He was quiet so long that she looked up to search his still features.

"Yes, it was all Caleb's idea," he said in a rush. "Shall we see what goodies my good brother missed out on in that two-ton basket of yours?"

Melly pushed away from the tree, and Conrad stepped back to allow her to regain the path. But he did not offer his arm, did not touch her in any way. As she passed him, she glanced once at his set face. And she was suddenly certain that his brother had played no part whatever in Conrad's showing up this evening.

As Melly brushed past him, Conrad caught her warm, sweet scent. It was astonishingly familiar beneath the overriding soap-cleanliness, starch, and sunshine. Involuntarily a crooked smile touched his lips, and he inhaled deeper.

He felt the tenuous rein he held on his more base inclinations slipping, and he closed his right hand slowly into a fist, cursing silently as he sought control. God, but he was an idiot.

Regardless, he did not turn back toward the church and its crowd. He knew he should, for Caleb's sake as well as Melly's—not to mention his own. But it was a sacrifice he meant to avoid unless the lady insisted.

She didn't. As he picked up the basket and turned in the direction of the band pavilion, she followed. She seemed to be almost unaware of their direction as she walked beside him, kicking her skirts away from her feet in moody and pensive silence.

To ensure her continued distraction, he said after a moment, "I'm sure Caleb will be sorry he missed the social."

"I suppose." She sent him a brief glance, then looked away again.

"He's working like a demon, trying to have everything finished in time for the wedding."

"Yes, I know."

"Everything has to be perfect—the house, the sheds, the barn. He's been trying to get his crop in so he won't have to worry with it.

I think he's happy to have me around now, because I'm another pair of hands to help."

"Which is not exactly what you expected to be doing while you were at home, I would imagine," she suggested.

He shrugged. "Frankly, it's not what I expected from Caleb either. I never thought he'd make a farmer."

"You thought he'd wind up a blacksmith? He didn't care for it much more than you; he was just less outspoken about it."

"More diplomatic, you mean? I have to say, the old man seems to have taken it well enough."

"You broke the trail for Caleb, I think. Your father didn't want to lose him the way he lost you. He—cares about you, you know, and worries when you're so far away."

Against his will, Conrad was touched by her attempt to mediate the old rift between father and son. He said quietly, "It can't be helped. As for how he feels, well, distance and time, not to mention a little more maturity on my part, has shed a little light. We've actually managed to say a few words without fighting since I've been back."

"I'm glad." As they reached the pavilion, she turned toward the wide steps, indicating that she would set out the food there. She settled onto the top step in a sighing of skirts and reached for the basket as she went on. "Tell me about the places you've been, the things you've seen."

Her suggestion was a bit more than just polite conversation, he thought. Something in it reminded him of his old yearning after things new and different. Recalling what Lydia had said of her and Melly's urges to roam, he said, "There was some mention of Tahiti the other night. I was thinking about the islands this evening when the sun was going down."

"About going back, you mean?"

He shook his head. "The ways the sun sets there, actually. It's huge and turns blood red as it drops into the sea. Then it washes the whole world with paintbox colors: vermilion and orange, rose madder and pink and gold. The ship's deck and rails, the sails above you, the water—everything is so drenched with color it almost hurts your eyes. You can't look away, don't even want to move because you're afraid you'll make it fade. I don't know how to tell you—it's almost as if the sun sets inside you, warming and coloring your heart."

"Oh, Conrad," she said with a catch in her voice as she sat with a napkin-wrapped chicken breast forgotten in her hand. "It sounds glorious."

It had been, but not nearly as glorious as the woman sitting there beside him in the dusk. Watching her face, seeing the longing in its pure, perfect lines, he felt a savage need to snatch her up and spirit her away with him, to show her all the wonders he had seen and then to find more to spread in front of her. The ache of it was like a knife turning in his soul.

Impossible.

He had to remember she was Caleb's, that nothing he could do would change that. That nothing should.

He had lost his chance years ago. He had gone away and left her to Caleb.

Caleb was the better man, always had been. Soon he and Melly would become man and wife. Then he would drive away with her to his farm, carry her inside, and close the door.

Caleb would bungle the wedding night. It was inevitable. What did he know of women and the tenderness they required? Caleb wasn't too strong on imagination, mistrusted the instincts that might guide him. How was a man like that to know what Melly needed? How could he touch and hold her with the required patience when he had not even understood how she might feel about being left alone tonight?

Or maybe Caleb would be fine. Maybe thinking his brother was wrong for Melly just made him feel less at fault for what he was doing now.

Caleb deserved better from him. So did Melly.

He didn't want to attend this wedding.

No. But he must.

Afterward, the sea would call him back, and he would go. He would rove the world, testing nerve and daring, building his fortune. And never come home again. Never.

But not yet.

FIVE

"I never did!" Conrad said with indignation.

"You did, too! Just because I ran through the spot where a horse had been standing. You whispered that odious name plain as day. *Smelly Melly.* I'll never forget it!"

"It was Caleb, I swear." Conrad crossed his heart with a swift wave of the chicken leg he had been nibbling. They had eaten their fill long ago and were only pretending now as an excuse to linger. And a good thing they had finished, too, considering the subject under discussion. Not that it bothered him a bit, but Melly's straight little nose was wrinkled in such a comical expression of distaste that it made him long to kiss it.

"It was not Caleb!"

He pointed the chicken bone at her. "You just don't remember. You were only five years old; you said so yourself. You didn't learn to tell us apart until you were at least six."

"And you were almost fifteen—old enough, surely, to have some consideration for the feelings of a little girl. I was so mortified by the experience that I cried for hours. And I still check my shoes every time I come in from the street."

"Oh, Melly," he said softly, his chest tight. "I'm so sorry."

"There! You did do it!"

He gave a definite shake of his head. "I meant I was sorry it happened, not that I take responsibility."

"Well. Caleb would never have done such a thing."

"My brother may be a paragon, but he's still human. And he's never been above pretending to be me when it suits him. Anyway, it had to be him, since there's only two of us and it wasn't me! I would never have dreamed of saying such a thing, because I used to think you were the sweetest-smelling little thing—"

He stopped abruptly as she swung her head to stare at him in the dimness.

"You what?" she demanded.

"Absolutely. And I still do." He folded his lips over the words, stubborn and unrepentant, though he shielded his gaze with his lashes. "Lavender and roses and spice. The scent is always with you; it's one of the things I remembered most when I was on the other side of the world."

"I—it must be Aunt Dora's potpourri. She puts it in the dresser drawers, the wardrobe, everywhere," Melly said, apparently at random.

"Don't ever let her stop." Avoiding her gaze, he reverted to the previous subject out of sheer self-protection. "Anyway, I've done enough in my short life that I deserved a good hiding for without taking the blame for things I didn't and don't do. It plain wasn't me who called you names."

She watched him a moment, then took another pickle slice on the end of her fork, popped it into her mouth, and slowly chewed it. After she'd swallowed it, she shook her head. "I can't believe it. All this time I thought . . ."

"Don't be too hard on old Caleb. It was only a tiny slip of the halo."

Melly watched the crooked smile that curved Conrad's mouth, heard the trace of bitterness and old pain in his voice. With their families living so close together on Main Street, they knew a great deal about each other's lives. She could remember Conrad always being in trouble of some kind, could remember people calling him a scamp and worse, while Caleb was known for being polite and staying out of trouble.

She could also recall angry scenes when Conrad had shouted at his father in protest over being blamed for everything. Once, she had come upon him crying after a terrible quarrel that had ended in a visit to the woodshed. She had wanted to put her arms around him, to help ease his awful grief. But he had been older, and she knew he would not like knowing she had seen the tears in his eyes. She had crept away without a sound. Yet she had felt a special sympathy for him afterward, even when everyone else in town shook their heads over him.

She said now, "Caleb doesn't claim to be an angel."

"No," he agreed on a sigh, "a body can't even hold that against him."

"Still . . ."

"What?" he said when she did not go on.

"It makes me wonder what else there might be that I don't know about him."

He watched her a long moment before he tossed the chicken leg away and began to wipe his fingers on his napkin. "Not a thing," he said deliberately. "Or if there is, all you have to do is ask, and he'll tell you all about it. He's a good man, the best."

"I know that," she said simply.

"Yes, well, I wouldn't want you to think I was suggesting otherwise."

She nodded her understanding of his loyalty. "On the other hand, I don't believe that you're exactly Satan's second in command."

His gaze touched her mouth and lingered there. Then he said, "I wouldn't bet on it."

Looking away, he began to pick up their picnic and pack it back into the basket. Darkness had fallen while they ate, and it was time to be returning to the others.

They cleared everything quickly, working together with an economy of motion and little need for words. Melly tucked the tablecloth they had used over the last of the food. As she reached for the basket handle, Conrad beat her to it. Rising with the lithe flexing of taut muscles, he transferred his burden to his left hand. Then, extending his right, he closed her fingers in his warm grasp and drew her up to stand beside him.

It was just then that they heard the soft scrape of footsteps on the sandy path. Caleb loomed out of the dark, square-shouldered, wearing his displeasure like a Greek mask.

"How cozy," he said. "And how incredibly dumb. I guess you know you'll have the whole town gabbling like a flock of geese."

"Not if you'll keep your voice down," Conrad said in stringent censure.

"Keep my voice down? Why, when most everybody else has gone home? Good God, Conrad, this isn't some free-and-easy heathen land. What were you thinking of when you led Melly way down here? Or need I ask?"

Conrad stiffened. As Melly tried to pull her fingers free, he tightened his hold. His voice carried a warning note in its deep timbre. "I suggest that, you think carefully before you say any more, brother. All I was doing was enjoying Melly's home cooking, since it didn't look as if you were going to show up to appreciate it.

As for the rest of the fine citizens of this town, I doubt they'll say a word—unless you want to keep shouting until they realize I was the one who ate the pound cake she made for you."

Caleb jutted out his chin and put his hands on his hips. "You mean you let everybody think you were me."

"More or less. I had this notion your reputation could survive an hour alone with your bride-to-be."

"And just what did Melly think?"

Caleb appeared to be speaking to his brother, but Melly thought his words were for her as well. She said tersely, "I knew exactly who he was."

"Good," Caleb said on a hard-drawn breath. "That's good, since it means Conrad couldn't take advantage."

Melly glanced at the man who stood protectively at her side; she couldn't help it. Not only *could* Conrad have taken advantage, but he *had*. And she had encouraged him, in a way. By the same token, she thought he had meant nothing harmful; it was just his way to be forward.

In any event, she resented being forced to stand there while Caleb glowered in righteous indignation. It gave her a vivid idea of what it must have been like for Conrad all those years, accused with little to say in his defense, always facing someone so certain of moral superiority.

Voice taut, she said, "I would remind you, Caleb, that this whole thing would not have come about if you had been here. Or if you had taken me with you on today's outing."

"I've already explained what I was about," Caleb said brusquely.

"So you have," she took him up, "but if my reputation can survive tonight's small indiscretion, I'm sure it would have weathered the short time we'd have been alone together on the road."

"It isn't just that," he said.

"Oh? Are you saying you don't trust yourself to be alone with me any more than you do your brother?"

"Melly," Conrad said in soft warning beside her.

"No, I want to know," she insisted. "Because if that isn't it, then I can only assume that I'm the one Caleb expects to misbehave."

"Oh, for heaven's sake!" Caleb said, running a hand through his hair. "You can't expect me to take this business lying down."

"I 'expected' you to be here. Or I thought you might join us before we finished eating. It even crossed my mind that we might all laugh about the joke. I never dreamed you would come storming up in a rage because I shared a few pieces of chicken with your twin."

Caleb was silent for long moments. Then he sighed and shook his head. His voice low, he said, "You're right, I shouldn't have flown into such a lather." He lifted a hand to rub the back of his neck. "It's been a long day, and I didn't find any of the things I wanted. Then to come back and see you and Conrad out here— well, anyway, maybe you can overlook my temper?"

It was as near an apology as he could come, Melly knew, and a fine reflection of the generous man she had always known, the Caleb she had agreed to marry. Stepping forward, she took his arm, smiling up at him. "I'm sorry, too; I know we shouldn't have wandered so far. But I was glad Conrad was here, since otherwise I might have had to eat with Leamon Stotts!"

Caleb smiled with the easing of facial muscles that indicated a return to his usual even temper. "I suppose you'd have been even more aggravated with me then."

"Indeed I would!" she agreed, and went on in that rallying tone. The two men joined in, if somewhat stiffly, and the moment passed away.

As they were nearing the church and the last of the buggies gathered around it, however, she realized an important fact. Caleb had absolved her of blame, but the courtesy had not been extended to his brother. In fact, he had hardly spoken to Conrad other than to condemn him.

Conrad was well aware of his brother's displeasure, but it was not a matter of grave concern to him. Though he felt sure he would hear more on the subject of his sins once they had seen Melly home.

He did not wait while Caleb walked her to the boardinghouse door. With a polite good night on the sidewalk, he jammed his fists into his pockets and continued in the direction of the livery stable and the river. If his brother was going to kiss Melly, he had no desire whatever to stand and watch. Self-torture was not his pleasure.

He must be mad. What had possessed him to pretend to be Caleb this evening? He should be past such juvenile tricks.

Yes, but Melly had been so lovely, so lovable, and so apparently accessible, that he had lost his head. And he'd be lucky if that was all. Not that it mattered a sailor's damn.

She wasn't for him. Soon, she would be his brother's wife, a tired drudge of a farmer's helpmate. Caleb would plant a child in her belly that she would bear in agony, and he would keep on doing it until her glorious body was a memory, until she was exhausted and faded, with lines in her face and gray in her hair.

She would become exactly like his mother—and Caleb's—had been before she died. His brother might care, but would feel no more blame than their father had before him. If Melly died in her early middle age, Caleb would miss the clean house, the good food, the convenient female body. But he would never miss the woman, because he would never have bothered to know her. Worse, he would think that was the way it was supposed to be, since it was all he had ever known.

"God," Conrad whispered, staring up at the night-black sky

with its silver dusting of stars. If he had Caleb's chance, he knew he would learn every thought and need and dream that Melly possessed. He would discover everything she had ever done or felt, her sorrows as well as her joys. He would take endless delight in sparring with her to find out her views on everything under the sun. He would tempt and tease until she had no secrets.

Nor would her pleasure be hidden from him. Nothing, nothing would stop him from exploring her lovely form inch by careful inch, while using every wile he had ever learned from foreign females, ever heard, ever imagined, to delight her. He would protect her from the ravages of endless childbearing, serve her rather than expect to be served, and it would be his greatest pleasure.

That was, of course, if he was intending to take a wife and settle down in Good Hope. But he wasn't. Couldn't.

"*God*," he said again.

"Blasphemy, brother?" Caleb inquired with heavy irony as he caught up with him again. "I can't say I'm surprised. Maybe cursing like a sailor will help you feel more like a man."

"The problem," Conrad said with succinct precision, "is not how much of a man I may be."

"Oh, I think it is," Caleb said. "Or have you forgotten I could always beat you in a fistfight?"

"You could once, thanks to fifteen pounds' more weight and hours spent hammering iron on an anvil. Things have changed."

"I doubt it. But we'll find out if you ever take my place again with Melly."

Conrad gave him a laconic look. "If you don't want it filled, then don't leave it vacant."

Caleb put out a hand to bring him to a halt, then squared off to face him. "Meaning?"

"Don't take Melly for granted. Don't disappoint her. Don't leave her alone."

"You're telling me how to treat my future wife?" Caleb's stance was belligerent in the dark.

"You could use a few pointers from somebody." The words were even, hard.

"Melly and I were fine until you came along, and we'll be fine again when you're gone. In the meantime, don't forget which twin you are."

Caleb, his warning given, turned on the heel of his heavy farm boot and stomped away. Conrad propped his fists on his hips as he watched him go. He didn't much care for ultimatums, never had. They brought out the devil in him.

For two cents, he'd show his brother exactly how to go about taking care of Melly. It would be a cheap and much-needed lesson.

Hell, he might even do it for free.

Six

The drive out to the new house with Caleb was, Melly considered, the direct result of events at the church social. That he had asked her was a surprise; that the two of them went alone was nothing short of amazing.

She had ridden out once with her aunt, driven by Mr. Seymour Prine, just after Caleb bought the land. Her many hints since then that Caleb should show her how the house was progressing had never borne fruit. She had come finally to believe he really didn't want her to see it until it was completed.

She did not expect a great deal. Caleb could not afford anything grand, and the two of them had agreed that it would be best to start small and add on as their family grew. The house, then, was to be a simple cottage made of vertical boards with a porch across the front and an attached kitchen on the back. There would be a proper parlor, however; Melly had insisted on that. They would need someplace other than the kitchen to entertain their guests, particularly in the heat of summer.

It was certainly hot today. Melly, jostling on the wagon seat, blotted her face with her handkerchief and slanted her parasol to block a little more of the sun's rays. The wind felt as if it were blowing from the devil's own forge. It swirled the plume of dust that boiled up behind them, enveloping them in a gritty fog that gathered in the folds of her skirt and settled on the tired weeds and sunflowers edging the road. Sweeping onward, it spun drying milkweed silk and thistle down across the road, and the drying cornstalks in the fields they passed rustled with the touch of its hot breath.

Following the wind's path across the picked-over cornfields, Melly caught sight of a landmark hill looming on their left. "We're almost there, aren't we?" she said, turning to Caleb with a smile. "I was woolgathering, I suppose. But I didn't know you had finished gathering your crop."

"Conrad has been giving me a hand this week. It made a difference."

Conrad. A small tremor ran over her at the unexpected intro-duction of his name, though she did her best to ignore it. "That was good of him. Did you get a fair yield?"

"Better than expected," Caleb answered with a nod. "It's been a fine growing summer, with the rains coming at the right time."

The corners of her mouth turned down. "We could still use a shower to settle the dust and cool things off a bit."

"Wouldn't hurt," he said in laconic agreement, adding, "but not this afternoon. We don't want to get wet."

Melly felt so hot and grimy that the thought of being rain-washed sounded like a wonderful thing, though she didn't say so. "Maybe it will rain and get it over with before the picnic on Satur-day. You mean to come, don't you?"

"Picnic?"

"To celebrate our quilt, which should be finished by then. I told you about it at the social, remember?"

"You must have told Conrad," he said in hard tones.

He was right.

"Oh. Yes," she said as color rose in her face. "Anyway, it's nothing elaborate, just a simple outing down by the river. We thought first of a fish fry, but it's too hot to hover over a fire. Mostly it's just a chance for my friends and me to enjoy each other's company, since it's the last time we'll be together before the wedding."

Feeling as if she had been babbling, she stopped abruptly. Her explanation seemed to mollify him, however, for his frown relaxed, and a teasing light rose in his eyes.

"My dear Melly, you can still see your friends after we're married. It's not as if you're going to be shut away like some female in a harem."

For a brief moment he looked and sounded so much like Conrad that she blinked. The next instant, she wondered if he was not repeating something his brother had said. But that was uncharitable and she knew it.

Flustered, she said, "I realize that, but things won't really be the same. We won't be running back and forth, in and out of each other's houses a dozen times a week. And I'll be different. A married woman has different concerns, different ideas and—and feelings."

"I should hope the last at any rate," he said, leaning closer with warmth in his eyes and his shoulder pressing hers. She smiled, though she hardly knew how to answer.

Still, rolling along with their bodies touching and the rattling of the wagon in her ears, she thought she caught a glimpse of how their life together would be, its shared understanding and quiet pleasure. It was comforting, yet disturbing at the same time. There should be something more, it seemed. How was it that she had never felt the lack before?

The wagon topped a slow rise and started down. Turning to glance ahead, Melly saw the farm that was Caleb's pride and joy.

The cottage was charming, a white-painted doll's house with scrolled brackets at the tops of the two posts that supported the porch and dark green shutters on the windows. It was perfectly placed, facing the road beneath a great oak tree, yet convenient to the barn and other outbuildings.

Regardless, Melly was disturbed. Her gaze was drawn to the barn. Spreading wide and deep and tall, it was a massive structure that overwhelmed the farmhouse, making it seem puny and insignificant.

"What do you think?" Caleb's voice was rich with satisfaction.

"I think—well, it's a dear little house. Just—just perfect." She could not stop looking from it to the barn and back again.

Caleb gave her a fond and approving glance. "Just wait until you see inside."

"You've been busy. It looks ready to move into."

"It is. I meant to show it to you on our wedding day, sort of bring you home to it, but—well, I couldn't wait."

"And you finished the barn, too?"

He gave a firm nod. "Working with Conrad is like having four hands; I hardly have to think what I'd like to do before he's there with it half done. And he's a demon for keeping after things until they're perfect, I'll say that for him. The responsibility of being a ship's captain has been good for him. There was a time when I could work circles around him, but not anymore."

It almost sounded as if he had tried. She wondered if the two men had spent the last few days competing with each other. If so, they had certainly accomplished miracles in the process. With some care, she said, "Where is Conrad today?"

"Resting, I hope," Caleb replied with a wry laugh.

It was good to hear the respect and even affection in Caleb's tone. She hadn't liked to think of the two brothers being at odds because of her.

Looking toward the outbuildings again as they drew nearer, she said, "I didn't think about the barn being so much bigger."

"Didn't you? That's the way it is, you know—lot more animals on a farm than people."

He had a point. The crops and animals the barn would have to shelter would be their livelihood. Yet looking at the barn overshadowing the house gave her a peculiar suffocating feeling, as if it was she who was being overpowered.

As they drew up in the yard before the house, Caleb climbed down and came around to help her from the wagon.

She leaned to put her hands on his shoulders, and he caught her waist, lifting her free of the wagon bed with easy strength before setting her on her feet. Her body brushed his, but he did nothing to prolong the contact, seemed not to notice. The disturbance inside her increased.

With a hand on her elbow, he guided her toward the porch steps. They reached the front door and he flung it wide, then stepped aside for her to enter ahead of him.

The house was simple but well designed. The walls were painted white except for the parlor, which was given some interest by a rose-patterned wallpaper. The kitchen was large and convenient to the back garden area. There was a fireplace in the parlor as well as the bedroom, and both wood mantels had been painted to look like gray-streaked white marble.

It was a pleasant house, everything considered, but it lacked color, had little character or warmth. Then again, these things could be added, Melly thought. She could paint flower and ribbon designs on the bedroom door and stencil the floors to look like rugs. She could make curtains and cushions and antimacassars, frame the needlework samplers she had done as a young girl and hang them on the walls. Of course, her precious Friendship Quilt would have to go in the parlor. Then there was the furniture. She would choose chairs and tables with some life to them, and a pretty oil lamp as well.

"I think," she said as they returned to the front of the house, "that I would like to buy a parlor set first."

"Not bedroom furnishings?" Caleb asked with the lift of a brow.

She colored a little as she moved ahead of him into the parlor. "We will have my bed and wardrobe. They are good quality, my mother's and father's set that Aunt Dora kept after the accident. She sold most everything else and put the money in the bank for me. I don't mean to spend all of it, but I saw a model for a rosewood parlor set brought to the mercantile by a drummer. Mr. McDougall could order—"

"There's no hurry for such folderols," Caleb said with a decided shake of his head. "What we really need is a good hay rake if the money's on hand."

"A hay rake." She heard the flatness of her tone, but could do nothing to prevent it.

"The better our machinery, the more I can do and the better things will be for us. We've talked about this before, Melly."

"Yes, I know," she said in some distress. "I understand that you want to build a good life for us, and it's not that I don't appreciate all your hard labor in building the house and trying to make it nice, the way you've worked in the fields out here as well as helping your father at the livery. But I would like something of my own, and this is my money—"

"Your money?" he said, face grim. "What I have is yours, Melly, and I expected you to feel the same way. That's what being married is all about."

"I do feel it!" She flung out a hand in a pleading gesture as she sought words to explain. "But you're making all the decisions for our future. You bought the land, chose the house design; you picked out the paint and wallpaper and arranged the kitchen. You aren't letting me be a part of what you're doing at all. Is this what marriage is supposed to be?"

"You don't like the house?" he said, his voice tight.

"Of course I like it! That's not the problem."

"You want to change the kitchen?"

"The kitchen is fine!"

"Then I don't know what's wrong with you. We want the same things, Melly. We have the same dream of a good, solid life here on the farm, working the land and watching our crops and our children grow and prosper year by year. It's all we've talked about, all we've ever felt was worthwhile."

"I still want those things," she said in desperation. "But don't you see that it isn't all I need?"

His face hardened. "I see you've changed since Conrad came home."

Had she? Or had she just remembered the way she used to be before she'd agreed to marry Caleb? Before she'd learned to be practical. Before she'd been forced to accept the fact that the things she'd conjured up in her mind, the places she yearned to see and the things she longed to do, were impossible.

It was not really so much that she and Caleb had the same dream, she thought with sudden insight, but rather that she had given up her own so that only his was left.

That was often the way of it, she knew; she had seen it before with her aunt's friends. So many women became faded shadows of their men, without a view or opinion that was solely their own. And yet she had not expected it with her and Caleb.

The hardest thing, however, was not giving up all the things that made her different, but knowing that her future husband had no idea she had ever thought of anything else. Or that if he did, he actually felt the sacrifice was natural, the way things should be arranged.

He was wrong.

He wouldn't accept that, she knew, would never believe that their disagreement wasn't really over furniture or money. It didn't matter, she told herself. It was necessary to make a stand somewhere, and it might as well be here.

She stared at him, her eyes dark and a little bleak. Lifting her chin, she said plainly, "I am going to have the parlor set."

She turned away without waiting for an answer. Walking through the open front door, she crossed the porch toward where the wagon stood with the horse cropping at a patch of dry grass. She climbed unaided to the seat, then settled her skirts and sat staring straight ahead.

Caleb came out of the house, secured the front door behind him, and crossed to the wagon. The vehicle rocked as he gained his seat. He unwound the reins from the brake handle and sat holding them for a few moments before he turned his head to look at her.

"Does it seem I'm putting the farm ahead of you, Melly? Is that it?" he asked in low tones. "I didn't mean to. It's just that there's been so much to do. I wanted it all perfect for you when you came here as a bride. There's a lot I'd like to give you someday—another room or two on the house, a nice organ for the parlor, all the pretty doodads and gewgaws that you deserve. It's just that first things come first, to my mind." He transferred both reins to his left hand and reached out to place his right on the fists clenched in her lap. "But I want you to be happy. If you've got your heart set on parlor furniture, then that's what I want you to have. I do love you, Melly."

"Oh, Caleb," she said quietly, but could not go on for the lump in her throat. He was trying his best to be reasonable, and to show her he cared.

She looked up at him, letting her gaze roam over his strong, regular features, meeting the straightforward devotion in his eyes. There was so much fondness between them, so many years and memories, so many good times. She had danced her first dance with him, shared her first grown-up kiss with him behind the door of the livery stable. He knew her so well, knew that she loved blackberries and cream, kittens and Christmas, but despised yellow squash and baying hounds. He knew she was fearless when it came to snakes and spiders or thunder and lightning, but terrified of deep water after having nearly drowned in the riverboat disaster that killed her parents. Surely that was a firm enough foundation on which to build a life?

"I love you too, Caleb."

A soft exclamation left him. He leaned closer and pressed his mouth to hers.

It was a kiss of warm and careful affection. The dry smoothness of his lips was pleasant. She felt the abrasion of his beard stubble at their ridges as he caressed her mouth with gentle movements. Then he drew back and sent a quick glance around, as if checking to be sure no one had seen them. They were safe. He lifted the reins and slapped the horse into motion.

He looked down at Melly once more and smiled. She felt her lips curve in a faint response.

Yet all the while she was distracted, almost fearful. It was wrong to compare the staid embrace of her future husband with the wild, reckless kisses of his brother, but she could not help it.

SEVEN

The day of the picnic dawned breathlessly hot. The air was still and heavy, with a sulfurous scent to it. The molten sunlight that poured over everything had a metallic, brassy sheen.

The very idea of building a fire in the cookstove to fry chicken, roast corn and make apple pie was enough to make Melly feel light-headed. To actually do it was like descending into the pits of hell.

She was all for calling off the outing. There was a thundery, oppressive feeling in the air that she did not like. Moreover, the chance of any enjoyment being gained from sitting beside the river seemed remote if they would have to spend the whole time fanning themselves or swatting at heat-drugged flies.

Aunt Dora laughed at Melly's misgivings. This little spell of heat, she declared, was like a breath of spring compared with the ones she had endured in her younger days. The only problem might be if the hot weather broke with a cloudburst. Anyway, it was bound to be better beside the water.

It was, indeed. The site chosen for spreading the picnic cloths and pallets made of old quilts was a couple of miles out of town. It was an oak-crested ridge that merged with the river's natural levee to form a wooded platform higher than the water. A hot breeze wafted over their vantage point now and then. It ruffled the glassy surface of the water below so that it sparkled in the sun like millions of glass shards. Whispering in the leaves of the oaks overhead, it stirred the leaf shadows that patterned the quilts where they sat. The touch of it fanned their moist faces, sifted through their hair with delicate, cooling fingers, and lifted the light summer skirts of the young women in indolent billows.

A steamboat churned past, spreading a froth of foam over the water, the *Cincinnati Star* on her way down to New Orleans. It gave them a blast of its steam whistle that startled a nearby flock of crows into flight. Passengers on the boiler deck and deckhands and chambermaids on the deck below waved and called across the water. The steamer's wake rocked an old piece of raft tied up just along the way, causing it to thud against the levee's bank with a sound like distant thunder.

Still, nothing could banish the heat-induced lethargy that held them in its grip. When they had eaten, they all sat around in a kind of daze, talking in fits and starts and staring out over the endless glide of the river.

"Oh, I ate too much," Biddy said, pressing her hand to her abdomen.

"My, yes, we can tell." The wry comment came from Esther as she surveyed the other girl's tiny, corseted waist and slender shape under her full black skirts. "You really should get yourself right up and walk it off."

"Good idea," Biddy returned with alacrity. "Let's stroll along the levee a way." She waited expectantly for volunteers.

Esther rolled her eyes at her. "Don't be daft."

"Melly will come," the smaller woman said as she turned in her direction. "Won't you?"

Reaching up to smother a yawn, Melly said, "Maybe. In a little while."

Biddy glanced around at the others lounging here and there on the quilts, her gaze hopeful. "Doesn't anybody want to walk?"

Aunt Dora groaned as if even the suggestion were excruciatingly painful. No one else answered.

They were eleven in number. Besides Melly, her aunt, Caleb, and Conrad, there were the four bridesmaids: Biddy, Esther, Lydia, and Sarah. Aunt Dora's boarder, Mr. Prine, had somehow attached himself to the party. Esther had invited the Reverend Milken as well, since he was at loose ends and always looked in need of a home-cooked meal. Sheriff Telford rounded out the group; he had happened by as Sarah was leaving the house, and she had asked him to come along.

The extra men had been more than welcome, since Aunt Dora never skimped on food. The only problem, or so the older woman claimed with mock seriousness, was that the few poor souls remaining in town were left with no one to keep the peace or pray for them—assuming, of course, that anybody found the energy to get up to mischief. But that wasn't likely, Aunt Dora pointed out, since they had the worst mischief-maker with them.

She was referring to Conrad, though he appeared unlikely to cause trouble of any kind. He was stretched full length on the edge of the quilt near Melly. His eyes were closed, his gold-tipped lashes meshed, his head turned toward her so that his cheek rested on the hem of her skirt. He looked for all the world as if he were fast asleep.

Caleb, on the other hand, was talking quietly with the preacher. Melly wondered if the discussion had to do with the wedding ceremony. The impulse to join them nudged her, but she couldn't quite make herself move. Besides, she didn't want to wake Conrad.

A faint, far-off booming, different from the rocking of the old raft, caught her attention. Glancing toward the southwest, she asked of no one in particular, "Was that thunder?"

"Too far away to do any good even if it was," her aunt allowed with a sigh.

Caleb glanced over at her and smiled a little, as if in agreement. As his gaze fell on the long form of his brother, however, a muscle tightened in his jaw. A moment later, he turned back to listen to something the Reverend Milken was saying.

Sarah appeared to notice the byplay from where she sat idly braiding a long silvery blond tress that had fallen forward onto her breast. Her gaze lingered on Caleb, and her face softened in a way that startled Melly for an instant. Then the fleeting impression was gone as her cousin glanced her way and shook her head with a look of comical sympathy.

The tall blond girl flung the strand of hair she was toying with back over her shoulder as she asked, "Did you get the binding sewn on the quilt?"

"Yesterday afternoon," Melly answered. Covering the edges with bias binding made from strips of blue material had been the final step. "I brought it, of course, since the picnic is in its honor."

Aunt Dora waved in the general direction of the pile of cushions behind Melly. "It's in the pillowcase there, I think."

Moving cautiously so as not to disturb the man sleeping so near, Melly reached for the stuffed pillowcase, then pulled the quilt from it and spread its silken folds. "Didn't it turn out well? I'm so proud of it."

"Lovely," Biddy said. There was real feeling in her voice, and it was echoed by the others in turn, each in her own way.

"It's the most beautiful thing I've ever laid eyes on, is what it is," Aunt Dora said in downright tribute. "And I've seen plenty, believe you me."

Melly flushed at the praise. Still, the quilt really was quite glorious as it lay with its soft fabrics gleaming in the muted light falling through the tree canopy overhead and its fine stitching tracking over it in regular and precise patterns.

The motifs of the bridesmaids' squares made lovely corner accents. The rich aquamarine blue of the sea waves beneath the clipper ship in full sail that Lydia had stitched. The shades of pink and rose which her cousin Sarah had used to embroider a rose wreath to indicate the bouquet of late summer blooms she would make for Melly to carry up the aisle. The sweet simplicity of the daisy Esther had cross-stitched on her square along with the Shakespearean phrase *Love comforteth like sunshine after rain.* The swirls of silver-gray embroidery in a running chain stitch of Biddy's eloquent and moving Biblical fragment, *Whither thou goest . . .*

Each of her friends had adorned her square according to her own taste and personality; therefore each square was a vivid and unique reminder of the person who had sewn and initialed it. Melly would have cherished the quilt for that reason alone, but the exquisite workmanship and fortuitous blending of colors and fabrics made it a treasure to be cared for and handed down through the years.

"I'll need to be careful of it," she said with a misty smile. "But I will be, always. And I'll never, ever part with it, not for anything."

Caleb, glancing over at it, shook his head. "I give it five years. After that, the babies will be spitting up on it while they use it for a napping pallet."

"Caleb Wells! What a thing to say!" The rebuke came from Biddy.

"That's right," Lydia said with an indignant glance. "You hush your mouth."

"Five years," Melly's fiancé repeated with an unrepentant grin. "Mark my words."

Conrad roused himself from his somnolent enjoyment of the sound of Melly's voice and the pleasurable torment of breathing in her unique fragrance while feeling the silky softness of her dimity skirt against his jaw. He didn't care for Caleb's superior tone or the suggestion that eternal motherhood would leave Melly too tired and harassed to care about fine things. More than that, he was curious.

Levering himself to one elbow, he cast an eye over the finished quilt, then gave it a closer look. The squares were pieced from scraps of the silk he had sent to Melly; he recognized the goods. Strange he had not noticed earlier, but then he'd had other things on his mind.

A crooked smile tugged at his mouth as he said, "What you need is a special box to protect it. I have a small chest on my ship made out of carved teak that I picked up in Hong Kong to keep moisture and bugs out of my papers. I'll send it to you, if you like."

"She won't need it," Caleb said, cutting into their quiet exchange. "I can build Melly a box out of cedar."

Melly sent her future husband a quick look. "What I would really like is a rack of some kind to display the quilt in the parlor, if you—"

"Sketch out what you want," Caleb said brusquely. "I'll see to it."

There was a small silence during which Conrad very carefully did not look at either his brother or Melly. He had wanted her to have the chest, and couldn't see that offering it to her violated any rules about presenting personal items to unmarried females. Caleb apparently felt otherwise. Or maybe it was just that he didn't want Melly accepting anything from him.

Did Caleb know he had provided Melly's wedding gown? Somehow Conrad doubted it. The groom wasn't supposed to see the thing before the wedding, after all.

Conrad hated to think of the way his brother might find out. It could easily be on his wedding night as he stepped close enough to his new wife to see the small Oriental figures in the brocade, to touch the heavy silk, to slide it from Melly's slender body. His hands closed slowly into fists as he pictured it.

It was Aunt Dora who filled the lengthening breach in the conversation. Turning in his direction with lifted brows, she said, "And just what do you know about boxes for the fine things women like to keep anyway, my lad? I thought you'd been at sea these many years, far from the company of women."

"Don't know a thing, Aunt Dora," he said, giving her a bland look from under his lashes.

"Go on with you. I'll just bet there's been a woman or two traveled a few miles on your China tea clipper."

His amusement faded. "Not my ship."

"If you say so. Still, you must've consorted with them somewhere, because you didn't learn your tricks in Good Hope. Not that I'm blaming you, mind. A man's a man wherever he may be, and a bear don't pass a honey tree without trying to climb it."

"Good Lord, Aunt Dora!" He drew back in a pretense of shock.

"Now don't go trying that innocent stuff on me, boy, because it won't work. I expect you'd just rather not take females to sea."

"I might take a wife if I had one," he said in tentative tones. "Some captains do; I know a lady who always sails with her husband. Once when he was laid up in his bunk, half out of his head with fever, his ship ran into a hurricane. His lady took charge, giving orders she claimed to be relaying from her husband. The ship sailed right through the storm, when every man jack on board had thought she'd surely go down. The captain laughed himself hoarse when he heard, because he hadn't been able to give a sensible order for five solid days."

"Sounds like a woman with a head on her shoulders to me," Aunt Dora commented with a notable lack of amazement.

"A man of sense, rather, for marrying the right one in the first place."

The older woman pursed her lips. "Still, not every female is cut out for a life afloat."

"Or every man."

"No, but most of the ones who take to it become sea rovers who can never settle down to one woman or be satisfied with a quiet life tending hearth and home. I think you're one of them, my boy. What do you say to that?"

He met the woman's wise eyes, saw the purpose there and also the anxiety that forced her to it. His gaze flickered to Melly, then returned to her aunt. Grimly he said, "You may be right. Or close to it."

"I thought so," the older woman said, then sighed. "You always were about half pirate."

Caleb said, "More like three-quarters."

"Humph," Aunt Dora said, giving Melly's fiancé a brief glance. "And the other quarter of you both was always two-year-old brat."

Conrad had to laugh. At the same time, he glanced at Melly again. She was staring out over the river, her teeth set in the softness of her bottom lip. Caleb, on the other hand, showed no signs whatever of regretting his brother's future absence.

It was a short time later that Biddy finally prevailed on Melly to go for a stroll. As he saw Melly gathering herself to rise, Conrad sprang up and pulled her to her feet. Once upright, he decided he might as well amble along with the two ladies as escort. That got Caleb moving. Then the Reverend Milken elected to join them. Next thing they knew, everyone was meandering off along the levee in the hot afternoon sun as if it made perfectly good sense.

Everyone, that is, except Aunt Dora and Seymour Prine. Melly's aunt watched them with openmouthed incredulity before lying back on the pile of cushions and closing her eyes. Mr. Prine shifted his position so that his body blocked a shaft of sunlight falling on her face. Then, taking a small book from his pocket, he settled himself for guard duty.

The group of picnickers turned downriver, talking in fits and starts, rambling with no real destination. The breeze off the water was stronger than earlier, and carried humid promise in its breath. Conrad sniffed the air and lifted his gaze to scan the heavens. There was a bank of clouds creeping above the trees from the southwest that quickened his weather senses.

As they neared the old abandoned raft that lay at the water's edge, Sheriff Telford detached himself from the others and stepped down the slope of the levee, digging in his heels for purchase. He put his hands on his hips as he surveyed the sorry craft. Glancing at Conrad as he came to stand beside him, he nudged the water-soaked logs with a booted toe. "We ought to sink the thing before some kid takes it out and drowns himself."

Conrad cast a practiced eye over the raft. Its logs were beginning to rot on the ends, and the ropes lashing it together were black with mildew. But the majority of the center logs, where it counted, were solid. The hemp fibers of the ropes seemed strong enough, and the knots were firm and tight. The rough steering oar attached at the stern appeared fairly new.

He said, "Whoever put it together knew what he was doing."

The rest of their band were straggling down the slope. As Caleb caught their exchange, he said, "The whole thing looks rotten to me. Sheriff's right, the best thing would be to chop it into kindling."

Conrad sent his too-rational twin a frown. "Some kid must have spent hours building it."

"Time that he should have spent helping out at home, I expect," came the unsympathetic reply. "I'd rather not be responsible when he winds up floating facedown in the river." He looked around at the other men. "Anybody bring an axe?"

The preacher looked dubious, but Telford nodded. "Might have one in the toolbox of my buggy."

Caleb and the two other men swung around and started toward where the buggy was tied up next to Caleb's wagon and the rig rented by Mr. Prine.

Conrad knew he should back off. This was no longer his town or his people. He wouldn't be around if the boy who built the raft should drown one fine day. But he remembered too well the things adults did to young boys in the name of saving them from themselves—the lectures, the whippings . . . There had even been a raft, once, that had disappeared. He wondered suddenly if Caleb had helped dismantle that one, too, for his brother's own good.

The raft was tethered to a stake pushed into the ground only inches from Conrad's right foot. A basic seaman's knot held it fast.

It only took an instant to jerk it free, toss the line onto the logs, then shove the raft off. As he straightened, he was caught and held by Melly's wide gaze.

She was watching him, her face a little pale and her lips parted. She looked toward Caleb, as if deciding whether she ought to call out and tell him what his brother had just done.

It might have been the reminder of the past that roused the devil in Conrad, or just the fact that his brother was so determined to override him. Maybe it was being forced into a public avowal of his need to roam that did it. Or perhaps it was the perverse determination to live up to what everybody so obviously expected.

Then again, there was a lesson he had vowed to teach.

The distinct possibility existed that he needed no excuse, however. The urge toward outrageous action was simply there, and he succumbed without a qualm.

One moment he was untying the raft, the next he was at Melly's side. He bent to thrust one arm under her knees and the other behind her back. She gave a low cry as he lifted her against him.

Swinging hard, he splashed to the craft that was easing out into the current. He hoisted her to the wet, uneven surface, then pushed farther from shore with a strong surge. As she wrenched over, clawing at the slippery logs, he pulled himself up beside her and swung his legs on board.

Lydia screamed. Esther yelled. Sarah called Melly's name in horror. The sheriff, the preacher, and Caleb swung around, then pelted to the water's edge. The first two stopped, but Caleb kept coming, cursing as he plunged in waist-deep and began to swim.

It was too late. The river current caught the raft, swung it around and away from the bank, and sent it skimming downstream.

"Don't worry!" Conrad called across the water. "We'll be fine! I'm three-quarters pirate, remember?"

Chuckling at his own mordant wit, he reached for the crude steering oar at the stern and put his back into swinging it, helping the dipping, gliding raft along. He reached the main channel, let it take the rough craft. The yells and cries died away. Caleb, never a particularly strong swimmer, began to fall back.

Within a few short seconds, the raft was rounding the next bend. A half dozen more strokes of the steering oar and all trace of the others vanished.

Water and trees, all around. Nothing but trees and water.
Conrad felt the rise of fierce exultation.
He had the river to himself.
Yes. And he had Melly.

EIGHT

For the next several minutes Conrad concentrated on putting distance between himself and any possible pursuit. His blood was up, the rising wind was in his hair, and he was sliding smoothly over the river's surface, guiding the raft with a rhythmic play of the stern oar that was as natural to him as breathing.

He had escaped, and the woman he loved was with him. His satisfaction couldn't last; he knew that. But for this small piece of time he was a contented man.

The woman he loved.

God, yes, beyond doubt.

He had not meant it to happen. But then, he had learned early in his ventures at sea that things seldom went as planned. A crooked smile curved his lips as he glanced down at Melly.

His pleasure vanished. She was huddled on her side in the center of the raft, knees drawn up, eyes tightly shut, face white as death.

He remembered her cry as he'd hauled her aboard the raft, the stiffness of her body against him, the way she had clung to him before he'd set her on the wet logs. He had thought her reaction only surprise and revulsion at being on the dirty, water-slicked craft.

That wasn't it at all.

Melly was afraid to the point of terror of deep water. The old, half-forgotten knowledge bloomed like a fiery explosion in his mind.

Releasing the oar, he plunged to his knees beside her. The movement rocked the raft with a violent tilt, and he heard her soft moan. The small sound cut deep, sliced into his heart. He caught her shoulders and dragged her up, folding her into his arms.

"Oh, Melly, I'm sorry, so sorry. I should have remembered. I'm an idiot, a criminal idiot, but I've been gone so long, and you seemed so— No, I should have remembered. How could I forget? God, how could I?"

He was jabbering, but couldn't stop in his bone-deep remorse. She was so cold and racked by shudders, and her pretty dimity dress was stained and wet where water was washing through the logs. His fault, all his fault.

"Please, Melly, open your eyes. Look at me. Please . . ."

She heard him, for she burrowed closer, but that was her only response. He lay back, braced against the support column for the oar, pulling her against the length of him. His hands shook as he rubbed her arms in an attempt to warm her chilled flesh. She pressed her face into his chest, and he felt her warm breath through his shirt. She moved nearer to fit the curve of her hip more firmly into the cradle of his legs.

Conrad sucked air into his lungs and stifled a groan at the sudden stir of fervid heat in his lower body. With wide unseeing eyes, he stared at the clouds mounting in massed darkness overhead.

Dear God, but he wanted . . .

He couldn't. No. What kind of bastard was he to even let it cross his mind? This was not what he had intended.

Or was it?

A shudder of denial rippled over him. No. His needs and desires were not important. He had to help her. There had to be a way.

"Oh, Melly, sweet Melly, it's only water," he murmured in low and unsteady supplication. "It's cool and wet and deep, but not evil. Men are evil; they'll take your life and maim your soul and mangle all your pretty dreams. You must not trust any of them, ever—least of all me. But water is life, just life."

She seemed to grow more still, as if she was attentive to his words. Dragging air into his lungs, he went on, giving her his hard-earned knowledge of the thing he loved most, after her.

"Water quenches our thirst, cleans us, comes raining down to save the parched green things of this earth, to save us. And it's beautiful. It holds all the colors of the world—yellow, brown, gray, blue, yes, and green in tropic lands. It gleams and sparkles like liquid sapphires far out to sea, and like emeralds and aquamarines close to shore. Sometimes it's as clear and still as the finest mirror; other days the waves billow and roll, riding as high as the sky. Water can take a man down, hold him, drown him if he isn't careful. But it's a gentle death compared to most. And no harm is meant, ever. The river, the sea, the ocean is only there. Wild or calm, deep or shallow, it's only as nature made it."

She was shaking less, he was sure of it, though fine tremors still coursed over her. Was there a little more color in her face?

At least her breathing was no longer so frantic. It was surer, deeper, so deep it flattened the firm globes of her breasts against him, threatening his sanity.

His voice not quite even, uncertain what he was saying in his need to reassure her, he continued. "The sea to me is siren and mistress and all the other things that men who love it call it. The sound and feel and look of it is inside me, a part of me. Yet it's just water all the same. It can harm us if we let it, yes, but also serve us. This raft floating along on the river can carry us to all the wide, free reaches of the world. If we let it, it could carry us past all the towns and right on out to sea, steadily taking us wherever we wanted to go. I wish it would. . . ."

He trailed off, his breathing ragged as he fought for control of the ache that had filtered into his voice.

Melly stirred and sighed, her warm breath fluttering across his throat. "So do I," she whispered.

The words were so soft he might not have heard them if he had not been straining so hard for some sign, some sound. But he did hear, and his heart kicked into a hard beat.

At the same time, he was unbearably moved that he could reach her with his words. That he could banish her fears even for a moment was a gift beyond price, one that helped ease his guilt for having forced her to face them.

Holding her in his arms seemed to fill the emptiness in his soul, to soothe the loneliness he had carried with him for years. It was as if they belonged together, as if he had always known it. Still, the fierce grip of possessiveness he felt inside stunned him.

The top of his head felt on fire. The muscles in his arms corded. He lay perfectly still while he fought impulses too dark to be named.

Safe. Melly felt so safe within the strong, confining circle of Conrad's arms. The horror in her mind receded, drifted away to nothing. Her last small shiver faded, along with the goose bumps on her arms. The core of warmth remaining inside her began to radiate outward again, leaving languid weakness in its wake.

The rocking of the raft and its steady glide were oddly soothing. The firmness of the shoulder under her cheek, the planes and ridges of muscles against her breasts gratified her in some way she did not care to consider. The need to lie as she was forever, happen what might, was astonishing.

Then the internal echo of the words she had spoken half in delirium reached her. As she recognized their startling truth, she opened her eyes and lifted her head to look at the man who held her.

There was torment in the rich, sea blue of his gaze, and something more that made her draw a strangled breath through parted lips. Suddenly every fiber of her being was awake, alive, and aware.

She felt the quick rise and fall of his chest, the thud of his heart under her breast, the taut muscles of his abdomen and the sheer, hard strength of him. His scent, made up of starched linen, bay rum, fresh air, and heated male, assailed her, inducing such mind-swimming pleasure that the muscles of her belly contracted. The river gurgled and slurped around the raft. The wet logs rubbed together with a steady rhythm, rocking her against the firm apex of his thighs.

Warm, she was so warm. Somewhere deep inside a rich, languid urge stirred, stretched, tingled along her nerves. Her lips felt swollen, sensitive. She was sinking in the deep-sea darkness of his eyes, buffeted by the storm she saw brewing there, drowning in its fury. And she didn't care.

Then Conrad's thick, gold-tipped lashes came down to shield his expression. He turned his head to stare at the passing shoreline.

"Hell and damnation!"

He shifted to sit erect. Then he cursed again in soft, foreign fluency.

"What is it?" she said, her voice husky and not quite even. She dragged the black, wind-whipped silk of her hair out of her eyes as she stared toward the featureless green shore. A brisk wind had sprung up, ruffling the water that lay between them and the land.

"We've drifted past Good Hope. I meant to pull in there at the landing, be waiting when the others got back."

"How far past?" Her question was punctuated by a rumbling sound of thunder that was much closer than earlier.

"I'm not too sure, though I recognize that big dead tree over there from the trip upriver the other day. I should have been keeping track, but—" He stopped, folding firm lips over whatever he had meant to say.

Melly had always stayed as far away from water craft as she could get. Still, she knew there was a big difference between traveling upstream and down on a raft, even with a steering oar. The crude paddle at their stern could guide them but would not propel them upstream against the river's strong current.

She said, "We'll have to land and walk back."

"No other choice," he agreed with a nod as he disentangled himself and rose to his feet. Squinting against the rising wind, he scanned the bank some distance ahead of them for a suitable place to put ashore.

In that instant thunder boomed again. Lightning crackled immediately afterward, streaking down toward the water in a crooked line like a crack in the overturned bowl of the sky.

Melly flinched. As the brightness faded, a sharp, almost singed odor drifted on the wind.

Clutching at a knot in the binding ropes, she stared around her, frowning as she noticed how the weather had changed in so short a time. Dark clouds blotted out the sun, leaving the sky almost as black as night. White-capped waves dotted the wide river's surface. A fog of mist torn from their crests made it difficult to see the distant shoreline. Water slapped over the logs on which she lay, wetting her to the skin.

"Conrad—" she said with a shading of alarm.

"Right," he said in grim agreement. "Whatever we're going to do, we'd better be quick about it." Then, swinging with strong grace on the pitching square of logs, he reached for the rear oar.

She shuddered, feeling exposed and bereft without Conrad's

protection. Her old terror hovered, threatening to swamp her just as the river seemed intent on swamping the raft. Yet at the same time she could sense the slow unfurling inside her of something near excitement.

There was a peculiar beauty in the gathering storm, a majesty in the fury of the elements. And the man who stood over her was part and parcel of these things. Feet braced, he rode the raft as if it were a living thing. With his hair whipped into a wild golden tangle and his shirt plastered to the hard sculpting of his body, he was fearless as he faced the late summer gale. With him there was the assurance of security, and intimations of a consummate glory that pounded in her blood, swelled like a storm tide in her heart.

Conrad pulled with teeth-clenched effort at the steering oar, but they made scant progress toward the west bank. The wind was too strong from that direction; it was holding them off. The yellow-brown river surged and frothed around them, threatening to upend the raft. The ropes lashing the shifting, rubbing logs together creaked under the pressure. The air was thick with spray and laden with the scents of ozone and ancient effluvia stirred up from the river bottom.

As they rounded the next bend, lightning pitchforked down the sky again, hissing as it struck in the water beside them. Melly heard Conrad's low oath. A bare moment later, he shouted, "We've got to get out of this!"

The raft changed directions. Melly swung around, narrowing her eyes to gaze ahead of them. There was an island looming ahead in the middle of the river. The dark green mass was much closer than the western shore. Conrad, she could see, was going to attempt to land on it.

It was then that the rain began, sweeping toward them in a thick, gray curtain. It peppered down around them as the raft grated over the sandbar that angled out in front of the island.

Conrad ignored the hissing clatter as he leaped over the side and splashed ashore with the rope tether in hand. He dragged the waterlogged craft higher, grounding it on the bank and lashing it to a willow that leaned down from the stand of trees along the water's edge.

Melly struggled to her feet, staggering against the blowing rain, half blinded by bits of flying bark and leaves. Conrad swung to scoop her up in his arms. Head down, he waded ashore, then fought his way through weeds and willows, emerging beneath the sheltering canopy of maple and sweet gum trees.

The rain rattled down through the leaves, fragmenting into a fine mist. The smells of wet earth, bruised greenery, and musty lichen rose around them. Conrad pushed deeper, not stopping until he reached the center of the isolated spit of woodland. There he set Melly on her feet under the spreading limbs of a great oak.

The sound of the rain beating the river surface to a froth came plainly to where they stood, yet at the same time seemed remote. The tops of the trees above them swayed and groaned, moaning with the wind, but Melly and Conrad were protected from its force. Sheltered by the great umbrella of oak branches, they were out of the worst of the storm. The thunder and lightning had subsided, making it unlikely they would be struck dead where they stood.

Conrad looked down at her. For long moments, they stood still, lost in the perilous moment and the currents of emotion that shifted between them.

Then wry amusement crept into the brilliant blue of Conrad's eyes, pleating the skin at the corners into tiny, endearing fans. Melly felt an answering smile curve her own mouth. They stared at each other, at their wet hair plastered to their heads, their sodden, mud-stained clothes, the raindrops spiking their lashes and dripping from the tips of their noses.

Suddenly they were laughing, holding each other in the relieved aftermath of peril—and the certain knowledge that, beyond all logic or sanity, they had not only survived their adventure, but enjoyed it.

Then just as abruptly they were silent. The rain splattered and sang, whipping in gusts. It dripped around them, wetting the ground beyond the oak's edge, forming runnels that oozed and spread and became freshets heading toward the river. The cooling air brushed Melly's wet skin with coolness, beading it with goose bumps. Against that chill, she could feel the intense body heat of the man who held her. The need to move toward it, toward him, was so strong that she felt light-headed with it.

She inhaled in sharp dismay and stepped away from him. He let her go. Turning from her, he braced one hand on the trunk of the oak while he raked his hair back with the other. She thought his stance relaxed—until she saw the bark crumble under the pressure of his white-tipped fingers.

Whirling away, Melly dropped down to crouch at the base of the tree. She rested her head on her drawn-up knees and clasped them with her arms. Closing her eyes tightly, she did her best to hold her treacherous impulses at bay while keeping body and conscience together.

Time became elastic, stretching and contracting until it ceased to have meaning. It might have been twenty minutes later, or two hours, when the sky began to lighten. The wind dropped. The pounding rain slackened at last, became a drizzle, a sprinkling. Thunder grumbled still, but it was fading away to the east. High overhead, a bird called. The trees dripped, clouds remained to dim the light and threaten another small shower or two, but the worst appeared to be over.

Conrad left the oak's shelter while the last raindrops were still pattering down. She thought he meant to check the river to see if it had settled down enough to chance the raft again. The day was waning. They would need to get going soon if they were to cross to the bank, then land and walk back to Good Hope before dark.

He returned almost immediately. There was a taut set to his shoulders and grim irony in his face as he stopped a few feet from where she sat.

"Better make yourself comfortable," he said, his voice flat.

"What do you mean?" She tried to decipher his closed expression.

"The tree I tied up to was undercut by the river and washed away."

"I don't see . . ."

"The raft went with it."

It was an instant before his words penetrated, before her befuddled brain made sense of the laconic syllables. Then she saw what he was saying, and an odd, fatalistic horror shifted through her.

The raft was gone.

They were stranded.

NINE

Marooned by the river like the rawest greenhorn. Conrad silently castigated himself with a few of his more choice seaman's epithets.

There was no question of how he had come to make such a stupid mistake; the answer was all too clear. It was sitting across from him, on the other side of the signal fire he had kindled in this willow-circled clearing near the river's edge.

It would be some time before the others found them. They had also been caught by the storm, so would have slow going on the muddy river road back to town. Everyone would expect him and Melly to be waiting for them there; it was the logical solution. How long would it take before they realized the two of them weren't there and weren't coming?

Thank God for the oiled pouch of sulfur matches that he had stuffed into his pocket. Such preparedness was second nature rather than planned, but was no less effective for that. The fire would not only alert whoever came in search of them, but would dry their clothes and help keep the mosquitoes and gnats at a reasonable distance.

Melly had taken down her hair to dry it. Watching her comb the tangles from the long, waving strands, staring at the way the soft, night-dark mass gleamed in the firelight, made his guts twist with pure, aching need. He wanted to gather her hair in his hands, bury his face in its warm, damp silk, and breathe the essence of her into his very being.

The bonfire crackled, leaping higher in a small explosion of sparks that spiraled into the purple twilight sky. Melly looked up at the sound, then glanced over at him across the flames. Her eyes reflected their red-hot glow, while the pure planes and angles of her face were enameled in blue and gold like some exquisite, fabled mask of enchantment. He held her gaze, absorbing it, and for a single instant there was nothing between them except smoke, wavering heat waves, and the aching mystery of desire.

Her throat moved as she swallowed. She lowered her lashes and bent her head. Picking up a small stick, she gouged absentmindedly at the dirt beside her. After a moment, she asked, "Do you remember the time we were walking along the levee and we saw that man throw a grass sack into the water?"

It was an effort to redirect his thoughts, but he nodded as he recalled the incident.

"There were kittens in the sack; we could hear them crying as it started to sink. I wanted to rescue the little things, but the water was too deep—and I was so afraid. You dove in and brought the kittens out to me. Vanilla, Aunt Dora's boardinghouse cat, was one of them."

A reminiscent smile creased one lean, sun-bronzed cheek. "You always were tenderhearted."

"And you always knew it. But do you remember that you were pretending to be Caleb that day?"

So he was. He looked away from her. "Maybe."

"Why?"

He lifted a shoulder in a moody shrug. "You were so young, only six, maybe seven. You wanted to go with me, and I—well, I wanted the company. Your aunt trusted Caleb." He heard the old pain in his voice, but could do nothing about it.

"That was the day I learned to tell you apart," she said softly.

His heart took on a trip-hammer beat. "How?"

"Some of the kittens drowned. You held me while I cried. From then on, all I had to do was touch you."

"But you never said a word . . . so I figured—"

She gave an emphatic shake of her head. "Caleb picked me up once to put me in a wagon, and another time he'd helped me into a rope swing. When you held me that day, it felt . . . different. Later on, I could see the difference in your eyes. I didn't under-stand why everybody couldn't see it. I used to follow you sometimes, just to see the way your face changed when you turned and saw me."

He couldn't have spoken if his life depended on it.

She went on after a moment, her voice tight, forced. "But you went away for so many years. It seemed you were never coming back." She stopped, took a deep breath. "Caleb is a fine man, a good friend, and he loves me in his way. To look at him is . . . very nearly the same."

Around them the insects and night frogs made their pleas for love and immortality. The wet, earthy smell of the woods, the fishy taint of the river, were strong in their lungs. The air was moist and cool after the rain, so that the acrid smoke from the fire lay on it like a drifting shadow, now concealing, now revealing, their faces. Yet between them, in still and perfect clarity, was an understand-ing that had no need for words.

She knew why he had come from so far across the sea to be with her before she was wed. He knew why she had been able to conquer her fear of deep water enough to endure the storm. They were two parts of a whole, in spite of her promise to Caleb or the pull Conrad felt inside from far distant horizons.

Nothing would come of it. Soon they would be rescued, and the pace of their days, so briefly interrupted, would resume their steady, inevitable course. It was not meant that they should be together. Time and circumstances had prevented it until this moment, and their loyalties demanded that nothing change that now.

Yet for a single, heart-stopping moment they were able to look into each other's eyes in the dancing firelight. And see in bright-hot glory the things that might have been.

She closed her eyes and tossed the small stick she held into the fire. Abruptly the stacked and glowing heart of the fire collapsed on itself. A burning branch tumbled from the heap, skittering, trailing coals and smoke. It spun toward Melly's skirts to lodge in the soft, crumpled folds.

Conrad moved in the same instant, lunging with a swift uncoiling of taut muscles. Stretching, reaching without conscious thought beyond the need to prevent disaster, he snatched the smoking limb from the fragile cloth and flung it back into the fire. Then, using the palm of his hand, he beat out the small flames licking at her spread hems.

Melly cried out, reaching toward him. He raked his gaze over her—her bare feet and arms, her face—in search of injury. Finding none, he demanded, "What is it? Where are you hurt?"

"Nothing. I'm not," she said with a violent shake of her head that set the ends of her hair to dancing. "But you—your hand . . ."

Reaching to catch his wrist, she turned it to the light of the fire. The skin was blackened, stinging, but protected from real harm by a layer of calluses. He had endured far worse many times from rope burns.

"It's nothing," he said, and meant it.

"Not to me." Her voice was quiet. Bending her head, she pressed her lips to the tender center of his palm.

For endless eons of time, he could not move, had no power over the assorted bones, tendons, and sinews of his body. He felt as if the entire surface of his body was mantled in a hot flush of need. His brain was baking in his skull, on fire with the violent internal conflict between brotherly fidelity and his own need, between honor and fate.

All that was left was instinct. It was that alone which set him in motion finally, only that which guided him as he reached to draw Melly to him. Some part of him looked on with remorse but lacked the power to stop what was happening. Only one thing could now.

"I want you," he whispered.

"I—know."

The catch in her voice shook his heart. "Tell me to stop."

"I would," she said, her gaze fastened on his in fearful honesty, "if I could."

"Please. I don't want to hurt you."

Her smile was at once tremulous and pitying. "You couldn't."

He could, he knew, and so easily, though it would be against his will. Still, he could not resist the lure of her trust. "If I do," he said in low entreaty, "will you tell me?"

"Yes. If." The soft words were both a promise and unspoken permission. They were proof that she knew him from his twin, wanted him for himself.

Her skin gleamed with the soft luster of the pearls of the Far East. It was smooth and firm and warmly resilient under his hands. Her kiss as he took it tasted of the sweetness of the Spice Islands, and was as layered with wonders. He marveled, yet restrained the wild urge to plunge in and take everything at once. He wanted her to know every delicate sensation of which the flesh was capable. That would be his gift, one directed by the force of his deep, abiding love. She would, he vowed to himself, have no regrets.

He knew full well that his own would come soon enough. But he would save them for the time when they were all he had left.

The ground near the fire had been cleared of sticks and debris but was still muddy and wet. He cushioned it with his trousers and shirt, hastily removed, before he laid her back upon it. Then he eased down beside her and drew her against his aching body.

Melly closed her eyes tightly, losing herself in the mindless pleasure of the moment. She would not think, only feel. She touched her fingers to his flame-gilded shoulders, enjoying their warm, hard shaping, sensing the strength he held so carefully in check. No, he would not hurt her.

Under her hand, she felt his muscles shift as he began to open the buttons of her bodice. One by one, they gave under his fingers, allowing the cloth to fall away. He skimmed over her rib cage to cup a breast. She ceased to breathe for long seconds as his gentle kneading sent magic sensations tumbling through her. Only as he drew her camisole aside to take the nipple into his mouth did she let the air in her lungs escape on a soft, strangled sigh.

He knew exactly what he was doing. More than that, he meant to enjoy all the small, encroaching preliminaries. Secure in that knowledge, she felt the release of the stiffness in her muscles.

She wanted to learn his body as he explored hers. She yearned to thread her fingertips through the whorls of golden-brown hair on his chest, touch the small nubs of his paps so they knotted as her own were doing under his ministrations. Her fingers trembled as she brushed them across his chest.

Sensing her need, he gave her access, guided her hand to him, then left her free to do as she pleased. She accepted the invitation, timidly at first, then more boldly.

As he nuzzled the small hollow beneath her ear, she sighed and arched her body toward him, nestling her breasts more securely in his hand. Accepting that mute gesture of need, he cupped their fullness, suckled them, draped them in long, cool strands of hair and licked the pouting rose-red nipples that peeked through. Then, he surveyed his handiwork. And he smiled.

If this was loving, she knew why everyone tried so hard to keep it from young women. They could grow too easily to crave it, following mindlessly after the man who could make them feel such splendor. There was no embarrassment in it, only voluptuous, spreading wonder.

Entranced by Conrad's deftness and her tingling reactions to it, she barely noticed as he drew off more layers of clothing as if he were shucking an ear of corn to reach the tender kernels inside. He tasted her as he might a freshly roasted ear also, nibbling as he went, gathering her flavor with his tongue.

Amazement rasped in her throat. She cried out, pleading, reaching convulsively for him. Her fingers pressed into his shoulder until her nails bit the skin.

He answered her need, enclosing her in the protection of his arms even as he slid between her thighs. For an instant her tight, desperate constriction prevented entry. He did not force it, but aided her with gentle stretching until she could accept him. Even then, he eased inside by heart-melting degrees, filling her so slowly that her veins pounded with the maddening escalation of glory.

She wanted, needed, all of him, could not bear to be denied an instant longer. Sliding her hands down the powerful curve of his back, she pressed the palms of her hands to his hips as she arched against him.

The pain stung. It was so unexpected that she tightened around him and fell back, taking him with her to impossible depths. He made a short, winded sound in his chest and then was still. He hovered above her and she heard him grit his teeth, felt the slow bunching of his muscles as he fought for control. A moment later he put his hand under her and lifted her, tilted her hips a little while he eased from her, then lowered himself into her again with shuddering slowness.

The abrupt beatitude was so overwhelming that a soft sob rasped in her throat and tears streamed from her eyes into her hair. And suddenly nothing was too deep or too hard or too much. She wanted all of him, needed him with desperate yearning. It was not mere lust but something deeper and more elemental, a passion for love and the life that he could give her by kindling that love inside her.

She moved with its ancient rhythm, hesitant and awkward. He felt the tentative accommodation, accepted it, molded it to his own efforts. As he drew back to carry her higher, she opened her eyes and looked into his face.

The firelight in his eyes was echoed in her heart. She loved him, and spoke the words though her lips did not move and she made no sound. Never would she forget this moment. Never, not even when she was old and bent and had dismissed all else from memory. In this eternal instant he was hers and she was his, and nothing would ever take that from her.

Then he sank into her, banishing thought with his surging power. Together they moved, rising, falling, while their skins glowed with the fiery heat of their blood and their hearts beat in thudding syncopation. Her very being rose to meet him, rushing toward him, pouring out to him like the river that coursed past where they lay. Higher it flooded, deeper, wider. She took his strength and gave him hers until their two beings were merged, so tightly and deeply mixed that there was no way to tell where one ended and the other began. No way, ever, to wrest them apart again.

And abruptly she was caught in the surging tide, racing with it, flowing with it in a run for the sea. She reached its depths and spread, voluptuous, serene. He pressed deep as he met her, welcoming her with hard, enclosing arms.

Afterward, they held each other, staring wide-eyed, glorified yet desolate into the encroaching darkness as they stroked, touched, soothed, sought answers that could not be found. They did not move until the fire died.

Later, when it was no more than a bed of orange-red coals, they rose and struggled into their clothes, tried as best they might to make themselves presentable. Then Conrad searched out more wood to build up the flames again.

They were leaping high, burning in hot tongues far up into the dark heavens, when Caleb found them.

※

"Fight! Fight!"

Melly heard the cries from the street as she emerged from the semidetached kitchen at the back of the boardinghouse. She had been heating water, getting ready to launder the dress and petticoats that had been so mistreated the day before. She abandoned the task as the yelling broke out, then hurried toward the front porch.

Sarah was standing outside the mercantile with a shopping basket on her arm, shading her eyes against the morning sun as she stared toward the river landing.

Glimpsing Melly as she moved out onto the porch steps, the other girl swung toward her. "It's Caleb and Conrad!" she called, her face as green and pale as a pattypan squash. "They're killing each other!"

Melly had suspected as much, but the anguish of it nonetheless washed over her in a wave. She had to stop them, or at least try.

Picking up her skirts, she began to run. Sarah hesitated only a second before she pounded after her.

There was no way they could miss the confrontation. The shouts and whistles, the cries of encouragement, and the barking of excited dogs carried plainly down the street. Some idiot was even ringing a bell as if the fight were a spectacle for all to come and see. Gray-beards, farmers, drummers in flat-crowned hats, and gentlemen wearing tailored frock coats gathered around the combatants in a wide circle. Some were laying bets, while others spat tobacco juice and showed their companions how they had dealt with past opponents themselves. Several boys crowded between them, though one enterprising towhead stood on a hitching post for a better view over the shoulders of his elders.

Melly did not pause, but waded into the men, with Sarah behind her. There were some scowls and mutters, but they made way for her. Every single one of them knew she was embroiled in this dispute between brothers.

Yet to call what was taking place a fight was totally wrong; the contest was far too one-sided. It was, instead, a punishment. One brother was dealing it out, the other taking it.

Caleb, his face a mask of rage, was pummeling Conrad with his fists. Conrad weaved and ducked, blocking the blows when he could, rolling with them when he couldn't. It was apparent that more than a few had connected, for there was a spreading bruise on his cheekbone and a cut at his brow that streamed blood into his right eye.

"Stop it!" Melly cried out above the noise. "Conrad! Caleb! Stop it this instant!"

If either of the two heard her or noticed her presence, they gave no sign. They circled, one advancing, the other retreating, each identical gaze intent on the other's face. It was disorienting and even macabre to see them, like watching a man battle his mirror image.

"Stand and fight like a man!" Caleb growled, his expression twisting in frustration as he stalked his twin.

Conrad kept moving, his eyes watchful as he spoke. "What I did was wrong, and I've admitted the fault. If you want blood for it, fine. But I won't make a brawl out of it."

"It never stopped you before." Caleb's scorn was plain.

"I don't have anything to prove."

"I think you do. I think that's why you took Melly out on the river, to spite me."

Conrad shifted from his brother's path in a glide of well-oiled muscles. "Taking Melly on the river was a stupid trick that went wrong, nothing else."

The words were laced with pain and self-blame. Melly thought they were for her, that at least Conrad was aware she was witnessing their dispute.

"Oh, I don't think that was it at all," Caleb growled, swinging a hard right as he moved in on his brother. "You're a man of the sea, with a trained eye for weather. You saw the storm signs and took advantage. You know water, read landmarks, remember things like the island because your life may depend on it. You knew exactly where you were going yesterday."

Clasping her hands tightly at her waist, Melly frowned. Could Conrad have known there would be a storm? Had he planned from the first to land on the island, arranged for the loss of the raft?

Caleb was right in one thing at least: Conrad was a seaman, and a good one. Surely he should have known better than to lash the raft to so flimsy a support? Did it follow, then, that her seduction had been planned?

Conrad, watching Melly's face, took a hard punch squarely over the heart. He gasped, reeling with the blow, but the worst of the pain was in his mind. He could not allow Melly to think that what they had shared had meant so little to him.

Lashing out at his brother with words in place of blows, he said in breathless derision, "It's not really Melly you're concerned about, is it? If it was, you wouldn't be making such a noise about what happened."

"What I'm doing is teaching you a lesson!"

"Are you, now? What kind? To watch out for bad luck? Or would it be about brotherly love?"

"To leave what's mine alone!"

Though his ribs hurt where Caleb had pounded them, Conrad laughed. "Here I was thinking it might be respect for the lady."

"Melly will be my wife in a few days. That's all the respect she needs."

The arrogance of that riled Conrad's temper. "You think so? How generous, giving her your precious name after such a terrible disgrace as being caught in the rain with another man. But I'd say something more is needed if she's to be happy."

"What do you know about it? Nothing, and you never will! I'll give her everything she needs: home, children, a good, solid life at my side all the days of our lives—and nights."

Caleb meant the last as a death blow. Against the pain of it, Conrad said, "She might prefer just to be loved."

"By you, a shiftless sea rover?" Caleb grunted his disbelief as he jabbed at his brother.

"By a man who might trade all the oceans of the world for the right woman."

Rage flashed in Caleb's bright blue eyes, so like his brother's. "She'd be a fool to take you. Unless you proved, out there on that island, that she's really no better than you are."

Conrad hit him then, a hard right with every ounce of his

power and anger behind it. And he kept on hitting Caleb until they pulled him off. But it could not erase what had been said, or ease the torment he felt for bringing this final insult down on Melly. Or eliminate his fear that she might believe it.

TEN

Within twenty-four hours, Conrad had made his decision to leave and packed his trunk to go. It was time: he had outstayed his welcome. Remaining could only make matters worse.

Anyway, his ship would be out of dry dock, outfitted, and ready in Baltimore. The steamer *J. B. Cates* was scheduled to put in at the landing again tomorrow at sundown on its run up to Ohio, with connections from there to the Maryland shore. When it left again, he would be on it.

He would miss the wedding that would take place the next day, on Saturday. That was definitely by design. He didn't think he could bear to serve as his brother's best man, even if Caleb still wanted him, which was doubtful.

The event was still going to take place. At least there had been no announcement to the contrary.

Caleb had apparently made his peace with Melly. He had paid

a formal call on her the evening after the fight and stayed some time. What they had said to each other was anybody's guess; what Conrad did know was that Caleb had been whistling on his return. Conrad would have liked to damn him to hell for it, had he not understood the elation too well.

All that was left, then, was saying good-bye to Melly.

He put it off as long as possible. It was forced upon him, finally, on the afternoon of his departure.

Melly, being the lady she was, made it easier for him. She saw him coming up the walk, all rigged out in his gray broadcloth with his hair freshly barbered and his hat in his hand. Rising from her chair, where she had been putting tiny stitches into the hem of a handkerchief, she stood waiting, grave expectation on her lovely face.

"So you're going," she said in clear, musical tones. "Caleb said you would."

Conrad didn't care for the sound of that, but could hardly argue. As he came to a halt on the step below her, he said simply, "It seems best."

"Yes." She swallowed, a visible movement in the graceful line of her throat.

"Melly—"

"No, please, I understand. There's nothing to keep you here."

"There's everything—" he began in fierce contradiction. Then he stopped. Taking a deep breath, he began again without quite meeting the shadowed darkness of her eyes.

"Caleb had a perfect right to be upset over what happened the other day, and I hope you won't blame him. I served him a shabby trick and wound up hurting everybody. Whatever he said was . . . in the heat of the moment and because, well, because he had so much to lose. He didn't mean any of it."

"I know," she said quietly.

He cleared his throat of a troublesome obstruction. "About the way I shanghaied you . . ."

"You forget that I also know you." Her smile was only a flicker across her lips. "I'll admit that I thought for an instant you might have meant to be caught by the storm. But then I remembered what you said on the island and I knew you would never set out to hurt me."

His pent-up breath left him. He pushed his hand into his pants pocket to hide its shaking. Against the ache in his throat, and in his heart, he said, "I did it anyway, in spite of everything. For that I'm desperately sorry."

"Don't be. You didn't—that is . . ." She stopped, began again. "I think we hurt each other, whether we meant to or not. And Caleb most of all."

She met his eyes then, and her own were clouded with regret. Seeing it, he gave a slow nod.

"Caleb will make you a good husband; it would be wrong to think anything else. He's decent and honorable and will do his best to make you happy. More than that, he's my brother. Though you will never be far from my thoughts or my heart, I can't take my own happiness at his expense."

"I understand," she said, the words barely above a whisper. "At least—I know that Caleb is not the only decent and honorable man in this."

His resolve and his voice almost failed him. Straining for control, he said, "Then maybe you can understand why this is good-bye. I can't stay and watch—"

"No." She looked down at her hands, still clutching her piece of sewing, then up again to meet his gaze. "For me it's easier. I will see Caleb, and it will be nearly like seeing you. I'll always know what you look like wherever you are, no matter how much you change. And sometimes when I shut my eyes at night I can imagine—"

"Don't!" he exclaimed, a sound of stark agony.

She stopped, closed her lips, pressed them tightly together. When she looked up again, her lashes were rimmed with wetness. "That was unfair, wasn't it? Forget it, please."

How could he, ever? "Melly, I—"

"No!" she said again. "I'm bound, too, don't you see? I made my promise, and Caleb has built so much on it. I can't take that away from him any more than you can. In any case, you're better off alone. You always were."

Once he would have agreed. No more. Here, right this minute, was the time to tell her so. Now was the time to say how much he adored her, how much he needed her beside him. It was the perfect moment to beg her to come with him.

But he couldn't; he had no right. He would never know what answer she might have given him—a more fitting punishment, it seemed to Conrad, than anything Caleb had managed.

"I expect you're right." The breath he drew hurt deep in his chest, which had nothing to do with the drubbing he had taken from his brother.

She made no reply, but unshed tears glistened in her eyes. He looked into them long seconds, memorizing their color, their shape, their forthright honesty. Remembering the way they had once darkened with desire, for him.

Then he took her hand and removed the piece of sewing from it before raising her fingers to his lips. He closed his eyes as he felt their coolness, the faint tremors that shook them. Then he released her, turned, and walked away.

He was halfway down the street before he realized he was still holding the handkerchief she had been stitching. He spread its folds, staring down at it as he walked. She had just set the last stitches of an embroidered motif: Caleb's initials—or his own—done in gold thread and enclosed in a blood-red heart.

A wedding gift for the groom, no doubt: He should return with it, he told himself, hand it back to her.

Conrad snapped the needle off from the thread, leaving enough length for a finishing knot. He dropped the small, sharp length of steel into the street. Folding the fine linen into a careful square, he put it in his pocket, over his heart. And kept on walking.

❧

"Aunt Dora? Do you ever wish you had married Mr. Prine, after all?"

Melly spoke into a lull in the animated gathering of bridesmaids that took place on the front porch later that evening. She had been subdued yet jumpy, starting at the blast of the whistle from the *J. B. Cates* as it came into the landing, paying more attention to the sun sliding down the slope of the sky toward the featherbed of lavender and gold on the horizon than to the final details of her wedding being discussed around her. Her gaze was pensive now, far away, as she waited for her aunt's answer.

"You asking if I've got regrets, child?" Aunt Dora sent her a shrewd glance as she looked up from the peas she had brought out onto the porch to shell for supper.

Melly gave a slow nod. "Something like that."

"Now and again. Wouldn't be human if I didn't."

"But you never thought of doing anything about it?"

The older woman grimaced. "Not a lot. There was so much against it. Then you came to me."

Melly looked around at her friends, who were watching her with obvious concern in their faces, when they were not exchanging uneasy glances. "Yes, and now I'm going," she said. "You'll be alone."

Down at the river, the three-note steam whistle of the *J. B. Cates* assaulted the air in token of its departure within the half hour. Melly's aunt waited for the sound to die away before she said, "Sounds as if you're trying to arrange my life for me, honey."

"Not really, but I was just thinking—"

"Don't," the older woman recommended. "Don't trouble your brain about me. You got enough to worry about just taking care of your own problems."

"Too true," Melly said with a smile.

Her aunt looked past her as a buggy came down the street, then drew up at the hitching post outside the front yard gate. "Here comes the main one now."

It was Caleb. He was due for supper, the last time she would see him before the wedding. Though she had bathed and changed her dress earlier, she had not expected him to arrive for at least an hour.

Caleb declined Aunt Dora's offer of cherry cordial, spoke politely to the other young women, then took a chair next to Melly. His unease was plain, however, and he seemed to have something on his mind.

The older woman heaved herself to her feet. "Time I was getting these peas on to cook if we're to have them for supper. Sarah, you and Biddy can set the table if you don't mind. Esther and Lydia can peel a few potatoes for a nice salad. Come along now, girls. It's getting late."

As the sound of the women's voices died away in the direction of the kitchen, Melly sat looking at her hands and searching her mind for some comfortable subject for conversation. So many things were unacceptable: the storm and the cooler weather it had brought; the steamer down at the landing; the lack of a best man for the wedding ceremony. Conrad.

Almost as if he could read her mind, Caleb said abruptly, "I guess you know Conrad is leaving this evening."

"Yes." She was hardly in need of a reminder, with the steamboat whistle signaling every few minutes.

"You said your good-byes?"

She nodded, looking away from him.

"And you're content to see him go?"

How was she to answer that? Perhaps a half-truth would do. "Since he could not stay."

"He might have, if you had asked."

The words, so quietly spoken, had such a sound of Conrad that she turned her head to stare. How unfair it was that even their voices should be so near the same. Could she stand it? Could she?

His smile was wry as he met her gaze, as if he understood what she had been looking for all her life, what she was thinking now. "You do love him, don't you? I didn't want to see it or believe it, but it's so plain since the picnic. I can't help wondering if it was him all along."

"Don't," she said on a quickly drawn breath. "*Please.* Just—don't."

"Why? Because I might say something I'll regret? Or because you might?"

"This isn't necessary, Caleb. I'm going to marry you tomorrow. I promise I will try to make you a good wife."

"I expect so, but I don't know if I want that if it's going to be so hard for you. Anyway, I've fooled myself long enough. Conrad was right: I've been too sure the things I could give you were everything you could possibly need."

"It would be," she said miserably, "if I were different."

"But you're not." He shook his head. "I don't know if I would love you quite so much if you were."

"Oh, Caleb." She shook her head, at a loss as she wondered what it was he wanted her to say.

A crooked smile tugged his mouth. "Never mind," he said abruptly. "If you hurry, you can still make the steamboat."

She returned her gaze to his face. "How—what do you mean? I can't do that!"

"Can't you, for Conrad? He's waiting for you."

"What did he tell you? I don't—don't understand."

"He hasn't said anything. We haven't spoken about it at all. Still, I know how he feels—he's my twin, remember? He's dying inside. He needs you."

"But the wedding—I told you I wanted to marry you."

"You did, and I honor you for it." His smile was weary. "I'm just not fool enough anymore to be certain you mean it. You still have time—just—to change your mind, though you have to make it up once and for all. Stay, and you marry me tomorrow. Go, and Conrad will take you with him to Baltimore and the *Queen of the Sea.*"

"Yes, but what if—"

"He'll do right by you; I know that much, because he's my brother and—but never mind. You can be married at the first town you come to tomorrow. After that, who knows? Foreign places, strange climes, then maybe the life of a riverboat captain's wife when the babies come." Caleb's smile was grim. "Conrad thinks he can plan his family, but I've seen the way he looks at you and expect he's more fool than I am about that part."

"He said nothing when he came by a little while ago." She rose to her feet even as she voiced the protest. Her voice held an edge of doubt amounting to near panic. Yet the light in her eyes glowed like the sunset.

He stood also. "I figured that out, which is why I'm here. Make up your mind, Melly. Do it now, or I swear I'll take back everything and hold you to your word."

Distress invaded her features. "Oh, Caleb! How can I leave you to face this alone? What will everyone say?"

He shook his head with a wry twist of his mouth. "It isn't as if they haven't guessed."

"Yes," she whispered. Still she hesitated, searching his face. What she saw there gave her courage, and a slow smile bloomed across her features.

Whirling abruptly, she ran into the house.

What must she take with her? she asked herself.

So much had been packed and removed to Caleb's house already. Aunt Dora could send it after her. Still, there was her wedding dress; she must have that. It would go in the top of her small valise, which stood ready, her underclothing and nightgown neatly folded inside. What else? Her hairbrush and comb from her dressing table, her toothbrush.

The steam whistle was blowing again. She must hurry, hurry.

Her quilt! She could not leave that behind. It would be a reminder of home and friends when she needed it. The initials set into her bridal square were the same, and the date, pray God, would be right. She had thought so often of Conrad, sailing the seas, buying the silk for her in far-off Cathay, as she was sewing the quilt, and had stitched such dreams and idle fancies into it. Perhaps that was why they were coming true.

Yes, she must take it. She snatched it up in her arms.

What else? She turned this way and that in distraction. Then she stopped.

Nothing. She needed nothing, so long as she had her love.

Aunt Dora was waiting for her on the porch. Caleb, Melly realized, must have told her already; her eyes were suspiciously red, and she had her hands wrapped in her apron. Yet she was smiling bravely. Melly set down her valise and quilt for a quick, fierce hug.

"You write now, you hear?" the older woman said, the words thick. "And take care, honey. You—take care."

"Oh, yes, I will, I will. . . ."

Then Sarah and Lydia, Esther and Biddy crowded around, laughing, crying, all trying to hug her at once. Good-bye, good-bye, so many good-byes. She didn't want the tears to fall, but she was leaving so much behind. So much. Yet there was so much ahead.

Caleb was still there also, waiting behind the others, coming forward as they drew back. Melly turned to him.

"Here," he said, taking her hand and thrusting something into it.

It was a gold wedding ring. Inscribed inside were their initials, just as they were written on her quilt. "Oh, Caleb."

"You can use it until he buys you another, or keep it to remember me. I won't need it."

She loved him then as she never had before. And because of it, she knew she would indeed keep his ring. There was a loose stitch in the center square of the quilt next to the wedding date; she had noticed it at the picnic. She would slip the ring in there, as a remembrance, and sew it up safe and tight, for surely Caleb was as much her friend as any of the others.

Abruptly she stepped close, flung her arms around his neck, and kissed him full on the mouth. He raised his hands, but did not quite touch her before he dropped them again. She moved back, her lips curving in a tremulous smile. Then she picked up her things and was gone, leaving him staring, white-faced, behind her.

The *J. B. Cates* blew a last long blast as she ran headlong down the street. She saw it ahead of her, a great wedding cake-like pile of lumber lying nose-in toward the dock. Its white paint gleamed pink with the light of the setting sun. A black cloud of smoke was flying from its stacks to smudge the lavender sky. Men on the dock were loosening its lines, flinging them into the water as deckhands on board the boat began to coil them.

"Wait!"

Her voice broke as she called. They couldn't hear her for the beat of the paddle wheel and the cascading of water. The pilot in the small house above the texas deck was watching the river instead of the dock. The boat was drifting away with the river current as it built up steam.

Her side ached as she ran pell-mell with the valise beating against her leg and the long quilt in her arms threatening to trip her with every step. Her lungs were bursting, her heart shuddering in her chest.

"Wait for me!"

Now the passengers on deck were calling, pointing at her. Her hair was coming down as she lost her pins. Her arms ached with the weight of the valise. Tears rose to blur her vision. She ran harder.

But on the upper deck, a man was whirling to stare, sprinting to the railing. Conrad!

He saw her, waved, then spun around and disappeared. Seconds later, he appeared on the main deck at the gangplank. He did not wait for it to be lowered again, but climbed to the end of the raised planking, using its rope guard rails. While passengers shouted encouragement or yelled up to the pilot to stop, the deckhands leaped to crank the gangplank to a level position. Conrad rode it down, weighting it, holding it steady.

But the boat was pulling farther away, getting ready to back into the river's current before swinging to head upstream.

Then Mr. Prine was beside her, come from the saloon nearby. "Give me your stuff, Miss Melly! I'll chunk it on board for ye!"

She pushed the small bag at him, and he swung around at once to give it a hard heave. It landed on the deck and skidded against the bulkhead. An instant later, the quilt followed the same way, rippling, shining, as it sailed over the water to catch on the railing. Eager hands grabbed it and drew it to safety.

Now Conrad was holding to the gangplank railing, grinning with joy, gladness brilliant in his eyes as he leaned out to her. "Jump, Melly! Jump! Now!"

But the gap was widening between boat and land. The water was swift-running, murky yellow-brown. And deep, so deep. A shiver ran over her, tracking down her back with the chill of old terror.

She couldn't do it. She couldn't.

"Jump, Melly, love. Come on, I'll catch you," he called again, his voice deep and true as he held out his hand. *"Jump if you love me. . . ."*

She squeezed her eyes shut, turned away. She took a step back down the dusty street. Then another. Another.

"Melly!"

It's only water. . . . Life, just life.

Whirling, she picked up her full skirts and began to run. She did not look at the water, but fastened her gaze on Conrad's face and the aching love in his eyes. Harder, faster. At the edge of the landing, she gathered her courage and her strength and leaped as hard and far as she could go.

The water, the deep flowing river, was under her, its widening stretch between bank and boat dancing in the last glow of the sun. She glimpsed it for a blinding instant before she fastened her gaze on the man who reached for her.

Then Conrad's strong arm whipped around her waist like a steel hawser. He staggered with the force of her momentum before swinging her onto the gangplank and dragging her roughly into his hard arms. Holding her so tight she could feel the hard thud of his heart against her ribs, he pressed his cheek to her temple. Overhead, the passengers on the decks cheered and shouted in congratulation and approbation.

"Dear God, Melly," he whispered. "I was so afraid."

He did not say of what, but she knew he meant many things. She tilted her chin as she said, "Not me."

He smiled down at her with aching tenderness. "I adore you, sweet Melly Bennington, and will my whole life long. Come away with me and I'll give you the world tied up in a ribbon. I'll show you sunsets and storms, white sails in moonlight and dark nights on a black sea. I'll sing you a chanty and let the waves rock you to sleep in my arms. And always, wherever you may be, there will I be also, and I will be home."

"I love you, my captain," she whispered. Then smiling, she put her arms around his neck, holding on as if she meant never to let go.

The *J. B. Cates* blew a deafening blast on its whistle and eased backward into the river. Conrad and Melly paid no attention.

It was miles before they noticed that the voyage had begun.

Forever Annie

JO ANNE CASSITY

ONE

WHISKEY, MISSOURI—JUNE, 1853

The quilt was the loveliest Annie O'Neil had ever seen.

The background was tissue silk, once white, now cream with age and adorned with different weaves and shades of blue silk and satin. It was edged in gold-thread featherstitching, and the outlining squares were embroidered with names, written sentiments, and pictures of tokens. In the very center of the quilt was a large multi-pointed starburst, embroidered with the date September 10, 1843. Above the date were the initials AB, and below were the initials CW. One square bore the cross-stitched words *Love comforteth like sunshine after rain*, and another read, *Wither thou goest . . .*

Horace Haney, the traveling peddler, held the quilt up higher for all to see. "Lookee here, folks!" he called out. "We got us a quilt, and a real special one it is, too—"

"One dollar!" came an instant bid from the man who stood

beside Annie. He stole a quick glance in her direction to gauge her reaction.

Without looking at him, she countered with a bid of her own. "Two!" She kept her voice level and cool, carefully camouflaging her desire to own the quilt.

A quiet spread over the crowd as they waited in patient silence for the bidding to continue. They'd gathered, at the far end of town to see what wares Horace had brought down the river to Whiskey this time.

A few seconds passed, then Horace hooted and slapped his pant leg, creating a small dust cloud. He was thin and lanky, with skin so brown and wrinkled it looked like cracked leather. "You two sure make things interestin'!" he said in his usual jovial tone. "Never thought dickerin' for a quilt could be so lively!"

Walker McGregor slid another glance in Annie's direction. He studied her expression, then smiled, suppressing a chuckle. She wanted the quilt with every inch of her starched and proper body, and he knew it. "Two dollars and fifty cents!" he called out.

Time slowed, and once again the crowd waited. They knew what was coming, and she didn't disappoint them. She turned to Walker, hands on hips. "Damn you, McGregor! You don't want that quilt any more than you want the pox."

Walker affected his most innocent expression. "Why, Annie," he drawled in that whiskey-soft voice that made her skin prickle with irritation. "Listen to you carry on now. 'Course I want the quilt. Why else would I bid on it?"

"'Cause I am, that's why!" She spat the words at him, her freckled face blooming as scarlet as a summer sunrise.

He shook his head, folded his arms over his chest, and gave a soft, short chuckle. "Annie O'Neil, tsk, tsk, tsk, I'm surprised at you. A fine upstandin' Christian woman like yourself entertainin' all those evil thoughts inside your pretty little head."

Her green eyes rounded and darkened, then narrowed into thin angry slits. She charged him like a bull, poking him hard in the chest with her forefinger. "Don't you play games with me, McGregor. I know what you're up to."

He lifted one dark eyebrow in question.

"Every time Horace comes to town, you try to outbid me, and you know it!"

"As you do me—"

"The hell I do—"

"The hell you don't! What about that rifle?" His voice rose an octave. "What the hell would a woman like you want with a gun like that?" He gave a short snort and looked her up and down. "Hell, Annie, that Sharp is almost as big as you."

She straightened her back, plunked her hands down on her hips again, and tried to affect her most earnest expression. "I might have need of a gun like that in this town." She looked toward the crowd for affirmation.

Several of the womenfolk murmured agreement, while the menfolk took the safe route and remained silent. The menfolk of Whiskey were well acquainted with Annie O'Neil and her temper, and since their womenfolk had taken quite a liking to her . . . well, they figured it was in their best interest to offer her a measure of respect.

Walker ran a handful of fingers through his dark, wavy hair, and his clear blue eyes crinkled at the corners. "Hell, you'd shoot your goddamned foot off 'fore you'd get around to shootin' anyone else."

Unable to help themselves, the menfolk broke their silence, and a small ripple of laughter skittered throughout the crowd. Annie shot an icy glare toward the sound. Edith Crowley, like many of the women present, elbowed her husband hard in the ribs. Ernest choked on his chuckle, and the laughter around them died.

"Three dollars!" she called out to Horace, then turned her scowl on Walker once again. She waited for time to save her, desperately hoping Horace would end the bidding before Walker could challenge her.

Walker grinned—a very big, very white grin. He was enjoying himself immensely, and he didn't bother to hide the fact. "Five dollars for the quilt, Horace, right here and now." He slapped his thigh. "Let's be done with it. I got work to do and a store to run!"

"Sold!" Horace's grin ate up his face. "For five dollars to Walker!" He took the quilt down off the end of his weathered buckboard and folded it into a haphazard square. Around them the crowd took to buzzing like a nest of busy bees.

"You can't do that!" Annie squawked in disbelief. "We aren't done bidding yet!" For a moment she forgot herself and allowed open longing to show in her expression. A quilter herself, she recognized quality workmanship when she saw it. But it was more than that—somehow she felt the quilt was special, very special indeed.

"It's done!" Walker stated. "It's mine!"

"Yep!" Horace quipped. "It sure as hell is." He was happier than a possum in an egg-filled chicken house. Five dollars was far more than he'd ever expected to get for the quilt.

Annie's temper boiled over. "Well, that's just fine!" She faced Walker, her eyes alight with fiery anger. "You're a cheat, McGregor! And you," she said as she turned on Horace, "are no better!"

"Now, Annie—" Horace began, looking truly repentant.

"Don't you Annie me, you no-good peddler! You're in cahoots with this worthless gambler, and I should have figured it out long ago—"

"Aw, Annie, now that ain't true a'tall," Horace said, looking more wounded by the second. "I like you both just fine, and besides . . . I let you win the bid for the gun last time I was here. You got to understand, I got miles to go 'fore sundown, and everybody knows

you and Walker could bicker over this quilt all goddamned night."
He shot a soulful look toward the horizon and the huge orange ball
that was already sitting on top of the trees. When he looked back
at her, his expression softened further. "You can't afford to pay so
much anyway after what you put out for that gun, Annie."

Her freckled cheeks flamed even brighter. She silently acknowledged that Horace was right. She'd bid far too much on the rifle,
and she'd done it out of spite—simply because she hadn't wanted
Walker to have it. Yet her pride was such that she'd be the last
person to admit her folly or her financial woes. "What I can afford
to pay is my business, Horace Haney, and no one else's." Her voice
was soft, but there was a hard, proud edge to her words.

She lifted her gaze to Walker's, and their eyes locked. They stood
face-to-face in the late afternoon sun, their gazes frozen in battle,
as they'd done so many times in the past two years. The tension
between them was as thick and palpable as two-day-old grits.

Walker read the disappointment in her face, and for a moment
his conscience pricked him. She was right, and they both knew it.
He had as much use for the quilt as she'd had for a Sharp rifle. She
suddenly looked much younger than her twenty-eight years, dressed
in her white blouse and starched skirt, looking Sunday-school
clean, her red-gold hair tied back from her face. Something about
her eyes, defensive yet large and vulnerable, made him sorry. He
almost wanted to give her the quilt.

Almost.

But he knew he wouldn't.

He knew she would take no gifts from him.

Annie O'Neil would not tolerate pity from anyone, especially
the man she held responsible for her husband's death. So he willed
his conscience into oblivion and gave her something she would
expect from him. Something that would set the town to buzzing
for at least a week.

He grabbed her arms, yanked her close, and planted a kiss squarely on her lips.

She sputtered and squawked, but he held her tight and worked her mouth beneath his. Around them the ladies gasped with horror, and the men chuckled with amused satisfaction.

Then, quite abruptly, he let her go.

At a loss for words, she stared up at him, her face blazing, her teeth clenched tight.

Walker McGregor was known for being a scalawag, for his lack of convention, yet for the most part he'd always conducted himself with propriety—at least with the decent women of Whiskey.

Until today.

"Walker McGregor," she finally choked out in a hoarse voice, "you are no gentleman!"

He threw back his head and laughed heartily. "I never claimed to be, Annie." His voice was silky and smooth, his grin cocky and sure.

Infuriated, she spun away. With her head held high, she stalked across Whiskey's dusty Main Street, her arms pumping, her full skirt sweeping out behind her, her long hair trailing down her back almost to her waist.

He watched her go, and though his expression did not give him away, his victory felt very hollow.

She strode past the millinery and the post office, then turned and glanced over her shoulder at him. Their eyes locked for an instant before she turned away and headed directly for the little store that boasted a sign that read: O'Neil's Mercantile.

It was only after she'd disappeared through the door that he felt a rush of irritation swell up from within. "Dammit," he swore quietly. He took the quilt from Horace's hands and paid him. "Thanks, Horace," he said, then followed in her wake, past the barbershop, in front of Martin's Boardinghouse, and on into McGregor's General Store—the store that sat directly across from Annie's.

༒

"Do you feel it, Sister!" the Reverend Leroy Sloan bellowed, his dark eyes blazing holy fire.

"Oh, yes!" the woman cried, her expression one of surprise and ecstasy.

"Do you feel the spirit of the Lord movin' on you?" He threw back his thick mane of silver-blond hair and his entire body took to twitching as he placed his elegant, long-fingered hands on the head of the woman who knelt before him.

"Yes, Preacher, oh, yes!" the woman cried, as she began to weep and sway back and forth on her knees.

Then quite suddenly, her eyes rolled back in her head and she fell over at his feet. She lay unmoving, slain in the spirit, as they called it. The preacher waited a brief moment, then moved on to the next needy recipient of his gift.

Around him the entranced crowd swayed and moaned, and a chorus of "amens," "hallelujahs," and "go to it, brothers!" rang out into the night, amidst bouts of writhing and weeping.

The crowd was taken with the Reverend Sloan. He was a sight to behold, as handsome as sin and every bit as appealing. This group of townsfolk was no different from any other. It didn't matter what town he rode into, he never lacked for attention, and his revivals never lacked for attendance. When the Reverend Sloan held a revival, everyone came, and anybody who dared not attend was considered bound for hell.

Leroy paused before the next anxious soul and repeated the words he'd spoken just moments ago. Within seconds this woman, too, fell over in a faint.

He smiled inwardly.

This work of his was special indeed, and he knew it. It had to be. It was his livelihood.

⁂

Later that evening, after the crowd had dissipated, Leroy entered his tent and packed the last of his preacher clothes into his bags. When he was done, he turned and walked out into the fading sunlight. The June evening was warm; fireflies twinkled and danced.

The huge tent would be down and ready for travel within the hour, and he and his entourage would be on their way. As he walked over to the wagon, he hummed out the melody of "Amazing Grace," one of his favorite hymns.

He thought about the people in the town he would leave behind. They were good people. He had given them what they wanted—faith, hope, a miracle or two; and they'd given him what he craved most—money.

He felt no guilt about taking their money. After all, he'd earned it.

"Ready, Reverend?" Brother Randy Ramp called out from behind the tent.

"Pack it up, Randy," Leroy answered. "God willin', we'll be in Whiskey by Saturday next."

"Amen," Randy said, then turned to the others. "Let's pack it up. The reverend wants to be in Whiskey by Saturday!"

A small commotion ensued, and the ragtag group of ten worked together to bring the tent down and pack the last of their earthly belongings into the three covered wagons.

Then Leroy Sloan, preacher and healer, worker of miracles, was on his way to the next town, and to his destiny: Annie O'Neil.

⁂

Charlotte McGregor's husband had built her a lovely little house at the end of Cork Street, and most of the time she stayed there, fussing in her flower garden and holding tea parties, unless she was attending a prayer meeting or something else of similar interest. In rare cases, when she could find absolutely nothing else to occupy her time, she climbed up into her buggy and ventured on down to the store.

So it was on this day that she rode into town just as Horace Haney rode out.

She entered her husband's store in a fluffy whirlwind of gingham and lace. Her eyes invariably spotted anything out of place or anything that had been added to the store since her last visit. Immediately her gaze found the quilt where it lay folded over the back of a chair near the window. She went over to it directly. She snatched it up and shook it open, then examined it slowly, her pretty brown eyes lighting with pleasure. "It's lovely, Walker."

Standing behind the long polished counter, Walker nodded, neither agreeing nor disagreeing. He'd come to find either option a difficult choice with women like Charlotte.

"Horace was peddling this?" Her eyes found his.

"Yep."

"Hmmm . . ." She thought about that a moment, then said, "It looks like something Annie O'Neil would be more interested in owning than you would."

Walker met his sister-in-law's gaze squarely, then shrugged a thick shoulder and walked over to a shelf where he busied himself with straightening several bags of flour that were already stacked quite neatly. "I thought we could hang it up in the store for now. It might brighten the place up some."

She continued to study him from beneath thick lashes. "I suppose we could." She paused a moment, then added, "'Course, I might like it for myself." She waited for his reaction, and when it didn't come, she decided to let the matter rest. She had learned early on that Walker was nothing like his brother John, her dearly beloved late husband. Walker could not be prodded, provoked, or manipulated into doing anything he didn't want to do, and if he gave something to someone, he gave it simply because he wanted to, and for no other reason. She also knew he'd only stayed in Whiskey out of a sense of duty, and that in order to keep him here, she would have to win him.

Charlotte was no fool.

She felt certain that in all of his thirty-four years Walker McGregor had never been won by any woman.

Yet.

TWO

Whiskey, Missouri, bordered the mighty Mississippi River. It was a friendly little town that attracted a variety of travelers and commerce, which was the very reason Annie's late husband, George, had decided to pack up their small store in Boardman Township in rural Ohio and head west.

Whiskey's Main Street was lined with wooden buildings that boasted many fine establishments: a bank, a respectable town hall, a little red-brick schoolhouse, Edith Crowley's millinery, a post office run by Tucker Hopkins and his wife Josie, Haag's Hotel, Jake and Mabel Martin's Boardinghouse, Eugene William's Barbershop, Josh Adams' Livery, the Whiskey Jail, operated by Sheriff Delbert Nagy, and of course McGregor's General Store and O'Neil's Mercantile.

Near the river, along the outskirts of town, ran River Road, which harbored a couple of establishments that the good folks of

Whiskey considered not so fine, such as Sally's Parlor and Otis Quinby's Saloon, both of which gave Preacher Elmo Fire, pastor of Whiskey's First Baptist Church, plenty of fuel for his Sunday morning sermons.

On down River Road was Perry's Landing, which served the community well, transporting folks back and forth across the mighty river. Daniel's Road and Cork Street, the town's other two roads, were lined with many of the locals' homes.

Annie's decision to make her home in Whiskey had been ambivalent. But George had been dead set on coming, and she'd been raised to believe that a good woman—that is, a godly woman—always respected her husband's wishes.

Now, however, she wished she hadn't tried to be so godly or so good and had fought against his decision. Had she done so, she felt, George might be alive today.

Despite the loss of her husband, however, Whiskey was her home now. Their settling in Whiskey had brought her many friends and the enjoyment of sharing the quilting craft she loved.

Whiskey's quilting circle consisted of seven ladies, sometimes nine, depending on whether the spinster sisters, Gertrude and Gladys Baker, were feeling sprightly enough to attend. There was Annie, Edith Crowley and her daughter Clara, Hester Haag, Mabel Martin, and two fifteen-year-old girls, Emma Thomas and Adelle Hill.

The ladies met every Tuesday and Thursday evening at seven-thirty sharp at O'Neil's Mercantile. They quilted and gossiped over tea and cookies, while across the street at McGregor's General Store their menfolk gathered to gamble, tell jokes, and drink whiskey.

The ladies didn't approve of the menfolk's choice of activities, but then, the menfolk of Whiskey thought the ladies' quilting circle boring and silly.

Yet week after week nothing changed.

This night was no different.

Annie eased the curtain aside and peered through the twilight at the half-opened window in the store across the street. The lights from McGregor's General Store shone brightly, and the sound of male laughter and the soft slap of cards floated in on the breeze.

She gave a huff of disgust. If George were alive today, she mused, he'd be across the street—squandering what little profit they'd made that day.

The thought made her angry.

She believed she'd loved him as much as any woman could love a husband. Yet she'd always felt there was something lacking between them. She didn't know what it was and, now that he was gone, she wasn't sure she wanted to know. Her greatest regret was that they'd had no children. She desperately loved children, and she knew they would have been a great comfort to her. She also knew that time was pressing in on her, that her chances of having children grew smaller with every passing year. Sometimes, in the loneliest hours of the night, her heart ached with that knowledge.

"They're at it again," Hester Haag said from behind, peering over Annie's shoulder.

"There's nothing new about that, dear," Edith Crowley said, then maneuvered her ample body around the quilting frame and bent over to take another stitch on the design she was working on. Edith was a good-natured woman with a pair of high, mountainous breasts whose very presence seemed to sap her energy.

Hester turned away from the window and walked back across the floor to her chair. Hester was Edith's best friend and her opposite in every way. She was thin and small and, more often than not, her face was screwed into more wrinkles than a raisin. "I ought to go over there and drag Joe out of that place by his ear!"

Inwardly the other women winced and held their breath, hoping Hester would not follow through with the threat. Although they disapproved of their men gambling and drinking, they preferred to have them doing such things across the street, where they could keep an eye on them, than to have them down at Sally's Parlor or Otis Quinby's Saloon, where they could engage in any manner of debauchery. After several tension-filled moments, Hester gave a tortured sigh and reached for the square of quilt she'd been working on. She took a series of careful stitches, and the other ladies gave a soft whoosh of relief.

"I don't see why Charlotte allows such goings-on," Hester said. "After all, it is her store."

"But Walker runs it." Edith looked up from her work. "And Charlotte isn't about to challenge Walker." Edith lifted one furry gray eyebrow. "She hopes to marry him, you know."

Gertrude's and Gladys' stitches halted, and their heads came up. At eighty-two and eighty-three years of age, they both claimed to be deaf as fence posts, yet at times like these, their hearing was miraculously restored.

Hester gave a loud snort. "Why, that's ridiculous!"

"What's so ridiculous about it?" Edith asked.

"Walker is her husband's brother. Besides, he's a scoundrel."

"He's the kindest scoundrel this town ever saw," Edith said with purpose. "He's given generously to every charity event we've ever held, and he's always been polite to me. And everyone knows that the Johnson family would have starved to death last winter if he hadn't given their oldest boy work in the store." Edith gave a great huff, her huge breasts rising and falling with an almost audible thump. "And his rascally ways are just an act, if you ask me."

Annie stared out the window and thought about the subject of their conversation. She and Walker had been competing for business ever since he'd taken over the store for his deceased brother three years ago, but the competition had intensified since George's death.

She watched a shadow walk across the floor, then stop in front of the window. She knew the shape, the very width and size of him, and she felt a quiver deep inside her stomach. He was not an excessively large man, rather average in height and very lean. But his shoulders were wide and strong and his arms muscular. She'd always felt dwarfed by him.

She remembered the feel of his mouth on hers, and a hot shiver coursed through her.

Clara Crowley stood up from her chair. At twenty-two, she was a pretty, pleasantly plump young woman with soft blue eyes and sunshine-blond hair. She and Annie had become fast friends when Annie and George had moved to Whiskey four years ago, and now that George was gone, when she wasn't helping her mother out at the millinery, Clara helped Annie out in the store. "Mama's right about one thing: Walker is a good man. But I doubt that Charlotte will win him. What do you think, Annie?"

It took a long time for Annie to answer, and when she did she lied. "I try not to think about Walker McGregor at all."

"Well," Hester said, "he was terribly indecent yesterday, kissing Annie like that in front of the entire town."

Edith lifted her head from her work. "Of course we all know he was only trying to get the best of you, Annie, but Horace shouldn't have allowed him to outbid you on the quilt like that. It really wasn't fair."

Adelle Hill and Emma Thomas, both fifteen, looked at each other and giggled. The quilt hardly warranted a thought as far as they were concerned, but the kiss, now that was something they wanted to hear more about.

Annie shrugged and forced her voice to sound nonchalant. "If he wants the quilt so badly, let him have it. I doubt he has much use for it anyhow."

"He could give it to Charlotte, I suppose," Gertrude Baker put in, speaking much louder than was necessary.

"What's that?" her sister Gladys yelled, cocking a hand behind her ear.

"I said he could give it to Charlotte!" Gertrude yelled into her sister's face.

"I don't think he will," Clara said softly.

"Why not?" Gladys asked, hearing the last statement quite clearly.

"Oh, I don't know." Clara shrugged a shoulder, then looked over at Annie once again. "I just don't think he bought it for that reason."

Disgusted with the topic of conversation, Annie turned away from the window and faced her friends. "Do we have to discuss Walker McGregor? For heaven's sake, I can't get away from that man no matter where I am!"

Edith smiled indulgently. "All right, then, let's talk about Mary Adams' new baby."

"Oh, yes," Hester said gladly. "Did you see that child's eyes? Did you ever see anything bluer? . . ."

Walker stepped out of the store and into the darkness, closing the door behind him. The card game had ended hours ago, and though he was tired, he was too restless to sleep. He leaned a shoulder against a porch post and plunged his hands deep into his trouser pockets. The night air was cool, a welcome change from the heat of the day. Spring had been warm and dry, and summer promised to follow suit.

Walker was glad most of the men had left happy tonight, having won enough money to satisfy their egos, though there were a couple of rowdies: young Terry Longer and Big Bufus Myers, who bet heavier than most and got a bit surly when they had to pay up.

Walker's card games rarely saw high stakes and were considerably more civilized than those that took place down at Otis Quinby's Saloon. Otis tended to attract most of the boatmen and professional gamblers off the river—a coarser variety of men—whereas Walker's clientele, for the most part, consisted of the citizens of Whiskey, men who were out for the evening while their wives quilted across the street. Every now and then, however, one or two of the boatmen and gamblers trickled up from the river to play a hand or two. And once drunk, these men, men like Terry Longer and Big Bufus Myers, often brought trouble.

They reminded Walker of George O'Neil.

George had been more than a little drunk the night he'd taken off for the river.

After the card game was over, he'd provoked a fight, calling the man who'd bested him a cheat, and if Walker hadn't intervened, that gambler, instead of the river, would have ended George's life then and there.

Walker knew Annie blamed him for George's death. And when he was honest with himself, he knew he blamed himself a little, too. He'd tried to curtail the stakes that night, but things had gotten out of hand. How could he have known that George would bet so heavily and then, after losing, take off for the river and drown himself?

Folks said it was an accident, that he was skunk drunk and fell into the Mississippi; they said that the mighty current had taken him on down to the muddy bottom. But Walker wasn't so sure, and he knew Annie wasn't either.

Walker tipped his head back and looked up at the stars. They blinked like fireflies against a midnight sky.

Missouri was a pretty place indeed—a moonlit sky at night, and miles and miles of lush, verdant land and wildflowers as far as the eye could see during the day.

Yet, with all that, he wondered what he was doing here in Whiskey and how much longer he would stay.

He'd been asking himself that same question for over three years now.

Whiskey had only been a place to visit up until then. It was the little town John and Charlotte lived in with their two children: David, eight, and Susan, six.

Then, on one of Walker's rare visits, his brother had died suddenly.

Now Whiskey was Walker's home, and he felt he had little choice in the matter. He was not the settling kind, and did not claim to be. Yet here he was, living in the back room of a store he didn't own, in a town that was far too small to supply him the pleasures he'd always enjoyed.

But John was his brother. So he'd do right by him. He'd do what he could. He'd run the store and take care of Charlotte and the children until she married again.

He just wished she'd hurry up about it and quit looking in his direction. He liked Charlotte just fine, but that was as far as it went. He knew most men would think he was crazy. Charlotte was a beautiful woman.

But he thought of her as his sister, the wife of his brother and nothing more.

As for Whiskey—it wasn't so bad. He liked his neighbors, and provoking Annie O'Neil had become quite a pleasurable pastime. So much so that he barely thought about Ginny and New Orleans any longer.

He wondered what it was about Annie that fascinated him. Did he dislike her so much? Or did he like her so much that he was really only hoping for a chance to vindicate himself?

He knew the answer. He'd always known the answer. He'd

wanted Annie O'Neil from the very moment he'd laid eyes on her, and that was why, when her husband had killed himself, he'd felt a terrible guilt all his own. He would never let Annie know about his feelings; it would serve no purpose. She was not his type of woman. He was far more comfortable with a woman who had no expectations beyond those of the evening, like the girls down at Sally's Parlor.

He'd once felt differently, with Ginny, but that was a long, long time ago, another lifetime ago.

From out of the past came the memory of New Orleans and a young girl with dark hair and large dark eyes. He would have died for that girl, had almost died for her, had in fact killed a man for her, only to learn that she did not want him, that she was in love with another. He'd been merely the pawn she'd used to get rid of the man her father had chosen for her. Once he'd done the deed, she'd cast him aside and walked away with another.

Fifteen years ago. God Almighty, he'd been such a young heartsick fool.

When he heard the door open across the street, his thoughts returned to the present.

She stepped out into the moonlight and stood a long moment, breathing deeply of the night air. Her hair, a river of red and gold, hung full and loose around her shoulders. She was dressed in a long white nightdress. She couldn't see him, he was sure, shadowed as he was, so he remained still and silent and took his time studying her. She walked across the porch, in front of a pale strip of light coming from her window. The light shone through her nightdress and gave him a glimpse of her curves, soft and feminine. He felt a swift rush of arousal.

She sat down in the rocker, leaned her head back against the wooden frame, and set it in motion. He heard the slow rhythmic creaking from where he stood, and that, too, was arousing and tantalizing. With slivers of silvery moonlight shining down on her, she was lovely.

He thought it a shame that life had dealt her such a hand. He imagined her as she should be—a happy, sweet girl, her green eyes shining with hope instead of sadness.

He stifled his thoughts and took a long, deep breath, then very quietly turned and went back inside the store.

Hank Davis swung down from his horse. He walked over to the hitch rail and secured the horse's reins.

A white-hot sun beat down on his head without mercy. His clothes were clammy and wet with sweat. He was stiff and tired and so hungry he couldn't think straight. Worst of all, by the looks of the campfires he'd seen on the outskirts of town, he was too late.

Again.

He walked into the sheriff's office and stood for a long moment, letting his eyes adjust to the dimness.

Sheriff Sam Wells looked up from his desk. He tipped his hat back and squinted, trying to identify the man before him. Then quite suddenly, recognition dawned, and a smile flashed across his weathered face. He stood, extending his hand. "Why, if it isn't Hank Davis. What brings you to town?"

Hank shook the sheriff's hand firmly and smiled, his dark brown eyes crinkling at the corners. "I'm lookin' for a man."

"Ain't ya always?" Sam asked, then chuckled.

"I suppose I am."

"Who is it this time?"

Hank paused a moment, and his smile slipped a little. "I'm

lookin' for a preacher. The Reverend Leroy Sloan, to be exact. Real handsome fella with almost white hair."

Sam sat down on the edge of his desk. "Well, Hank. You're two days too late."

The grin returned to Hank's face. "Two days ain't so bad. Last time it was four. Time 'fore that it was nine. You don't happen to know what direction he was headed?"

"Well, I can't say for sure, but folks say he was headin' south." The sheriff's face sobered. "He cleaned this town out, Hank."

Hank nodded. "He usually does. Well . . . I got an old friend south of here in Whiskey. I just might look him up."

"Well, there ya go," the sheriff said, his smile returning. "Hey, why don't ya stay for the night, and I'll buy you supper."

"Wish I could, Sam, and I'm mighty obliged for the offer, but I been trailing this preacher for over three years now, and I'm gonna perform a miracle of my own: I'm gonna catch him. It's time for a reckoning."

With that said and a smile on his face, Hank turned and strode back out into the blazing Missouri sunshine.

THREE

The Reverend Leroy Sloan rode into Whiskey on Saturday morning.

The sun was high, and the streets were crowded. Saturday was the busiest day of the week in Whiskey. Folks came in off the farms and from across the river to stock supplies, do their banking, and sometimes just sit and visit awhile along the walk in front of the mercantile and general store.

Leroy's arrival caught the attention of everyone who was out and about that morning.

Annie was outside sweeping the planked walk in front of her store when Harold Hollins passed by in his wagon and called out a warm howdy-do. She smiled and waved a greeting.

From inside the store Clara called out, "Did you order the bolt of material for Gertrude Baker?"

"Yes, last week."

Clara stuck her head out the door. "How about the thread for Hester?"

"Ordered," Annie said, and began to sweep the walk.

"Good," Clara said, relieved. "I don't need those two hens clucking after me."

Annie chuckled. "I doubt they'd come after you, dear."

Clara made a face. "When they can't find you, they come after me."

Just then the door to McGregor's General Store opened, and Walker stepped out onto the walk. Seeing him, Annie's pleasant mood evaporated.

Walker's eyes found her immediately, and a wide grin stretched across his face. "Morning, Annie!" he called out.

"McGregor," she acknowledged with a stiff nod.

"Nice one, ain't it?"

"You could call it that."

"How's business?" He hooked his hands on his hips, his eyes snapping with enjoyment.

"It could be better."

"And how are you?"

"I was better a minute ago," she answered coolly.

He paused a moment, then threw back his head and roared with laughter. When finally he quieted, he said, "Aw, Annie, you never fail to amaze me with your diplomacy." He leapt down the two steps to the dusty road and swaggered across Main Street. "I have something for you." In one agile movement he took the steps up to where she stood, then held out an envelope. "Tucker dropped this off with my mail."

She considered his offering a short moment and then, spotting her name on the front, took the letter from his hand with a terse "Thank you." She dropped her gaze and placed the broom between them, wrapping both hands around the handle.

He stared down at her. Her pretty green dress fit her nicely. Her waist was nipped by the waistband of a starched white apron. Her bright hair was pulled back from her face and hung in gentle waves down her back. Shorter tendrils curled around her face. She looked as fresh and sunny as the morning itself, despite the scowl that marred her face. "You look mighty fetchin' this morning," he told her, though he knew the compliment would make her prickle.

Her eyes lifted and sought his. She was used to his barbs and teasing, and she knew how to counter both. But the sincerity she heard in his voice now made her feel vulnerable. Though he stood a respectable distance away, he suddenly seemed very close.

Too close.

His broad shoulders stretched the red work shirt he wore. It was open at the neck, exposing his thick tanned throat. His dark trousers were tucked neatly into worn but polished black boots. Wide black suspenders dented his shoulders, and his hair, black and wavy, contrasted appealingly with his clear blue eyes.

Annie knew most women found him handsome, devilishly so, and she could almost understand why.

Almost.

Then sanity returned with force. "Thanks for the mail, McGregor, but if you don't mind, I have work to do." Holding the envelope in her hand, she returned to sweeping the porch with a fury, creating a dust cloud worthy of her efforts.

"You're welcome, Mrs. O'Neil," he said, but didn't move.

Out of the corner of her eye, she caught sight of his grin. Ignoring him, she jammed the envelope into her apron pocket without taking time to look at the postmark and swept a vicious circle around his boots, covering them quite nicely with a thick layer of dust. Still he made no attempt to move, so she glanced back up at him.

Their gazes met and held.

They stared at each other a long, long moment, both refusing to back down, and time stretched on, until a commotion up the street drew their attention away from each other.

From the north end of Main came a small train of three wagons. The first was led by a man driving two horses. His bearing was noble. He wore a spotless white shirt and black trousers. The breeze caught at his silvery hair and blew it back from an aristocratic temple. As he drew closer, the activity in the streets seemed to slow and eventually halt; then, entranced, the crowd parted to either side of the road to allow the wagons to cut a path down the center.

The men of the town studied the train with suspicion, while the womenfolk openly gaped at the gentleman leading the train. He was as handsome as any man could be.

Curious as the next person, Walker crossed his arms over his chest and leaned his shoulder up against the porch post to observe the new arrivals.

In time, the wagons drew abreast of O'Neil's Mercantile. The man in the first wagon slowed his horses' gait, while his dark eyes seemed to search Annie's entire building with purpose. Finally his gaze landed on her. His eyes bored a hole straight into her. He nodded, rose slightly from his seat, and bowed, then seated himself once more. He gave his reins a short flick and on down Main he and the other two wagons went.

Walker chuckled. "Well, hell's bells, Annie. Looks like you got yourself an admirer."

Annie's cheeks flamed. "Go to hell, McGregor!" she hissed under her breath. She felt like beaning him with her broom, but a crowd had begun to gather, and after the spectacle he'd caused just a few days ago, she didn't want to be the fuel for next week's gossip as well.

"I most likely will," Walker said, his eyes following the stranger.

Something about the man was oddly familiar. Walker's smile faded, and he frowned. He felt a chill shiver through him.

"Well, glory be," Clara said, coming out of the mercantile behind them. She wiped her hands on her apron and took a place to Annie's left, staring after the retreating wagons.

"What is all the fuss about?" Edith Crowley asked, sticking her head out the door of her millinery. "You'd think this town never has visitors."

Tucker Hopkins and his wife Josie came out of the post office next door and joined the others. "Not like the likes of him, we don't," Josie said with a sly wink at Clara.

Her wink earned her a snort and a frown from her husband. "Who do you imagine he is?" Tucker asked Walker.

Walker shrugged. "I ain't got a clue, but I have a feelin' we're about to find out."

Annie felt oddly disconcerted. She thought about those dark, dark eyes, and a shiver ran down the length of her spine.

Walker glanced over at her, then over his shoulder at Tucker. "I'll bet my bottom teeth, though, he's trouble."

Rousing from a dazed-like state, Annie shot him a disgusted look. "You have a lot of room to talk."

He angled her a wicked grin and wiggled his eyebrows. "Don't I, though?" He paused a second, thinking, then his smile faded once more. "I got a feelin' this fella's a different kind of trouble."

"You don't know that," she countered, challenging his presumption.

"No," Walker said, "I don't know anything for sure." He clumped down the steps, then turned to face her. His eyes took on a mischievous glint. "But when I get a feelin' about something, I'm rarely wrong." He paused, considering his next words. "And I'd be willin' to bet that quilt I got against that Sharp rifle of yours that I'm right."

Annie glanced at the back of the receding wagon train. Walker was no fool, she knew; he'd only place a wager on something he felt confident about. But, she told herself, Walker was as human as the next person, and therefore he could be wrong. Despite her aversion to gambling, she thought about his offer. The desire to own the quilt was sharp and tantalizing, the desire to best him even more so. Before she could stop herself, the words were out of her mouth. "All right, McGregor. You're on. The Sharp against the quilt."

"Done." Walker nodded, then turned on his heel and strode across the dusty street to his store. He climbed the stairs, chuckling to himself. Before summer passed, he thought with satisfaction, he'd own that rifle, by God.

❧

The late afternoon sun stretched a stream of sunlight across the wooden mercantile floor. Dust motes danced like sparkling fairies in the beams of golden light. Annie straightened rows of jars filled with pickles, beets, and peppers on the tall shelves beside the counter.

Standing behind the counter, Clara untied her apron and pushed a lock of sunny hair back from her face. "I wish you'd change your mind and come on down to the river tonight."

"I don't think so," Annie said, pretending disinterest, though her curiosity was as high as the next person's. Gossip had fired a path through town by early afternoon, and word had it that the handsome stranger was the Reverend Leroy Sloan, traveling revivalist and healer. The first revival would be held that very evening, and the entire town was in a stir about it.

The menfolk thought all the hoopla ridiculous, but planned to attend the revival to see what all the fuss was about. The womenfolk thought God had heard their prayers at last and had sent them a prophet to lead their men to salvation. And, truth be told, the womenfolk thought salvation had never looked so good.

"Well," Clara said, "Mother is determined to go, and to be quite honest, I'm a little curious myself."

Annie shot a glance over her shoulder. "It wouldn't be the handsome reverend you're curious about, would it?" Her green eyes were teasing.

"Humph," Clara huffed, her cheeks turning pink. "I never really got a look at him. And even if I did, I doubt it would do me any good. Everyone said he was quite busy eyeing you."

"He was being friendly," Annie said, though she, too, had been taken aback by his obvious interest. She didn't for a moment fancy herself a beauty and was quite puzzled by the stranger's attention. With a silent shrug, she returned to dusting the shelves and straightening her jars.

The bell above the door tinkled, and Edith Crowley and Hester Haag entered the store. Edith, along with her daughter, Clara, had appointed herself Annie's guardian after George's passing.

"Hello, dearies," Edith called out breathlessly. She glanced in Clara's direction. "Ready to go?"

"In a minute, Mama. I was trying to persuade Annie to come with us."

"Oh, yes, Annie, do come. You should get out. The fresh air will do you good, and a good old-fashioned revival never hurt anyone." She lumbered across the floor to Annie's side.

"Yes, Annie," Hester put in. "We all could stand a little soul-searching and confession now and then." Her words were spoken meaningfully. She liked and respected Annie, and she believed that Annie was a Godfearing woman, but she'd also overheard Annie's use of vulgar language when provoked by Walker McGregor.

"Not tonight," Annie said.

"Oh, pooh, Annie," Edith pouted, "the entire town will be out. Even Preacher Fire will be present to hear what the young reverend has to say."

Clara hung her apron on a peg on the wall behind the counter. "I doubt the young preacher can outpreach Preacher Fire. Nobody spouts hellfire like our preacher." She gave a short giggle and winked at Annie.

Edith frowned her disapproval, while Hester gasped her shock. "Don't be blasphemous, Clara," Edith reprimanded gently. "Preacher Fire is a fine preacher."

"Yes, Mama, I know, but he's been pounding that pulpit and preaching those same three sermons since I was knee-high to a tadpole."

Edith agreed with a nod. "But he has the salvation of his flock at heart, and he's a good, God-fearing man."

"He is that," Hester put in piously, "which is more than I can say for most of Whiskey's menfolk."

"Come with us, Annie," Clara pleaded, trying once more.

"Not tonight," Annie repeated with a smile, then tried to placate them with, "Maybe next time."

"Oh, all right," Edith conceded, anxious to be on her way. "Let's go get some supper, Clara. Then we can go on down to the river. Your father's probably so hungry he's chewing the hitch rail by now."

Clara laughed and gave Annie a hug. "See you in the morning."

"Bright and early." Annie patted her hand.

After the three others left, Annie went in the back of the store to her rooms. There were three rooms, one very large one that she used for supplies and two others that were her home. One was a bedroom, the other a combined sitting room and kitchen. They were cozy and charming, though a bit crowded. The bedroom housed an impressive brass bed that had once belonged to her grandmother, and the sitting room was furnished with her mother's rocker, a small settee, and many of Annie's quilt creations.

She sat down, untied her apron, and cast it over the end of the bed.

Silence echoed around her and from out of the past came the memory of George and herself holding each other in this bed. Though their times of joining had been infrequent and rarely satisfying, this particular memory was bittersweet. He had promised to build her a house here in Whiskey, a house that would be a real home—a home for their children. His intentions, though she believed them sincere at the time, had never seen fruition.

The memory made her sad, and she found herself missing him. She lay back on the bed and closed her eyes.

In time, thoughts of George faded and were replaced by the disconcerting memory of Walker's lips on hers, soft and hard and demanding. A shock rippled through her body, skittering to the ends of her fingers and toes. Surprised by the intensity of her reaction, her eyes popped open, and she sprang from the bed, shaking off the memory, along with the feelings it evoked.

What is wrong with you, Annie O'Neil? she silently scolded herself. *Thinking about that man! He's a murderer. He killed your husband.*

No, a small voice within answered, *George killed himself.*

Annie dropped her chin to her chest and sighed. It was true, and she'd known it for a very long time. But it was easier blaming Walker. Blaming him, unfair as it was, put to rest the odd feelings he aroused in her.

Having no further argument against the truth, she rose and fussed around the rooms, straightening things that were not out of place, until pale blue twilight began to seep through the windows and steal away the daylight's sun.

Then she stepped out onto her porch and lowered herself into her rocker.

❧

The last thing Walker wanted to do was attend a revival.

But as evening descended, his curiosity had grown, and the niggling feeling that he'd seen the reverend somewhere before would not let him rest.

He found the tent set up at the far end of Cork Street, behind town hall, along the riverbank, positioned at the opposite end of town from the First Baptist Church of Whiskey. It was a huge structure, a half-tent of sorts, completely open in front so that everyone could see inside. The entire area was lit by lanterns that had been hung in the trees. The area was further illuminated by a large campfire that flickered and hissed to the left of the tent.

From the size of the crowd, Walker knew it had been gathering for some time. An almost festive air of anticipation crackled throughout, while the sharp, pungent smell of the river rose up and mingled with the scent of the animals present. Frogs burped and fireflies winked, oblivious to the event that was about to take place.

Walker stood on the outer edge of the crowd, arms crossed over his chest. He heard a sound to his right and turned to see Sheriff Delbert Nagy coming up behind him. The sheriff took a place at his side. Delbert was tall and lanky, with overly large hands and feet that looked extremely awkward. But when he walked he was as graceful and smooth as butter flowing over a hot ear of corn, and everybody in Whiskey knew he could get a gun to his shoulder in one agile movement that was nothing short of a blur.

"What do you make of all this nonsense?" the sheriff asked Walker in his quiet voice.

"Hell, I don't know, Delbert."

"It's looks mighty shaky to me," he said. "He's too damned pretty to be a preacher." A hint of amusement shone in the sheriff's pale blue eyes. He pushed his hat back from his forehead. "Never did trust a pretty preacher."

A wry smile touched Walker's mouth. "I got a feeling I've seen him before. I don't remember where, though."

"Hmmm . . ." Delbert rubbed his whiskered chin thoughtfully. "You'll come see me if you remember?"

"You can count on it."

Delbert nodded and walked away, and Walker's gaze followed him as he worked his way through the crowd.

FOUR

Annie stood on a hill beneath the limbs of the ancient oak tree, listening to the Reverend Sloan lead the crowd through the second stanza of "Amazing Grace." Though she had not planned to attend the revival, the restlessness that had plagued her earlier had not eased, and to quell it, she'd ventured out.

The night was warm and steamy, full of night sounds and shadows and mosquitoes that buzzed around her head. Though she'd bathed and donned a fresh dress, her clothing already felt damp and uncomfortable. She pushed a curling strand of hair back from her face and searched the crowd for familiar faces.

It seemed the entire town had turned out for the revival. Through a break in the sea of bodies, she spotted Clara, Edith, and Hester standing near the front. Edith's husband, Ernest, and Hester's husband, Joe, their expressions tortured, were in attendance, also.

Annie contemplated joining them, but before she could decide to do so, she felt his presence.

"Hello, Annie."

"McGregor," she greeted grudgingly, casting a quick glance over her shoulder.

He smiled down at her, his face shadowed by a thick tree limb. "So how's business?" he asked.

"Could be better," she answered, then gave him an appraising stare. "This is the last place I expected to see you."

He chuckled, his blue eyes amused. "I wouldn't have missed it for the world. I got a wager on this fella, if you remember." He paused a moment. "So what brings you out?"

"Couldn't sleep," she admitted honestly, and turned to watch the spectacle taking place before her.

Without saying more, he took a place at her side, leaned a shoulder up against the oak, and pushed his hands down deep into his pockets.

They stood side by side on that Missouri hill, while time ticked by and the fireflies flitted around them. As the seconds stretched on, they grew very aware of each other.

"Nice night," he finally said, glancing over at her. The evening breeze caught at her hair and blew it back from her face, revealing her throat and the tiny little pulse that beat at its base. He allowed himself a moment to study her. She wore a yellow dress that fit her snugly through the bodice and waist; the skirt was full and loose. His gaze quietly shifted to her breasts.

"Hmmm, yes, but warm," she answered at length, her gaze still fixed before her. He smelled clean and spicy. His was a tantalizing, seductive scent that was as pleasant as it was unnerving. She glanced over to find him staring at her. She held his gaze long enough to acknowledge silently that he looked very handsome tonight in his plain white shirt and dark trousers.

She tried to distract herself from the nearness of his presence by once again searching the crowd for familiar faces. Her gaze settled on the Reverend Sloan. As though he knew she was watching him, his head lifted, and their eyes locked. He smiled slightly and nodded. Her cheeks warmed, and she glanced away.

"Like I said before, looks like the preacher's got an interest in you, Annie." There was a smile in Walker's voice, carefully masking his growing concern about that observation.

She ignored him and defiantly returned her attention to the reverend, who began to pace back and forth in front of the crowd. "Are you ready for a miracle, folks?" he called out, his voice like thunder, his eyes flashing black lightning.

A low murmur filtered throughout the crowd.

"Let me hear you, folks!" he hollered, raising his arms high into the air.

Most of the men remained silent, but many of the women humored him with weak "hallelujahs."

Behind the reverend stood a half dozen people, men and women alike, his disciples, singing and cheering him on. They were dressed in their Sunday best and seemed well acquainted with the part they would play.

In time the song came to an end, and the reverend bowed his head. Most of the crowd followed suit. "Our Father," he intoned solemnly. "We need a miracle. We ask that your spirit move over this crowd, Father. That you touch the hearts of these sin-ridden people—"

"Amen!" someone called out.

The prayer eventually came to an end, and the reverend began his sermon. As he pranced and paced in front of the crowd, his voice took on a magical cadence that began to weave a web around the people of Whiskey. The lamplights flickered in his face, and his eyes took on an unearthly glow.

A current of anticipation rippled through the air. Annie felt it, too, and she shivered despite the warmth of the night. Beside her Walker was silent. He crossed his arms over his chest and waited.

"Is there anyone out there who needs the power of the Lord to lift away their infirmity?" The reverend paused a moment, waiting. "Come forward *now* if you believe in the power of the Lord!" Leroy's deep command thundered with authority.

A young blond-haired man stepped out of the crowd, and a quiet began to spread. He hobbled toward the reverend, the sea of townsfolk parting, as though the hand of the Lord was pushing them back. The young man dragged his nearly useless left leg behind him in his slow and arduous trek.

When finally he reached Leroy, he halted.

"Do you believe the Lord can heal you, son?"

"Yes, Preacher. I believe," the young man answered humbly, and awkwardly dropped to his knees. He bowed his head and waited.

Leroy stood in front of him, his expression solemn. The flames from the campfire flickered, and the lanterns swayed in the trees, casting shadows over the sharp angles of Leroy's face. His hair gleamed bright, like a shining halo around his head. The crowd became entranced. He widened his stance and, very slowly, stretched out his hands and laid them on the young man's head. Time seemed to stop while everyone watched in anticipation. Many held their breath; a few wept softly.

After several tension-filled seconds, the reverend began to shake, and huge droplets of sweat broke out on his forehead. "Dear Father, Holy Jesus," he began softly, "touch this young sinner with Your powerful hand and make him whole. Scare the devil out of him!" Leroy shouted, now shaking violently. The young man began to sob and writhe on the ground.

Several people wailed openly, and a chorus of "hallelujahs" rang out.

Leroy lifted his head and threw back his hair. His fine features were drawn tight, as though pained. "Rise and walk, son," he commanded in a voice that made bones shiver, "and reveal to your brothers and sisters the power of the Lord!"

A pregnant silence fell over the crowd once more. Everyone waited.

Minutes ticked by, and the young man didn't rise.

On the hill, beneath the protective arms of the giant oak, Walker and Annie watched.

Suddenly the young man lifted his head and awkwardly rose up on his knees. He wiped a tattered sleeve across his damp eyes, then took Leroy's outstretched hands and struggled to rise to his feet.

The crowd held silent.

"Go on," Leroy urged, turning him to face the crowd. "Walk, son!"

The young man took a hesitant step toward the crowd. His boyish face mirrored his uncertainty, then slowly his expression turned to wonder. Gaining confidence, he took another step, then two more, each one stronger and less labored. His eyes filled with tears, and he began to sob openly, his expression one of surprise and ecstasy. He took a couple of quick steps, and all who watched could see that his lameness was gone.

"Praise God Almighty!" someone cried out.

"Glory hallelujah!" someone else yelled.

"Sweet Jesus!" Edith wailed.

The young man walked by Hester. He looked at her and smiled. "It's a miracle, Sister," he said quietly, his voice shaky with emotion. Hester blinked twice and wobbled, then her eyes rolled back in her head and she went down like a rock. Her husband, Joe, noticed her descent and caught her a mere moment before she hit the ground.

Leroy's disciples stood on either side of the fire, waiting for the master's signal. When the young man was almost through the throng, Leroy sent them a meaningful look and cried out, "Now, folks, in order for us to continue to do the Lord's work, I'm gonna need some help from you. We're going to pass the collection plates now, and you all know how the Lord loveth a cheerful giver. Look deep in your hearts and give to the glory of the Lord, brethren, and remember: Satan don't want you to give nothing to the Lord. No, he doesn't! That evil wily old serpent wants your money for whiskey and gambling and whoring!"

Whiskey's womenfolk got smug looks on their faces and aimed meaningful glances toward their menfolk. The menfolk reddened and dug down deep into their pockets.

Leroy's disciples began to sing, and two of them took off their hats, tipped them over, and very slowly worked their way through the crowd.

Leroy waded through the throng, shaking hands, clapping shoulders, and laying his hands on the heads of the children. Soon his disciples' hats were filled to overflowing with money.

Annie watched in confused wonder, not sure how she felt about the drama she'd just witnessed.

Walker watched in cynical amazement, still haunted by the feeling that he knew Sloan. As he observed him working the crowd he grew angry. He was no saint himself and never claimed to be—in fact, he'd taken a certain pleasure in nurturing his reputation as a scalawag. But he'd always dealt fairly and honestly with his customers. Many of those customers were his neighbors and friends, and as he watched the man before him take their money, he felt a quiet rage build within. "I've seen just about everything now," he said, shaking his head with disgust.

Hearing the sarcasm in his voice, Annie turned a scorching glare his way. "Don't you believe in God, Mr. McGregor?"

A wry grin touched his mouth. "God is one thing, Annie. What we just witnessed is another."

"There are miracles, McGregor."

"Maybe," he agreed quietly. The grin left his face, and his expression turned flat and cold. "But what we just saw wasn't one."

"He's a man of God, Walker," Annie defended, challenging Walker's skepticism.

"So he claims."

She tipped her head in challenge. "How can you judge him without knowing him?"

"I'm not judging him. I just said that what we just witnessed was no goddamned miracle." His voice carried a hint of irritation. He had not thought Annie O'Neil to be so gullible.

A movement to their right caught their attention. "Anybody know the name of the young man he healed?" someone asked over Walker's right shoulder.

Walker turned. He was silent for a moment, then recognition lit his face in the form of a wide grin. "Hank!"

Hank Davis clapped Walker on the shoulder. "Walker, it's good to see ya." Hank was a tall, broad man a few years younger than Walker, with dark brown hair and friendly brown eyes.

"You too! What brings you to these parts?"

"It's a long story." He glanced down at Annie and touched the brim of his dusty hat. "Ma'am." He glanced back at Walker.

Walker followed Hank's lead and introduced the two.

Annie nodded. "Mr. Davis." She paused, then said, "I'll leave you gentlemen to renew your acquaintance—"

"I'll see ya home, Annie," Walker interjected quickly, taking her arm, fully expecting her to protest. But he was reluctant to see her leave alone. It was all too obvious that the reverend was interested in her. And Walker trusted the reverend about as much as he trusted a rabid dog.

Annie bristled visibly and gently disengaged her arm from his hand. "Thank you, McGregor, but I can see myself home just fine."

Walker lifted one eyebrow and shot her a wicked grin. "I'm goin' your way, Annie. Ain't every day I offer to see a pretty girl to her door."

"Thank you just the same," she repeated with forced politeness, "but I believe I'll say hello to Clara before I go home."

"Nice to meet ya, ma'am," Hank said, his smile warm and sincere.

"Mr. Davis," Annie returned, then left them and made her way through the crowd toward her friends.

The two men watched her go. When she reached Clara's side, Hank whistled softly. "My, my, I'd surely love to meet up with the one with the pretty yellow hair."

Walker smiled, his eyes still on Annie. "Her name's Clara Crowley, and she's as sweet as she is pretty. Stay away from her, Hank," he said good-naturedly, "she's not your kinda girl."

Hank shot him a wounded look. "Aw, Walker, it's been a few years since you and me hooked up. I've been doin' a lot of thinkin', and I ain't gettin' any younger. Maybe she's exactly my kinda girl."

Walker's brows lifted, and he gave a short disbelieving chuckle. "Well, now, if that's true, I guess we do have some catchin' up to do. Come on. I'll buy you a drink, and you can tell me what brings you to Whiskey."

FIVE

The bell above the door tinkled.

Annie looked up from her books. It was nine o'clock in the morning, and she did not expect Clara for another hour.

He was much taller than she'd thought, his hair lighter, his eyes blacker and more mysterious. "Mrs. O'Neil," he greeted in his deep reverend's voice, and closed the door behind him.

Annie stepped out from behind the counter. "Reverend," she returned politely, then paused a moment, eyeing him curiously. "How did you know my name?"

He smiled. "I asked your neighbors."

She thought it odd for him to have done so, but she didn't comment on it further.

"I need supplies for myself and my people." He pulled a piece of paper from his coat pocket and held it out to her. He was dressed as though ready to deliver another one of his stirring sermons: spanking white shirt, black tie, black coat, and trousers. "I was told to visit McGregor's General Store or O'Neil's Mercantile." His lips curved into a slight smile. "I thought the Lord would bless my choice of this store over the other. I've heard about your competitor and his activities."

She felt a stuffy surge of satisfaction. Even though she knew it was wrong to nurse the grudge she held against Walker, she did so with petty determination. She hugged it to her heart, like a protective armor.

"I need everything on the list if you have it in stock."

She took the list from his hand and studied it: beans, flour, sugar, coffee, and the like. She glanced back up at him and offered him a smile. "I think we can take care of you just fine."

"Oh, I'm sure you will, Mrs. O'Neil." His dark gaze found and held hers. "Did anyone ever tell you that you have a lovely smile?"

Flustered, she blushed beneath the intensity of his gaze. She hesitated a second before saying, "Thank you." Then she busied herself with filling his order.

"I'm told you are from Ohio." He leaned a hip against the counter and watched her move about the store.

"Yes, I am." She looked over at him, and a small crease formed between her eyebrows. "You've been asking a lot of questions about me."

"As a matter of fact, I have." He paused a moment. "There aren't many women with your character and beauty, Mrs. O'Neil."

She tilted her head the slightest bit. "Don't you think you're being a bit presumptuous, Reverend Sloan? You don't know anything about me."

"The Lord reveals His wonders."

Annie was silent.

"He works in mysterious ways, Mrs. O'Neil. Don't you agree?"

She thought about that a second and returned to the task of filling his order. "Yes, I suppose He does."

"He has led me to Whiskey for a reason. . . ." He let the sentence hang.

"Indeed, and what would that be?" Annie dared to ask.

He smiled, as though he harbored some great eternal secret. "In time, you too will understand, Mrs. O'Neil."

Amused, she gave a soft huff and smiled. "There you are, Reverend," she said, packing the last of the items into a burlap sack.

He pulled a stack of folded bills from his pocket and peeled off several, laying them on the counter between them. "Will that cover the debt?"

Annie picked the money up and counted it out. "Yes, thank you."

"Thank you, Mrs. O'Neil. It's truly been my pleasure."

He picked up the sack, turned, and walked to the door. Then, his hand on the doorknob, he turned to her once again. "I would very much like the pleasure of your company for a ride out into the country tomorrow. Would you accept my invitation?"

She opened her mouth to refuse his offer. But she remembered Walker and the wager, and her mouth snapped shut with the speed of a snapping turtle catching a fly. There was only one way to prove she was right and Walker was wrong, and that was to get to know the reverend well enough to be sure of his character. She was a stubborn woman, and she meant to win the quilt and keep the Sharp rifle as well. "Yes," she said before she could change her mind. "I would like that very much."

❧

A week passed, then two, and Leroy's weekly revivals continued, as did his sporadic courtship of Annie. Annie kept a careful distance between them, refusing to see him as often as he would have liked, though the reverend worked hard to win her over. Summer steamed on into July, and the rain held off. The townsfolk and farmers began to worry. After the stone-scorching summer of two years ago, they feared that if it did not rain soon their crops would be burnt to stunted cinders.

The warm balmy nights brought forth a different crop, however, as salvation found many and miracles abounded. But those folks who ventured forth to receive the greatest healings were, more often than not, strangers to Whiskey. Though some of the townsfolk wondered about that, Leroy's fame and popularity grew nonetheless. He was the talk of the ladies' quilting circle and the subject of the men's card games.

On Sundays and mid-week, too, however, Preacher Fire took to preaching a new message about sheep and their foolish tendency to stray. Oddly enough, he'd lately been seen going in and out of McGregor's General Store with regularity.

This news sent a fresh surge of gossip pulsing through town.

Hank Davis stayed on in Whiskey, though no one really knew why. He took a room over at Martin's Boardinghouse, next door to Walker's store, and he, along with Walker, Sheriff Nagy, and Preacher Fire, attended Leroy's revivals religiously, not missing even one.

Hank had other interests, also. He took to dropping by the mercantile after ten in the morning, when he knew Clara would be there. He bought something every now and then, but most of the time he merely browsed and smiled a lot. Then one day he asked Clara to a barn dance, and she accepted. It wasn't long after that they were courting regularly.

❧

Walker was livid with Annie.

He told himself he was only concerned about her welfare; he told himself she was an innocent, unable to discern the ways of a man like Leroy; he told himself many things, all of which were true. But the truest factor of them all was that he just couldn't stand the thought of her with another man. Jealousy had a sharp sting to its bite, and though he thought he'd exorcised the demon from his heart when he'd left New Orleans and Ginny all those years ago, he learned he was still vulnerable to its power—especially when it concerned Annie O'Neil.

One evening, the second Tuesday of July, after closing the store for the night, he could stand it no longer and decided to pay her a visit.

He stalked across Main Street and burst through her door without bothering to see if she was still open for business. Once inside, he slammed the door behind him so hard the little bell above tinkled once, then dropped to the floor with a clang and died.

Stunned, Annie looked up from where she stood beside the quilting frame, her hand paused in mid-stitch. She opened her mouth to speak, but he descended on her like the wrath of God.

"What the hell do you think you're doing?" he shouted.

She forced her expression into one of impassive indifference. "I believe I should ask you that question." She returned her attention to the quilt and finished the stitch before saying, "What do you think *you're* doing, bursting into my store in such a rude manner?"

"I thought you had more sense," Walker went on.

"I beg your pardon?" She lifted her eyebrows but refused to look at him.

"Don't play coy with me, Annie! We've known each other too long for that." He leaned toward her. "You know exactly what I mean!"

Annie huffed softly and continued her work. She was working on a quilt for Abigail Stanford's new baby boy. The background of the quilt was soft blue. The outlining squares were etched with bright red and yellow stitching. In the very center was a yellow duck. "I'm afraid I don't, Walker."

"Are you out of your mind?"

"No," she said as she glanced up at him. "I'm quite sane, thank you." She seemed so calm and assured, which inflamed him even more.

He shook his head in disgust, his black eyebrows drawn together into a furry frown. "I know you want the quilt, but courtin' the man—"

Annie caught his gaze and held it. The impassive look faded from her face, and a little crease formed in the center of her forehead. "Is that what you think this is all about?" She rolled her eyes in disbelief. "This is not about the quilt, Walker."

He gave her a sharp, discerning look, and a grin touched the corners of his mouth. "You're lying, Annie. I know you want that quilt so bad you'd just about sell your soul to the devil to get it."

"I would not!" She straightened her shoulders and lifted her chin a notch. "I'm spending time with Leroy because I enjoy his company."

Frustrated, Walker's grin faded, and he let the air hiss out of his lungs. So she liked him, then. The knowledge hit him like a blow to his gut. He was silent a moment, weighing the wisdom of telling her what he knew about Leroy Sloan. "He's not who you think he is."

Annie gave him a sly glance. It was her turn to be amused. "Do tell."

He stared at her in silence, trying to decide how much to tell her.

When he didn't answer, her curiosity got the best of her, and she huffed a little laugh. "He's not wanted for bank robbery, is he?"

"No," Walker said quietly.

"Then what?"

"Maybe it would be best if you talk to Hank and Delbert about this."

"What would they know about Leroy?"

Walker searched her face, his mind outlining every detail—the spray of freckles across the bridge of her nose, the sparkle of her green eyes. . . . She was so pretty it hurt him to look at her.

She gave a short laugh. "There's nothing to tell, is there? You just want to provoke me. Well, it's not going to wor—"

"Hank is a bounty hunter. He's been trailing Sloan for two years," Walker interrupted quietly, "and Delbert has been doing some checking up on him, too."

The smile slid off Annie's face. For several moments, her face remained as blank as a freshly washed chalkboard. Then, quite suddenly, her expression turned to one of disgust. "My God, Walker! You must be desperate to make up a story about a decent man just so you can win a bet and get your hands on a gun!"

Anger got the best of him. "I don't give a goddamn about that gun right now, Annie! I'm tellin' you the man is trouble." He was silent a moment, then said, "Didn't you ever wonder why our townspeople rarely get healed, that most folks who do get healed are strangers none of us know anything about?"

She had indeed been puzzled by that very thing, but she'd kept it to herself, mulling it over and over in her mind. "Yes," she answered truthfully, "I have wondered about that."

"Then use your head." He took her by the shoulders. "He's a fraud, Annie, a parasite who feeds off the generosity and gullibility of decent people. Don't you see that?"

"Then why hasn't Delbert arrested him?"

"Because without some kind of proof, he could have half the town in an uproar. Delbert doesn't want a fight with his own neighbors. He's waiting for some papers, some 'Wanted' posters from some of the other towns he's passed through. He and Hank want to prove his guilt without a question of doubt, then Hank plans to take him back to Charleston to stand trial."

Stunned, she stared at him, trying to digest everything he was telling her.

"There's more, Annie, but I think you should talk to Hank or Delbert."

"Why are you telling me all this?"

His eyes lost their anger. "Because . . ." He paused, searching his heart for the truth, searching his mind for the right words. "Because I care about you," he finally said in a very quiet voice.

Her eyes were suddenly large and vulnerable. "Because of what happened to George?" she asked, surprised at how her heart had leapt at his words.

"Hell, I don't know," Walker said, knowing it was much more than that. "Maybe that's part of it. . . . Does it matter?"

"It does to me," she whispered. "I don't need or want your pity."

He stared down at her for a long moment, then reached up and brushed a strand of red-gold hair from her face. "Pity is the last thing I feel for you, Annie."

She lowered her gaze and thought about what he'd told her. "What do you want me to do?" she finally asked.

"We don't know what he wants from you, but until we do we don't think you're safe with him."

The tone of his voice was so sincere, so concerned, it touched a tender spot deep inside her heart. She looked back up at him. His face was darkly handsome. Her thoughts churned. Was he telling her the truth about Leroy? Would he make up such a wild story merely to win a wager? Surely not. She closed her eyes, and her mind ran on. When she opened her eyes and looked up into his face, there was a tenderness in his expression and something else, something she did not recognize, that made her heart go still.

Twilight kissed the panes of the windows, and time ceased, though the clock on the shelf behind her ticked out a hypnotic harmony. It was crazy, she knew, but she wished he would kiss her. She'd denied her attraction to him for so long, carefully cloaking it behind a layer of distrust and resentment, and she was suddenly very tired of the effort it cost her.

As though he read her thoughts, he gave a muffled groan and pulled her into his arms. She felt good against him. Soft and feminine and sweet. One arm held her close, while his other hand found her hair and plowed through its soft thickness. His body reacted to her nearness, and he quickly grew hard with desire. She pulled back a little, and his hand tugged her hair, gently tilting her face up to his. Her eyes darkened to deep green, like a midnight forest after a long summer rain, and her lips parted, inviting him to taste of their sweetness. He lowered his head and kissed her. The kiss was long and lingering, tender and sweet. His lips were gentle, moving lightly over hers, learning her mouth as he had not taken the time to do on that warm day in June.

She trembled in his arms, and the kiss deepened and grew heated. It felt good and right and better than anything she could ever remember. His body was hard and warm against hers. His tongue touched her bottom lip, and she opened her mouth further, granting him entrance. She felt wonderfully alive, and when his hand left her back and slid around her rib cage to a place just beneath her left breast, she shuddered, but did not pull away.

She groaned, half afraid of the intensity of her response, and he lifted his head, knowing that if he didn't stop now, they would go much farther than was wise. He laid his jaw against the soft crown of her hair and held her against his chest for several moments, quietly, gently, while time ticked on again, and their hearts settled. Finally, he lifted his head and set her away from him. "Think about what I said, Annie. Please."

She nodded. Her lips were swollen, her hair loose and flowing around her shoulders. She did not want him to go.

He walked toward the door, then stopped and turned to her. "Annie, I—"

Suddenly the door opened and Charlotte blew into the store, bringing with her a gust of hot air. An overly bright smile was pasted across her pretty face. "Annie, hello!" she called out warmly, as though they were the closest of friends.

"Hello, Charlotte," Annie returned, feeling more than a little uncomfortable.

Walker felt no such discomfort. He was simply curious about why Charlotte had ventured out so late in the evening.

"I've been meaning to stop by and see how you are," Charlotte rushed on. "But as Walker can tell you, I don't come into town all that often. The children keep me busy." She turned her honeyed smile on Walker and fluttered over to his side. "I've been looking all over for you." She pressed a kiss to his jaw. "Thank you so much for the quilt, darling. It looks lovely on my bed."

SIX

"The quilt is not for you, Charlotte," Walker said as kindly as he could manage once he was inside the door of McGregor's General Store. His back to her, he lit a lamp and took a long deep breath. He was trying valiantly to rein in his temper, having no desire to hurt his sister-in-law, but the pain he'd seen in Annie's eyes had sent a dagger to his heart, and he knew it would take a great deal of work to earn her trust back again.

"I don't understand," Charlotte said, disappointment evident in her voice. Walker turned to her, and she lifted a hand in a defensive gesture and shrugged. "I found it in the back of the store, wrapped in tissue. . . ."

"I wrapped it."

She stared at him for several seconds and allowed herself a moment to compose herself. Then she lifted her chin a notch. "May I ask what you intend to do with it?"

"What I should have done with it in the beginning," he answered in a quiet voice. "It belongs to Annie."

"You want to . . . give it to her?" She'd suspected for some time that Annie O'Neil was her rival.

"Yes."

"I see," Charlotte said stiffly. She swallowed her wounded pride and lifted her chin another notch. The hope she had nurtured for a joining between herself and Walker died. She now knew for certain that he did not want her. He did not love her.

She did not love him, either.

But that little fact was not important. Propriety called for her to have a husband to take care of her and her children, and though she'd always known she would never own his heart, she would have settled for the respectability of his name. She sighed. Life was so much easier with a husband.

She still needed Walker, though, and could not afford to anger him. He could leave Whiskey anytime he wanted; there was nothing to tie him here. And the last thing she wanted was to be stuck with the responsibility of operating this blasted store. She looked around at the shelves, stocked with bags of flour, sugar, and coffee, and wrinkled her nose in distaste. She'd always hated the store, though her husband and Walker's success with it had kept food on her table and had dressed her and her children far more fashionably than most of Whiskey's residents. She enjoyed her teas and her flower garden, however, as well as her prayer meetings, and she had no desire to work her fingers to the bone in a store all day long.

Walker turned down the lamp and walked to the door that led to his quarters. "I'd appreciate it if you'd return the quilt to me as soon as possible, Charlotte."

She thought about her answer for several moments and finally forced herself to say, "Of course." Then she turned and walked out the door.

Walker decided then and there that once Leroy Sloan left town and things were back to normal, he would move on, too.

It was time to leave Whiskey.

That next morning Walker paid Leroy a visit.

The sun was high when he rode into the camp. The campfires were cold and lifeless, the residents of the camp still asleep. The horses stood beneath the trees, their tails whisking back and forth in constant motion, whacking flies off their rumps and bellies.

Walker swung down off his horse and tethered the reins to a tree branch. He called out a hello, but heard no response.

He walked over to the largest tent and peered inside. Leroy, his limbs entwined with another's, was fast asleep.

Walker cleared his throat. "Sloan," he called out.

A soft feminine moan sounded, and Leroy jerked awake with a start. He propped himself up on an elbow. "Yeah. Who's there?" The tone of his voice was thick and southern, much different from his normally deep, resonant preacher's voice.

"McGregor."

"Yes, Brother." Leroy cleared his voice, adjusting it to his reverend's intonation.

"I'd like to talk to you."

Silence, and then, "Just a minute."

Walker turned away and waited.

When Leroy emerged from the tent, his eyes were bleary, as though he'd had too much to drink the night before. He extended his hand and forced a saintly smile. "Mr. McGregor. How nice of you to visit. I don't believe we've ever formally met."

Walker ignored the reverend's hand. "I'm not so sure about that."

An alarm went off in Leroy's head, and his smile slipped a little.

He dropped his hand to his side. "What brings you out today, Brother? Do you have a prayer request?"

"You might say that."

"Well, you're a wise man to bring your requests to the Lord," Leroy said, and nodded, trying his best to shake off the effects of the whiskey he'd drank the night before. "Yessir. The good Lord hears and answers all prayers."

A cool smile touched Walker's lips. He stared at Leroy a few seconds, then plunged his hands deep into his trouser pockets. "I want you to stay away from Annie O'Neil," he said bluntly.

Surprised, Leroy was silent a moment. "I beg your pardon?"

"She's a good woman, and I don't want to see her hurt."

Leroy feigned his most pious expression. "What makes you think I'd hurt her? I'm a disciple of the Lor—"

"Save it for your followers, Sloan."

Leroy's face reddened, and a foxlike sharpness came over his features. "Don't you think it's Mrs. O'Neil's choice as to whom she sees?"

"Normally I would think that. This is not a normal situation, however. And you are not a normal preacher, are you, Sloan?"

Leroy smiled then, and it was a terrible smile. "I'm afraid you've lost me, sir." The word "sir" came out sounding very much like "suh."

An icy cold passed over Walker, and fifteen years fell away. Once again he was in New Orleans on that early morning before dawn. Leroy's voice of a moment ago became a voice of the past: "I'm afraid you've lost, suh," the young silver-haired man had said, as he walked away with Ginny, while Walker had stood over the bleeding body of a man who had not deserved to die.

Walker had never clearly seen the face of the silver-haired man who'd stood in the early morning shadows, watching, waiting, like a vulture, for the duel to be done.

But Walker saw him now, and he now knew why he'd felt that tug of familiarity the day Leroy rode into Whiskey.

Walker's mind came back to the present, and his eyes turned hard. "What happened to Ginny?"

"Ginny?" Leroy's smile remained an awful thing to behold. He tapped his chin with a long thin forefinger, as though the name evoked no memory. Then his face lit, and his dark eyes narrowed. "Oh, yes, the fair Virginia Ewing. Did you know that the old man was just weeks away from his death and that our Ginny stood to inherit everything? Which she did, of course. The old man never had time to change his will. Ah, well, a pity, though. She never lived to enjoy her inheritance. I'm afraid my dear wife died at a very young age, under very unusual circumstances. . . ." Leroy paused, his face becoming the picture of sorrow and affliction. "I was quite grief-stricken, as you might imagine. . . ."

Walker's eyes sank shut. Ginny was dead. The thought filled him with a soul-deep sadness. All these years he'd been bitter about the way she'd used him. But her actions had rendered her a retribution far worse than what he'd suffered, far worse than she'd deserved.

A searing anger rose up within, and he wanted to kill the man before him, squeeze the very life from his throat. But reason prevailed, and he thought of Annie. He willed himself under control. "Leave this town, Sloan. Move on and leave these people alone."

"I think the townspeople might have something to say about that." Leroy smiled his victory. "They've grown quite fond of me, you know."

"They don't know who you are."

"They wouldn't care if they did." He lifted his hands to the heavens. "I've been cleansed by the blood of the lamb. I'm redeemed. The fact that I'm like them, capable of sin in my foolish youth, will only endear me to them."

A muscle twitched in Walker's jaw. "Don't be too sure about that." His blue eyes turned to shards of glass. "Stay away from Annie O'Neil. If you hurt her, I'll find you. There won't be a place far enough away for you to run." Then he turned and walked off.

꿎

Two weeks slid by, and August rode in on a ferocious heat wave.

The drought continued, and Whiskey grew drier. From time to time a few dark clouds gathered on the horizon, and the towns-folk grew hopeful, but the clouds eventually dissipated, as did the townsfolk's hope.

Annie sympathized with her neighbors. If the harvest was poor, they would all suffer.

At the same time, other matters pressed in on her. Though she had tried to exorcise the memory of the night Walker had come to see her about Leroy, she was still nursing her injured pride, feel-ing very much the fool. She had allowed Walker to get past her defenses and, for a moment, she had actually believed that he cared about her.

He had stopped by the store to see her three times since that night, but she'd refused to talk to him and retreated to her rooms, leaving Clara to deal with him.

On one such day, Clara turned to her and said, "You should at least listen to him. Maybe there is an explanation."

Annie looked up at her. Her green gaze was hard and deter-mined, carefully masking her hurt. "He lied to me. He told me a preposterous story about Leroy, and I'm ashamed to say I almost fell for it. He was so sure he could convince me of the story that he'd already given the quilt to Charlotte. He probably thought he'd have the rifle that very night." A fist squeezed her heart, and Annie shook her head in disgust. "There is no need for an explanation," she said, her voice dull with finality.

Clara shook her head in disbelief. "There has to be more to it than that. Walker is a decent man; we all know that. I can't imagine him doing such a thing. . . ." She paused a moment. "In fact," Clara said hesitantly, "there's something I've been wanting to tell you. Something you should know about Walker—"

"There's nothing else I want to know about that man," Annie said to cut her off abruptly. "I will never have anything to do with him again," she vowed.

❧

The third Saturday in August, Annie broke that vow.

It was early morning; the sun was just beginning to bathe her bedroom in shades of pink and gold.

She'd decided to give her rooms a good cleaning and, wanting to air the mattress, she began with taking the bed apart. And then she saw it.

The letter.

She picked it up and sat down in the chair near the window, surprised that she had so completely forgotten it.

The postmark was from Ohio; the handwriting was that of her brother-in-law, Joseph. She tore the envelope open, took out the letter, and read:

Dear Annie,

It is with concern for you that I write this letter.

I am sorry to tell you that Father has passed on.

Though this news is sad, it is not the source of my concern, however. You see, dear sister, Father had named you heir to his small estate, and I was so angry I fear I may have placed you in danger. My conscience has stung me sorely ever since.

One evening in early May, I spent several hours playing cards and drinking with a stranger. Without thinking, I revealed your widowed state and the fact that you would soon inherit an amount of money.

After he left town, another man came through looking for him. His name was Hank Davis. He told me and the sheriff why he was looking for the stranger. Apparently this man claims to be a reverend and is wanted for several crimes: fraud and bigamy, possibly even murder. I am told he preys upon widows, marrying them, then running off with their money. His name is the Reverend Leroy Sloan.

Annie, I fear for you, as he seemed especially interested in you and where you lived.

Please forgive me for putting you in danger this way. I would never intentionally harm you. I know Father left you the money because he thought you would put it to better use than I. I would have gambled it away, and we all know that. The money is in a bank here in safekeeping for you.

Please write me and let me know that you are safe.

With affection,
Joseph

Annie lowered her arms to her lap, her hand still clutching the letter.

The sun sifted through the window and touched her face with a warm kiss. Walker had told her the truth. She felt a surge of gladness to know that he had not lied to her. As for Leroy, she felt a flood of anger and disappointment that a man as gifted as he would use his charisma to deceive others. She laid her head against the back of the rocker, and her eyes sank shut.

She stayed that way for a very long time.

SEVEN

Annie showed Clara the letter later that morning.

Clara read it in silence, then handed the letter back to Annie. "What are you going to do?"

Annie shrugged and sighed. She felt no pain at discovering Leroy's deception, only anger. If she were to be honest, she knew, she would have to admit that she'd always sensed there was something sinister about him. But in her desire to best Walker, she had closed her mind to what her common sense had been telling her. Now, however, for the sake of her friends and neighbors, she could no longer ignore the truth. "I'm going to talk to Delbert, of course." She paused, then added, "Hank, too."

"What about Walker?"

Annie's gaze was direct, her expression somber. She was a proud woman, but not so proud that she couldn't admit she was wrong.

"I owe him an apology. Despite our wager, I believe he was truly concerned about my welfare." She gave a sad little smile. The knowledge that Walker had given the quilt to Charlotte still stung sharply. She didn't want to think about why it hurt so much. It would be better, she supposed, that she never put solid thoughts or words to her feelings concerning Walker.

Clara's eyes softened. "Oh, Annie. . . . you care for him, don't you?"

Annie's cheeks reddened. She gave a little huff and looked away. "Of course not. I have nothing in common with the man, other than the silly competition we've entertained these past few years."

Clara thought a moment, then very quietly said, "I still believe there is an explanation about the quilt—"

"It doesn't matter," Annie interrupted. "Really."

Clara put a hand on Annie's arm. "Annie, please listen. The other day I tried to tell you something, but you wouldn't let me."

Annie waited.

"I don't know how to tell you this, but I think it's time you knew." She took a deep breath, then went on, "When George died, we all knew it was very hard on you. . . . No one wanted it to be any harder for you than it was . . . especially Walker."

"Walker?" Annie's brow knitted. "What are you talking about?"

"George lost everything you and he owned in that card game that night, Annie." She waited for Annie to digest her words. "He even lost the store."

Shocked, Annie shook her head. "That can't be."

"It is."

"Then why didn't the new owner come forward to claim it?"

"Because someone paid him not to."

"I don't understand."

"Oh, Annie," Clara said, obviously distressed, "Walker paid George's debts and bought the store back for you."

Annie stared at Clara, stunned. "Are you sure?"

"Yes."

"How do you know this?"

A sad smile touched Clara's mouth. "Almost everyone who was there that night knew the extent of George's loss. It didn't take much to figure out who took care of his debt so that you would never know what George had done."

Annie sank down onto a stool behind the counter. "Oh, Clara . . ." She suddenly felt very, very tired. She ran a hand over her face, a gamut of emotions flooding her: renewed grief at George's foolishness; embarrassment that she had been so cold to the man who had protected her home and business; gratitude that he had never even hinted at the truth or tried to exact repayment; confusion at the warm rush of tenderness she felt for him. "Oh, Clara," she said again, sadly realizing that the rush of warm feelings was much more than simple affection. "I never would have guessed. I've treated him so badly at times. . . ."

Clara came around the counter and gave her a hug. "You shouldn't feel bad." She smiled and chuckled. "He has always enjoyed provoking you, or have you forgotten?"

"Of course not, but—"

"But nothing. You can't be blamed for what you didn't know."

Annie's pride pricked her. "I'll have to pay him back, of course," she said almost frantically. "Every penny. I can't accept his charity."

"I don't think he considers it charity, Annie."

Her entire body snapped to attention. "Well, I do!"

"Well, that matter will have to be discussed between you two. Besides," she added with a lighter tone, "I have other news: Hank has asked me to marry him."

Annie's face lit up like a ray of sunshine, and for a moment she forgot her own inner turmoil. "Oh, Clara . . ." She was off the stool in a heartbeat, giving her friend a great hug. "I'm so happy for you!"

Clara laughed and returned Annie's hug. "Can you believe it? He wants to get married before Christmas. But he said he had something to take care of first." Clara pulled back and made a face. "I have a feeling that something is more like someone named Leroy Sloan."

❧

That night, after the ladies of the quilting circle had all gone home, Annie closed the store and retreated to her rooms. She filled the tub with water and took a cool bath.

She stayed in the tub a long time, thinking about a lot of things. Mostly she thought about Walker and what he had done for her.

In time, she rose from the tub and dried off, then dressed in a simple gray skirt and white blouse. She brushed her hair out and pulled it back from her face with a ribbon. Then she took the letter from her bureau drawer and sat down and read it once again.

❧

It was well past eleven when she knocked on Walker's door. The night was lit only by a silver of silver moon, but a chorus of crickets sang, and a slight breeze stirred the tree-tops, offering a measure of relief from the close night air.

After what seemed like a very long time, he opened the door.

"Annie!" He was surprised to see her. He held the lantern up to see her face.

"Hello, Walker."

He was wearing only his trousers; his chest was bare. He looked sleepy, and she deduced that she had woken him.

His surprise quickly turned to concern. "Is something wrong?"

Annie O'Neil, he knew, was not one to pay a visit to his door at any time of day, let alone at this late hour.

"I need to talk to you." She paused. "May I come in?"

"Of course." He stepped sideways and gestured her in, then closed the door behind her.

She stood in his shadow, realizing she hadn't been in the store in a long time. She'd come over from time to time to trade with John before he died, but she had not stepped foot inside since Walker had taken over.

"Come, sit down," he urged, his expression still puzzled. He led her toward the back rooms.

She shook her head. "I can say what I've come to say right here."

Walker turned to her, and his eyes grew mischievous. "I promise not to ravish you, Annie. Come on back and have something to drink."

Annie thought about what he'd done for her, and she decided she had nothing to lose. She followed him.

The room he lived in was large and comfortable. It was totally male, housing a bed with a shirt thrown over the rail at the foot, a bureau with a couple of books stacked on top, and a spindle-back chair that sat beside the bed with his boots placed neatly beneath it. At the far end of the room was a cookstove. A small wooden cupboard hung on the wall behind the stove. The room was lived in and lacked feminine touches, but it was not untidy.

They were barely inside the room when the words poured from her mouth. "You own my store."

He stopped in his tracks and turned. He regarded her in silence, then gestured to the chair and in a quiet voice said, "Sit down, Annie."

She did, and the seconds stretched on while she waited for his response.

He walked to the cupboard and took out a glass and a bottle of whiskey, then poured out a small amount of the liquor. His back still to her, he asked, "Can I get you something?"

"No, thank you." Her heart was pumping wildly. Being in his room, while the rest of Whiskey slept, unnerved her to the point of panic. After the night in her store, she was all too aware of the power he had over her and her body. "About my store . . . ," she began.

He turned to her and leaned his backside up against the stove, lazily crossing one ankle over the other. "I don't own your store, Annie." His clear blue eyes were kind, bereft of any teasing.

"You paid George's debt—"

"The deed was never changed."

"But—"

"But nothing. The store belongs to you. Nothing has changed."

"I'll pay you back, of course—"

"That's not necessary." He took a slow sip from the glass of whiskey.

She went on as though she hadn't heard him. "It'll take some time, though." She lowered her gaze to her lap and studied her hands. "I don't want your pity, Walker. And I don't need anyone's charity."

He knew she was right about that. Annie O'Neil was a survivor. His heart swelled with tenderness for her. Walker set his whiskey glass down on the small table, then crossed the room and stopped before her. He took her by the shoulders and gently pulled her to her feet. "Annie, you don't understand. I did what I did because I wanted to. That's all there was to it. I didn't do it so that you would find out one day and feel indebted or embarrassed."

She stared up at him and thought about that for a few seconds. "Thank you" was all she could think to say, though her heart was full of so much more.

She took the letter from her pocket and held it out to him. "You should read this."

He lowered his hands from her arms and took the letter. He read it in silence, then without a word folded it and handed it back to her.

"The gun is yours," she said. "You won the wager fair and square."

He realized at the moment that he cared nothing for the gun or for the quilt beyond what they meant to her, that the entire wager was just a ploy to have contact with her, that he would gladly give them both to her if she would have them. "Annie, about Charlotte and the quilt . . ."

She lowered her gaze, not wanting to hear what he would say.

"There is nothing between Charlotte and me. In fact, when this thing with Sloan is taken care of, I'm leaving Whiskey."

The words he'd spoken were much worse than she'd expected. The thought of never seeing him again made her heart constrict with sudden pain. Her eyes found his. "But why?"

"It's time." His gaze was tender on her face.

The words escaped her mouth without warning. "I don't want you to go." It was a whisper, a very softly spoken plea.

"Aw, Annie," he said, and roughly pulled her into his arms. He expected her to pull away. But she didn't. "About the quilt—"

"Shhh," she whispered, and cast prudence aside. She didn't want to think about Charlotte and the quilt, about the gun and the wager, about Leroy and the letter. She didn't want to think about anything except this one moment and the hunger that ate at her soul. "Just hold me for a little while," she pleaded, and pressed her cheek into his shoulder. Her eyelids closed and she sighed. He smelled of night and sleep and maleness, of all things right and good and strong.

Her childlike plea sent his heart thumping. He buried his face in her red-gold hair, knowing he should send her home, knowing he could not. The lantern cast shadows that danced along the walls, while he held her and felt the flutter of her heart against his own. "Annie, maybe you should go," he tried in one single heroic effort.

She raised her face and pulled back slightly. "Do you want me to?" Her deep green eyes held a secret promise.

He swallowed, hard. "No." The word was a hoarse whisper.

He pulled the ribbon from her hair and lowered his lips to hers. She met his kiss with a heated passion. Her arms entwined his neck, and her fingers pushed into his thick dark hair. His tongue dipped against hers, and her knees felt weak, her stomach jumpy. She felt as though she was molten liquid and was melting in all her deepest parts.

He lifted his mouth from hers and, cradling her head in his hands, nipped at her nose, cheeks, and neck. She arched against him, ever aware of his body clothed only in his trousers, warm and hard and pulsing against hers. His lips slid to her shoulder. "You smell so good," he groaned, sliding his hands down her back to clasp her waist, then lower to bracket her hips. He pressed himself into her, and she caught her breath as a delicious series of shivers rippled over her body.

His fingers found the buttons of her blouse and worked them open. "I want to see you. I want to touch you all over."

She murmured a wordless reply. He pushed her blouse open, pulled it free of her skirt, then slid it off her shoulders and down her arms. His hands found her waist once again, and he undid the button on her skirt. In seconds that, too, pooled in a puddle at her feet.

She stood clad only in her chemise.

He stared down at her, his gaze traveling to the dark tips of her breasts where they pressed against the thin fabric. His hands came up to cradle her rib cage, then very gently his palms skimmed upward and his thumbs found her hard nipples. She caught her breath and met his gaze. His eyes were heavy-lidded and dark with desire. "Oh, Annie. You are beautiful," he said. His palms cupped and lifted her breasts. He rejoiced in their roundness, their weight and fullness. His lips found hers once again, and his tongue swept her mouth, as though he couldn't get enough of her sweetness. He wanted to taste all of her, smell all of her. His hands rode her body again, impatiently now, untying the ribbons on the front of her chemise, and then, with his mouth still on hers, he sent the chemise to join her other garments on the floor.

She stood before him naked and unashamed. His gaze scorched her. She felt flushed and feverish and more alive than she'd ever felt. His eyes roamed her body while he undid the buttons on the front of his trousers and slid them down over his narrow hips. He stepped out of them and wordlessly took her hand and placed it on his body. He was hard and smooth and wonderfully male.

He took her other hand and gently tugged her down on the bed beside him. They stretched out and lay beside each other, belly to belly. He stroked her cheek. "I've thought of you this way for such a long time."

She took his words and cradled them in her heart. "I didn't know."

"I couldn't tell you."

"Why?"

"You were married."

"Oh," she said in a hushed voice. Then, "You thought of me . . . like this . . . way back then."

"Yes."

She felt no repugnance, only wonder that she had never guessed.

She smiled. "I thought you didn't like me much."

"I did." His smile was wicked. "I sure as hell did."

His mouth found her neck and nuzzled there, then traveled down to her breasts. His teeth tugged at her nipples tenderly until he brought forth soft moans of pleasure.

She closed her eyes, holding him to her, marveling that this—this wonderful thing they were doing—was so different from what she had known with her husband. It was a beautiful thing, a dance of joy.

His hands learned her body, all of the hollows and curves, until at last he found that secret place. She was wholly aroused, all sleek and swollen.

"Annie," he said hoarsely, "you're as sweet as I knew you'd be." He withdrew his touch, and she moaned a soft protest. But he answered her protest by rising above her and pressing his flesh to hers. She stared up into his face and wrapped her arms around him. She felt the smoothness of his back, the hard leanness of him beneath her hands, and she wanted to tell him all she felt, all of the secrets of her heart; but those secrets would have to wait, she could see, for his control was fading. "Walker," she said, a little smile tipping up her swollen lips.

"Yes, Annie?"

"Business is getting better, Walker."

The chuckle was a deep rumble in his chest. He smiled down into her eyes and said, "You're one hell of a woman, Annie." Then his expression sobered and he pressed his mouth to hers. His entrance was slow and lovely. She drew him in, tears gathering in her eyes. He moved within her tenderly until at last she arched and tensed around him. His thrusts grew hard and hot and fast, and she caught her breath as shivers of sensation washed over her. She clasped him tight, and he gave a hoarse groan and cried out her name, then collapsed on her, his jaw resting against her temple. They lay together in silence for a long time, drifting off to a special place that belonged to them alone.

And the night pressed in against the window, and the crickets hummed.

EIGHT

The following saturday evening, the people of Whiskey gathered down near the river. Everyone came, even Horace Haney, who'd arrived in Whiskey that afternoon with more wares to sell.

The crowd gathered around the huge tent. They were anxious for a glimpse of Leroy. August was fast sliding into September, and it had not rained since the second week of June. The dry weather and scorching heat had taken a toll on the crops. Now, however, it was not their crops that was the townsfolk's main concern, but their livestock.

As they waited, the evening shadows deepened. The lanterns hanging in the trees cast an eerie shimmering light over the crowd. The heat hung heavy in the air, and low, dark clouds gathered on the horizon. No one paid them much attention, however. Clouds had gathered in the same manner for weeks, and it had not rained.

Annie stood between Clara and Edith. She tugged against the

collar of her dress, wishing for even the slightest breeze, but none came. The treetops stood still and silent this night.

She was restless. There was an odd tension in the air. She knew her friends had come hoping for a miracle, the miracle of rain, but she had come for another reason.

She turned, and her gaze rose to the hill behind her. Beneath the sheltering arms of the huge oak tree stood Walker, Hank, Sheriff Nagy, and Preacher Fire. Her gaze settled on Walker. He winked and smiled at her, and a slow warmth lit within her chest and spread until it encompassed her entire body. She'd seen him only once since the night she'd spent with him, and that one time they had met with Sheriff Nagy, Hank, and Preacher Fire.

She knew Walker would leave Whiskey soon, and that knowledge filled her with a sadness that went far beyond grief. She loved him. She loved his smile, his generosity, his warmth—even his unmerciful teasing. And it hurt terribly to imagine a life without him. She knew if he stayed with her she would love him more with each passing day, with each passing year. But she also knew she could not ask him to stay. She would hold tight to the memory of that one beautiful night they had shared. He had loved her with both a tenderness and a fierceness that she had never known, and when she woke the next morning in his bed, he was gone, but she'd found that he had covered her with the quilt—the one she'd thought he'd given to Charlotte.

She heard a murmur of excitement rush through the crowd, followed by an explosion of clapping and cheering. She turned to face the tent. Leroy was wading through the throng, shaking hands and calling out greetings, looking as elegant as always. His disciples followed behind, and when he took his place at the front of the tent, they took theirs at his side.

He raised his arms, and the crowd hushed. He waited a long moment, then boomed, "Good evening, brethren!" He paused a moment, then led the crowd through a long rambling prayer, punctuated by people calling out "hallelujahs" and "amens." When he was finished, the crowd looked up, ready for an explosion of preaching.

They weren't disappointed. His handsome face contorted, and he shouted, "There is *sinnn* among us tonight!"

The crowd gasped, and the sound of his voice made Annie tremble.

"Yes, brethren, *sin!* Why do you think the Lord has withheld His bountiful rains? *Whyyyy,* the devil is so strong in Whiskey he's burning the entire town up with the power of his breath!" He pointed a finger at the crowd. "*Satan's* got you, people of Whiskey!"

The townsfolk cast quizzical glances at each other.

Leroy waited for his words to take effect, then thundered on, "But there isn't a sin in this world the good Lord can't cast out if you repent."

"Amen, Preacher!" chorused the townsfolk.

"No sir, brethren!" cried Leroy, punching his fists to the sky. "You can fight that devil, but it's going to cost you. Yessir, it's going to cost you! You got to *confess* and *repent!* Confess, folks!" Leroy roared. "Shake the devil from your souls!"

"Amen!" cried the townsfolk.

"Are you repentant?"

"Yes, yes!"

Then Leroy's expression grew solemn, and despite the heat, Annie felt a shiver pass over her. He was silent for some time, waiting for the crowd to settle. "Now, folks," he went on at last, "if you're gonna win the war over sin and evil you'll have to starve Lucifer. If you want Him to bless you and this land, if you want Him to give you the rain you need, you've got to give back to the Lord. That's right, give, and give generously, from the very bottom of your hearts." He raised an arm and pointed to the horizon.

"Look at the sky, folks, and see the hand of the Lord ready to grant your prayers!"

And, sure enough, the twilit sky was growing ominously black and a low rumble sounded far out in the distance. A few seconds later, lightning forked across the sky, and the crowd gasped. An angry growl of thunder followed, closer this time, and from the west came a sudden cooling gust of wind.

"Hallelujahs" rang out. Leroy's disciples started to make their way through the throng with their hats upturned, and sure enough, the people of Whiskey dug deep.

Anger surged through Annie, and though she was supposed to wait for a signal from Walker and Hank, she could take no more. She began to work her way forward. The crowd parted to let her through, and in seconds she was standing before Leroy.

He stopped his ranting and stared down at her in surprise. Using every ounce of strength she possessed, she drew her arm back and slapped his face so hard his head snapped sideways.

There was a sudden stunned silence.

"You're a fraud, Leroy Sloan!" Her voice, strong and sure, rang out over the crowd.

Leroy's face reddened, and his black eyes grew cold with fury. He wanted to strike her, but his gaze lifted to beyond her shoulder.

"I wouldn't if I were you," Walker warned quietly, coming up behind Annie. He took her hand and pulled her back a little, putting himself between her and Leroy's venomous gaze.

Leroy's eyes flicked back and forth over the crowd to see what damage Annie's words had wrought.

Annie turned to face the crowd and drew an envelope from her pocket. "This man is a fake! I have a letter from my brother-in-law in Ohio. This man"—she pointed at Leroy—"has come from there. He preys on people like us, in towns like ours, and uses widows like myself for his own gain. He came to Whiskey to take your money and to steal the money my father-in-law left me."

A ripple of questions raced through the crowd.

"Silence!" Leroy raised both arms in the air, and his handsome face contorted into an ugly mask. "Listen to me! The devil is talking through this woman!"

"No!" Preacher Fire roared, and raised his fist into the air. He left his spot beneath the tree and waded through the townsfolk. "Listen to Annie," he ordered in a voice every bit as powerful as Leroy's. "She's telling you the truth!" Behind him, Sheriff Nagy and Hank followed.

A rumble of astonishment arose from the crowd. The townsfolk shared glances of confusion and disbelief, and with her heart pounding, Annie went on. "Isn't it funny that the only 'miracles' we've witnessed have been granted to folks we don't know?"

Thunder cracked above them, and a few light raindrops hit the dusty ground. Leroy smiled his victory. "Behold the glory of the Lord!" He tipped his face to the heavens.

The three other men reached Annie and Walker, and they all faced the crowd.

Preacher Fire's face turned red with fury. "This man is the spawn of Satan himself! Are you such foolish sheep you can't see the truth? The people he's claimed to have healed are among his traveling troupe of followers."

A low ugly hum skittered through the crowd.

Sheriff Nagy held up a hand to silence them. "Show them the posters, Hank."

Hank held up several "Wanted" posters. One had Leroy's face in the center, while others were stamped with the faces of his disciples.

Walker turned to Leroy. His eyes glinted like cold blue diamonds. "You're done, Sloan. You might as well give it up. If God is just, you'll rot in hell for what you've done to decent people." He paused a moment, then added, "And for what you did to Ginny and others like her."

Thunder boomed and lightning lit the sky, illuminating the angry faces of the crowd. The low hum of moments ago erupted into loud shouts.

Leroy swallowed. Sweat broke out on his face. He looked out at the sea of people and sensed their mood, and he knew what he had to do. He took a few steps away from his accusers, then broke into a run, heading for the oak tree on the hill. Behind him, Hank reached for his gun, but Delbert was faster. His gun left his holster in a blur, but he couldn't fire at Leroy for fear of hitting someone in the crowd. Instead, he lifted his gun to the sky and pulled the trigger.

At once a loud crack sounded, and the heavens opened. Rain began to pelt the earth with fury. Leroy stopped a few feet from the oak and tipped his chin to the sky. The rain washed over his face, and he smiled triumphantly.

"Brethren," he shouted victoriously, raising his arms into the air, "I give you your mirac—"

Thunder boomed, and the sky was lit by an awesome tangle of lightning, forking wildly across the sky. And then a jagged bolt shot downward and struck Leroy where he stood near that old oak tree. He arched and jerked, then gave an angry, defeated scream and fell to the ground.

A shocked stillness descended.

Leroy lay on the ground, his clothing smoldering, even while the rain beat upon his lifeless body.

Annie's emotions got the best of her, and a sob tore from her throat. Walker pulled her into his arms and turned her head into his shoulder.

"Oh, dear Lord," she whispered.

He held her tight against his chest and stroked her wet hair back from her face. "It's all right, darlin'. Everything's gonna be just fine now."

His gun in his hand, Hank walked up the hill to where Leroy lay, still and silent. Walker and Annie, and Delbert and Preacher Fire, followed him.

When Hank reached Leroy, he stood over his body for a moment, then dropped to one knee and rolled him over. "I've never been one to claim I was a godly man, but seems like the Lord couldn't wait for us to mete out justice. He wanted to do it all Himself."

"Amen," Preacher Fire whispered.

Sheriff Nagy shook his head and looked up at the crowd that had followed. "Let's go home, folks," he finally said.

NINE

The rain fell all night long, but in the morning the sun was bright and a light breeze whispered through the treetops. The sky was the hazy blue of late summer, and birds sang out sweetly.

Just about every soul in Whiskey was in church that morning. Sally gave her girls the day off, and even Otis Quinby, having witnessed what he believed was the Lord's fury, closed his saloon's doors for the day. Preacher Fire delivered a scorching sermon on false prophets, and the townsfolk were glad to see him pounding his pulpit once again.

Afterward, the townsfolk gathered at the far end of town to see the wares Horace Haney had brought down the river this time.

Dressed in the pretty pale green dress she'd worn to church that morning, Annie made her way down Main Street.

Walker had left her at her door last night with a light kiss and a promise to talk to her today. She'd been too exhausted to ask questions about when he planned to leave Whiskey. But it was more than exhaustion that kept her silent. She really didn't want to know the answer to that question.

When she reached the throng of neighbors who had gathered around Horace's wagon, she instinctively scanned the crowd for Walker's face. He was not there, and the disappointment she felt was sharp. Her heart ached, knowing he would soon be gone.

Horace came out from around his covered wagon. "Howdy, folks," he called out in a cheerful voice. Seeing Annie, his smile faded a little. He hadn't forgotten the dressing-down she'd given him in June. He nodded and touched the limp brim of his dusty old hat. "Annie."

"Hello, Horace." Her smile was warm and gentle, her anger at him long forgotten.

Horace reached inside the back of his wagon and began pulling out the items he hoped to sell. "Well, lookee here," he said after several minutes. "Seems we got us a quilt."

Annie's eyes widened.

"Special one it is, too," Horace went on, holding it up for all to see.

The quilt was the loveliest Annie had ever seen. In the very center was a large multipoint starburst, embroidered with the date September 10, 1843. Above the date were the initials AB, and below were the initials CW.

She didn't know how Horace had come to be in possession of the quilt again, but this time she would have it. She raised her hand to offer a bid, but before she could, someone called out behind her, "Five dollars for the quilt, Horace, right here and now!" They were the very same words Walker had spoken in June.

She spun to see him wading through the crowd, a broad grin on his handsome face. His blue eyes were snapping with merriment.

"Wait!" Annie shouted, confused.

"Sold!" Horace said without hesitation. "To Walker for five dollars."

Walker strode past Annie and up to the wagon. He paid Horace and took the quilt from his hands.

"Now wait just a minute!" Annie yelled, heat flooding her cheeks. Time turned back, and they were as they'd always been, competitors trying to outdo each other. She pushed her way through the crowd, arms pumping. When she reached Walker she poked his shoulder hard.

"Well, howdy, Annie," he drawled in that whiskey-soft voice of his that set her teeth on edge. "How's business?"

"Walker McGregor," she said, tipping forward and anchoring her hands on her hips. Her green eyes flashed fire. "I don't know what you're up to but I mean to buy that quilt!"

"I'm sorry to hear that, Annie."

She waved an impatient hand at him. "There's no need to be sorry." She pointed at Horace. "Just give it back to Horace."

He shook his head sadly. "Afraid I can't do that. You see"— he paused a moment, his expression sobering—"it's a wedding present."

She was silent a long moment. "Oh" was all she could think of to say.

"I bought it for the woman I plan to marry."

She stood in stunned silence, confused, afraid to hope, even though his deep blue eyes were full of love and promise.

He stared down into her pretty, freckled face, and he felt a moment of uncertainty. What if she refused him? He'd lain awake all night long with the future yawning before him. The future was a long lonely road leading to a kaleidoscope of different towns and places. The layout of the towns would change, but the colors would remain the same. And he knew that a life without Annie would be nothing more than a drab, empty journey. He wanted to go to sleep at night holding her in his arms; he wanted to wake up in the morning with her pressed to his side; he wanted to see the faces of their children. "I bought it for you, Annie," he finally said. "I love you. I don't know how good a husband I'll be—I've never been one. But I can tell you this. I'll do the best I can for you and our children, and I'll love you forever."

A hush fell over the crowd.

Annie's heart hammered inside her chest, and his words sang out a magical melody in her head: *I'll do the best I can for you and our children, and I'll love you forever.* Imagine that, she thought with wonder, and closed her eyes to savor the precious promise.

After a few seconds, she opened her eyes, and her gaze found Walker's once more. A slow, lazy smile pulled at his mouth. He held the quilt out to her. "Will you marry me, Annie?"

Tears stung, and she swallowed thickly.

A twitter of excitement zinged through the crowd.

He leaned in close, his eyes teasing. "If you don't, I'll tell everyone what we did the other night, and they'll *really* have something to talk about."

She looked up at him, her heart billowing. A smile trembled on her lips. "You wouldn't dare."

"Wanna bet?" He lifted one eyebrow in challenge.

"Oh, Walker . . ." It was a hoarse, heartfelt whisper.

"Say it, Annie," he urged.

And so she did. "I love you, too, Walker."

He smiled down into her eyes and pulled her close, wrapping the quilt around her shoulders with slow tenderness. "For you, Annie. It was always for you."

She wanted to thank him, but the words got stuck in her throat. She swallowed again, afraid she would begin blubbering all over him.

"So will ya?" he asked.

She tipped her head to the side and smiled. "Will I what?" She wanted to hear him ask one more time.

"Marry me?"

Her smile became full blown, and her green eyes sparkled with happiness. She walked up against him and hugged his neck tight. "You bet I will."

He kissed her then, while they stood swathed in sunshine, and Whiskey's townsfolk cheered.

Horace chuckled. He couldn't remember ever selling the same item twice, and selling it to the same man at that. He almost felt guilty for taking Walker's money. But business was business, and as he'd said, the quilt was special indeed. . . .

Hand-Me-Down Hearts

LINDA SHERTZER

"Mommy, I miss Aunt Cora," Willow whispered.

"Me, too," Russell agreed.

"So do I, pumpkins," Elise Barker said as she tucked around her children the old quilt Miss Cora McGregor had bequeathed them.

If it weren't for Cora's generosity, the children would probably be tucked in at either end of the sofa, and she'd be sleeping on the floor—and they'd be considering themselves lucky.

"She was awful sick, but now she's gone to a better place."

"Wif da angels?" Russell offered.

"With the angels," Elise repeated, nodding. She reached over and tousled his pale brown hair. "She didn't want us to miss her too much, so she left this nice quilt that'll always remind us of her."

"When you die, can I have it?" Willow asked, her blue eyes shining with hope.

"No, me!" Russell protested.

Elise feigned a look of horror. "My goodness, I hope that's a long time from now—and we'll have worn out this old quilt years before."

"No, it's too pretty," Willow protested. "I'm going to take good care of it, and make sure Russell doesn't wet the bed on it."

She gave the quilt a tug, pulling it off her brother.

"I don't no more!" he wailed, clutching at the edge. "Gimme!"

"Don't tear it!" Willow cried, yanking it back again.

"Stop teasing him," Elise scolded. She disentangled their fingers from the delicate fabric and patted the quilt back in place around them. "He doesn't do that. He's a big boy now."

Willow shot her brother a haughty sneer, then turned back to her mother. "Did Aunt Cora make the quilt?"

Elise thought a moment, trying to remember some of the many things she and the frail, lonely woman had talked about while Elise was cleaning her house.

"As I recollect, she said her father bought it from a traveling peddler for her mother before they were married. How the peddler got it is anyone's guess. So I don't know who actually made it. I don't suppose anyone ever will."

"I like it anyway." Willow's fingers ran lightly over the tiny stitches that held the pieces of faded blue and cream silk together in close layers. "It's pretty."

Elise's fingertips, too, slid across the fabric, touching individual patches in the various squares.

"I can almost make out someone's name on this block." She peered at it more closely. Her voice brightened with the challenge of the quilt and its temptingly mysterious array of patches. "It looks like L, Y—and is that a D? 'Lydia'?"

She turned a questioning look to her children.

Willow shrugged. "We can't read yet. Was she the one who made the quilt?"

"I don't know. But they were probably all friends."

"That doesn't look like a name." Willow pointed to the patch in the center.

"It's a date." Elise looked more closely. "September. But I can't tell if that's a *ten* or a *sixteen*. Eighteen-forty . . . eight? Three? Five?"

"Then this month is the quilt's birthday!" Willow exclaimed.

"I guess so."

"We need cake," Russell said.

"We'll see," Elise told him. She might be able to get together some white flour, eggs, milk . . . some cinnamon, slice up some apples.

"Well, even if we can't read it, it's still pretty," Willow decided. "I'd like a dress like this to wear to a Christmas party."

"This looks like someone's wedding gown," Elise said. "This could've been a Sunday-Go-to-Meeting dress. I wonder if this was a ball gown."

"Like Cinderella's?" Willow's eyes lit up as her imagination, as usual, began to run wild. "Oh, Mommy, wouldn't it be wonderful if you had a gown like this?"

She pointed to a patch of pale blue silk unlike any of the others.

"You'd go to a fancy ball and be the prettiest lady there. You'd meet Prince Charming, and he'd marry you, and we'd ride in a golden carriage to live in his castle—with lots of servants so you'd never have to clean house ever again!"

Elise laughed at her daughter's unbridled enthusiasm.

"That would be nice. But Cinderella lived a long, long time ago. . . ."

"In a castle?"

"Far, far 'way?" Russell added with a big yawn.

"Oh, definitely. There just aren't a whole lot of Prince Charmings around here." Elise gave a deep sigh to fuel the children's imaginations.

"There aren't a lot of dragons, either."

"I haven't run into one in years."

"Well, there *should* be Prince Charmings," Willow said very seriously. She pressed her lips together and, in spite of the flattened pillow her head rested upon, tried to give an emphatic nod.

Yes, there should be, Elise thought. Almost two years ago, she'd lost her husband in a farming accident, and then lost the farm, and everything else, when she couldn't pay the mounting bills.

With what little she'd managed to salvage of her life, she'd bought this two-room house on the outskirts of town where Cork Street became a dirt road and trailed away into the fields. They had to share a well and an outhouse with the Dorn family next door, but at least the floor was sturdy and the roof didn't leak much.

Elise managed to keep food on the table and clothes on the children's backs by cleaning other people's houses. And she didn't see any sense in being too proud to accept an occasional hand-me-down, either.

She figured she was about as close to being Cinderella as a woman could get without having ugly stepsisters.

"Well, don't lose any beauty sleep over it," Elise warned her daughter. "Maybe you'll be the one to find Prince Charming."

Willow giggled.

"What 'bout me?" Russell demanded.

"Oh, you *are* my little Prince Charming." Elise bent down and kissed both children on their foreheads. "Good night, my pumpkins."

"Night, Mommy."

"Night-night, Mommy," Russell said with a big yawn.

Elise pulled the threadbare curtain across the doorway to the side room that served as the children's bedroom.

Prince Charming, indeed. Maybe it was her own fault for having given Willow such a fanciful name. Maybe she should've called her something sensible, like Ann or Jane or Mary. On the other hand, when her children possessed so few material goods, maybe a vivid imagination was the best—or even the only—thing she could give to them.

Elise longed to snuggle down on the lumpy sofa that served as her bed and rest her weary bones. It had been a long day, but she wasn't finished yet. She'd remade a dress of Cora's into a dress for Willow. All she needed to do was stitch the hem.

She looked at the two chairs—another bequest from Cora—placed on opposite sides of the fireplace. They were pretty, but her bottom had worn a comfortable hollow in the seat of her old rocking chair that suited her perfectly, so she'd decided to save the good furniture for company.

After settling in, she picked up her sewing from the basket beside her and started to rock. The crackling of the fire in the hearth and the rhythm of the creaking chair in time with her small, even stitches gave her a feeling of, if not luxury, at least comfort and security.

The pounding on the front door so startled her that she dropped her needle.

"Oh, tarnation!" she muttered, falling to her knees to search the bare floor. "My last sharp needle."

The shadows and the flickering flames conspired to disguise each crack and grain in the floorboards until everything looked like a needle.

She groped around with the palms of her hands. A stuck finger was worth it if she could find her needle.

The pounding on the door continued.

"I'll be right there," she called cheerfully, while muttering much less pleasant thoughts under her breath as she continued to search. Nobody in his right mind would come calling at this hour—leastwise nobody who could possibly be more important than her last sharp needle.

The pounding grew more insistent.

"I'm coming! I'm coming!" she called with exasperation, but still paused for one last glance over the floorboards.

It suddenly occurred to her that Mr. Fitch down the road might be having trouble with his palpitations again. Or that maybe Molly Dorn's baby had decided it was time to make its entrance into this world.

She sprang to her feet. Molly's first baby had been stillborn. One more loss, Elise feared, would drive her insane. She'd try to do what she could, or run for the doctor if she had to.

In a mere two steps Elise was at the door. She pulled it open.

The stranger's dark figure surprised her. His long black coat made him appear very tall. His black homburg was pulled down over his eyes so that she could barely make out his features in the night.

"Who—"

"It's about time you opened that door," he pronounced as he strode into her house. "I don't relish standing outside in a section of town as disreputable as this."

Elise blinked, trying to regain her senses. The stranger's lack of manners had startled her even more than his mysterious appearance. He gave a cough of disgust as, without another word, he turned his back on her and looked around the room.

The coat was a good device for intimidating people, she decided. Not only did it make him look tall and forbidding, but it also made his shoulders look so broad that she could scarcely believe anyone would dare to correct his terrible manners.

He removed his hat, but kept it tucked in the crook of his arm. He looked as if he might sit down uninvited in one of her company chairs. Instead, he rubbed his gloved finger across the mantel, then peered with distaste at the fingertip, as if her house were too filthy to bear.

Perhaps her house and its furnishings were a little threadbare. But no one could say she didn't keep her home and her children spotlessly clean.

Elise decided she'd already had more than enough of this fancy-dressed stranger.

Her next thought was to run for Sheriff Hopkins. But then she hesitated.

Only last year she'd read the newspaper accounts of Miss Lizzie Borden in Massachusetts and her misadventures with an axe. What if this stranger had escaped from some asylum for the insane? Why else would he wear a big coat and a hat that covered his face if not to hide his identity? Did she dare leave her children alone with him? Suppose she returned to find their lifeless little bodies in a blood-soaked bed? She'd never be able to forgive herself!

She couldn't risk leaving until she knew more about this man and why he was here. She'd have to take care of this all by herself.

"Who are you?" she demanded, trying to sound as stern as her intruder. "What do you mean, coming here this time of night? What do you want?"

"My name is Ryder McGregor—although I doubt that would mean anything to you," he replied, gazing at her disdainfully.

"Oh, no, Mr. McGregor," she contradicted.

She could barely discern the features of the rich little boy who wouldn't play with anyone under the stern features of this man who had changed so much.

"I didn't recognize you at first, all covered up like that. But I grew up in this town, too, and I remember you *very* well. You're Miss Cora's younger brother."

He didn't seem surprised.

"Your sister passed away a month ago. Why are you here now?"

"I'm here at this ungodly hour because the miserably slow excuse for a locomotive that services this one-horse town just arrived. I'm here at all because I want the priceless family heirlooms that I understand you now possess, thanks in no small part to my late sister's excessive generosity. And, no doubt, thanks to a great deal of conniving on *your* part."

"What?" All his quickly spoken words hummed in her ears.

"Are you deaf, hard-of-hearing, or stupid? Shall I repeat myself?" He stared at her from his formidable height, his gaze holding her entrapped.

"I heard you perfectly well the first time. I just couldn't believe my ears," she said, returning his angry glare. She'd faced down enough bill collectors; this man didn't intimidate her at all. "I just didn't remember you being so rude."

"I really don't care what you—or anyone else—thinks of me."

Elise nodded. "No. I sort of figured you wouldn't."

"Then shall we proceed with the business at hand?"

"I don't have any business with you."

"Yes you do," he insisted. "My sister was a foolish old maid who mistakenly bequeathed to you pieces of furniture and a valuable quilt that rightfully belong to my family's estate."

"Estate?" she repeated with a laugh of ridicule. "Your family lived in a big house over on Daniels Road, but it wasn't exactly a castle. I don't know what *you* consider an estate, but this isn't some kingdom, and you're certainly not the lord of the manor."

His squared jaw was set in a firm line as he dispassionately examined his surroundings. He didn't seem to be paying any attention to her protests.

"You sure as shooting aren't Prince Charming, either!"

"What?" He stopped and stared at her.

"But you might make a passably good dragon."

"What?"

His outbursts and puzzled expression told her she'd finally managed to surprise this haughty man. She tried not to smile with satisfaction.

"I have no idea what you're talking about, and I highly suspect you don't either. However, there is the matter of certain property . . ."

He dipped his gray-gloved hand inside his overcoat and into the breast pocket of his jacket. He pulled out a long document, unfolded it, and proceeded to read.

"A mahogany bedstead circa 1810, two Duncan Phyfe chairs—"

"You came here just to get back that old bed and two old chairs?" Elise demanded incredulously.

"A quilt . . ."

"She gave me some old dresses of hers, too. I suppose you'll be wanting the clothes off my back as well."

Mr. McGregor's gaze flickered over her body, then returned to meet her eyes. In the dim firelight, it seemed to Elise, his green eyes glowed with all the intensity of a demon of greed and avarice. Was he judging her monetary worth, just as he seemed to appraise everything else? What could she possibly have left worth taking— except her soul?

"That won't be necessary," he replied coldly, folding up the document.

She couldn't let him think he and his green-eyed stare had left her speechless. She had to say something!

"You're darned right it won't be necessary," she muttered.

He turned and strode about the room, tapping both chairs from his sister with the folded paper, but scrupulously avoiding Elise's furniture.

"I see the two aforementioned chairs. The bed and quilt are missing, however."

He stopped and glared at her accusingly. "You haven't sold them, have you?"

"Of course not! Who'd buy those old things? Cora had to *give* them away."

He glanced at the fireplace. "Or chopped it up for firewood?"

"Good gracious, no!"

"Then where are they?" he demanded harshly.

She pressed her lips together tightly and stared at him. She wasn't about to tell him anything.

His eyes darted toward the curtain. "Is *that* a room?" he demanded with obvious disdain. Boldly he marched up to the curtain and yanked it back. Willow and Russell lay fast asleep. "Oh! By the Almighty!"

"Hush!" she scolded in a hoarse whisper.

She pulled the curtain out of his hand and spread it across the opening. Then she stationed herself in the doorway. If this man thought he was going to snatch the quilt right off her sleeping children, he'd have to do it over her dead body!

"I'll thank you to at least leave my children undisturbed."

Mr. McGregor was tucking the document back into his pocket and shaking his head.

"Don't think you can use your pitiful urchins or your lamentable status as a widow to induce me to stop," he warned. "I intend to retrieve my possessions."

"Look, Mr. McGregor, as far as you coming here and bothering me so late at night, it's not my fault that the trains don't always run on schedule."

She moved past him to place one of Cora's chairs between them. She rested her hand on the back, hoping that the loving spirit of her friend could give her some kind of moral support.

Yes, Cora must be urging her on, Elise decided. She could almost hear her friend telling her to teach her spoiled little brother a lesson.

"I don't know who this Duncan Phyfe fellow is, or what he has to do with this business. As far as I'm concerned, your sister gave me the quilt and furniture very legally—"

"I doubt that very much."

He looked at her, one dark brow raised skeptically. This man was full of doubts, fears, and uncertainties, Elise realized. In spite of all the wealth that she knew must line his pockets and swell his bank account, he seemed completely empty inside. His eyes were fiery and intense, but there was no love, no joy, no tenderness in them. For just a moment, she could almost feel sorry for him.

But she knew she mustn't weaken. She could pity him, but the welfare of her children was at stake. This man didn't stand a chance.

One bold step brought her close enough to peer up into his narrowed eyes.

"You may not remember me. We never played together—"

"I chose my playmates very carefully."

This stuffed shirt definitely needed some deflating.

"The truth is, you were such a little snot, no one wanted to play with you!"

He said nothing.

"Your sister spoke of you often—and rather fondly, too. She even seemed to miss you, although now that I've seen you again, I can't imagine why. I can't even believe you two are related."

Even now, confronted with her tirade, he showed no emotion on his lean, tanned face. He just looked down at her and demanded, "What do you mean by that?"

She hesitated just a moment. Her mother had raised her better than to be rude.

"I could be polite and say I mean you don't look anything like her."

Cora had been pale and fragile, with limpid blue eyes and red hair, but none of the proverbial redheaded temperament. Mr. McGregor, on the other hand, had dark wavy hair, and green eyes that snapped with fire. He might even be considered handsome—if he weren't such a pompous ass!

"Let's not allow mere common courtesy and the strictures of society to stand in the way of our being perfectly frank with each other," he stated sarcastically. "I believe I've already been more than forthright with you."

Mr. McGregor was just asking for this, Elise decided, and he deserved it, too.

"Miss Cora was the sweetest, kindest, most generous, warmhearted person in the whole world."

"Yes, I can see how you'd believe that." He glanced at the coveted chairs again. "And how you'd take advantage of the fact."

Elise could feel her anger swelling, causing a dreaded lump to form in her throat. It made scolding this man even more difficult. It also brought all her tears dangerously close to the surface. She wouldn't cry now! She had so much more to say to Ryder McGregor.

"*You*, on the other hand, must be the meanest, pettiest, greediest, most suspicious, heartless vermin ever to infest the face of the earth!"

She swallowed several times, but the lump in her throat refused to go down. She blinked furiously and hoped that, in the flickering firelight, he wouldn't notice the tears waiting to tumble from her lashes.

"Are you quite finished with your appraisal? I really had expected more."

"No," she replied quickly. "But I don't think you're worth wasting my breath on."

He twisted his lips into a wry sneer and gave a little snort. "If you're quite finished, you may turn the quilt over to me now. I'll have someone bring a wagon around in the morning for the furniture."

"That's where you're mistaken. Your sister gave me these things fair and square, and I'm keeping them."

She crossed her arms over her chest, just to show him how determined she was.

"You can't."

"Yes I can. Possession is nine-tenths of the law—and *I* possess the furniture."

"Not for long."

"We'll see about that."

"Yes we will."

"You won't take my quilt or my furniture."

"Yes I will."

"No, you—" Goodness gracious, she suddenly realized, they sounded worse than Russell and Willow bickering. "Mr. McGregor, it seems as if our argument has degenerated into 'yes I can' and 'no you can't,' which is childish, and very pointless. So for now, considering the lateness of the hour, I'll thank you to leave my house."

She strode boldly toward the door and pulled it open. The air of the late September evening was growing increasingly chill. She knew she shouldn't leave the door open and allow what little heat the meager fire gave to escape; she and the children would need it to stay warm tonight. But she had to show Mr. McGregor she wasn't afraid of him or his threats, and that he was very unwelcome.

"Without the quilt," she stressed.

He drew himself up. For a moment, she was afraid he'd refuse to leave. Then how would she get him out of her house?

"This isn't the end of the matter, Mrs. Barker," he promised as he strode toward the door.

"I never for a minute thought it was, Mr. McGregor."

Suddenly he stopped and turned back to her. Standing on the doorsill, Elise met him eye to eye.

His cold green eyes stared at her, unblinking. He seemed to be able to peer deep into her mind, to search out her weaknesses in order to take advantage of in his insatiable quest to possess everything.

She tried to return his stare with equal chill, but she was afraid she wasn't succeeding. Something in his cold, steady gaze made the heat rise across her breasts, up her throat, and in her cheeks. Yet at the same time his gaze made her want to shiver.

"I'll warn you now—I'm a man who always gets what he wants."

"And I'll warn you I'm a woman who's learned to hold on to what I have."

He gave a scornful sniff. "You can have what's yours, but you won't have what's mine."

"Your threats don't mean anything to me." She lifted her chin defiantly. "You might be a little taller now, but you still act like a child. And just like a child, you need to be taught that no matter how big a temper tantrum you throw, you *can't* always have everything you want."

He gave a bitter laugh. "And you intend to be the one who teaches me?"

She nodded.

He placed his hat on his head and turned away from her. He was chuckling, but she didn't detect any true humor in his laugh. In fact, it seemed to Elise as if he were trying too hard to do something he didn't do very often, and wasn't very good at. What a sad, sorry man he was!

Then he glanced back at her over his shoulder.

"I'd really like to see *you* try to teach me a thing or two." He gave another bitter laugh. "I'd really like to see that."

"You will."

❧

People needed to guard against the cold and rain, Ryder thought as he pulled the collar of his coat up closer around his neck to ward off the chill evening air that whistled down the street. He wished he'd brought his cashmere scarf.

Even the healthiest people had to be careful. Who would have suspected his beloved bride, Frances—young, beautiful, healthy— would catch a chill one October evening in the San Francisco fog and be dead of pneumonia by February?

He glanced cautiously around as he strode quickly down the dirt road toward Whiskey proper. The chill wasn't the only thing he had to worry about.

He didn't remember this outlying section being so squalid. Even though the main line had bypassed Whiskey, the town had still managed to grow. They'd built many more houses, some of them fairly nice, he'd noticed as he'd passed through Whiskey on the way from the little spur train station to Mrs. Barker's.

But why did they also have to build little hovels like hers? There were usually skinny, dirty men hanging around outside, and fat, greasy women lolling around inside. Such places always smelled of cabbage, sweat, and urine. Why didn't these people take baths and get jobs?

He supposed that's what happened when a town went sprawling out across the prairie. Or when people like Elise Barker and her grubby little offspring stayed in town.

She said she'd grown up in Whiskey, too, although for the life of him he couldn't remember any girl named Elise or any man named Barker. Of course, if they'd come from the wrong side of town—and it seemed pretty evident that these people had—he wouldn't have paid much attention to them anyway.

He grimaced. Cora had always been a little different—so pale and fragile compared to him and his brother and other sister. She'd never married, but had stayed home to care for their parents until they both passed away several years ago, within months of each other. Leave it to Cora—always too kindhearted—to hire a woman from this part of town. It was a wonder the woman hadn't stolen them blind.

He should've hired a carriage, he thought with regret as he walked down the rutted street. It was a long way from the shacks at the end of Cork Street to the homes of the well-to-do on Daniels Road.

Maybe he should've rented a room in the local hotel, too. It wasn't the Palace Hotel, but at least it would be clean. He didn't have any idea what condition the old house was in now.

He grimaced when he saw the weeds springing up through the brick walk leading to the front porch. His mother would turn in her grave if she could see her rosebushes trailing lanky canes along the ground, and her chrysanthemums leaning over each other like drunken revelers because no one had bothered to pinch them back. He guessed the gardener hadn't been by in quite a while.

He stepped cautiously onto the porch, half expecting it to collapse under his weight. He pulled out the big brass key and stuck it in the lock. It turned with surprising ease.

Ryder pushed the door inward. The vestibule was much too dark to make out anything but the vaguest shadows. Even with the moonlight streaming in the two long, narrow windows on either side of the door, he could barely see.

Slowly he reached out his right hand and eased it along the wall beside the door. His fingers fumbled around the brass fixture until he found the key and turned it. The jets flared to life, casting an eerie pall over the entrance.

"Well, I'll be . . . ," he whispered, his voice trailing off in surprise. The place looked exactly the same as the day he'd left it ten years ago.

He couldn't find a single dust ball on the floor, not even in the corners or clinging to the edges of the turkey carpet.

There wasn't a speck of dust on the round table in the center of the vestibule. The crystal vase his mother had always kept full of flowers was empty, but it was still sitting in the middle of the table, catching the gaslight and reflecting it back from every dazzling facet.

As he stood staring at his surroundings, Ryder fully expected to see his parents coming toward him in greeting, with his brother and sisters merging on the entrance from other places in the big house. He even half expected to meet the shade of himself as a child creeping through the house. The thought unnerved him.

To his left was the shadowy dining room. If he summoned enough courage to go in there and turned up the gaslight, he'd see the table that had been big enough for the whole family and their guests, too, to gather round. Would he hear the laughter and chatter of family and friends, mingled with the clink of china and glasses? Would he smell the roast turkey, lima beans, and candied sweet potatoes of their traditional Christmas dinner?

To his right, he could see into the darkened parlor. If he went in there, would he hear the fading notes of Cora and Martha's piano duets? Would he hear the echoes of long-ago toasts drunk to the health and happiness of himself and his new bride before they'd set out for San Francisco?

In San Francisco, Frances was the only one who haunted him. Here, they all ganged up on him, painfully reminding him of everyone he'd lost.

"Gone. They're all gone," he said very loudly, as if his shouting could chase away all the ghosts.

He headed for the stairs.

"Mom and Dad are dead." It seemed out of place to call them Mother and Father in his childhood home. "Aunt Charlotte's dead. Cora's dead."

Their names rang in time to the dull thud of his footsteps on each tread.

"Henry moved to Chicago with his wife. I never hear from them except at Christmas."

The long hallway that led to his bedroom at the back of the house was dark and echoed his footsteps back at him.

"Martha married that traveling salesman from Albany," he muttered. "I hope they've finally settled down someplace decent."

The door to his old room gave just the tiniest squeak as he pushed it open.

"I don't know if Aunt Charlotte's children are still living in Whiskey, or even if they're still alive. I haven't heard from my cousins in years."

He didn't want to investigate too deeply into whether he or his cousins had stopped corresponding first.

He was angry and frustrated, and tired right down to the

soles of his feet. He'd thought this was going to be a quick trip to reclaim the inheritance. Then he could go back to business again. He had a bad feeling this was going to take a lot longer than he'd expected.

He turned the gaslight up just enough to enable him to see without tripping over things. "Even Frances didn't stay around," he muttered as he prepared for bed. Frances, who'd promised to love, honor, and obey, in sickness and in health, and to stay with him until death parted them. Even when confronted with the inarguable fact that death eventually claimed them all, how could he have foreseen that death would claim her so quickly?

He removed his jacket and tie. He unfastened his cuff links and moved, out of long-forgotten habit, to place them in the small tortoiseshell tray on his dresser. It was right where he had left it. There wasn't a spot of dust on it, or on anything else in the room.

His bed, his dresser, his desk and chair were all in the same place. The evidence of his juvenile mania for rock collecting still rested on a spotless shelf. Even after an absence of ten years, he could move around this room blindfolded and lay his hands on every object he'd cherished as a youth.

In all this time, not a thing had changed.

"But no*body* stays the same," he argued aloud with circumstances. "Nobody ever stays around."

He scooped the handful of coins out of his trouser pocket and placed them in a wooden bowl on his desk. They clinked against each other and clunked as they came to rest in the bottom of the bowl.

"This is the only thing a man can ever really count on—and then only if he holds on to it as tightly as he can."

Just to reinforce his belief, he picked up the coins and clutched them tightly in his fist until his nails bit into the flesh of his palm.

"Not like my silly, sentimental sister, giving away perfectly good things for no logical reason." He dribbled the coins back into the bowl.

As he settled into bed and leaned back against the pillows, he noticed how the sheets smelled like lavender.

But Cora had passed away over a month ago. Certainly the smell would have dissipated by now. And dust would have accumulated.

Had Elise Barker been coming back to clean this place, even after Cora passed away? Obviously, he decided, his feelings about the industrious woman softening just a bit. Was she still expecting to be paid? Probably, he added to himself with a wry grimace.

"Well, that's just one more thing I'll have to discuss with Mrs. Barker when I take the sheriff there tomorrow."

❧

"Oh, wow!" Russell exclaimed, dashing for the front window. "Look't da big wagon!"

Elise finished scooping the oatmeal into three bowls and hurried to the window. "Yes indeed. That's a big wagon. Now go eat your breakfast while it's still warm."

The only people in town with a wagon like that were the Martin brothers, who waited at the train station every day to hire out to people who needed big things moved to their house. Elise didn't need three guesses to know who'd hired them this time. She didn't need to ask why, either.

She knew exactly who was knocking on her door. But when she opened it, she never expected to see the sheriff there as well.

"Good morning, Mrs. Barker."

Without waiting for her to return his greeting, Mr. McGregor strode into the house.

Sheriff Hopkins remained in the doorway and, grinning apologetically, said, "Mornin', Mrs. Barker. I hate to be botherin' you at this hour." Hat in hand, he looked more like a little boy begging for cookies than a lawman come to arrest some renegade cleaning lady.

"Yes, it's pretty early, but I never sleep late. Anyway, I was expecting him. I just didn't think he was serious enough to bring *you* here. Come on in."

The sheriff stepped inside and nodded his head toward Mr. McGregor. "I tried to talk him out of it, but he can be awful gol-durn pigheaded."

Elise glared at Mr. McGregor. "I'm sure he can."

"I even told him he might get a little more cooperation if he came by a little later in the day. . . ."

"Cooperation?" she repeated with a brief laugh. "I don't intend to cooperate one bit with that scoundrel."

"You'd be wise to cooperate with me, when I have the law on my side," Mr. McGregor warned her.

"You might have a lawman with you," she pointed out to him, "but that doesn't mean you have the law on your side."

What was Mr. McGregor thinking, she wondered, as he studied her so closely? It was hard to tell, since his face was always so devoid of any show of feelings.

She glared back at him, trying to add more menace, as she did when Willow and Russell would continue to bicker during church services, even after several warnings.

"I have a list here."

Once again, he pulled his precious paper from his breast pocket. He held it out in front of her, just out of reach. Was he afraid she'd snatch it from him and destroy it in a desperate attempt to keep him from regaining his property?

"My goodness!" Elise exclaimed. "You carry that around with

you like it was Holy Writ. Or like you were a little kid hanging on to his blanket."

Sheriff Hopkins chuckled. Elise laughed, too. But Mr. McGregor wasn't laughing.

"How did you get these items to your house?" he demanded.

"I carried the chairs."

Elise noted the lift in his eyebrows.

"Don't look so surprised," she told him with as much arrogance as she could manage. "I can't afford to hire the Martins' wagon, but I'm not some weakling who just sits around waving a fan and eating sweets. I can do my fair share of work."

"I have no doubts about *that* whatsoever."

How could he make the fact that someone worked hard sound like an insult? she wondered.

"'Course, you had to get Purdey Meekins to help you move the bed," Sheriff Hopkins reminded her.

"But he owed me a favor anyway, for the time I watched their kids when Elva had their third one."

"You still have no right to keep these things," Mr. McGregor insisted. "They're valuable family heirlooms that—"

"Valuable," Elise repeated with a laugh of ridicule. "Did you stay awake last night thinking up this stupid stuff? Most folks just count sheep."

Mr. McGregor still wasn't laughing. "You can just thank your lucky stars I'm not pressing charges—yet."

She glared back at him. "I don't have *anything* to thank *you* for. You've been nothing but a nuisance since you came here."

"I tried to tell you, mister, but you were too dang stubborn to listen," Sheriff Hopkins said. "You don't stand a Chinaman's chance o' gettin' that furniture back. Your sister had that lawyer write it down, all legal and businesslike."

"I've seen the document, but I'm not convinced of the legality of it."

"Figurin' out what's legal, and what ain't, ain't my line o' work. Maybe you should've checked with that lawyer first."

"I suppose you want the clothing back, too?" Elise asked.

"The clothing is the one thing that *isn't* of any value."

The sheriff chuckled. "I don't think none of it'll fit you, neither."

Elise giggled.

"Darn shame, too," the sheriff added, obviously prodded on by her appreciation, "since that blue gown might've been right becomin'."

Elise laughed again. She noted that Mr. McGregor never showed even the tiniest smile at the sheriff's jokes.

"I doubt the quilt is worth anything, either," she told them. "Except to me."

"How do you figure that?" Mr. McGregor demanded.

Elise hesitated. She already regretted the fact that Mr. McGregor was a part of her life, even temporarily. She didn't want to let him into any more—her thoughts, her memories.

"Your sister and I were good friends."

"Odd." Mr. McGregor gave a doubting sneer. "I don't remember her mentioning you in any of her letters."

"Maybe you would if you'd written to her more often," Elise countered.

"How did you two manage to become such 'good friends'?"

"I started cleaning her house shortly after my husband died. I was lonely. She was lonely. We started talking about one thing and another. Next thing we knew, we were good friends."

"How convenient," Mr. McGregor remarked sarcastically.

"The quilt helps me remember her," Elise said, trying to ignore his sour disposition. "And it'll help keep my children warm this winter."

"These little houses do get mighty drafty," the sheriff agreed. "Couldn't you see your way clear just to let her keep the quilt?"

"Sheriff!" Mr. McGregor exclaimed. "Don't tell me you've fallen victim to her sly little game, too."

He clapped his arms at his side in exasperation. The heavy black material flapped, making Elise think he looked like some greedy vulture, just waiting for another poor creature to die so he could feast on the bones.

"I wasn't playing any game when my husband died, you heartless wretch!" she cried.

"You must admit—"

"I'm not admitting *anything* to you!"

He ignored her outburst. " 'I was lonesome, she was lonesome, so we became friends' is a convenient excuse for swindling someone out of her property."

"You miserable polecat!" Elise wanted to throw one of those darned chairs at him. "I didn't swindle her. She gave these things to me."

"And 'I need to keep my children warm this winter' is an excellent use of pathos and guilt."

She was just about ready to pound in frustration on Mr. McGregor's head.

"It wasn't any game when I lost the farm, the bed my children were born in . . . their cradle, my hope chest . . . my mother's dining room table . . . I remember your sister telling me how you married and moved to San Francisco, how you lost your wife like I lost my husband."

Mr. McGregor barely nodded his acknowledgment. She should've figured he was incapable of sympathy.

"You don't know what it's like to lose everything!"

Her voice trailed off in a cracking sob. She'd only thought to laugh this fool out of his pretensions and send him on his way empty-handed. But he'd struck a deep wound in her that hadn't yet healed.

"Sheriff, will you at least take possession of the quilt now?" Mr. McGregor asked.

"Nope," the sheriff answered, crossing his arms firmly over his paunch. "Can't rightly take away what might be the only thing keepin' them kids warm."

Mr. McGregor fumed in disbelief. "I should've known her pathetic tales would make you take her side."

If this was the way he wanted it to be, then she'd stopped playing games, indeed.

"Get out," Elise ordered coldly. She had control of her voice now, and—she hoped—her emotions. More important, she wanted to keep control of the situation.

She stood in the doorway, her right arm extended and index finger pointing out into the street. She felt like a tableau of some maudlin lithograph entitled "Never Darken My Door Again." She never realized how much she could really mean it.

"Get out now, Mr. McGregor, before I take that quilt and smother you with it!"

Mr. McGregor grimaced. "Then arresting you for my murder will *finally* give the sheriff something to do!"

Elise almost grinned. Was there hope yet that Ryder McGregor might have some life in him? Nope, not a chance.

❧

Ryder shifted his seat uncomfortably on the hard boards as he and the sheriff rode up Cork Street with the Martins. Imagine him riding in the back of a wagon!

In San Francisco, he had several carriages for his various

needs. He'd even toyed with buying one of those newfangled, gasoline-powered automobiles he'd heard they were building in France and Germany. But they seemed too unreliable to waste his money on. One thing Ryder McGregor *never* did was waste his money.

He'd taken the humble family general store and turned it into a large shipping, importing, and exporting business. He knew his competitors—and associates—considered him a lone wolf, and also a bit of a pirate, a reputation he relished. Thank goodness none of his business associates could see how far he'd sunk in *this* illfated venture.

But suppose someone from town saw him—someone who knew him when he was a child. What would they think had happened to him to reduce him to riding in the back of the wagon? Did they know he could probably buy and sell this entire town?

Or were they more likely to recall the time the Crowley boys had called to him, urging him to cross their backyard? He hadn't known they'd moved the outhouse but hadn't yet filled in the old pit and dug the new one. He'd come running and fallen right in. Of course, the darn Crowleys had laughed their fool heads off, drawing quite a crowd, before someone figured they ought to pull him out. It had taken several baths with harsh lye soap to get rid of the smell. Was it any wonder he never again wanted to play with any of the kids in town?

Why was that the kind of thing people tended to remember, instead of the good things—like the time he won the county geography bee?

Elise Barker had said she remembered him, even though he couldn't recall her. No doubt the outhouse incident was one of her favorite recollections.

"Clever little minx," he muttered under his breath.

"Who? Mrs. Barker?" the sheriff asked.

"I believe that's who we've just been to see," Ryder snapped. "The woman takes up housekeeping for one of the richest spinsters in town, insinuates herself into her good graces, then takes whatever she can get from her."

"What? An old quilt?"

"If that's not being a clever little minx, I don't know what is."

"I'd sure hate to see a dumb one then," the sheriff mumbled.

"At least my sister had the good sense not to leave the woman cash."

"Now *that* she really could've used. I think she's still tryin' to pay off the doctor's bill from her husband's accident."

Still paying the doctor's bill? Why hadn't she finagled his sister into paying that off? Cora could be that softhearted; why hadn't Mrs. Barker been that conniving? The woman was a puzzle!

The wagon pulled to a stop in front of the jail.

"Never could see how Miss Cora could stand livin' all alone after your parents passed away," the sheriff said as he jumped down. "Mrs. Barker and her kids sure had a grand ol' time in that big house."

"You mean she actually invited *all* of them . . . actually enjoyed them coming for a visit?"

"Oh, lots o' visits."

Ryder shuddered to think of those grubby children romping through his parents' beautiful home. His father had built it for his mother. She'd spent a lifetime filling it with beautiful things. Cora had done her part, and he expected to do his now, too.

On the other hand, the house didn't look as if it had suffered. It looked spotlessly clean, and nothing seemed to be missing.

"Yeah, she really liked those little rascals."

Ryder couldn't imagine anyone liking children unless he

absolutely had to—for instance, if the child was one's own. *After* he or she had learned to walk, talk, and be civilized, of course. And then only for short periods of time.

"I always wondered why she didn't just invite them to come live with her. She had enough room. But I guess Mrs. Barker's right stubborn about her independence," the sheriff remarked as he walked away.

Ryder watched the man with disdain. Lawmen were supposed to be tough, wary, and hardheaded. How could this man fall for Mrs. Barker's pathetic stories? He was as gullible as Cora!

Ryder jumped down from the wagon. He hadn't jumped off the back of a wagon in years. There was just the tiniest feeling of pride in realizing he was still in good enough shape to do it.

He handed the Martin boys a few bills.

"You need us for tomorrow, too, huh?" Bobby Eugene asked.

Ryder hesitated just a moment. He wasn't about to let these yokels see him again refused by a mere cleaning woman.

"I'll let you know," he answered at last.

"Whatever you say, mister," Billy Joe said.

Ryder walked away. Walking was so much more dignified, he thought, than riding through town in a wagon that probably hauled everything from bathtubs to manure.

He held his head high as he strode down Main Street. He was looking for one particular door, but he wasn't sure he remembered exactly where it was. Maybe they'd moved their offices. Maybe they'd died, like almost everybody else he'd known.

Then he saw the lettering on the door—Anderson, Anderson and Cole, Attorneys-at-Law. The letters were slightly faded and peeling, but the office appeared to look pretty much the same. He opened the door and walked in.

Elise gave the pinafore a hard shake, then held it up to the line and pushed the clothespin down. In the space between her house and the Dorns', she saw the Martins' wagon pulling to a stop.

"Oh, for Pete's sake!" she grumbled. "Not again."

Russell and Willow were playing in the pile of sand just behind the house.

"You two stay here," she told them. "Mommy has some things to take care of inside."

"Is that nasty man here again?" Willow asked.

"Yes, I'm afraid he is."

"My mommy's not 'fraid o' nothin'," Russell said.

"I'm not afraid of *him*, pumpkin," Elise said as she walked into her house.

At least, she didn't think she was. Her heart beat faster when she saw him because she knew she was in for a fight, she reasoned. She checked her reflection in the tiny mirror on the kitchen wall and patted her hair into order. After all, she had to look firm and businesslike—not as if she'd just gotten out of bed.

Bed. She shouldn't put Ryder McGregor and a bed in the same thought. It was because he wanted to take the only bed her children had, she told herself. There were absolutely no other connections she could—or wanted to—make between Ryder and a bed.

Before he had the chance to knock, Elise pulled the door open.

"Well, at least this time you had the decency not to call at the break of dawn," she said in greeting.

"Good morning to you, too, Mrs. Barker," Mr. McGregor said pleasantly. "May we come in?"

Elise was surprised when he remained on the door-step, politely awaiting her invitation.

Her gaze slid from Mr. McGregor to the man at his side. She recognized him as the lawyer Miss Cora had write up her Last

Will and Testament. She knew with certainty Mr. McGregor had brought him here now to back up *his* claim.

Preacher Elmo Fire always said the Lord giveth and taketh away. She wondered when the Almighty had extended that privilege to lawyers.

The whole thing was ludicrous! She supposed it just showed that if the price was right, some lawyers would argue for anything.

"I can't imagine why you want to come into my house," she said as she moved aside for them to enter. "We've already said everything we possibly could to each other."

"That's why I've brought my attorney."

"So, he's going to do your talking for you?"

"I always do my *own* talking," Mr. McGregor said sternly. "Mr. Anderson is here to clarify some points of law about my sister's will that you might not be aware of."

The two men sat on the sofa. Mr. McGregor couldn't know he was sitting on her bed, she thought. But she knew where she fluffed up her pillow just before she laid her head down at night, and that made her even more uneasy as she sat in her customary rocking chair.

"Now, Mrs. Barker," Mr. Anderson began.

She turned to the lawyer, one eyebrow raised in question. She hoped she looked stern, knowledgeable, and worldly-wise—the kind of person nobody could fool.

"Regarding this matter of the quilt, the bed, the chairs—"

"Mr. Anderson, you know darn good and well Miss Cora gave those things to me of her own free will. They're all I have. Why would Mr. McGregor try to take them away from me when he already has so much?"

Before the lawyer could answer, Mr. McGregor warned, "Don't try to dupe Mr. Anderson as you did the sheriff with your poor-widow story."

"It's not a story. To me it's all too real."

They sat there glaring at each other.

"Mrs. Barker, the will clearly states that you are to receive these items," Mr. Anderson said, breaking the silence. "However, there are ways in which members of the family may contest the terms of this will."

"Yes?" Loud alarms were going off in her head.

"Particularly since Miss McGregor was bedridden and infirm, and perhaps not quite in complete possession of her faculties—"

"No! Oh, no! Doc Wilson can tell you she was perfectly sane when she passed away. Tell me, Mr. Anderson, how much money did he offer you to make this more complicated?"

"Mrs. Barker, please!" the lawyer declared, looking completely affronted.

"It doesn't have to be this way, you know," Mr. McGregor said. "You're only making it more difficult for yourself."

"Funny. Things were going just fine for me before you arrived," she replied. "I'd say *you're* the one who is causing my problems."

"Don't make me make things even *more* difficult." His voice grew deeper with warning.

"If Mr. McGregor decides to contest the will, we can go through months of hearings," Mr. Anderson explained.

He sounded as if he were already looking forward to it—as well as to the fat fee Mr. McGregor undoubtedly could afford to pay him.

"Do you have an attorney, Mrs. Barker?" Mr. McGregor asked.

"You must be joking!"

"An attorney, as you've probably gathered by now, can be very expensive."

She nodded. How could she afford a lawyer? Offer to clean his law offices once a week—for the rest of her life?

"It could end up costing you more to keep the quilt, the bed, and the chairs, *if* you get to keep them," Mr. Anderson gloomily predicted, "than to simply give them up and buy replacements."

Elise sat for a moment, drumming her fingers on the arm of the chair as she tried to think. She didn't have enough money for a new sofa, let alone a lawyer. She felt lucky if she had enough money to buy the children a piece of penny candy each when they went to the general store once a week. And how could she replace her memories of Cora?

A man like Ryder McGregor had enough money to keep her in court for the rest of her life—and feel no compunction about doing so, either.

She didn't play poker, but she knew instinctively she had to call Mr. McGregor's bluff. Suddenly she rose from her chair.

"All right, Mr. McGregor." She crossed her arms over her chest and glared down at him. "Sue me."

She could almost see little dollar signs rolling around on Mr. Anderson's eyeballs. She could see Mr. McGregor was exerting all his self-control not to let his jaw drop open in surprise.

"Mrs. Barker, are you sure?"

"I've never been more certain of anything in my life."

"I don't think you understand. . . ."

"I understand better than you'd imagine."

She uncrossed her arms and began to stride purposefully back and forth in front of the sofa.

"You see, while you were running around town hiring wagons and lawyers, I've been doing some work of my own."

"Such as?" He spoke very slowly and cautiously.

Good, she figured. Let him be the one to worry for a change.

"I've been remembering what Cora told me about you."

"Please, continue."

"I figure there's nothing else you can take from me, Mr. McGregor," she announced.

"Oh, please . . . not the poor-widow story again."

"Why do you think it's so strange that I refer to myself as a poor widow? That's what I am."

"But you use it to your own advantage with such skill."

"I haven't even begun yet."

"I don't think Mr. Anderson is as gullible as the sheriff."

She stood in front of him, her feet set apart in a firm stance. She needed to remain as balanced as she could. She drew in a deep breath.

"Go ahead and get all the lawyers you want, Mr. McGregor. Try to take away from me what little I still have. I'll go to Waldo Emerson."

"Who?"

"The newspaper editor."

"Oh." Mr. McGregor grimaced. "I suppose he owes you a favor, like that Purdey Meekins fellow."

"I clean his offices for him once a week," she replied with a shrug. "He's a smart man, and real interesting to talk to. He's always looking for a good story for his paper. It increases circulation, you know."

"I know," Mr. McGregor muttered.

"Mr. Emerson would be real interested in printing a story about this rich man trying to take away the last few possessions of this poor young widow and her two fatherless children."

"Oh, please."

"Did you know that most local papers all over the country get their news stories by reprinting them from the big-city newspapers?"

"Yes, I did."

"But what you might not know is, local newspapers all over the country take stories from other local newspapers, too. It might start out as just a small story from Whiskey, but pretty soon, my—or should I say *our*—story, Mr. McGregor"—she gave him her sweetest smile—"will be in St. Louis, and then on over to Wichita, Kansas City, Chicago, Albany . . ."

"I get your point, Mrs. Barker." He frowned. He looked as if he was trying to sit very still, in spite of an urge to shift uncomfortably in his seat. "But I see little use of it. After all, I've already told you I don't really care what others think of me."

Elise didn't believe him for one minute, not anymore. But she wouldn't tell him that—not yet. "I know," she replied instead. "But don't forget Preacher Fire."

Who could forget Preacher Elmo Fire? The man seemed to walk around carrying an air of fire and brimstone with him.

"What about him?"

"People in small towns don't forget as easily as you city folks do. Your parents and sister, and your aunt—may they rest in peace— are still fondly remembered in this town. Your cousin David is president of the Grange chapter. Your cousin Susan married Lester Haag, and leads the women's Bible study class over at the First Baptist Church. I wonder what the folks in town would think of Preacher Fire's sermons about the rich man who slaughtered the poor man's lamb, or perhaps the widow's last mite, and how they might pertain to a certain man whose parents used to live here."

"That's enough!"

Mr. McGregor rose so fast, Elise barely had time to get out of his way before his body could make contact with hers. She felt a jolt at the very thought that he might actually touch her, and took a step backward.

"I was wrong, Mrs. Barker. Very wrong."

Now she had to look up at him. She didn't like that, not when she had to do battle with him. She especially didn't like the way his closeness made her heart beat faster. It wasn't a good idea to get this close to a man she was trying to defeat.

She took another step backward, and still felt she was much too close. She wanted to back farther away, but wouldn't allow herself. She'd suffer, she figured. She wouldn't want him to mistake her actions for retreat.

"I'm just now beginning to see how much I've underestimated you as an opponent," he confessed. "I won't make that mistake again."

Elise sank down on the sofa, her head resting in the palms of her hands and her elbows resting on her knees. She closed her eyes and tried to knead some of the ache from her temples.

She'd only meant to tease and cajole this humorless man out of his complacency. He needed to learn how to laugh—especially at himself.

But the man took everything, including himself, far too seriously. Now she was engaged in a full-blown, knock-down-drag-out fight with him.

What in the world had gone wrong? And how in the world could she fix it?

Her mother had always told her a person could catch more flies with honey than with vinegar. Should she try being nice to this grim man? Maybe he could use somebody to be nice to him.

Then again, would it even be worth the try?

"I don't have time to have Anderson start a lawsuit against this woman."

Ryder ripped off his coat so quickly he turned the sleeves inside out. He was too angry to bother to hang it up. He rolled it into an uneven bundle and tossed it at the chair in his bedroom. It missed and ended up in the corner instead.

"I have better things to do than involve myself in this battle of wits with a cleaning woman!"

He pulled off his shirt, a little less violently than he'd removed his coat. One of his gold cuff links went rolling under the bed.

"Oh, tarnation! I'll get it tomorrow."

He flung his shirt carelessly at the same chair. But it ended up in the corner, too. He slumped down on the bed and began to remove his shoes.

"I need to get back to my business. I don't like to leave it for so long."

Oh, he trusted Oscar Porter; his personal secretary was very competent at carrying out his express orders. And he trusted his other employees to follow their routines and their instructions from Mr. Porter to the letter. But there was really only one way to make a company truly work and earn the kind of money he enjoyed. It was a motto he had tried to live and work by: If you want a job done exactly the way you want it, you've got to do it yourself!

That was the problem, he decided in a sudden flash of insight. He never should have tried to overwhelm Mrs. Barker with the authority of the sheriff or an attorney. He realized now that people like her weren't impressed with badges, diplomas, and certificates.

He knew now what he should have known all along. If he wanted a job done right, he should have done it by himself.

He also realized he'd made a big mistake in assuming that Mrs. Barker was just a simple-minded country woman. He'd figured out she was almost as shrewd as he was, and he'd also figured out exactly what she really valued.

She needed money. He'd just offer her enough to replace the bed, the chairs, and the quilt.

He hated to pay for items that were his by rights, but he was losing money each day he was away from his work, and it was worth it to him to put an end to this madness. Heck, he'd even throw in a few extra dollars so she could buy a cord of wood to keep herself and her children warm this winter.

Then he'd return to San Francisco and go on about his business as usual. He'd never have to worry about that stubborn woman again.

This time he wouldn't bring along a sheriff or a lawyer. He wanted his family heirlooms. He'd go do it himself.

❦

"Oh, my." Mrs. Barker gave a deep sigh when she saw him standing in her doorway once again. "What do you want now?"

She'd probably already figured he hadn't come here to ask if they could be friends.

He'd have to be very circumspect about everything he said and did. Everything hinged on not frightening her again, or insulting her intelligence. He had to keep everything unemotional and businesslike.

"I'd like to talk to you. May I come in?"

She looked around him. "Where are all your little friends? Did you come out to play all by yourself?"

He was just about ready to turn around and get his lawyer. Then she grinned. How could she tease him while she continued to argue with him? Most puzzling was the fact that she really didn't seem to mean him any malice.

"I decided to come by myself this time," he replied, being sure to keep his voice very even. He might accept her good-natured jesting, but he himself would remain businesslike.

"Well, come in and have a seat."

After the way she'd already kicked him out twice, he hadn't expected an invitation to come so easily.

"But I can't talk long," she warned.

She sounded almost apologetic. That was even more surprising than her unexpected invitation.

"I'm supposed to clean Mrs. Chaney's house today and I should be leaving soon."

She wore a plain blue cotton dress. Her light brown hair was pulled back in a single braid that hung down the center of her back until it came to rest at the gentle rise of her buttocks.

She was definitely ready to clean something. Then why would she smell like lavender? It wasn't just a scent she applied to her body—she herself seemed to smell like the tiny flower. Why hadn't he noticed it before?

Why hadn't he noticed before that, even in her plainness, she was pretty? Her face was oval and delicate. There was a slight flush to her cheeks, as if she'd been working outside without her bonnet.

Her eyes were deep blue. Her lashes were long and dark. She appeared too slender to carry chairs down the street or to be scrubbing other people's floors.

She didn't belong in this humble setting. She looked like some captive princess, held hostage to do the work of an evil wizard.

Good heavens, what was he thinking? He hadn't read a fairy tale in years, and even when he had he'd considered them all a lot of hogwash. Knights, fairy godmothers, and damsels in distress—such things didn't exist in the real world. In the real world, the only thing he'd found that worked any real magic was money.

"What I have to say won't take long."

"Good. I've got just enough time to finish breakfast and drop the children off with Molly Dorn. Would you like a cup of coffee?"

"No, thank you," he answered automatically. He immediately regretted his decision.

"Then please excuse me while I finish my breakfast."

❧

She moved toward the long table at the back of the house. He guessed that was as much of a kitchen as she could afford.

He thought he detected the smell of blackberries. Suddenly he found a piece of jam-covered toast shoved under his nose.

"What the! . . ." As he jumped, his shoulder hit the child's arm, almost shoving the toast up his nose.

"Hi. Want some?" the little boy asked.

"No, thank you."

He reached out and moved the boy's hand away. At least it wasn't sticky. Surprisingly enough, neither was the child's face. He didn't smell bad, either. He supposed Mrs. Barker must bathe them on a regular basis. She probably just tied a rope around his ankle and dipped him in the well.

The child climbed over the back of the sofa and perched on the arm, to his right. He began to eat his toast by himself.

"It's really good," the little girl told Ryder. She, too, seemed to have materialized from nowhere. He supposed she'd been hiding behind the sofa, too, lying in wait for him.

"I'm sure."

"My mommy made it," she said. "It's got to be good."

"I'm sure."

"She said she'd teach me someday, too."

"How nice."

"She said you can make jelly out of blackberries and huckleberries and apples and all kinds of stuff."

"Indeed."

"But I like the blackberries best."

"I pickeded dem," the little boy said.

"My name's Willow." She sat down on the sofa to his other side.

"How do you do?"

"That's Russell." She indicated her brother.

"Hello, Russell."

" 'Lo," the boy mumbled between mouthfuls of bread.

Ryder wasn't about to say "Pleased to meet you" when he wasn't—not for one minute. He had very little use for children. They couldn't buy and they couldn't sell. He couldn't see any other use for them.

Where in the world was their mother? He looked around the room, but she'd disappeared.

"I seeded you 'fore here," Russell said.

Why can't these creatures speak English? he wondered.

"Yes, I've been here before."

"Are you still trying to take away our stuff?" Willow demanded, glaring at him.

"I believe that business is between your mother and myself."

"Nope. It's our bed. It's our business," she stated firmly, crossing her arms over her chest.

"It's not exactly your bed," he tried to explain.

"I sleep in it. It's mine," Willow insisted.

"Mine!" Russell declared. "Mine!"

"Not exactly—"

"*Mommy* said it's ours." Her round little face was deadly serious.

She was a stubborn little thing. She'd undoubtedly inherited this quality from her mother, Ryder decided.

"I suppose you want my quilt, too?" she asked.

"You don't understand. It's a valuable antique. It's been in my family for two generations."

"Mine, too."

"Excuse me," he asked. "How—"

"It's Mommy's, and she told me I could have it when she died, so it's mine, too. That's two. Two generations."

Ryder frowned. "How old are you?"

"Five."

"Are you sure?" He wasn't.

He felt surrounded by malevolent pixies, and he didn't know quite what to do. Tarnation, where had their mother gone? When was she coming back to save him from these little beasts? Was this her way of getting even with him for bringing the sheriff and the lawyer to her house?

"Mommy don't got no bed," Russell said.

"Well, that's not my fault . . ."

"Mommy sleeps on the sofa," Willow said.

Ryder rose quickly.

"Oh, sit down, Mr. McGregor." Elise suddenly reappeared, carrying her cup of coffee, and sat in her rocking chair.

He sat back down. He tried to look her straight in the eye and tried not to think that he was sitting by day where Elise Barker slept at night.

"I have a business proposition for you, Mrs. Barker."

She began rocking back and forth. "What sort of business proposition?"

"A sort of an exchange between us."

"What are we exchanging?"

"The bed, the two chairs, the quilt . . ."

"For?"

"Money."

She stopped rocking and silently watched him. Ryder thought maybe he ought to check to make sure she was still breathing. Had his proposition shocked her that badly?

At last she began to rock again, very slowly.

"My, my, my," she murmured. "You really want those things badly, don't you?"

"I'm tired of playing games, Mrs. Barker. I'm tired of insulting the intelligence of both of us with useless tactics."

"So am I."

"You need money."

"That's pretty evident," she said, glancing around the room.

"I want my property."

She fixed her gaze on him again. "That's *very* evident."

"I'll see to it that it's a fair and equitable exchange, one that enables you to replace those articles I've reclaimed, as well as a little extra to allow you to buy a few . . . treats for yourself and the children."

"That's very generous of you, Mr. McGregor."

"Do we have a deal?"

"No." She sat and rocked.

He had expected a bit more of an answer.

"I'm offering enough for you to buy a new bed—not just a secondhand one, but a brand-new bed. And two new chairs."

"No."

"You'll be able to buy a dozen new blankets for you and your children."

She laughed. "What would we do with a dozen blankets."

"Then buy something else you need. A bed for yourself," he suggested.

"Where would I put it?"

"You won't accept my offer?"

"No."

"Why not?"

"You just don't understand, do you?" She gave her head a little shake, then watched him with sympathetic eyes.

He was the one with the business in San Francisco and Hong Kong and the substantial bank account. She was the one with two grubby children in a two-room hovel on the outskirts of a small town. Why should she be feeling sorry for him?

"Why don't you explain it to me," he challenged.

She reached out and placed her hand on his arm. "I don't think I can."

Her small hand was gentle, but so strong he felt as if he were shackled to the sofa. She and her blasted stubbornness were beginning to make him very angry again.

He managed to slide his arm away from her grasp, but strangely enough, he still didn't feel free of her.

"Try. And I'll try my very best to understand. I can't believe it's only because you know I want them. You might be stubborn, but you don't seem to be the cantankerous, vindictive type."

"I'm not."

"You clearly need the money. Why are you depriving your children—"

She pointed her index finger directly at his heart. "Don't *ever* tell me I've deprived my children!"

"Yeah!" Russell shouted. The little fellow was pounding his heels against the bottom of the sofa and glaring at Mr. McGregor belligerently.

"Mommy got us a nice bed," Willow joined in with the ferocity of a Teutonic battle maid.

"Yeah!"

"And makes us pretty clothes and good food."

"Yeah!" Russell waved his fist in the air.

Ryder was glad the children were eating toast and not anything that required the use of forks, or knives.

"Well, Mrs. Barker, I see you're well defended."

"Better than your sheriff or lawyer," she acknowledged with a little grin. "You see, you're never just fighting me, Mr. McGregor. You're fighting my whole family."

She was right. He realized he'd looked rather foolish bringing those useless men along. He found the corners of his mouth twitching, a very uncomfortable feeling—he was tempted to grin back at her! He couldn't do that. If he revealed something even as simple as a smile, she'd think she'd triumphed over him—and maybe she'd be right.

Pulling his lips and his composure back into place, he said, "I can see family is very important to you."

"To us," she corrected as she glanced at her children, who were still throwing dagger-glares at him. "Family sticks together."

"Yeah, stick!" Russell declared.

"Look, Mrs. Barker," he said, making his voice intentionally deep and serious.

This time he reached out to place his hand atop hers. He wasn't used to touching prospective business associates. He was even more unused to touching anyone as delicate and soft as Elise Barker. He wanted to believe he'd held her hand to show that this time he was in charge of the situation. But deep inside, he had to admit he'd done it just because it felt good.

"My offer is more than fair. What reason could you possibly have not to accept?"

Elise drew in a deep breath and looked into his eyes. She looked as if she was getting ready to tell her children a fairy tale. Ryder glanced quickly at the two rascals sitting on either side of him, still watching him with eagle eyes. From the looks of them, they'd probably be cheering for the Big Bad Wolf!

"Do you have any feelings, Mr. McGregor?"

"Feelings?" he repeated. What in the world was she getting at now? He felt his fingers twitching nervously about hers. Could she feel it, too?

"You know. Happiness, sadness, envy, regret, love, hate?"

"Yes, I know what feelings are," he replied impatiently.

"But do you have any?"

"I . . . I suppose so."

"How much are your feelings worth to you?" she asked. "Can you put a price tag on them?"

She paused just a moment, as if giving him time to answer. She was watching him with her dark blue eyes. They appeared fathomless, as if she were very accustomed to swimming in waters that were way too deep for him. Waters that he wouldn't even dare to wade in up to his knees. Strange creatures, he feared, lurked in these deep waters, creatures that he wouldn't know how to combat.

She placed her other hand atop his. Now that his hand was caught between both of hers, he feared she might drag him into those waters, and under.

Before he could open his mouth to reply, she continued.

"Are some feelings worth more than others? Are some people's feelings worth more than those of others? Are feelings about some things worth more than feelings about others?"

"What in thunderation are you talking about?" he demanded in frustration. He pulled his hand back and sat firmly against the back of the sofa.

"I don't know about you, Mr. McGregor, but I have feelings—lots of them."

"I've noticed that." He resisted the impulse to rub away the sensation that she was still holding his hand. "I can just imagine what you're thinking of me right now."

"Don't bet on that, Mr. McGregor," she replied. Her face remained serious, but her eyes twinkled with mischief. "I feel very good when I'm with my children and my friends."

"Well, good for you, Mrs. Barker."

As much as he'd tried to follow his intentions to be pleasant, he couldn't keep the sarcasm from his voice.

He didn't need family or friends; after all, they were the ones who'd left him. He could get along without them all. He might not have too many personal friends, but he had business associates who respected him. He didn't need love in his life. People's respect—and a healthy fear for one's job—served him much better.

Ryder knew Elise was the one who had to go to work, but now, suddenly, he was the one who was anxious to leave this unsettling woman and all her probing questions.

"Is there a point to all this, Mrs. Barker?" he demanded.

"How can anyone put a price tag on sentimental things?" she asked.

"Very easily. They're completely worthless."

"Do you really believe that?"

He rose without answering. "I take it you're not going to sell me the furniture or the quilt."

"No, I'm not."

"Not even for—"

"Not for all the money in the world," she stated very adamantly.

"How could you know what I'd be offering?"

She laughed. "What else would you be offering, Mr. McGregor? Money is the only thing that actually means anything to you."

"Well, I must admit, Mrs. Barker, you're one of the most intelligent women I've ever met."

"Thank you, I think."

He liked the way her eyes blinked, and the way her delicate eyebrows rose in surprise.

"Oh, I do mean it as a compliment." Strangely enough, he thought, he actually did. "I must also admit you're absolutely right. Money is the only thing that means anything to me. With love or happiness—or whatever other silly sentiments you might want to name—I might have a bit of contentment. But with money, I can have everything I need."

"You think so?"

"I know so."

"You can't buy love."

"That may be true, but I've found love isn't really worth what you pay for it. It doesn't last very long. You and I both know that, Mrs. Barker."

She slowed her rocking just a little. He'd hit a weakness, and he knew it. Now he just needed to see how far he could push her before she finally gave in.

"There must be something that will induce you to return my property to me. I've always found that everyone has a price. I haven't found yours yet, but I think I will. And I think I'm closer than you're willing to admit."

The sudden pounding on the front door—and not his words—startled her. He was surprised, too. Who could be coming here that he hadn't sent for?

"Miz Barker, open up!"

He didn't recognize the voice.

"It's Odell Dorn!" she exclaimed as she jumped to her feet and bolted for the door. She pulled the door open so fast it creaked on its hinges.

"It's time, Miz Barker!" the slender man exclaimed. He was practically jumping up and down in excitement and nervousness. His bony fingers were shredding the cap he held in his hands.

"Are you sure?"

"'Course I'm sure! We been through this . . . before. I mean, I can't explain. It . . . it's all women's stuff, Miz Barker. Come see for yourself. You'll know it's for sure."

She turned. "Willow, run and get Doc Wilson. Then go tell Mrs. Chaney I'll be a little late this morning."

Willow shot out the door at a run.

"What 'bout me?" Russell demanded.

"Willow will . . . I'll . . ." She glanced frantically between Russell and the man fidgeting in the doorway. Then she turned to Ryder. "Mr. McGregor, I realize this is a great imposition, but . . . would you stay with my little boy?"

His face must've shown more shock and distaste than he'd intended.

"It's only while I check on Mrs. Dorn. I'll only be next door. I'll be right back—I hope. He's very well behaved." She babbled her explanation, all the while still glancing between Russell, Odell, and Ryder.

At last she stepped up close to him and grasped his hand. He could feel the urgency in her fingers. He could see the worry in her eyes, torn as she was between concern for her neighbor's welfare and her child's well-being.

"Please, Mr. McGregor. Willow's too young. There's no one else . . ."

He couldn't believe he heard himself telling her, "I'll stay with him until you return."

"Oh, thank you!"

She squeezed his hand. For just a moment, he had the strangest impression that she was going to stand on tiptoe and kiss him in gratitude! Then she released his hand and rushed out the door as quickly as Willow had.

Ryder stood in the little house, alternately staring between the little boy and the empty doorway, trying to decide what to do next.

"Sit," Russell commanded, patting the place next to him on the sofa.

"I think I'll stand . . ."

"Sit!" The boy patted harder.

"Your mother will be back soon."

"Sit!" Russell pounded on the seat and drummed his feet against the sofa.

"Now see here, young man!"

Russell grinned up at him. "Sit. Tell me story."

"What do I look like, a nanny?" Ryder demanded. "I don't know any stories."

"Ma'up."

"Excuse me?"

"Ma'up story."

"I'm afraid I neglected to bring along a translator this trip, young fellow," Ryder quipped. He doubted even the Cantonese translator he hired for his buying trips would do any good in this situation.

"Pease."

The little boy looked up at Ryder. His wide eyes were twinkling in anticipation. They were as blue as his mother's. His hair was about the same color, too, only a bit thinner, and curled in little baby wisps instead of waving long and luxuriously, as his mother's did.

"Pease," he repeated.

Out of all the single words in the English vocabulary the little rapscallion could pronounce with even the slightest degree of clarity, it had to be this one. This one Ryder understood perfectly well.

He grimaced and shrugged. Slowly he sat down beside the little boy on the sofa, though not too close. The last thing he needed was blackberries on his camel-hair coat, and not a reputable dry-cleaning establishment around for miles.

"I'll warn you, young man, I don't know any stories."

"Tank you." The child scooted-closer to him.

Ryder raised one finger as if that could fend off the encroaching child.

"Let's not get too cozy," he warned. "I'm not used to this sort of thing."

"Story."

He let out a deep breath. What had he gotten himself—no, what had that Barker woman gotten him into? This was another matter he'd have to discuss with her.

"Well, no one could ever say Ryder McGregor didn't give it his best try. Once upon a time . . ."

Molly had a hard time of it, Elise reflected as she closed the door behind her. But in the end, after a lot of hot water, hard work, and prayers, both Molly and her new daughter were doing just fine. Tomorrow she'd return and give Molly her gift.

She and Cora had found some fine dimity in a sewing chest up in the attic. She'd washed it carefully and Cora had pronounced it fine enough to use. Elise knew she'd never need baby clothing again and that the material would be yellowed with age by the time Willow or Russell's wife might need a layette. She and Cora had decided it would make a wonderful gift for Molly, and they'd said a prayer that she'd actually use it this time.

Elise had worked on the tiny christening gown while sitting at Cora's bedside, chatting with her. Cora had even managed to sew a few of the little white ribbon rosettes onto the bodice before she grew too weak to hold her needle steady. The gown was finished a week before Cora passed away.

The sun was setting, and her house was completely dark. Willow was old enough to light the lamp; certainly Mr. McGregor was. Why is the house so dark? Elise kept asking herself as she walked faster across the rustling grass.

She pushed her front door in. The house was dark and empty, and silent as a tomb.

"Willow? Russell?" she called as she hurried to light the lamp.

She checked the sofa and each chair. She even checked under the sofa and chairs, just in case. They weren't there. They weren't in the kitchen.

"Willow? Russell?"

She rushed to their bedroom. Ripping back the curtain, she saw the empty bed. Her heart sank. She ducked to look under the bed. They weren't there. Where could they be?

"Willow? Russell?" she shouted as she ran for the back door. Were they playing outside in the sand, even though it was dark and she'd told them not to leave the house?

The sandpile was empty, too.

"Willow? Russell? Don't hide from Mommy," she called as she ran back into the house. "It's not nice to frighten Mommy like this."

No answer.

She sank down on the sofa in near exhaustion. Her feet ached, and her shoulders slumped. She'd just spent all day helping Molly bring her baby safely into the world, and now she couldn't find her own children.

She should've checked on them, but she'd been so busy helping Doc Wilson keep Molly's body and soul together, as well as the baby's. She'd trusted them with Ryder McGregor . . . Ryder McGregor!

She almost screamed with fear and alarm. She'd left her precious children with that hypocritical, smooth talking, fancy-dressed bandit. How could she have been so stupid?

He'd sworn he'd find some way to make her give him the quilt and the furniture. She'd sworn there wasn't anything in the world worth her memories of Cora. But there was. Her children. And he knew it.

He knew she'd sacrifice anything for their sake. The miserable, unscrupulous villain had taken her children hostage until she agreed to give him the quilt and the furniture!

She'd find Ryder McGregor, she decided as she rose and headed straight for the kitchen cupboard. She'd give him the darn quilt, if only he'd give her her children back. She'd shove it down his miserable, lying throat. She'd make sure the horrible man *never* forgot her.

She'd lost her husband's good Remington rifle on the auction block, but she'd managed to keep the shotgun. Of course, she didn't intend to shoot Ryder—not unless she really had to. But she'd put more fear of the Lord into him than Preacher Elmo Fire ever could in a month of Sundays!

"Mommy! Mommy!" Willow ran excitedly into the house. Russell toddled in behind her. "Guess where we were!"

Elise quickly shoved the shotgun back out of sight and slammed the cupboard shut.

"Merciful heavens! That's just what I've been trying to do," she exclaimed as she ran toward them. She bent down to gather them both in a tight embrace. "I've been so worried. Where were you?"

Mr. McGregor strode into the house, acting as if not a thing in the world was wrong.

She looked up at him. He seemed even taller when she was kneeling. Still, she wasn't going to let him intimidate her.

"What did you do with my children?" she demanded, rising to confront him.

"He took us out!" Willow cried, tugging at her skirt.

"Out!" Russell echoed.

She was beginning to calm down a bit more. She was able to speak in normal tones. "Out where?" She looked to Mr. McGregor for further elaboration.

"We went to the hotel to eat," Willow explained, grinning

widely. She gave a deep, impassioned sigh. "It was beautiful! There were lights—even more than at Aunt Cora's house."

"Lights!" Russell declared, spreading his hands out high over his head. "Lotsa lotsa lights."

"They had cloth on the tables, and dishes without cracks that matched each other. And cups that still had handles. Everybody had a knife, fork, and spoon, too."

"Dey had lotsa food."

"You didn't have to eat just what they gave you. You got to pick what you wanted. I had lamb chops."

"Lamb chops?" Elise repeated.

"Yeah, and nobody made me eat string beans." She stuck out her tongue and made gagging noises.

Willow hated string beans, but they were cheap. Did the child have any idea how expensive lamb was?

"I had pancakes," Russell told her.

"Pancakes?"

"Yeah, dey was real good."

Elise turned a questioning glance to Mr. McGregor. "Why did you do this?"

He shrugged. "He wanted pancakes. I didn't see much use in ordering him a steak."

"No, no. I mean, why did you take them out?"

"I couldn't just sit here all day," he answered. "I had to do something with them."

There was something very different in the tone of his voice. The children certainly seemed happy. Was it possible that Ryder McGregor could actually be happy, too?

"I thought you'd stay here."

Before Mr. McGregor could answer, Russell pleaded, "Do 'gain, Mommy."

"Oh, yes, Mommy," Willow said with a breathless little gasp as she clasped her hands in front of her, "We've got to do that again someday real soon. Oh, please!"

"Soon," Russell agreed. "Pease."

"*You'll* come next time," Willow told her. "You can't miss all the fun."

It *would* be a wonderful thing, but there was no possible way she could ever take her children to the hotel.

"I've missed a little fun before, and I'm none the worse for it. But my, my, we've all had a busy day," she said, trying to divert their attention. "Mrs. Dorn has a baby girl."

"Hooray!" both children shouted. "Can we see her tomorrow?"

"I'll ask her first if she's up to seeing visitors. But if you want to go tomorrow, you've got to go to bed now."

The children reluctantly headed toward their bedroom. Willow stopped and turned around. "Thank you, Mr. McGregor."

The curtain fell back in place behind her.

"Yes, thank you for taking care of my children today. I'm sorry I left so abruptly. You see, Mrs. Dorn had already lost one baby," she explained in a whisper. "It was very important she not lose this one, too."

"You were there a long time."

Was he scolding her for leaving her children? Or was he praising her for her loyalty to her friend? She couldn't tell from his expressionless face. All she could be sure of was that he was studying her face with a strange intensity.

Ryder McGregor was so difficult to understand.

"She's fine now. The baby, too."

He just nodded.

She gave a guilty little giggle. "I should apologize for some of the things I was thinking about you while I was wondering where my children were."

"I have a feeling I shouldn't ask, but I think I will anyway. What were you thinking about me?"

"I . . . I suspected you were holding my children for ransom until I turned over the quilt." She tried to smile apologetically.

"Darn, I never even thought of that!" he exclaimed. "Would it have worked?"

"Are you crazy? Of course. I'd give up anything for my children."

"Yes, I suppose you would."

For the first time, Elise didn't feel his remark held some sort of veiled insult.

"Well, it's too late now." He shrugged his shoulders in a gesture of helplessness.

She'd never expected to see Mr. McGregor admit any kind of helplessness.

"Why did you take them out to eat?"

"You certainly don't believe for one minute that I know how to cook."

He made a noise that sounded to Elise almost like a laugh. But she'd never heard him laugh—she wasn't even sure if he could—so she couldn't really tell for certain.

"No. But there's bread and apples in the cupboard." She gestured toward the kitchen. "There's butter and cheese and milk and apple cider in the spring house. None of these things require cooking."

"I'm sure it's fine food, and granted, I don't know much about raising children, but don't they need something more substantial? Like meat?"

"I can't afford . . . and I still wish you hadn't—"

"I didn't know what else to do with them. We were all hungry, so I did what *I* usually do. I must admit, I was very pleased at how well behaved they were. They didn't break a glass or spill food on anyone."

Suddenly his tone grew very serious. He was smiling at her, but there was a sincerity in his eyes that she'd never seen there before.

"You did a good job raising them, Mrs. Barker."

"Well, I'm not quite done with them yet, but thank you."

"I hadn't considered before how difficult it must be, raising them alone."

"I still wish you hadn't taken them out."

"Why not? They enjoyed themselves."

"Yes, they certainly look like they did," she had to admit.

"Don't they deserve a little treat?"

"But you heard them. They want to do this again."

"Yes? . . ." There was an unfinished quality to his response, as if he still didn't see anything wrong with what he'd done.

"Tell me, Mr. McGregor: How often do you think I can afford to take my children out to eat?"

"I . . ." He knew the answer to that question very well, so he just said nothing.

"You've shown them something I can never give them."

She stood directly in front of him and looked up into his face. He met her gaze evenly. The big dummy still didn't think he'd done anything wrong.

"Is that why you did it? To show them how people with money can live, the wonderful things they can do?"

"It was a simple meal at a second-rate hotel—not exactly something Andrew Carnegie or Jay Gould would come up with."

"But I can't do that for my children at all!" She gave a bitter little laugh. "Not unless I take the money you're going to offer me again. Isn't that what you intended all along?"

"No," he answered, very loud and very stern. Then, more softly, he continued. "I hadn't looked at it that way at all." He sounded puzzled and almost sincere. "No, that wasn't the reason I did it."

More softly, she told him, "Maybe you did think you were being kind, but it's not really fair, Mr. McGregor. My children have to know there are things they won't be able to do simply because we don't have the money for it. They have to learn to be content with what they have at home."

"All right."

Why was he giving in so easily?

"If you insist, I promise there won't be any more outings."

Ryder was still up to something; she could feel it in her bones.

Ryder couldn't wait to see the expression on Elise's face when she realized that the wagon in front of her house one more time wasn't there to take anything away.

The wagon had barely pulled to a stop in front of her house when she opened the door. Her eyes were wide with a confused mixture of dismay and disappointment. This wasn't quite the reaction he'd hoped for. For just a moment, he wished he had warned her first.

He hopped down from the wagon seat and strode boldly toward her. She began to back away, closing the door in front of her at the same time.

"Mrs. Barker, please," Ryder called. "Elise, wait!"

She kept the door open just a crack and peeked out.

"What do you want? Why have you brought that darn wagon again? I've told you before, I'm not giving—"

"No, no. You misunderstand me." He placed his hand on the door, close to hers. He wanted to hold it, to reassure her with more than mere words. "I haven't come to take anything."

"All right," she said hesitantly. "What are you offering for the quilt now?"

"Nothing." Ryder signaled for the Martin boys to start unloading the packages.

As she stared in disbelief at each and every package they carried into her little house and placed on the floor in front of the sofa, Ryder refused to give even the smallest hint of what any of the packages might contain.

"Goodness gracious, Mr. McGregor. You must think that blooming quilt is lined with gold!"

"I told you, I'm not doing this for the quilt."

"You sure could've fooled me." She stopped staring at the pile of packages long enough to look into his eyes. He was watching her with a softness and a light in his eyes that bespoke more than admiration. "Then why are you doing this?"

"I promised you I wouldn't take your children out anymore. You never said I couldn't bring you all things."

"Wow!" Russell exclaimed.

"It's not even Christmas yet," Willow said as she walked around the packages. "Even if it was, Christmas isn't ever this good at our house."

"Birfday," Russell said.

"That's right," Willow agreed. She tugged at the hem of Ryder's coat. "We figured out this month was the quilt's birthday. Is this the party?"

"I don't think so," Elise told them cautiously. But ever since Mr. McGregor had treated them to a night out, they weren't about to believe anything bad about him. Had she lost her only allies in this fight? The way she was beginning to feel about him, was there still a fight?

"Cake," Russell demanded.

"Yeah, where's the cake?"

"Sorry, no cake. Will you settle for this?" Ryder reached over and picked up a package wrapped in brown paper and handed it to Russell, who plopped down on the floor and excitedly tore it open.

"Crish!" His pudgy fingers clutched the licorice strings. "Tank you!"

He pulled a string out of the strand and offered it to Willow, who immediately stuck one end in her mouth and let the other end hang down.

Ryder handed Willow a package. With just a little more care, but no less excitement, she unwrapped it.

"Rock candy!" She dangled the encrusted string in front of her, watching the sunlight play across the lumps of crystallized sugar.

Two more packages yielded lemon drops and small, square lavender-flavored candies. A long thin package produced a treasure of peppermint sticks.

"Thank you, Mr. McGregor," Willow said. Then, clutching the hoard to her chest, she motioned with her head toward the door. "C'mon, Russell."

They scrambled to their feet. Ryder fully expected to see the two of them head for the kitchen or their bedroom, there to gobble everything down. He never expected to see them rush outside.

"Where? . . ."

"They're not like you. They have friends, you know," Elise told him.

He was almost ready to sweep everything up and head out the door again, until he noticed she was laughing.

"I'm still having a little trouble realizing when you're teasing."

"I'll give you a hint. If I'm smiling, I'm teasing."

"Thanks." He handed her a package.

She pulled the greasy paper aside. "Sweet rolls?"

He nodded.

"Why?"

"Why not? You do like them, don't you?"

"Of course. Who wouldn't? Thank you."

Package after package yielded tea and coffee, a packet of needles, even a roll of pink ribbon.

"Thank you very much for all this," Elise said as she started wrapping everything up again. "But I really can't accept any of it."

"Why not?"

"It's . . . it's not . . . proper."

"Come on. You don't think . . . I mean, let's not stand on old strictures."

"I . . . I can't give you anything in return, so I think it's best not to accept any of this in the first place."

"I know you think I'm doing this so you'll give me the quilt and the furniture. . . ."

"Aren't you?"

"Yes. No. I mean . . ."

She sat in her rocking chair and watched him for a moment.

"Go on. I'm waiting to see how you weasel your way out of this one."

"Look, Mrs. . . . Elise, I'm used to business dealings," he said, "where everyone wants what someone else has. I've done this for nine years. It's a little hard to do something that I'm so unaccustomed to—like giving something and not expecting anything in return. That's just not good business. But I'm trying."

Elise rose from her rocker and smiled at him. She handed him a package, then suddenly began piling all the packages into his outstretched arms.

"I'm sorry I was so suspicious of you at first," she said, peering into his eyes earnestly. "I truly do appreciate this. It's just that I don't need all these extra things."

"I've worked my entire adult life for these 'extra things' that you find so unnecessary."

"Well, I really could use the needles," she admitted. She pulled that packet from the pile and placed it in her sewing basket.

Then she extended her hand. He wrapped his hand around her fragile fingers. He noticed little calluses on her palm and across her fingertips. She'd probably gotten them dusting furniture and scrubbing floors. Why hadn't he noticed them the first time he'd held her hand? Maybe the first time he'd just been taken with her as a person. Now he was learning all the little things about her—and he liked it. She was so different from any woman he'd met before. He wanted to know her better.

"Come with me," she said as she led him toward the door.

She made a brief stop to pick up one more small package that was wrapped in white paper and sitting on the table beside the sofa.

"Wait a minute. I didn't bring that."

"I know. That's mine and Cora's."

"Cora's?"

"We made it together" was all the explanation she would give. Still holding one of his hands, she pulled him out the door.

It was difficult enough to walk trying to hold all those packages with one hand, especially when he couldn't even see his feet when he looked down. It was even more difficult to navigate through the throng of children gathered on the front step.

Willow and Russell sat in the middle of a group of children of various shapes and sizes, all happily sharing the candy Ryder had bought.

"What are they doing?" Ryder asked Elise, pointing at her two children.

"Something I don't think you've tried to do for a long time," she replied. "Sharing."

"But . . ."

"Oh, you're learning," she assured him.

"You're a good teacher, Elise."

They stood and looked into each other's eyes for just a moment. Then she smiled at him and moved along quickly to the house next door. She reached out and knocked.

Ryder recognized Odell at the door.

"How are Molly and the baby?" she asked.

"Come on in and see!"

Elise pulled him through the doorway.

Before Ryder could politely decline, Odell shoved a hand-rolled cigarette into his mouth.

"Ain't got none o' them fancy store-bought Cuban cigars to celebrate with. But I got some right decent homemade ones. Try it."

Odell pulled a stick from the fireplace and lit it. Almost choking from the pungent aroma, Ryder could just picture his load of greased paper going up in smoke, and taking him with it.

"Is Molly awake?" Elise asked. "Can we see her and the baby?"

"Yeah, sure. Come on through here."

Odell led them through the doorway to what served as their bedroom. Molly lay propped up in bed, holding her daughter beside her.

"She's beautiful," Elise said.

"We've decided to call her Cora," Molly said.

How many other people had been swindling his sister? Ryder was seized with the sudden notion to go home and study the terms of his sister's will a little more closely.

"Why would you name your daughter after my sister?" he asked.

"Why not?" Molly looked very puzzled. "She was a wonderful woman. We were all so sorry to see her pass on."

"Yes . . . yes, indeed," Ryder mumbled.

"We—Cora and I—made this." Elise extended the pure white bundle. "We want you to have it for the baby."

Odell picked little Cora up from the bed so Molly could use both hands to open her present. She gasped when she held up the delicate dimity christening gown.

"It's beautiful!" She started to sniff, then dabbed at her eyes with the edge of her sleeve. "Thank you both."

Elise leaned over and planted a kiss on Molly's cheek. "We're glad you can use it."

"I'll cherish it forever," Molly promised. "It's the only thing I have of Cora's."

"She made the little rosettes," Elise pointed out.

"Such fine work!"

"This is from Mr. McGregor."

Elise nudged him in the side, urging him to hand Molly the small package.

"Pink ribbon," Molly said as she pulled it open. "It's perfect. Thank you, Mr. McGregor. You're every bit as nice as your dear sister, may she rest in peace."

"Oh, Molly," Elise chided her good-naturedly. "You always were so sentimental—and very prone to exaggeration."

Molly was still exclaiming over the little dress as Elise and Ryder made their way out of the house.

As soon as the door closed behind him, Ryder spat out the cigarette and stamped out the embers with his heel.

"Did Cora leave them anything in her will?" Ryder asked.

"Why? Are you going to try to get that stuff back, too?"

"No. I . . . I was just wondering."

"No, she didn't," Elise said as she continued to lead Ryder down Cork Street, away from town. "Your sister didn't just leave things to people for no good reason. She left me the quilt and the bed because I didn't have any."

"Well, excuse me for noticing, but it didn't look to me as though the Dorns have much more than you do."

"You were looking at the wrong things."

"What's that supposed to mean?" he grumbled.

Elise stopped and faced him. "You look, but you still don't see, do you?"

"I guess not. Do you think you can explain it?"

Elise released a deep breath. "Your sister gave me what I really needed—a bed, a quilt, two chairs. Your sister could never give the Dorns what they really needed."

"What's that?"

"Cora."

"What?"

"I told you before, about a year and a half ago, Molly had a baby that was stillborn. All the money in the world can't replace that."

Ryder was silent. She could see his green eyes cloud over as he peered inside, into his own soul.

"Not all my money could replace Frances or my parents, or my sister," he mumbled.

At last Elise said softly, "I guess you're not as unfeeling as you thought you were." Then she grabbed his hand and laughed. "Maybe you're not even as unfeeling as *I* thought you were. Come on!"

"Where are we going?" he asked, trying to juggle the packages he continued to hold as she pulled him along.

"To see Mr. Fitch."

"Who?"

They approached a little house that wasn't much different from the rest. The old man sat rocking on his front porch.

"Morning, Mr. Fitch," Elise called.

"Morning, Mrs. Barker."

"How's the rheumatism today?"

"Going to rain soon," he predicted.

Elise looked skyward. "Good. We could use it. How's the palpitations?"

"Not bad." He nodded in time to his rocking. "Not bad at all."

"Well, I've got something here that's going to make your heart go pit-a-pat again," she warned.

"What you got, Mrs. Barker?" He grinned in anticipation.

Elise grabbed the top package, held it tantalizingly in front of

Mr. Fitch, and slowly began to fold back the brown paper, now translucent with gooey grease.

"Bless my soul and whiskers!" Mr. Fitch exclaimed. "Sweet rolls."

He leaned forward and smelled them. He stuck out a gnarled finger, scooped up a glob of icing, and put it in his mouth.

"Land o' Goshen! Where'd you come by these, Mrs. Barker? Have you been cleaning the bakery again?"

"They're a gift from my friend, Mr. McGregor—for you."

"Well, howdy-do, sir," Mr. Fitch said, raising his hand in a salute. "I do appreciate your fine generosity toward a veteran of the war to keep this great land of ours together."

"My pleasure," Ryder responded. Seeing the look of surprise and delight on the old man's weather-beaten face, he had to admit he did feel pretty good about giving him the rolls.

As they made their way along Cork Street, Ryder's burden continued to grow lighter. At last they returned to the door of Elise's house, empty-handed.

Elise could hear the sounds of the children playing in the sandpile in the backyard.

"Would you like a cup of coffee?"

"Thank you. I must admit I'm still very puzzled." He followed her into the house. "I bought those things for you and your children. Why did you give almost everything away?"

"I only gave them to folks I knew needed them more than I do." She went to the little cookstove and turned on the kerosene.

"But the ribbon for Willow . . ."

"You've seen her. You know what a little hoyden she is. Molly's little girl will look beautiful in pink."

"The sweet rolls . . ."

"Willow and Russell have enough with the candy. They don't need rolls, too. But Mr. Fitch hasn't had a treat in a long time."

"I guess I understood the reason behind your generosity all along. I even think it was a good thing to have done."

"I knew you weren't hopeless," she told him, smiling.

"I *was* wrong, though. You're not the greedy, grasping vixen I thought you were. Maybe you're not like everyone else—you don't have a price."

Elise laid her hand on his arm. He wanted to place his hand over hers and hold it again as he had while being led down Cork Street earlier. He wanted to see if the rest of her felt as delicate as her hands. He wanted to find out if the rest of her skin belied her work-worn palms.

"You know, I've never had the opportunity to ask what you do in San Francisco, Mr. McGregor."

"Run my business. Importing fabrics and pottery from the Far East. You have quite a talent for changing the subject."

"I thought we'd pretty much finished up that one. I guess you travel a lot."

"Yes. Next year, I'm planning a trip to Japan."

Elise listened as he outlined his plans. He talked of cities she could barely pronounce, much less find on a globe.

"I'll bet I know someplace you haven't been in years," she challenged. Her eyes grew even brighter. "If ever."

"Where's that?"

"Spooners Hollow."

"Spooners Hollow?" he repeated. "Where's Spooners Hollow?"

"If you'd ever been there, you'd remember it. But you'll have to wait until tomorrow to find out," she taunted. "Meet us here at ten o'clock."

"What should I bring?"

"Not a thing."

"This might be our last nice day for a while," Elise predicted.

"But look at that clear blue sky," Ryder protested.

"Mr. Fitch's rheumatism is never wrong."

"Let's go before it rains!" Willow pleaded.

"Yeah!" Russell agreed.

"Will you carry the basket, Mr. McGregor?" She indicated a large wicker basket resting on the kitchen table.

Ryder looked it over. "Do you think we might need to hire the Martin brothers?"

"Don't be silly. A fine healthy man like you can carry that."

She obviously thought he was fine and healthy. He wanted to get to know her better, so she'd realize there was more to him than just two arms for carrying packages.

He moved to pick up the basket. He figured there'd have to be enough food for the four of them—and anybody else Elise decided to feed along the way. But when he tried to lift the basket, it fairly flew off the table.

"Wait a minute. I'm a modest man—"

"You are?"

"But I didn't know I was *that* strong." He flipped open the top of the basket and peered inside. "It's empty!"

"Yes. Well, no, not exactly. I forgot something."

She disappeared behind the curtain, then reappeared carrying the old quilt. She stuck it into the basket.

"Wait a minute! You know that's valuable."

"It's not worth anything if you can't use it," she told him.

"Call me silly, but I still don't see how we can go on a picnic without food," Ryder said.

"Of course we can," she assured him. "You'll see."

He leaned back challengingly and fixed her with his gaze. "All right. I'm from Missouri. Show me."

Her eyes held an equal challenge. What else was he urging her to show him? At first she'd thought Ryder was after her soul. She knew she was in danger of losing her heart as well.

The children ran ahead up the dirt road that led through the fields out of town. Elise and Ryder followed at a more leisurely pace. He held the basket on his left arm, and offered Elise his right.

She slipped her hand through the crook of his elbow. He could smell the lavender again, now that she was so close to him once more.

If he drew his elbow a little closer to his side, would she call an abrupt halt to this picnic? he wondered. Or would she draw closer to him?

He'd wait until she tripped over a little twig or tuft of grass, he decided. Then it would look more like he was trying to help her maintain her balance, and less suspicious.

"Lovely day, ain't it, Mrs. Barker?" the man in overalls called cheerfully.

"Good day, Mr. Phelps." She waved at the man leaning on his fence by the side of the road. "How are the pears this season?"

Mr. Phelps shook his head, looking forlorn. "I don't know what's wrong with them, Mrs. Barker."

"But you always have the best pears in the county," she protested.

"I just can't seem to figure it out. Why don't you and the kids try these and let me know what you think?" There was a gleam in his eyes as he held out two golden pears.

"Thank you!"

Willow and Russell scooped up the fruit and dropped it in the basket. Ryder wasn't sure how good the pears were to begin with, but he was certain that after rolling around in the bottom of that basket for a few hours, they weren't going to be in such great shape. Neither was the quilt.

"Where's this Spooners Hollow?" Ryder asked as they continued to walk along.

"Just down by the river a ways."

They drew closer to a bright red mill whose busy wheel was splashing up sparkling droplets.

"Morning, Mrs. Barker. Fine day for a walk," the rosy-faced housewife called to her.

"Yes, it is, Mrs. Reuter."

"Where're you going?"

"Spooners Hollow."

"A body needs energy to go on such a long walk. Why don't you take along a few of these turnovers?"

"Apple?" Elise inquired.

"What else would I be using?" Mrs. Reuter answered. She nodded to the small apple orchard beside the mill.

"Thank you very much."

Willow and Russell dropped the turnovers into the picnic basket. Ryder thought they looked mighty tasty going in. Of course, after a few hours of being rolled on by the pears they might not be in such great shape. He wondered how the apple stains would blend with the blue-and-cream quilt. For a brief second, he suspected Elise might be doing this just to mess up the quilt so badly that nobody would ever want it again.

"How much farther is this Spooners Hollow?" Ryder asked.

Elise held out her arm and pointed ahead. "Just over the rise." She turned to him and laughed. "Don't tell me the basket's getting too heavy for you!"

"Of course not," he declared. He raised the arm she was holding and flexed his biceps.

Elise pressed her fingers into the fabric of his sleeve, testing his muscle. "Not bad," she conceded.

Ryder looked down on her as sunlight twinkled in her eyes and highlighted her hair. The shadow of the brim of her hat made her eyes look even darker, and more intense.

"Elise," he whispered.

She opened her mouth to say something, but no sound emerged. She closed her mouth and backed away just slightly. But she still hadn't released his arm. She hadn't slapped him. Maybe she wasn't completely offended by him.

"We're here! We're here!" The children ran ahead toward a small stand of beech trees.

As they drew closer, Ryder saw the little stream that trickled through the gentle rise of its banks as it ran on to join the Mississippi.

"So that's why they call it the Hollow," he said.

"Why didn't you know it was here?"

He gave a small self-deprecating laugh. "I guess I really *was* too much of a little snot to wander out into the fields to play."

"I think you've done some growing up since you were last in Whiskey."

"But who is Spooners?"

She laughed. "It's not a who. It's a what."

"What?"

"Or rather, *they're* a what."

"What?"

"Spooners—you know. Like two people courting. Spooners Hollow."

"Do you really think this is the best place to bring children on a picnic?"

"Silly. The spooners only come out at night."

"How could I not have known!" he exclaimed with mock dismay.

She released his arm to spread the quilt under a tree. After they'd eaten the pears and the turnovers, which to his surprise were undamaged, and delicious, they dipped their hands into the cool stream, scooping up handfuls of trickling water.

Elise and Ryder leaned back against the trunk. Willow and Russell were still running around the field.

"Where do they get their energy?" Elise wondered aloud.

"If I could bottle and sell it," Ryder responded languidly, "I'd be a millionaire."

"Wait a minute. I thought you already were."

"Just joking," he replied. He actually laughed.

"You *can* laugh. You do have a sense of humor," Elise said.

"I also have energy," he asserted.

"Do not," she challenged. Their teasing was beginning to remind her of Willow and Russell's.

"I'll show you." Ryder slipped out of his jacket and loosened his tie.

He hadn't run through fields like these since he was a very little boy. After a year or two in school, he'd decided it wasn't dignified for a fellow with his aspirations to romp like a common farmer. How odd that for all those years, he'd somehow forgotten how much fun it was just to romp.

But after several games of tag, none of which he won, he collapsed onto the quilt at Elise's side.

"What happened to you?"

"I ran out of energy."

"You *do* need to figure out a way to bottle them," she told him as they watched Willow and Russell, who were still running. "Then not only will you own the business, but you can be your own best client."

"Not a bad idea," he agreed. "But then, I'm so hot and tired, I think I'd agree with anything."

"Water!" Russell said.

He had already removed his shoes and socks and was wading with Willow along the shore of the gentle stream.

"I have some energy left. Do you have any buoyancy?" he challenged her.

"You bet I do. Turn around," she commanded.

Ryder obeyed. Before he could complain, Elise quickly slipped out of her shoes and hose, and headed for the bank of the stream.

"You're not timid, are you?" Ryder asked as he followed her.

"Not a bit."

"But you are," he countered. "Look at you, dabbling your toes along the edge."

He proceeded to wade in ankle-deep. Russell began to splash him.

"No fair, two against one!" he cried when Willow joined in.

When he splashed back, they squealed in delight and ran away, but always came back for more.

Elise laughed aloud at their antics. Between her laughter and the children's squeals, it was a wonder people in town weren't complaining about the noise.

Suddenly a deep, low cry split the air.

Ryder dropped onto the sandbar, clutching his foot. The sand below was turning crimson.

"Oh, my Lord!" Elise exclaimed, rushing over to him. "What happened?"

He pulled away his hand to reveal a jagged cut across the sole of his foot.

"Look!" Willow held up a sharp piece of rock.

"So that's the culprit," Ryder said.

He was trying to grin, but Elise could see small beads of perspiration across his forehead. She sat down beside him on the sand, lifted her skirt, and began to tear her petticoat into strips.

"Don't," he protested.

"That's all right. I'll let you buy me another one."

"That is *definitely* not proper."

"I know, but that's the trouble with going on these picnics. I never bring along bandages."

"It hurts like the dickens."

"I'm sure it will for a while. You're not really going to be in much shape to walk back to town."

"Maybe you should go back and bring the Martins out here," he suggested with a pained laugh. "I won't be going anywhere with the children while you're gone, that's for certain."

"That's not necessary," Elise assured him. "If we sit here long enough, one—or rather, two—*at least* two of the spooners will be by here later tonight. They'll take us back."

She wadded part of her petticoat into a pad that she pressed against the bottom of his foot. She wrapped the other strip around his foot and ankle until the pad was firmly in place and there was no more bleeding.

"Do you know what your problem is?" Elise asked as she finished tying off the last knot.

"Aside from the fact that I've just cut my foot?"

"You're soft, Ryder McGregor," she accused.

"Excuse me. I think I was the one who carried the picnic basket from town, as well as ran around here with the children while *you* sat on your . . . quilt," he finished with a mischievous grin.

"Nope," she insisted. "You've let your feet go soft from city living. Always wearing shoes. Always walking on smooth cement. Not letting your feet really feel the rough stones and cool grass beneath."

"Excuse me, but I just cut my foot on one of those stones," he reminded her. "I think I'll stick to wearing shoes and walking on cement where it's safe."

"You let your feet get soft, but you let your heart grow hard, Ryder."

One week ago, if anyone had said that to him, he would've gotten very angry. Now he just looked into Elise's eyes, waiting for her to tell him more.

"What made your heart so hard, Ryder? I know your parents couldn't have raised you that way."

"No, they were good people."

"What happened to your wife?"

"She caught a chill about four months after we were married that developed into pneumonia. She died four months later."

Elise was very quiet for a moment.

"I didn't know," she whispered. She reached out to touch his hand. "No wonder you're so sad."

"How could someone so young die so quickly?"

"I don't know. I asked myself the same question when my husband died."

"How could she leave me like that when she'd promised to stay with me? . . ."

"Until death do you part?" Elise finished.

"Exactly."

"But that was the only thing that parted you," she reminded him. "Wasn't it?"

"Yes."

"It wasn't as if she fell in love with anyone else, did she?"

"No."

"No one can control when we come into this world or when we go out of it. She didn't leave you deliberately, Ryder."

"When she died, there wasn't much else to do but work," he told her. "Making money was the only thing I knew I could do well. I could control money. I could hold on to money. I never would've believed . . . You've shown me that money isn't everything."

"It's not exactly nothing, either," she reminded him with a little laugh.

"But when you have your family and good friends, it's easier to do with a little less of it."

"A little," Elise conceded. "On the other hand, I wouldn't advise you to give away all your money and live naked in a tent on the side of a mountain."

"Don't worry—I won't," he assured her with a laugh. "There's something else I'd like to do with my money, though."

"What's that?" she asked.

"Share it."

Elise nodded. "Sharing is good. It's what I try to teach Willow and Russell. You know, I think I just might take back what I said about you not being a Prince Charming."

"I think there was also a remark about a dragon," he reminded her.

She laughed. "Yes. I'm sorry. But the children and I had been playing pretend, and you seemed to fit into the story so well."

"That's all right," he confessed. "I'd sort of cast you as the wicked witch."

"Have you changed your mind?"

He looked into her eyes. She felt his hand cover hers as it rested on the smooth blocks of the quilt. "Yes."

"What's your opinion now?"

"Oh, I still think you're some kind of sorceress."

"You mean you think I'm good at creating illusions?"

"No."

His hand slid up her arm until it came to rest on her shoulder. He leaned closer to her so that she couldn't have any doubts about the sincerity of his words.

"I think maybe what I've been seeing for the past nine years is the illusion."

He moved closer to her. She didn't draw away.

"I think I'm beginning to see what's real again."

He moved his hand across her shoulder and up to cradle the back of her neck.

"There's more than my money I'd like to start to share," he told her.

She watched his vivid green eyes. She remembered how they'd seemed to gleam with greed the unfortunate night they'd met. But now they shone with a clearer light.

"I know we haven't known each other very long, Elise."

"No, not really."

"Most of the time we've known each other we've spent fighting." He chuckled.

"You've got dimples!" she said breathlessly. Her hand flew up to touch his cheek.

"I do?"

"Yes indeed. I just never saw them before, because you never laughed, you old grouch!"

"I think I'm going to be doing a lot more laughing in the future—if you'll be there to help me."

"Only if you promise we won't fight."

"I can think of a lot of other things to be doing."

"Such as? . . ." she prompted.

"I don't think I'm in such a hurry to get back to San Francisco anymore."

"I'm glad to hear that."

"I think I'd like to take my time telling you what I want to share. I'd like to stay around here and get to know you better. I'd like for you to get to know me."

"I'd like that very much."

"Do you think you could ever learn to love me?"

She leaned back and fixed him with her stare. "Don't you think you're going a bit far now trying to get that quilt back?"

"No." He laughed and pulled her closer to him. He loved her teasing sense of humor, and he decided he'd make the most of developing his own, just to match wits with her, again and again. "There's only one way I want this quilt back now."

"What's that?"

"If you and I are under it together."

She felt her cheeks growing warm.

"I'm already in love with you," he confessed. "Do you think you could learn to love me, too?"

He leaned forward slowly. To his surprise, she met him halfway.

Her nose brushed gently against his as they drew nearer. She closed her eyes. She could feel the warmth of his breath combining with the warmth of the sunlight on her cheek.

His lips met hers, softly at first, in a butterfly-light caress. As she felt the growing pressure of his lips, she felt, too, her own being glowing from within with an ever-in-creasing brightness.

He broke off the kiss for only a second. Then he kissed her again, this time with more certainty. He reached around to entwine his fingers in the hair flowing over the nape of her neck. His other hand rose to caress her cheek.

"Do you think you might be able to spend the rest of your life with me, Elise?"

"Yes."

"Sometimes we'd be living in San Francisco. Sometimes we'd travel. Sometimes we could even live in my house right here in Whiskey. But I promise, you'd never have to clean it."

She laughed, then bent forward and kissed his cheek.

"Yes, Ryder, I could do all those things. You see, not too long ago, I discovered that wonderful part of you that you've kept hidden for far too long—the part of you that can laugh, and love, and share that love and laughter. Of course I can love you, Ryder. I've already fallen in love with you!"

A Ring for Remembrance

Christina Cordaire

ONE

"What's the matter with you?" Sara Blake spoke out loud. The woman hurrying along beside her glanced at her, startled. Embarrassed, Sara increased her pace. She was talking to herself again. That meant she was really under pressure.

And she was. As if getting the quilt exhibit ready to open wasn't enough, she had another problem of the first magnitude. Josh wanted an answer.

Sara Blake didn't know *what* it would take to enable her to commit to a relationship with Josh Conrad! Heaven knew the young CEO of one of the most successful software companies in the business was all a girl could possibly hope for. Tall and handsome, his sun-bleached blond hair expertly trimmed and his shatteringly blue eyes shining with intelligence, he was right up there next to irresistible.

But she was resisting him. She wished she knew why, because it was obvious to a doorpost that her highly eligible—and desirable—

suitor was running out of patience. She could see her rivals beginning to salivate hopefully.

Tall, svelte, sophisticated beauties that they were, they'd been too surprised to even put up resistance when Josh had started dating her. They'd been flabbergasted when it became apparent Josh preferred her company to theirs. Now that it looked like Joshua Philip Conrad was going to ask some sort of commitment from her, they were in absolute shock.

To make matters worse, Josh had dumped the whole matter in *her* lap, demanding an answer today. She groaned out loud and the man waiting closest to her for the light to change shied away from her, his eyes wide. Sara hardly noticed.

Sometimes she wished he'd just seduced her—Josh, not the man on the curb—and settled the whole matter for both of them himself! But Josh Conrad didn't operate that way. He was the kind of man who respected a woman's right to make her own decisions. The kind of man who demanded that the woman he loved come to him by a clearly thought out act of her own free will. He'd accept nothing less, and Sara, haunted by her mother's sad experience, couldn't seem to come to a firm decision. It was all she could do not to bite her fingernails over this.

Sara arrived at the museum feeling as if the short walk from her apartment had somehow lengthened by at least five miles.

With an effort, she pushed the whole commitment problem thing to the back of her mind. She had until lunch. She just wouldn't think about it for a while.

Now that she was here on the premises, she could feel excitement rising in her, and she knew that even this awful, weighty decision about Josh Conrad would take a backseat in her mind. Today, Elisia Wainwright's quilt was due to arrive.

Her secretary looked up as she burst through the door. "Meg! Has it come?"

"Good morning to you, too." Meg followed her boss into the inner office and grinned while Sara kicked off her Reeboks and pulled on a smart pair of sling-back, navy kid pumps.

"Of course good morning. But has it come yet?"

"Yeah. Receiving got it ten minutes ago."

"I can hardly wait to see it!"

"You a little excited, are you?"

"Yes. I can hardly believe it. A Friendship Quilt of such fragile construction, and it's still whole! How generous it is of Mrs. Wainwright to donate it to the museum." She shook her head in wonder. "When I wrote asking them if we could borrow it, I'd no idea they'd *give* it to us! Not many people want to part with family heirlooms, even to preserve them for posterity." Grabbing a clipboard and a pen, she beamed at her friend. "Oh, Meg. If it's half as lovely as the slides she sent, it's a prime example of the art."

Dashing out the door, she headed for the stairs down to receiving. Behind her, her secretary crossed plump arms over her chest and asked aloud, "Now why in the world can't she get that enthusiastic about Josh Conrad?" She shook her head. "Gotta be something wrong with that girl."

❧

Joshua Philip Conrad, CEO of Megatrends Computer Software, scowled at the sheaf of interoffice messages his secretary had just handed him. "Get as many of these scheduled before eleven-thirty as you can, Barbara. Give 'em ten minutes each and tell 'em they'd better be on time. I'm leaving at eleven-thirty sharp to pick up Sara for lunch."

"Thirty minutes isn't enough time to get to the museum by noon."

"It is in the Gull Wing."

"Not if the cops see you."

"You're a worrier."

Barbara let the space of a heartbeat pass. "I like her."

Blue eyes shot an intent look her way. "You do, huh?"

Barbara met his gaze with a level one of her own. "Yes, I do."

He stood there a long moment, never taking his gaze from his secretary's face. Then he swooped down to place a kiss on the top of her perfectly coiffed gray hair. "Go get these appointments set up."

Barbara left the room with the stack of messages in her hand, her eyes bright. He'd said "pick up *Sara*." All the others had been *Miss Whatever*. As she started making her calls, she was smiling.

❧

The quilt was all Sara had dared hope it would be! She cradled it lovingly in her arms as she walked to the exhibit hall where the showing of Nineteenth-Century Quilt Art was being set up. She was careful to keep all of it in her arms. She still shuddered when she remembered dragging part of one once. She had to be more careful than most of the staff—she simply wasn't tall enough to be careless.

Spreading the quilt carefully on a large square table, she began preparing the fragile piece for hanging. As her fingers brushed the center square, she found a lump. The delicate silk had deteriorated at that point, and her light touch was enough to dislodge the object.

She gasped in dismay to see the edge of something shiny peeping through the delicate silk of the quilt. Fearing that leaving it there might cause further damage, Sara carefully worked the rest of it out of the square. A moment later, she was staring at a bright gold circlet. A wedding band!

As she looked down at the plain gold ring on her palm, shivers and tingles ran along her spine. She could almost feel the hair on the back of her neck stir. Tears gathered, blurring her vision until the band was no more than a warm golden glow in the center of the indistinct outline of her hand.

Out of nowhere, in a room sealed from the outside to keep street pollutants from damaging the museum's treasures, a faint but insistent breeze encircled her. Her vision became further blurred. Goose bumps rose on her arms, and time ceased to exist.

"Hey! Sara!"

Sara gave a startled cry and almost dropped the ring. Clasping it tightly, she spun around to face Meg.

"You gonna dream over that quilt all day? It's ten minutes to noon, and Galahad will be here to pick you up, you know."

Sara fought her way back from unreality. How could the whole morning have passed? All she'd done was to go get the quilt from receiving, place it carefully on the table . . . and find the ring.

Again she'd given in to her ever-present urge to do all the work herself. The fabric experts the museum employed could have prepared the quilt for hanging, but she'd had to do it herself. She knew she had a problem with that. She had to be the best. Desperately, she hoarded all her time, all her energy, all her passion, to spend on being that best. She had to do everything faster. To do everything better.

She had to be the best so that she'd always have a place to belong, so that no one could ever discard her.

She couldn't afford to let anything else interfere.

Not even Josh Conrad.

And here she'd lost one whole morning.

Her eyes wide, she backed away from the quilt, slipping the wedding band absentmindedly into the pocket of her tailored shirt.

⁂

Josh was ten minutes late, and he'd driven his antique Gull Wing Mercedes. For an instant, she worried about the loss of another ten minutes from the schedule of her day. She'd already lost a whole morning, for Pete's sake.

Then, Josh smiled and kissed her lightly, and thoughts of her work and everything else dropped away and there was only the two of them in all the world. When she sat on the broad red leather padded window sill of the Mercedes to swing her legs into the car and he stared at them in frank admiration, her spirits rose. She pushed all chance of thoughts of work out of her mind. She was Cinderella, and this was her golden coach.

Sara settled herself for the ride, looking forward to the time she had with Josh and the exhilaration she always felt to ride in his marvelous Gull Wing.

Josh was grinning as he signaled the winglike doors to lower over Sara and him, changing the Gull into a rocket, then aimed the sleek black monster out into the heavy flow of cars. Only his excellent driving ability tamed the superbly powerful road car to drive in San Francisco traffic. They arrived at Fisherman's Wharf in record time.

The man Josh had sent ahead to take the car met them and accepted the keys. Sara gave him her sunniest smile. He'd probably spend their entire lunch hour trying to find a parking space. "Back here at one, boss?"

"One-ten's good enough." Josh took Sara's hand, and they made their way to the restaurant at the end of the wharf. There, they were smilingly escorted through the age-mellowed dark wood and red leather to their favorite table at the window. With only a hint of fog lingering on the bay, they saw the sea otter they always looked for lying on his back, gazing up at them as if he'd been waiting.

Josh spoke softly into her ear as he seated her. "Do you think we ought to give him a name?"

Sara shook her head, sad for a moment. The way the abalone

fishermen hated sea otters, this one might be gone one day. She'd miss him all the more if they gave him a name.

Josh ordered for them, his gaze never leaving her face. The minute the waiter had gone, he said, "Well?"

"Well, what?" But she knew perfectly well what and felt like a coward for equivocating. He wanted her answer about the approaching weekend.

Ignoring her hesitation, Josh went straight to the point the minute their wine had been poured. "What about this weekend? Is it a go or a no?" His blue gaze pinned her in her seat.

Sara sat struggling to find the words to explain how she felt. She found none. Instead of answering she asked, "What is it you want from me, Josh?"

"Everything, Sara. I want everything." His deep voice was tense, his gaze searching.

She closed her eyes an instant. When she opened them again she stared out at the otter, not at the intent face of the handsome man across from her. It was just as she'd feared. He wanted all she had to give, and that frightened her. She wasn't ready to give him all of herself, not yet, not now.

Sara moved uncomfortably in her chair. She felt as if she were being torn apart. She was being torn—torn between Josh and her dreams of security. She couldn't give any man, even this man, everything. Fear of doing so made her tell herself that she wanted . . . *needed* to keep a great deal of herself for her dreams. She needed time, as well. Time to become the best curator she could possibly be. Having seen her mother give passionately, fully to her father, she wanted to keep her own strongest passion for her job. Josh Conrad threatened her ability to do that.

And there was more. There was something else that she didn't want to face. There was the awful, haunting feeling that if she gave all that she was, all that she could be, it wouldn't be enough.

She shrugged out of her navy-blue suit jacket, suddenly warm under his steady regard.

"Well?" Josh Conrad wasn't a patient man, and he loved Sara. He wanted a relationship with her. He knew she loved him, so what was the problem? Hell, she was the only woman he knew who wouldn't jump at the chance to snag him.

Sara was the only woman he knew who loved him for himself. While all the rest cooed over his achievements and urged him to greater effort, to more power and wealth, Sara urged him to slow down.

Dammit, she was even worried about whether he got enough rest, or exercise, or the proper food. And she was always picking at him about it. So why wouldn't she make up her mind to take on the task of *personally* overseeing him?

All the rest of the women he knew had been hinting they'd love the job since he'd met them. Of all the females he knew, only Sara Blake didn't have dollar signs in her eyes. But that wasn't why he loved her. He loved her because she was caring and kind and touchingly vulnerable.

He thought he understood her. She was driven to make something of herself. Something big. Someone important.

He felt tenderness rush through him as he remembered another thing she wanted: something to fall back on. But, dammit, Sara wouldn't need anything to fall back on. Couldn't she see that he was hers forever?

He'd had Sara investigated, as he did all the women he dated for any length of time, and he could understand the reason for her drive to be a success from the story of her self-sacrificing mother. Mrs. Hamilton Blake had spent all her life making a home for her neurosurgeon husband and raising his children . . . only to be left for a woman half her age—a pediatric surgeon who had much more in common with her dapper husband than she did. Divorced now and with no life of her own, she was drinking herself elegantly to destruction at the country club.

He raked a hand through his hair. He could see why Sara wanted to establish herself in her own right, to create a life of her own. He just didn't want her ambition to keep them apart, to prevent them from living together. They belonged to each other. Why the devil wouldn't she commit to him?

This weekend was to have been their beginning. Her hesitation told him that she didn't want it as much as he did. The knowledge hurt, and that angered him.

His gaze dropped to the pocket of her white silk shirt. He could see the outline of a gold circle there. "Is that it?" He nodded toward the pocket. "Is that what you're holding out for?"

"What are you talking about?" Sara shook her head, puzzled.

"That ring. It's a wedding band, isn't it?"

Sara's hand flew to her breast to touch the ring.

Josh caught his breath on a shock of sweet desire. The longing to touch her there himself almost dizzied him. Silk and Sara. The combination was tempting beyond all reason. His gaze fastened on the pocket. Vaguely he could see lace under the little tailored shirt. Sara. God, how he wanted her.

Sara didn't even notice. Her hand dropped away from her shirt pocket and her brow creased in a frown. *Was* that what she wanted? No. Assuredly not. She wasn't going to make the mistake her mother had made. She wasn't going to marry anybody until she had a career that wouldn't quit! Especially she wasn't going to try to marry a man like Josh . . . a man who understood her and to whom she could so easily relate because he was as driven as she was herself. That very fact made him extremely poor husband material.

When she married, she wanted a man who had time for his

family, and all of Silicon Valley knew that Joshua Philip Conrad couldn't even delegate a fraction of the responsibility for his company, even to his department heads. Like her, he wanted to do it all, to be on top of it all.

She started to tell him that marriage was not what she wanted just now, that she wasn't ready for that kind of commitment. Suddenly, however, she realized that she might not want to make even the commitment of a relationship—or as her mother would no doubt call it, an affair—with a man who didn't love her enough to want to marry her.

She brushed her hand across her eyes, thoroughly confused. She'd never expected to find herself caught between her father's broad-minded attitude toward sex and her mother's old-fashioned values. She raised stricken eyes to Josh. "I . . . I don't know, Josh. I don't know *what* I want."

"You knew what you wanted the last time we talked." His blue eyes blazed at her. "You wanted me."

"Yes. Yes, I know." And she had. She *had* wanted to enter into a relationship with Josh. She'd meant to, truly meant to. Right up until the instant she'd held the wedding band in her hand and mysteriously lost a whole morning looking down at it.

Now she wanted something more. Something infinitely more.

She just wasn't clear yet as to what that something more was.

TWO

Back at the museum, Sara threw herself feverishly into her work on Elisia Wainwright's donated quilt. Knowing she was still infuriated by some of the hurtful things the very angry Joshua Conrad had said to her in the car coming back from lunch, she was being especially careful of the fragile fabric treasure.

Attempting to block the whole rather one-sided conversation out of her mind, she gathered up the quilt. Still fuming, she climbed the stairs to the balcony at the end of the hall.

With four spotlights focused on it, the quilt was going to be the first thing people saw as they entered the mammoth room. Elisia Wainwright would be pleased, Sara knew. And it was the least she could do to express the museum's gratitude at the elderly lady's having donated her quilt to their collection.

Sara put the quilt gently down on the shining clean floor and flipped the switches that would activate the spotlights that were going to highlight the space in which it was to hang. Then she dragged over and opened the ladder one of the maintenance men had left on the balcony for her.

The very idea of Joshua Conrad accusing her of leading him on! She slammed the ladder down in front of the lighted space. She'd never led a man on in her life!

"A tease. He called me a tease." She sniffed and dashed the back of her hand across her eyes. Josh knew very well she wasn't a tease.

Picking up the quilt, she climbed the ladder. It wobbled a little as she started up it, but she was paying all her attention to the quilt and barely noticed. It would be dreadful if she snagged the fragile silk on any part of the aluminum ladder.

The polished bar to which she was to secure the top of the reinforced quilt was almost twelve feet off the floor, and the ladder was only a six-footer. The maintenance men all thought she was incapable of handling a bigger ladder. Being petite had always been the bane of her existence, now it was interfering with the proper performance of her duties. She'd have to speak to Mr. Lumas, the man in charge.

Sara moved up to the second-from-the-last step in a gingerly fashion, hating the way she had to brace her shins against the very top.

Ladders obviously swayed a bit more the higher one climbed on them. "Either that," she muttered, "or my cowardly imagination is working overtime."

Darn! She was talking to herself again!

She heard the door open at the entrance to the hall. Looking that way, she saw the tall, broad-shouldered figure of Joshua Conrad striding purposefully toward her. From the heights she presently occupied, he looked the size of the Ken doll she'd had to go with her Barbie. What did he want! Surely he wouldn't interrupt her work to continue their quarrel!

Joshua had gotten over his anger minutes after he'd screeched away from the curb and left a year's worth of rubber on the street in front of the museum. Heartily ashamed of his childish behavior, he was determined to apologize to Sara.

He found her in the exhibit hall. Her short honey-blond hair haloed by one of the high spots focused on the wall, she was standing on the top step of a ladder. With a jolt of his heart, he saw that the ladder wasn't properly locked into place.

Seeing her so precariously braced on the ladder drove all thought of an apology, of anything but her safety, out of his mind. He was afraid to shout at her to be careful. The ladder was already wobbling enough to cheat him of seven years growth.

The fool woman had failed to lock it open!

If only she'd stay still—and safe—until he could get to her. He shifted into high gear and headed for the stairs leading to the balcony at a dead run. He had to get to her before that ladder fell.

Sara saw him break into a run and head for the stairs with a flare of annoyance. What caustic comment could he possibly have forgotten to make to her? She'd been sure he'd said it all.

She craned around to see him as he reached the top of the stairs. It was a bad move. She saw the horror on Josh's face even as she felt the ladder shift.

He was racing toward her when she began to fall.

Then everything began happening in slow motion.

She started to reach out and grab at the quilt, but she knew that if she did she would tear it to shreds. Even to save herself, she refused to close her hand on the fragile folds of antique silk.

There was nothing else to break her fall. The ladder lurched, and she went flying.

She thought she might be screaming, but all her attention was strangely focused on the shining gold wedding band that had been thrown from her pocket. It was sailing in a slow, bright arc through the air toward the edge of the balcony, toward the white-painted iron railing toward which she herself was falling.

She threw up a hand to break her fall as the railing loomed nearer, but her hand moved in slow motion also, and she was too late bringing it up to save herself.

Joshua reached out desperately, straining toward her. He could hear himself shouting "No!" His heart stopped. "Sara!"

Sara's head hit the railing. Bright lights behind her eyes exploded sharp pain through all of her. Her body went limp and thudded to the floor.

Josh Conrad skidded to a stop. Sara lay crumpled like a broken doll at his feet.

⚘

Sara knew there were people all around her trying to help her. She could hear Josh calling, "Sara. Sara, hang on. Hang on, darling." And then, his voice breaking with anxiety, "Sara, come back!"

She felt as if she were soaring out away from herself and fought to hold on to Josh's voice, but the effort was futile. A few minutes later, the scream of the ambulance mercifully faded to blend with other, softer sounds.

Spinning and spinning, she tumbled away from the hubbub of sirens and ambulance attendants and paramedics. In slow motion she fell down a silently whirling tunnel that seemed endless. Finally, after what felt like eons, her descent slowed and she heard the almost-forgotten sounds of breezes and birdsong.

⚘

Sara lay still as death, the hospital monitors glowing green behind her over her bed. Josh sat with his head in his hands, the beard stubble of the past two days on his face.

"You need some rest, Mr. Conrad."

"No." He didn't even look at the doctor. "I won't leave her."

"There's nothing you can do here. Nothing any of us can do." The doctor looked at him seriously. "The next couple of days will tell the tale."

"What the hell is that supposed to mean?"

"If she doesn't come around in the next day or so . . ." The doctor let his comment trail away, silenced by the agony in the man's eyes.

Sara came back to consciousness a piece at a time. Feeling returned to her body, and with it a headache to end all headaches.

Slowly, she opened her eyes. The bright light hurt them, and she frowned slightly. That wasn't a good idea. Pain caused her to moan.

"Sarah! Thank God you're awake. I'll go tell Pa." Sara watched the blond giant leave the room in amazement. Who was he? Where was she?

Listening didn't hurt as much as looking. She closed her eyes again and heard birds singing and the rustle of a breeze through tree leaves. There was the homey sound of chickens clucking and scratching outside. Listening harder, Sara heard more quiet than she'd ever heard in her life.

There was a sound in the room, and she opened her eyes again. A tall, gaunt man stood in the doorway, his strong-featured face full of concern under his shock of white hair. Two more men, younger than the one who'd gone to call him, stood behind him.

"Sarah, child. The Lord be praised! We've worried something fierce these last two days." He came over to the narrow bed on which she lay. "You just rest now, daughter. Your brothers and I will manage your chores. And I guess the four of us can do something for meals until you're yourself again."

Herself again! She didn't feel like herself *now*, that was for sure, but she felt enough like herself to know that this man wasn't her father. His rough clothes were nothing like the latest casual fashions her father sported, and at last count, she'd been one of two sisters, period.

The man patted her hand. "You just rest, Sarah honey. Get well for your papa."

Sara lay there stunned. What on earth was going on? She moved her hands restlessly over her covers and felt the outlines of squares of fabric. A quilt. Was she dreaming? Had her concern over the Wainwright Quilt caused her to dream this bucolic setting and to people it with large blond men, obviously farmers, but very like Josh Conrad? She turned her head carefully—it was time to look around.

In one corner of the sunny room she saw her most significant clue. It was a green-painted immigrant's trunk, its corners a little battered. Painted on it in letters six inches high was the name "Franks." From that, as the paint lacked the bloom antique paint acquired after a few decades, she deduced that her dream was taking place in the home of people named Franks, newly come to . . . the Midwest? Most immigrants came west.

She was terribly uneasy. She just didn't feel as if she were dreaming. Everything felt too real. Especially the pain in her head. She'd no idea what had happened to her, but she knew she'd better keep trying to figure it out!

The rest of the room was very simply furnished in fine country pieces that she recognized as early nineteenth century. She thought that if it were later, many of these lovely pieces would have been traded for the popular oak furniture found in the early catalogues.

Trying to guess at everything and deduce from those guesses, however, was difficult in her present condition. Her head began to ache intolerably, and she closed her eyes against the brightness of the day outside. A few minutes later, Sara was asleep.

When she awoke the second time, she found to her acute disappointment that she was still in the same strange surroundings. It was dark out and the chickens had evidently put themselves to bed. Someone had lighted an oil lamp and left it on the dresser across the room.

Rising carefully so as not to set her temples pounding again, she reached for the plain cotton robe at the foot of her bed, put it on over her high-necked flannel nightgown, and looked cautiously down for slippers.

There they were, peeping out from under the edge of the bed, beautifully embroidered with wildflowers. Whomever she'd mysteriously usurped the place of was a talented needlewoman. It was a shame to use such lovely things to walk around in.

The effort of looking down cost her her equilibrium for a moment, and she sat back down on the bed. "Well," she muttered, "what do you expect after a swan dive into an iron railing, klutz? You're lucky to be alive . . . wherever you are."

When the room stopped spinning, she rose again, slipped her feet into the narrow embroidered slippers, and cautiously made her way to the dresser. In the mirror hanging above it, she saw "herself." It was a distinct shock. Where was the gamin face with the slightly retroussé—that had been her mother's word; her father had offered her plastic surgery for her sixteenth birthday—nose? In the mirror she saw, instead, a lovely serene face, beautiful blue eyes, and a wealth of shining white-blond hair. She'd become a girl she'd never in her life seen before!

Butterflies rioted in her stomach. She felt like somebody out of *Quantum Leap!*

Telling herself she was only feeling light-headed because of

cranial trauma, Sara made her way out into the main room of the
farmhouse. Come what may, she was determined to discover what
in the world was happening to her!

❧

By the time she got back to the bed, her aching head was spinning anew with the world of facts she'd learned from casual
remarks made by her "father" and three concerned "brothers." She
was Sarah Franks, and she'd been kicked by the family milk cow
and sent flying backward into one of the support beams of the
barn.

Her brother Walter had found her and brought her into the
house, where they'd all taken turns sitting beside her bed for
the past two days. Days, Sara learned by sneaking a glance at the
older man's weekly newspaper, the *Good Hope Missouri Clarion,*
that were happening in the year 1843!

Somehow, she was one hundred and fifty-some years behind
herself! She was one thoroughly confused nineties woman.
Nineteen-nineties, that is!

In response to her "brother" Enoch's comment that she was
quiet, her oldest "brother" Hans remarked, "Ach, not to worry.
Our little sister is no more quiet than she is always."

Sara glommed on to that as if it were a lifeline. If the girl whose
body she was occupying were a quiet person, then there was the
possibility that she could hide behind her—her host's?—habitual
silence long enough to get by.

She'd no idea what had happened to send her back here to Good
Hope, Missouri. Until she figured it out, she was going to keep her
mouth shut. It didn't take a rocket scientist to get a big picture of
what would happen to her if she tried to explain to these very nice
men that she wasn't who they thought she was. She could see herself trying to explain that in reality she was a surprise guest from

the next century. Yeah. Sure. She'd be in the local loony bin before she'd even finished her explanation.

Exploring the mental health care system of the 1800s really wasn't one of her top priorities just now.

"Would you like me to drive you into town, daughter? I know your Cousin Melly would be much relieved to see you, and I think you girls are supposed to get together at your Aunt Dora's to work on the quilt for Melly."

Sara felt like a rat. This man was so obviously trying to please her, so obviously concerned, and she couldn't even tell him what had happened to his child. She couldn't offer reassurances that she was all right somewhere. She didn't even know when, or *if,* Sarah Franks would ever be back. Tears filled her eyes. She felt so *helpless.*

Mr. Franks misread her tears. "Now, now. You don't have to go if you don't feel like it, Sarah."

"No, it's not that. I-I'm just afraid I might . . ." She could hardly tell him she feared she might give herself away. Quickly she substituted, ". . . be poor company."

Enoch chuckled. "Heck. Melly and them never let you get a word in edgewise, Sarah. I don't see how you could be poor company."

Sara glanced his way, wondering if he and his sister were quarrelsome. She saw only affection in his face. Obviously, Sarah Franks was of a decidedly retiring nature. Perhaps, given that, she *could* go work on her "cousin's" quilt.

As she nodded her compliance at the man who thought he was her father, her thoughts went to the quilt. Somewhere deep inside, she knew with fatalistic certainty that the quilt in question was going to turn out to be the Friendship Quilt donated to her museum by Elisia Wainwright.

Sara knew, too, that the time had come for her to see if she could pass as the woman whose body she occupied. She had to, she simply had to—at least for long enough to discover the reason she'd been sent here. Because, suddenly, with a dreadful clarity, she knew that she would never get home to her own century again unless she accomplished whatever task it was she'd been sent to do.

THREE

The drive into town was pleasant, the early evening noticeably cooler than the day had been. Sara was enchanted by the variety of things she could see, really see, on the way.

Used to speeding along sealed up in a car, she was really enjoying the length of time the slow wagon ride gave her to drink in her surroundings. She could even hear the birds singing over the melodic jingle of harness and the dust-muffled hoofbeats of the plodding workhorses.

When they finally arrived in town, Mr. Franks drew his team to a halt in front of a house with a discreet sign proclaiming it a boardinghouse. Before she could figure out how to climb down from the high wagon seat, a lovely brunette ran down off the porch to meet her. "Oh, Sarah, we're all so glad you could come!" Helping her down, she gave Sara a big hug. "Aunt Dora's made us lemonade. You just come and sit and have some."

"I'll go pour another glass." A plump older woman with silver-streaked dark hair turned to reenter the house. "Mercy, it surely is good to see you're all right, Sarah."

"Yes." One of the three girls waiting on the porch stepped forward to hug Sara. "It's God's mercy that you weren't killed when that old cow kicked you into the barn post."

"Yes." The second girl spoke. "Esther's right, and we're all grateful you're still with us. I just hope you won't have any complications. I was reading just the other day that blows to the head can cause all sorts of harm, even migraines." She put her cheek against Sara's for an instant, then looked at her compassionately. "I do hope you won't have migraines as a result of this, dear."

The smallest of the three nudged her out of the way. "Hush, Lydia. Don't even suggest such a thing. Your migraines are worry enough for us aplenty. We don't need Sarah to start up her own." She looked Sara over with round, china-blue eyes. "You look as if you came through all right. You're not to have migraine headaches, Sarah Franks. Do you hear me?"

Sara smiled automatically. This petite girl was obviously the powerhouse of the group. "Yes. I promise."

"Biddy Zane, you stop plaguing Sarah and get her in here and make her sit down." Aunt Dora spoke from the doorway, warm lamplight behind her, a tall glass in her hand. "I have her lemonade all ready for her."

Sara smiled widely as she was ushered into the parlor and onto a chair at one corner of a quilting frame. So these were the girls who made up the core of Sarah Franks's circle of friends. They were all nice people. She heaved a small sigh of relief.

The sigh ended on an abrupt intake of breath. In the middle of sitting down, she saw the quilt that was stretched smoothly over the big quilting frame. A thrill shot through her. Pristine, new, and gloriously glowing with the undulled luster of new silks and satins, it was, indeed, the Friendship Quilt that Elisia Wainwright had donated to the San Francisco Museum of Americana, *one hundred and fifty-three years from now!*

⁓

Sara sat quietly listening to the banter about Dora's gingersnaps and Melly's wedding and plied her needle, hoping her skill with it was close to that of the girl she was supposed to be, in order to avoid suspicion. She'd always prided herself on her ability, but the needlework on the Wainwright quilt had been so beautiful as to cause her a touch of envy back in her own time. She hoped any lack she exhibited would be attributed to the blow to Sarah Franks's head.

She concentrated hard on all the others' conversation, listening with a small smile to her "friends." In listening, she learned that Melly was engaged to a man named Caleb, who had a brother, Conrad, who was a captain on a China clipper and who was thought of as something of a scamp. She smiled at all their pleasant recollections.

She pretended to be lost in her thoughts, a circumstance the other girls seemed not even to notice. Then the comfortable woman they called Aunt Dora came in from the kitchen with a kitten.

"All right, ladies, gather close around the quilting frame and push your needles. . . ." Aunt Dora went on to explain that the kitten would walk to the next to marry if thrown to the middle of the quilt. Then, according to tradition, the first man to come in the door would be the man the girl was to marry.

Sara didn't give a rip for the quaint tradition. It was all she could do not to cry out aloud in protest. The very thought of the little cat's claws on the precious quilt was enough to make her feel faint. No one seemed to notice her little movement of protest, however. In fact, she concluded, nobody seemed to notice her at all. She was beginning to think people didn't *notice* much about Sarah Franks in spite of their very evident fondness for the girl. She frowned, and something rebellious rose up in her.

Just then, Aunt Dora dropped the kitten on the quilt and told them, "Call to it, girls. Come on now, you want it to be a fair trial."

Sara obliged, trying to keep her irritation out of Sarah Franks's voice. What did she think she'd do if anything did happen to the quilt? Whop Aunt Dora?

The others called the kitten as well. There was laughter all around when it balked and sat licking a paw, then explosive mirth when the feline oracle launched itself straight into Melly's arms. When, an instant later, a blond giant of a man appeared in the doorway and Melly cried, "Caleb!" and leaped up to greet him, Sara's ears began to hum.

She shook her head a little, trying to dispel the odd sensation she was experiencing. Even as she did, she noted the fervor of the man's embrace, the enthusiasm with which they kissed. He was quite a hunk, and he really hung one on Melly. She watched with pleasure. This was going to be a happy marriage, indeed.

Then a carbon copy of the man who held Melly in his arms stepped into view. His voice harsh with shock and pain, he cried, "Melly!"

Sara felt the strange tingling and disorientation she'd felt when she'd found the wedding band in the center of the quilt. Fight it though she tried, it was overcoming her. As if from miles away, she viewed the scene before her. She saw Melly spring guiltily from the first man's embrace.

In the confusion that followed, the first blond man apologized, but Sara knew he didn't mean it. So did the man's twin. That must be Caleb, Melly's fiancé. He was clearly furious.

The tingling through Sara's body intensified. She seemed to see Caleb in sharp, startling detail. All the rest of the participants in the little drama receded into a fog, their voices becoming meaning-less murmurs.

It was he. He was her target. She knew it as sure as she knew her own name. Her own real name, Sara Blake. This man, this Caleb, was the reason she'd been sent back to September, 1843!

In a daze she heard Aunt Dora smooth things over. "Come in here, Conrad Wells, you rapscallion!"

So now she had a last name for the man she'd guessed was to be her project. Wells. Caleb Wells. She also had a pretty good idea from the embrace she'd just witnessed between Caleb's bride-to-be and his twin brother that Caleb Wells was soon going to be up for grabs.

Was she supposed to grab him? She panicked at the thought, con-fused for a moment. Surely not. She loved Josh. Twentieth-century Joshua Conrad. She had to find out how to get back to him.

She returned her attention to Melly and the other twin. The attraction that sizzled the air between the two guilt-stricken young people who'd just kissed almost took the paint off the parlor walls. Surely she wasn't the only one to notice that there was something more going on here than a casual, mistaken embrace?

Sara Blake was glad that Sarah Franks was the retiring type. Sarah's well-known reticence made it possible for Sara to sit quietly and hope that the strange feelings that harassed her would clarify her purpose for being a century and a half behind herself and lead her to some sort of a plan.

Now that she knew that it had something to do with Caleb Wells, she needed to figure out how to do whatever it was she'd been sent back in time to do. She also needed, desperately needed, to know what the heck it was!

Somehow they all got through the rest of the evening.

Riding home in the wagon with Mr. Franks, Sara, thinking feverishly, was given her first clue to finding a key to the puzzle. In the all but one-sided conversation with which Mr. Franks tried to fill the time, her "father" said, "I bet you'll have plenty to write in your journal tonight, won't you?"

"My . . ." Sara swallowed the word "journal" and said, "Oh, my, yes." Her heart soaring to discover a diary existed that might give her some insight into both Sarah Franks and what she was beginning to think of as her mission, she added, "I've certainly neglected it lately."

"I'll say that's so. Why, never a night went by that you didn't write something in your journal. Our cantankerous old cow Bessie has a lot to atone for."

Sara answered his smile, and they rode on in companionable silence. Excitement made it hard for her to be patient. She just *had* to complete this job, whatever it was, so that this nice man could have his daughter back.

The rest of the slow way to the Franks farm, she fought to contain her impatience. A diary! Somehow she knew she'd find it. She just had to. She knew that book, Sarah Franks's journal, would probably prove to be the most important thing she'd ever read in her life.

FOUR

It was only with the greatest effort that Sara retained the calm exterior expected of Sarah Franks when at last they got home to the farmhouse. She felt as if she'd explode with twentieth-century impatience. Somewhere in Sarah's room she knew she'd find the diary that would give her the clue she sought to her own presence here in the nineteenth century!

"Did you have a good time, Sarah?"

"Yes, thank you, Enoch."

"How's your headache?" Walter looked at her searchingly.

She pressed fingers to her temples, almost surprised that she did still have a headache. It was probably just the heat. After all, she was used to the coolness of San Francisco . . . and of modern air conditioning.

Hans grinned at her. "Just ignore him, Sis. He had to cook dinner tonight, so of course he wants you to be well."

"Of course." She made sure the smile she gave them was wan, hoping to delay her entrance into the culinary world. They wouldn't be so eager to get her into the kitchen if they knew that if she, Sara Blake, took over the cooking she'd probably poison four perfectly good men. "Good night."

"Good night, Sarah." It was a fond chorus. These very nice men seemed to love their sister very much. Sara longed to know that the girl would come back to them safely. Again she wished with all her might that she knew whether or not the real Sarah Franks were safe somewhere.

Longing for a modern shower, Sara washed the heat of the day from her body with a cloth wrung out in the tepid water she'd poured into Sarah Franks's flower-painted washbowl. All the while she got ready for bed, she concentrated fiercely on the missing girl. "Where are you, Sarah?" She sent the thought out with every ounce of her concentration. Then aloud she said softly, "Are you as frightened as I am?"

Suddenly with the strange tingling sensation she'd experienced earlier, she could feel Sarah reaching out to her. She shied away with a startled "Oh!"

Then she sensed the desperation in the girl. With tears in her eyes, she accepted this strange state of affairs, relaxed her habitual guard, and extended her whole consciousness to meet Sarah's, seeking to reassure her, striving to learn what had become of her.

And in an instant, she was there with Sarah.

Sarah Franks was trying to open her eyes, but she couldn't.

Sara was startled to feel and hear what Sarah Franks was feeling and hearing. It was all she could do not to draw back. Standing statue-still in the Franks's farmhouse in 1843, Sara Blake felt the brush of a kiss over Sarah's lips as if she herself were receiving it.

Josh. Through Sarah she could smell his aftershave, feel the roughened satin of his kiss.

It was Josh who'd kissed her. Over decades of time and hundreds of miles, Josh had kissed her.

If only he would speak. Never had she longed for anything as she now longed to hear his dear voice.

Sara's heart swelled to know that Josh was at her bedside and that he cared. Obviously it was her body that Sarah Franks occupied, just as she stood here in the tall silver-blonde Sarah's. They must have swapped places somehow. Why else would Sarah be hearing these things that were frightening and confusing her?

Sara could hear Sarah's frightened thoughts chasing around in her brain like jet-propelled butterflies. She could hear Sarah's wild, confused perception of her surroundings.

If only she could reassure the poor girl that the sounds were hospital monitors and San Francisco traffic and car horns. . . . No, that *wouldn't* be reassuring. While she knew all about Sarah's world from history, Sarah had no familiarity with the world of the twentieth century. It was only natural that the poor girl be frightened.

She could feel Sarah reaching out frantically, striving to make contact with something, anything, familiar. Stretching her mind away from the indecipherable sounds around her and toward the things she knew, Sarah thought of the cow who'd kicked her. Bessie. Bessie and the pail of milk.

Sara felt her decide she should be worrying about the milk.

Desperately the girl from the past concentrated on that, concentrated with all the force of her mind and every fiber of her body. Frightened by her strange surroundings, she locked her mind on Bessie and the milk. A calmness settled over her as she did.

Sara sensed her clinging to the fact that she didn't know whether or not the pail had been knocked over when Bessie kicked her. Sarah Franks was deliberately making the cow's milk her first priority, telling herself that she was only worried about whether or not it had spilled, rather than what was happening to her in this strange place. . . .

Sara's heart went out to the girl.

Then a low masculine voice murmured, "Ah, God, Sara. Wake up, darling. Please wake up."

Tears ran down Sara's cheeks. She whispered, "Oh, Josh, I love you so." The words were torn from her by a power beyond the careful logic by which she strived to live her life. She loved Josh Conrad. Time and distance had enabled her to admit it without reservation. Still, the thought of that love frightened her.

If only she could control this strange exchange of time and be again with him at their table at Tarentino's. Their quarrel would never have happened.

Then, of course, she would never have been so careless with the ladder, never have fallen, never have been brought back here to the nineteenth century. But again she was filled with a sense of destiny. Right now, she belonged here. She was here because there was something she had to do.

With all the determination she could summon, she resolutely set her mind to discovering the task she must complete before she could get back to Josh. A thought intruded. It glimmered tantalizingly at the edge of her mind, but she pushed it away. Sara ignored the suggestion that there was something else, some additional reason she had been sent back as well. She had all she could manage right now, she told herself, without facing that.

❧

Having searched everywhere else for Sarah Franks's journal, Sara drew the paisley shawl off the green-painted immigrant's chest almost reverently. Pausing, her hands ready to lift the lid, she breathed a small prayer that she'd find Sarah's diary inside.

The chest was filled almost to the top with fine linens. They looked to her like a bride's trousseau, all fine embroidery and exquisite cutwork. It wasn't the needlework that held her interest though—it was the little pile of notebooks bound with a red ribbon sitting on top of them. Carefully, Sara lifted the small stack of books out of the trunk. She felt as if she were handling some vital part of Sarah Franks's life.

Opening the topmost book, she read, *My beloved Caleb is to marry my dear cousin Melly on September 10th.*

My heart is breaking just a little. I suppose I have always hoped that there might be a chance for me, but now that I know there is not, I am glad he has chosen Melly. I love him so much. I want him to have only the best, and that is certainly Melly.

Sara's heart filled with sympathy for the girl who'd penned these unselfish words. She smoothed the cover of the book closed, reluctant to read further in it just now. Instead, she picked up the book just underneath it. She wanted to learn a little more about Sarah Franks before she finished reading the latest of her journals.

From the notebook she selected, she learned that Sarah loved her garden and tending her chickens and hoped that Melly would learn to take an interest in such things. Sarah knew that Caleb was about to ask Melly to marry him. *More than anything in the world, Caleb loves his farm,* Sarah wrote. *It's a wonderful farm, with enough land to make a good living for the family he'll have one day, and the barn he's building will be the grandest in the county. Melly will be so proud of all he has accomplished.*

"Oh, why must people be so blind?" Sara spoke aloud. "You're the one who's so proud of Caleb's farm, Sarah. You're the one so in tune with his dreams." She sat recalling and weighing all she'd learned since she'd arrived. "Evidently Caleb never saw that. He chose Melly, and Melly is too full of life . . ." she searched for the right word—". . . too questing to be a farm wife. Why couldn't Caleb see that?"

She sat remembering the look on Melly's face after Conrad had kissed her. She saw again in her mind's eye the hunger and longing she'd glimpsed in Conrad's.

Here in her lap she had proof of yet another person's hungering. Sarah longed to be Caleb's wife. It showed beneath her every written word, no matter how bravely she'd penned them.

And some of the passages Sara read were full of Sarah's desire for Caleb. *Love for Caleb fills me to the point of bursting, and makes my nights a torment. I would count it heaven to lie in his arms. More than anything in the world I long to draw from Caleb a passion equal to my own.*

Sara sat very still, embarrassed that she had just trespassed on another woman's soul.

How in Heaven's name could Sarah Franks, the girl who had written such words, stand meekly aside and let the man of her dreams marry someone else? And how did Caleb miss realizing that such passion burned for him when he was near Sarah? Without meaning any disrespect for Sarah, she would have thought it must have been like standing next to a blowtorch. How could he have been so unaware?

Maybe that was what she was here to do. Maybe she was to find an opportunity to show Caleb that Sarah Franks was a woman to be reckoned with. Sarah had been so quiet for so long, shyly guarding her deepest emotions from her houseful of jovial men, that she'd been unable to do it. Sara, with her freer sense of man-woman relationships, might just find a way to bring it off.

"A love such as Sarah Franks has for Caleb Wells comes along once in a lifetime. I must have been sent here to help Sarah attain her dream."

Without feeling the least bit foolish, she spoke aloud to the author of the diary. "Sarah, you love him, and Melly doesn't, and she's realized that at last." She hugged her knees. "Something has to be done. Your reticence has obviously locked you up so that you can't help yourself." Sara sighed and added, "So I'm here to do it for you."

There was no answer from Sarah, just a silent, breathless feeling of anticipation.

Sara sighed and got back to her reading. Sarah had written that more than anything in life Caleb loved his farm, and Sara believed it. To her sorrow, she hadn't seen anything but possessiveness and anger in Caleb's face when his brother and Melly had sprung apart after their kiss.

It was perfectly clear to her that Caleb Wells had not yet learned the meaning of true love. "All right, Caleb. Hold on to your horses. I'm here to get you started on the path to learning."

She didn't feel the least bit guilty about meddling in Caleb's life. It didn't take the personnel skills she'd learned in her management courses to see that the engaged couple were ill-suited. Caleb would make a drudge of Melly for the good of his farm without even realizing he was doing so.

Melly would set aside all that she'd wanted from life in order to fit into his world. She'd never attain her dreams of travel and adventure, dreams hinted at by the little sailing ship embroidered on one square of her quilt.

Sara sighed gustily. "What a shame. What a lousy, crying shame."

Suddenly, Sara thought of how she had put Josh Conrad on hold for *her* dreams, and frowned. She didn't want to think of that now, she had her hands full already. Shaking her head to chase away the sudden picture of Josh that filled it, she read on.

It was agonizingly clear that Sarah had never really believed that she had a chance with Caleb. Overshadowed by the vivacious cousin of whom she was so fond, she'd always hidden her love for him, in spite of the fact that inside she'd nurtured a passion that surprised Sara in its intensity. She hadn't even tried to make him notice her.

"Oh, for Pete's sake. Why didn't you at least make a play for him? It's better to go down in flames than to sit there and rust out."

She began to read again. None of her friends knew of her love for Caleb, Sarah wrote, and neither did her family.

"Oh, that's great. Just great."

Finally, she wrote, she'd started walking out with Theodore Frazier, and ultimately allowed her father to arrange a marriage for her with the young local carpenter. He was a good man, and would be a faithful husband and a diligent provider.

Sara wrinkled Sarah Franks's nose. It didn't give her the same feeling she got when she wrinkled her own. That was disconcerting, to say the least.

When, half a book later, she read that Sarah's carpenter had stepped on a nail while repairing an old barn and died of lockjaw, she could feel Sarah's pain at not having been able truly to feel grief over his death.

Sara read every last notebook. The underlying theme of all of them was Sarah's unrequited love for Caleb. Even so, that first entry she'd read had been filled with nothing but Sarah's hopes for her cousin's and Caleb's happiness.

Sara didn't know many people in her own time who could have been so generous. She was full of respect for the quiet girl.

She also had a desire to shake her until her teeth rattled.

"If you wanted him, why the dickens didn't you at least make one try for him, Sarah Franks?" She could hear her exasperation in Sarah's voice.

Then she felt the now-familiar tingling begin. The strange stirring of air she'd felt back in the museum when she'd first touched the Wainwright Quilt breezed around her. It blew the bright calico

curtains against the window she'd closed to keep moths from flying in to singe their wings against the hot chimney of her oil lamp.
It ruffled the edges of her long cotton skirt, and swirled errant
strands of long, silver-blond hair around her face.

With the breeze came knowledge. With a lift of her heart, she
knew. She could say now, "Don't worry, Sarah Franks. You'll come
back safely from wherever you are, I know it." For all at once, with
a shattering certainty, Sara Blake knew that she'd discovered her
reason for being here in Sarah Franks's century . . . and in Sarah
Franks's body.

She grinned as inspiration hit her. "Well, *you're* not here now to
make a play for Caleb, are you, Sarah the Solemn? *You're* not right
here to fight for the guy you love." She laughed. "But *I am!*"

She jumped up and went to the mirror over the dresser. She
studied the reflection she saw in the silver-backed glass carefully,
then whispered, "So long, Sarah the Silent. With that kick from
the cow to serve as my excuse, I'm going to give you a slight but
effective change of personality. And when I do, Caleb Wells is
going to notice you."

She turned "her" head first one way and then the other. "A little
pale, but I think I can jazz you up with a bit of aerobics to bring
some color to your cheeks." Her gaze swept downward as she backed
away from the mirror. "Everything else about you is already A-OK.
Nice willowy figure. Curves in the only place that counts."

Her gaze swept upward again. "You have long hair. Men love
long hair. Especially long, blond hair, and yours is beautiful. We'll
just have to get it out of that regal coronet of braids you wear. Too
formal, too stiff." She began pulling out hairpins.

She gave her reflection a conspiratorial smile. On Sarah's rather
sad face it looked almost sinister. She laughed again, and Sarah's
face brightened beautifully.

"My go-getter personality and your looks. That ought to do it.

Look out, Good Hope, Sarah The Retiring Franks is gonna come out of her shell and land the man of her dreams. Wish me luck, Sarah Franks."

By the time she fell asleep, her plans were taking form. Cool in a light summer nightgown instead of the flannel one her "father" had put her in when she'd been hurt, she fell asleep without any difficulty. She was quite pleased with the latest turn of events.

Her dreams, however, were disturbing.

In a haze, she felt as if she were in two places at once. She was sleeping restlessly on Sarah Franks's bed, and she was floating some-where else. She tried to see through the cloaking mist to determine her surroundings, but was unsuccessful. Then, out of the fog of her confusion, she heard Josh Conrad's voice!

"Sara, please wake up, darling. You have to wake up."

Sara could actually hear him. She could hear the tortured anxiety in his voice. She knew then that she was with Sarah and she wished Sarah could respond, but the girl seemed powerless to do so.

Something was keeping her from it. Whatever strange force was in charge of their lives just at this time had Sarah wrapped in a protective cocoon. She was waiting, merely acting as a conduit between Sara Blake and her proper time and place.

There was the sound of a muted phone bell. She sensed Josh's movement as he answered. Oh, why couldn't she push through this envelope she was in to speak to him, to tell him she was here?

"Hello?" A pause. "Yes. Have Jenkins handle that. No, not that, too. Give that one to Halloran." He paused, then "And Barbara? Just muddle along as best as you can. The department heads can take care of everything. They're all perfectly competent." There was a long pause before he said, "Yeah. It *is* a pity that Sara had to go to the hospital before I could admit that, but they are. All of 'em are good men."

Sara heard him shift impatiently. "Look Barb, I—I don't wanna think about business right now." He was quiet a moment, then Sara heard him speak again. "No. She's still in a coma." Again silence, then, "Thanks, Barbara. I appreciate your prayers for her." There was a soft click, and he sat back in his chair.

He sighed. Moments passed and then he told her softly, answering one of her old arguments, "You see, my very dearest, when you're my reason, I *am* able to delegate authority."

He groaned and twisted in his chair as if he were in pain. Sara felt, from a century and a half away, the grip he had on Sarah's hand tighten. "Please, Sara. Wake up!" His agony deepened and she heard him pray softly, "Oh God, please, bring her back to me."

Sara's heart ached with love for him. What he was doing in staying by her bedside meant the world to her. By doing so, he'd just reassured her that she was more important to him than his precious company.

Josh loved her. He really loved her. She couldn't think of anything she'd rather know just now.

As she drifted reluctantly back to the farmhouse, she clung to the comforting knowledge. He *could* delegate authority when she needed him. While she had no way of knowing whether he would in the future, it was a beginning.

It was time for her to take her own advice. Hadn't she told Sarah Franks to fight for what she wanted? She had every intention of doing so herself if . . . no, *when* she had the chance.

FIVE

Sara spent every minute that she was in their company carefully studying Melly and the twins. It wouldn't do for her to make a mistake, and she sure as heck didn't want to stay here forever. Not with Josh waiting.

The church social had strengthened her conviction that Melly felt more for Conrad than she ever could for Caleb. Clearly, though, the girl wasn't about to admit it, even to herself.

Caleb's failure to get back from some farm auction to squire his future bride to the social spoke volumes, too. Farm first, Melly second. Sara shook her head and muttered, "Bad move."

Sheriff Telford, who'd shared the supper she'd made and brought—heaven help him—hadn't even noticed her preoccupation with the others. Evidently he, like everybody else, was well used to Sarah Franks's reticent personality.

She thought it a pretty sad state of affairs that only Sara Blake, a stranger from another century, had any idea of the depths of Sarah Franks's nature. It looked to her like, as far as Good Hope was concerned, the tall blonde might as well be a doorstop.

Being ignored irked Sara's modern sensibilities. Sarah Franks was a very pretty girl, and from what Sara had learned from her journals, a very interesting one. That knowledge, along with suddenly finding herself no longer a petite, honey-blond museum curator but a tall, silver-blond earth goddess, got the devil up in Sara.

She hadn't been able to resist teasing the sheriff by flirting with him just a little. The results had been most gratifying. That little bit of flirting had gotten her the attention not only of Telford but also of more than a few others of the young men from the town.

Sarah Franks's hair, shining down her back to her waist for a change, seem to fascinate them all. Sara wondered why at least one of them hadn't realized the girl was a blonde before.

Well, Sara noted smugly, they all knew now.

Even playing her little game of heightening the interest of the male population in the formerly too-quiet Sarah, the modern Sara had somehow gotten through the evening without betraying herself. Now she was more confident as she went on to her second test—the picnic Melly's friend Lydia had proposed. She hummed contentedly as she dressed for it.

The day had dawned hot and bright and breezeless, with a sullen stillness that bespoke a gathering storm. It hadn't improved as it wore on, and Sara was putting on Sarah's lightest dress when her brother called out to her.

"Hey, Sarah! Sheriff Telford's coming along the road." Walter popped his head around the doorjamb and waggled his eyebrows at her. "If you were to invite him to the picnic, it would save me driving you into town." He grinned impishly.

Sara grinned back. "Done. Go call him in, and I'll do the deed." She peeped out the window and eyed the deeply padded seat of the sheriff's buggy, or whatever it was. "That thing he's driving looks a lot more comfortable than your wagon."

"Done? Do the deed?" Walter shook his head as he went to the door. "You surely do talk strangely, Sarah."

"It must be that knock on the head. I'm sure I'll come right before long."

She sure hoped she'd come right before long. Come right back to San Francisco and Josh . . . not to mention air conditioning. She scrabbled through Sarah's ultraneat dresser drawers, looking for a fan.

There were twelve of them at the riverside, but everyone seemed as enervated as Sara felt. No one bothered to make much conversation beyond "Lordy, it's so hot," so she was free to watch Melly and the twins.

To Sara, with her twentieth-century perception, it was obvious that Melly and Caleb were through. Whether or not they would ever admit it was another matter.

It was just as obvious to her that Conrad and Melly were in love, big time. The way he lay, pretending to doze, with his cheek on the edge of the hem of Melly's skirt told a poignant story to a person watching for such signs. The way Melly took care not to move and disturb him told another, and Sara was taking note.

Caleb was talking to the preacher. Sara could sense a baffled unhappiness in him. Still he made no attempt to engage his fiancée's attention, nor to amuse her.

Sara thought him an absolute jerk.

The conversation was desultory, the day humid and gnat-infested. Sara turned and looked long at Caleb. She felt her expression soften as she thought of how much Sarah Franks loved him.

He was one lucky man, and he didn't even know it. He just kept on talking with the preacher.

She caught Melly's glance, shook her head, and gave her a look of comical sympathy. You'd think the man would pay more attention to his very near future bride.

Caleb certainly did nothing to demonstrate his affection for Melly. It irked Sara.

What on earth was the matter with them? Why in the world didn't they realize that they simply weren't suited? If they'd been her contemporaries, they'd have broken up long before now.

Melly and Caleb didn't live in the twentieth century, though, they lived in 1843—a time when real commitment was the order of the day. Commitment to one another, commitment to marriage and the family, and commitment to the community. People *did* what they pledged to do. They did what was expected of them.

In this case, it could be a trap for all of them—herself included. . . .

Sara's stomach went into a knot wondering what Melly and Conrad and Caleb would do. All three of them. All three of them because this was definitely a triangle now.

That made Sara uneasy. Even in her promiscuous time, triangles could get ugly.

Things were already getting mock-ugly now.

The quilt, glorious in its shining blues and lustrous white, had been brought out of its protective pillowcase for everyone to admire. Shimmering softly, it seemed almost a living thing as the changing patterns of the sunlight through the leaves moved across it.

Sara could sense a resentment in Caleb that left her unsurprised when he said that he bet the quilt would be used for babies to nap on after five years. Sara understood. The even tenor of his life had been disturbed. Uneasy about his twin and Melly, he was spoiling for an argument.

Biddy and Lydia verbally attacked him.

She, Sara Blake, would attack all of them if they let anything happen to the quilt!

Tension, heat-bred, was building in their little group under the oaks.

Finally, Biddy Zane got up and stretched, and several of them wandered down to the river's edge where an old raft bumped against the bank. Then more of them were leaving the deep shade of the tall oaks, meandering off toward the river and slithering down the bank toward the old raft.

Sara sat where she was, toying with Sarah's long blond hair. It was too hot to walk anywhere. Besides, she could hear the grumble of thunder in the distance.

Suddenly, there was an outcry and Caleb went splashing into the water. She leapt to her feet to see what was going on.

She saw that Conrad and Melly were on the old raft and headed for the middle of the river. Conrad stood on the slippery old logs of the raft and swung the steering oar with confident grace, driving the craft out away from his twin.

Caleb was shouting and swimming after them.

Sara watched, her hand pressed to a stomach suddenly in knots. Caleb swam after his twin and his fiancée like a madman. He was furious at his brother's high-handed prank. He was humiliated, too, at having his bride abducted in front of all their friends this way. Especially by Conrad. Worst of all, Sara sensed, he was seeing his plan for his life being stolen away.

Sara could sense his frustration and fury as the distance between him and the raft widened. Helplessness overwhelmed and shamed him.

When finally he gave up, defeated, and swam back toward the group, Sara's heart went out to him. She watched as Caleb stood up and waded the rest of the way to the bank. He looked like a man who'd just seen his whole life swept away on the current of the river.

Still as a statue, she stood in the deep shadow of an oak and listened to the thunder roll closer. She looked out to where Conrad plied the steering oar to send the raft more quickly away down the river toward Good Hope, and electricity tingled through her and through the air.

A storm was about to break.

In more ways than one.

SIX

Sara spent a restless night wondering if everything was all right. In the morning, Enoch drove her into town to replenish the kitchen supplies at the mercantile. Sara left off thinking about the way Conrad had carried Melly away on the raft and turned her mind to her own immediate problem. She was frantically wondering what she'd do when she got to the store. She barely knew her way around a supermarket, much less an 1800s mercantile.

"Thank heavens," she breathed when she learned there was a standing order that Sarah Franks got filled every month and she didn't have to cope. Now she only had to worry about how to use the stuff if and when her "family" forced her to resume Sarah's duties as cook.

That would be such a shame. A crying shame. She'd really come to like the men of the Franks family, and food poisoning wasn't pretty.

She came out of the store annoyed and disquieted by the gossip she'd heard inside about Conrad and Melly being marooned alone and for hours and into the night on the little island downstream from the town. She shook her head over the malice of it as she read-justed the position of her basket on her arm.

Hearing shouting, she turned to see what the commotion down at the river landing was about. What looked like every dog in town dashed around a large group of shouting men, frantically barking. Shading her eyes against the morning sun, she saw that the crowd was surrounding two tall, identical men. It was Caleb! Caleb and Conrad were fighting! She heard a screen door bang shut and saw Melly on the steps of the boardinghouse. "It's Caleb and Conrad!" Sara called to her. She had no idea what to do. Brawls in her time were handled by policemen.

When Melly picked up her skirts and ran, Sara plopped her bas-ket down and was right behind her. She was still with Melly when the girl pushed her way into the resisting crowd.

She hadn't Sarah's long association with the town to buffer her feelings, and the shouts and whistles of encouragement to the com-batants sickened her. She clapped her hands over her ears to shut out all sound. The violence appalled her. She could only stand numbly watching until it was over and a battered Caleb rose from the dust.

Ignoring everyone else, she walked over and took him by the hand. "Come," she told him softly, "I'll wash your face."

⁂

"God, Sarah. What got into me? I slandered Melly. I attacked my own twin."

Sara reached out and patted his knee. She knew what his prob-lem was, but she also knew that this wasn't the right time to tell him. "Just be quiet and let me tend to your face, Caleb."

She hated to hear the despair in his voice, see the dejection in the slump of his shoulders. It was awful to know how his story ended, to know that he would lose Melly, but not to know whether he would ever be happy.

She wished she did know, wished she could comfort him, but the only thing of which she was certain was that the golden band that was to have been his wedding ring had been sewn into the center square of the Wainwright Quilt. That left no doubt in her mind that he'd lost Melly, because there was only one thing that putting the ring in her quilt could have meant. It meant that he was a friend, finally, not a husband. For a husband would have worn the golden wedding band to his grave.

Sitting here in the shade on the bench built along the river side of the livery stable, Sara sought for the words to make things better for him, but she could find none. He *had* said dreadful things to his brother, and words once spoken could never be recalled. They rolled along through time like the river across from them flowed on between its banks.

"Sarah." It was a cry from his very soul. "Why did I do it? What got into me?"

She sensed his bitter regret, but still she had no idea how to comfort him. Now wasn't the time to tell him what had gotten into him. Maybe in a few minutes, but not now, when the pain was so fresh. "Let me go wet my handkerchief at the watering trough." She rose. "Some of the cuts on your face are dirty. If we don't get them clean, they'll make scars."

She went to the front of the livery stable and wet her handkerchief under the pump for the watering trough. The dusty street was quiet in the heat of the morning. Empty almost. It was a far cry from what it had been earlier.

There was no sign to show that a man's life had been destroyed here at the river landing just a short while ago.

It was true. Caleb's whole life was in fragments, and Sara wasn't certain that she was up to the task of picking up the pieces.

Then, welling up in her, she felt a hope and a determination that didn't belong to Sara Blake at all, and she knew that somehow, Sarah was here, too, and helping Caleb was going to get done.

"Here. Hold still." She grasped his chin in Sarah's long slender fingers and began dabbing at his lip.

Caleb squirmed and tried to draw back.

"Hold still, Caleb. I have to get it clean."

"When are you going to answer my question?"

She stopped and looked straight at him. "Maybe you won't like what I have to say."

"Well, say it anyway. I don't much like what I'm saying to myself. I'll survive it."

"I was going to say that maybe you got so angry at seeing Melly with Conrad because it showed you that Melly isn't right for you."

"Melly not right for me?" He was incredulous. Manlike, he had no idea that choosing a girl didn't automatically make her right for him.

"Well, when you were younger, didn't Melly always dream of travel and visiting foreign lands?"

"Yes, but that was just silly young girl. Melly knows better now."

"Better than her dreams?"

He looked truculent. "Are you telling me that she wishes she could choose Conrad so that she could go off and see the world?"

"No. I'm telling you that maybe she was meant for Conrad all along and didn't ever know it until he came back the other night."

Caleb shot to his feet. "Have you lost your mind, Sarah? Melly made her choice of her own free will."

She sat and looked at him, never letting her gaze waver.

"What are you trying to tell me, Sarah Franks?"

"I'm not trying to tell you anything, Caleb Wells. I'm just waiting to see what happens when you decide to listen to your heart."

Caleb looked at her as if he'd never seen her before.

Evidently Sarah had never taken charge in a situation before. Not one that put her at cross-purposes with Caleb, at any rate. When he finished pacing and sat down with her again, she started on the cut above his left eye.

Looking at her with a frowning intensity, he told her, "You have your hair down. I've never seen you with your hair down before."

Sara seized the opportunity. Caleb had at last noticed Sarah. She lowered Sarah's long lashes, swept them up again, and gave him the full battery of Sarah's lovely blue eyes. Making her voice intimate, she asked, "Do you like it?"

Caleb sat as still as if he'd been turned to stone. "Ahhhh. Ummmm. Yes. I had no idea you had such pretty hair. It's—ah—long."

"Yes." She was careful to speak modestly. "It is, isn't it?"

Caleb stared out over the river for a long while. Finally he said, "What am I to do, Sarah?"

The temptation to tell him was so strong that Sara had to make a mighty effort not to. "I don't know what you should do, Caleb. But I'm here for you if talking it through with me might help."

He looked hard at her again, a slight frown between his brows. "You're different, Sarah. You've changed."

"Not really. You've just never really noticed me before."

He flushed at the truth in her words. "You *are* awfully quiet."

"Is that supposed to be some sort of excuse?"

That flustered him. "No." Then more strongly, "No, I don't think I need an excuse. You've just always been so—so quiet."

Sara put some of the warmth she'd found in the absent Sarah's diary into her reply. "No, Caleb. I assure you that underneath, I'm not quiet." She laughed, then almost laughed again to see the startled interest with which Caleb reacted to the change her laughter brought to Sarah's face.

After a moment he said, "I think I know what to do, Sarah." He sighed. "I think I have to let Melly go."

"Are you certain?"

He took a deep, shuddering breath. "Yes." Pain showed in his face. "It's Conrad she loves."

"She didn't realize it, you know."

"Yes, I know."

"When will you tell her?"

"Tonight. I can't leave it any longer."

"No." She smiled at him, fighting back the joyous elation she could feel emanating from Sarah. "You're a good man, Caleb."

"I don't feel very much like a good man. I feel like a jackass. I should have seen that Melly wasn't a farmer's wife."

"She's such a lovely girl. Any man would want her."

"Yes, but a man ought to have some sense about his choices." He grinned a little. "Especially such a sensible man."

"Yes."

He offered her his arm. "I'll walk you up to your Aunt Dora's."

Sara stood and took his arm. Their discussion was at an end. "Thank you, Caleb."

SEVEN

Good Hope had resettled itself after all the excitement. Melly had jilted Caleb and run off with Conrad Wells. The town was abuzz with the story of how she'd gone leaping out over the water—water the whole town knew she feared—to land safely in Conrad's arms. And how Mr. Prine had tossed Melly her carpetbag and the Friendship Quilt her bridesmaids had put together for her. It had been a three-day wonder. Then the talk had turned once again to crops and weather.

Sara, afraid that her "family" might discover that she was not really Sarah Franks, and anxious to do whatever she had to do to get back to her own time, went to her "father." "Pa, I'd like to go stay a few days with Aunt Dora." She used the speech patterns she'd learned since being catapulted a century and a half back in time. "Seems to me like she might be missing Melly pretty badly by now. Would it be all right with you?"

"That's a mighty thoughtful thing to do, daughter." He reached out and smoothed her hair wistfully, and Sara knew that deep, deep down he was somehow aware that this was only his daughter's shell, and he was mourning her. "I'll have Enoch drive you into town."

"Thank you, Father." Sara would miss this quiet man. She'd had more concerned attention from him in the few days she'd been in his time than she'd had from her real father all the days of her life. She'd be glad when her leaving could restore his real daughter to him. Impulsively she gave him a big hug and darted off before he recovered from the surprise of it.

She gathered a few things to use while she was in town, and went to tell her "brothers" good-bye.

"Why, Sarah." Walter hugged her gently. "Ain't no need for crying. You'll be back in a couple of days."

Enoch grinned at her. "Yah. And maybe you'll be good enough to remember how to cook again while you're at Aunt Dora's?"

She smiled through her tears. Big, loving dears. Knowing them had been another pleasure for which she owed Sarah Franks her best. She had no intention of ever coming back from "Aunt Dora's." She was determined to stay until she'd won Caleb Wells for their sister. By hook or by crook, she was going to get the job done and get back to her own life . . . and to Josh. She smiled and told Enoch, "You know, I just bet I will."

Hans shook her gently by the shoulder. "Hallelujah!"

❧

Sara stored up memories of the farm and the road into town to serve as background for the memories she would carry the rest of her life of the people in Sarah's time. She was going to win Caleb Wells for Sarah, she knew. She refused to consider defeat. She wished with all her heart she knew *how* she was going to accomplish it, though.

"Thanks, Enoch." She jumped down from the wagon in a flurry

of skirts. Too late to learn the proper way to get down off one of these things now. She didn't intend to be around long enough to ever get up into another wagon. "Take care . . ." Hastily she added, "Of yourself."

His regard became serious. "You take care of yourself." Was there a slight hesitation—or did she merely imagine it? "Sister."

She stood in the dust of the street and watched him drive off. She'd miss him, she realized with a pang. She'd miss them all. Resolutely she tightened her grip on her bundle and turned to go tell Aunt Dora she'd come to stay.

When Caleb walked her through the park on the way home from Wednesday night prayer meeting, Sara knew her work had begun in earnest.

"I got a letter from Melly today, Caleb."

She felt him stiffen, but went on. "It had a piece of bad news in it." She rushed on before he could get any wrong ideas. "She was married to Conrad just fine."

"Unnh." The tone of the single utterance was more expressive than a paragraph would have been.

"The bad news is that the chest that contained her lovely quilt that we all worked so hard on fell into the river as it was being transferred from the *J. B. Cates* to the ship that was to take them to Boston. By the time Conrad got a boat and rowed after it, some boy had fished it out, they think."

"Is the quilt all right?"

"It's lost. The boy told Conrad that he'd seen the chest sink in midstream. Short of calling him a liar and searching his skiff, there wasn't a thing he could do."

Caleb pulled her closer to him as the path narrowed and they passed through a group of bushes that intruded into it.

Sara, mindful of her project, stayed that close, even when the path widened again. She half turned toward him and marveled anew at how different it was to be tall and to be able to look a man in the face without getting a crick in her neck.

"Are you feeling better about things, Caleb?"

"Yes. I know I did the right thing." He kicked at a rock in the path.

Sara debated whether to say it, and did. "Melly wasn't the girl for you, Caleb."

"And I suppose you know who is?"

"You sound like . . ." She shifted away from saying "a child" and said, "Us when we were little."

He stopped and looked directly at her in the light from the boardinghouse windows. "Do I, Sarah?" He walked her up the steps. "Yes. I guess I am acting like a child." Suddenly a grin flashed across his face. "Been as mad because Conrad won as I've been sad to lose Melly."

Sara smiled to see the insight in his remark. It didn't seem like a good idea to tell him she was proud of him for noticing his feelings, but she couldn't help herself. Impulsively, she leaned over and kissed him on the cheek. "Sounds to me like you've done a lot of growing up in these last few days, Caleb Wells."

Caleb stared at her oddly for a long moment. Then he blurted out, "Sarah, will you go to the Williams's barn dance with me on Saturday night?"

Sara smiled radiantly. "Oh, yes, Caleb."

Caleb stared even harder. Funny, he'd never noticed how pretty Sarah was. And she was somehow so—he searched for the right word—comforting. He touched the spot on his cheek where she had kissed him. Sarah was a real beauty when she smiled so big and free like that.

"I'd love to go to the barn dance with you."

Caleb felt lighter all of a sudden. It was like he felt the weight of the world drop off him. He didn't understand why, but it sure felt real pleasant. "Good."

He started across to the steps. Abruptly he turned back. "Sarah."

"Yes, Caleb?"

"I'm not sorry the quilt was lost." There was no trace of bitterness in him as he told her, "That quilt was made for Melly and me." He peered at her, willing her to understand what he was trying to say. Just to be extra-certain, he said it real slow. "And Melly and me are done."

With that, he plunged down the few steps of the boardinghouse porch and disappeared into the night.

Sara stood thinking for a long moment, weighing the elation she felt, making sure it was based in reality. Then, as she reached for the door to let herself in to her "aunt's" brightly lighted parlor, she told Sarah, "I think we finally have a chance."

A delighted, tingling awareness was her only reply.

EIGHT

The night of the barn dance was clear and star-bright. Aunt Dora fluttered around while Sara dressed with excessive care. Taking the brush from her "niece's" hand, she brushed Sarah's shining blond hair until it glittered silver in the lamplight.

"I need more color in my cheeks, Aunt Dora."

"Here, dear." Aunt Dora reached into her apron pocket and brought out a square of red cloth.

Wishing for her own cosmetics and their brushes, Sara made do with the small square of red fabric from Aunt Dora. A piece of red-dyed cloth to rub on her cheeks and lips was nothing compared with what she could get from the cosmetic counters of the big department stores of her time.

Oh, well, she'd just have to make up in vivacity what she lacked in paint. She'd had pretty good luck with that system around town since she'd arrived to stay with her aunt. With Sarah's wonderful hair hanging in a silver-gold cloud down her back and the fun of being tall enough to look everyone in the eye, she certainly *felt* vivacious.

"Mercy, Sarah, honey," Aunt Dora told her when the girl came to the parlor. "I do believe you've positively bloomed since that old cow kicked you."

Her bright brown eyes were curious, urging Sara to tell her why and how she'd suddenly become the belle of Good Hope. She obviously approved.

Sara stepped out on faith, praying Sarah Franks would know to keep up the illusion when they swapped back. "I guess it was coming so close to getting killed, Aunt Dora. When I woke up safe in my bed out at the farm, I knew that I couldn't just sit still and let life pass me by anymore."

Aunt Dora patted her on the cheek, her eyes a little sad, as if she was sorry to be letting her own life, and Mr. Prine, pass her by. "Well, honey, you just keep right on enjoying being alive. Seems to me like it's doing this whole town a heap of good." Her eyes twinkled. "Especially one poor old jilted bachelor."

Sara grinned. She guessed she should have blushed at the insinuation, but she wasn't really Sarah, and she was rather proud of what she was achieving for the absent girl. "Thank you, Aunt Dora." She gave the startled woman a quick peck on the cheek. She'd miss her, too, when she went back. She'd even miss her lemonade.

Caleb arrived just then. He was driving the buggy from his livery stable, and was all spruced up in his Sunday best. There was no sadness left in his eyes when he smiled at Sara.

She was glad she'd taken such pains to dress Sarah. There was a light in Caleb's eyes that boded well for her project, true, but there was something a lot more important here than her project. There were two lives involved, and she must be careful that she do nothing to disturb this thing that was happening to Caleb.

"You look real pretty, Sarah."

"Thank you."

"It's funny I didn't know before how pretty you are." His brow was furrowed as he said it.

"I told you, Caleb—you never ever really looked at me."

"I remember," he said with a grin. "It was because you were always so quiet."

Sara pretended to scowl at him, then chuckled. Caleb was noticing Sarah. That was what she'd been sent here to do, to get Caleb to zero in on Sarah Franks. Surely it wasn't going to be long before she could go home.

Caleb was having trouble remembering how it was he could have ignored Sarah so all his life. He shook his head, wondering at his own lack of perception.

Sara turned suddenly as she was going out the door and gave her "Aunt Dora" a fierce hug. She had the feeling that she was never going to see her again.

"Mercy, child, what was that all about?" Dora laughed and waved them on their way.

Caleb promised to get Sarah back at a reasonable hour, and turned to go. Taking Sara carefully by the arm, he led her tenderly across the porch and down the steps to assist her carefully into the buggy. Finally, he slapped the driving reins lightly on the horse's back, and they were on their way.

❧

"Sarah." Caleb gave the horse its head on the way home and turned to look directly at the smiling girl beside him. "I could hardly get near you at the Williams's." No way around it, he was feeling just plain disgruntled. "You should have saved me more dances. After all, I took you."

Sara couldn't resist. "I didn't think you'd mind if I danced with the other men who asked me. I thought you might like the time to talk to the preacher . . . like you did at the picnic." She toyed with Sarah's long blond hair and hummed a snatch of a song they'd heard at the dance.

"No, I . . ." He scowled, trying to find the right words to express what he wanted to say. "I just think you ought to have stayed with me more than you did."

"I don't belong to you, you know." She said it very softly, not knowing whether she did it to tell him he was being a tad too possessive for an uncommitted man, or whether she was trying to jog him into making some sort of proposal to Sarah Franks. She only knew that she was trying to make something happen.

With all her heart, she wanted things to come to a head. More than anything, she longed to go back to Josh. She knew now that she was no longer afraid to make a commitment to him.

She was burning to get back. Not to her job, not to her ambition and her dreams, but to the man who was more important to her than all of them.

Sarah Franks had taught her that, she realized with a start. Sarah had never been afraid of the passions she felt for the man she loved. Sarah had put her man's happiness ahead of everything, even the love she had for him. All her dreams, all her ambitions had been aimed toward being his wife, and she'd never doubted nor feared for a single instant. Win or lose.

Now, neither would she. She'd discovered her "other reason" for being here.

Yes, she wanted her career. Yes, she wanted to be the best curator the Museum of Americana had ever seen, but she had learned something tremendously important from Sarah Franks. She'd learned to be unafraid, to put first things first.

And people were the first things in life.

All the material possessions in existence, all the positions, all the power and all the praise were nothing if you didn't get them in the proper order, didn't keep them in their proper place.

Josh was the first thing in her life. The most important. The top of her list. She saw that with perfect clarity now. And more than anything she wanted to get back to him to tell him so. She wanted him to know she'd never again hold anything back. She and everything about her were his. Totally, unreservedly his.

And if she didn't get knocked on the head so that she could go home to him soon, she was going to dive onto a rock!

Sara was so frantic with her thoughts of Josh, with aching to get back to him, that when Caleb said wonderingly, "Sarah, I think I love you. Will you marry me?" she launched herself into his arms and cried out, "Sarah loves you, too, Caleb Wells!"

With that, she kissed him with all the pent-up frustration she'd have used on her Josh if she could just have gotten her hands on him. And suddenly she *did* have her hands on him. With her spinning mind filled with the echo of Sarah Franks's voice crying, "Thank you, Sara Blake! Oh, thank you," and without even the smallest bump on her head, she'd made the leap.

The transition from 1843 to 1996 was so smooth she couldn't even feel a break in her kiss. She only knew that one minute she was kissing Caleb Wells for Sarah Franks, and the next instant the lips on her own were those of Josh Conrad.

Arms locked around his neck, she arched up out of the narrow hospital bed to glue herself to him.

His response was gratifyingly enthusiastic.

"Oh, Josh. I'm so glad to be back."

At the same time, Josh was saying, "Sara. Oh, thank God, Sara, you're awake. You're all right. Thank God."

She felt dampness on her cheeks and didn't know for a moment whether they were his tears or her own. She pulled free and sat back looking at him, devouring him with her eyes.

Holding his dear face in her hands, she looked and looked as if she would never get enough of the sight of him. "Oh, Josh. I love you so." She took a deep breath, and the words spilled out of her. "I have so much to tell you. I've met so many wonderful people. People who know what's really important in life."

She felt her love for him shining in her face, and was glad. The time was long gone—one hundred and fifty-three years and a fraction more gone—to hide any part of what she felt for him.

She could give it all now. She was no longer afraid. Reading Sarah Franks's diaries, learning of her courage, had taught her that fear had no place in loving. No place at all. She was ready now to entrust Josh with all that she felt, all that she was, just as Sarah had entrusted Caleb.

"Sara honey, oh, honey." Unashamed, Josh swiped his tears away and gathered her into his arms, rocking with her. "Take it easy, darling. You've been in a coma a long time. You have to take it easy."

"No. No I don't. I don't need to rest—I've just come from a lovely, restful place. I need to tell you all that's happened. I need to tell you so you'll understand. So you'll know that I can love you now. Really love you. With nothing held back."

She looked at him from under her brows and told him earnestly, "Sarah Franks wasn't afraid. She might have despaired, but she was never afraid. And I don't have to be either."

Josh sat there grinning at her, his heart full of relief and gratitude . . . and utter confusion. "Of course not. Of course you don't have to be afraid."

"I was at first. I was scared to death when I first got to Good Hope."

"Good Hope?" Josh brushed a hand across his forehead. A decidedly puzzled expression appeared on his face.

"Yes. When I woke up to find myself in a strange bed in another girl's body and in 1843 . . . well, you can surely imagine how frightened I was. I—"

Two nurses erupted into the room, followed by the best doctor Josh Conrad's money could buy. Rushing to Sara's bedside, they began an examination of their hitherto comatose patient that precluded conversation.

"Josh. I have to tell you."

"Please, Miss Blake." The doctor indicated his stethoscope, irritation plain in his voice.

Sara tried to see over the heads of the medical personnel. "Oh, drat. I'm too short again." She could have seen over them if she'd still had the statuesque Sarah's lovely height.

"Be patient, darling." Josh did his best to help the doctor. "Stay calm. You have the rest of our lives to tell me."

His words acted like a sedative. Calm descended on her, and she finally, and with as much patience as she could manage, let the doctor tell her and Josh what she already knew perfectly well. She was fine. She'd come out of her coma without any ill effects and she was fine.

"Thank you." She glared at the doctor through the hank of her tousled honey-blond hair that had fallen on her forehead. The man had sounded almost disappointed that she didn't have anything wrong with her.

When he patted her lightly on the head and told her she could go home in the morning, she wanted to bite his hand. She'd spent glorious days in the body of a willowy blond earth goddess, and here she was back to being treated like a pet.

Josh laughed at her truculent expression and came to sit on the edge of her bed. "It's all right, my little love. They're all gone."

Sara leaned her head on his shoulder. "I know." She sighed, then startled her true love by declaring plaintively, "But it was so wonderful to be tall, if only for a little while."

NINE

The wedding, one of the outstanding social events of the year, had been thoroughly planned and everything was all set to go. Sara's father had pulled out all the stops. "Nobody is going to say that I didn't give my little girl the finest wedding of the year."

Her mother had immediately signed herself in at the Betty Ford Clinic. She'd told Sara, "Now that there's finally a chance I might someday be a grandmother, I really must see to it that I become a better example, dear. I'm sure they'll let me come out for the ceremony."

The whole of society was abuzz. People thought it a bit odd that the couple planned to honeymoon in Good Hope, Missouri, but, except for several very beautiful and once-hopeful women with a tendency to be bitter about Josh Conrad's upcoming nuptials, everyone was too fond of the bride to comment on it.

Josh Conrad was happily delegating authority to his department heads so that he could spend more time with the petite dynamo who was soon to be his wife. He had found a fly in the ointment of his content, however. Never one to let such things fester, he picked up the nearest phone and dialed Sara. "How about taking an afternoon off?"

"Hmmmm. I'd love to, if I'm to spend it with you."

"Good. Pick you up in half an hour."

Sara settled beside him in the Porsche. For just one nostalgic moment she wished it had been the Mercedes Gull Wing. It seemed to her somehow that all of this had started in the Gull Wing.

As if he'd read her mind, Josh said, "This one's easier to park."

Sara laughed, delighted. She loved the way they seemed so often to be on the same wavelength. She put her hand over his on the knob of the gearshift and sat, just letting the strength of their love flow back and forth between them.

Josh headed for the section of San Francisco they most enjoyed wandering in. "I thought you might like an afternoon of raiding the junk shops."

"They're not junk shops," she corrected him as she always did. "They're antique shops. And they're crowded with treasures just waiting to be discovered."

Josh grinned over at her. "I thought maybe you'd like to find something to commemorate the big event."

Sara nodded thoughtfully.

Josh frowned. The dusty antique shops never failed to interest them both, but until today, Sara had always been the one who looked forward to them more eagerly.

Over the past few days, though, she'd seemed almost listless. He was desperately concerned about it. "Honey? You aren't getting cold feet, are you?"

She looked up at him, startled. His profile had something a little grim about it, and Sara realized that her preoccupation with her own thoughts was talking a toll on Josh. How could she have been so selfish?

"Oh no, darling." She turned in her seat so that she was facing him. "I love you more than anything in the world, Josh. I want more than anything to be your wife."

Josh began to relax. Pride at her declaration began to swell in him.

For every balloon there's a pinprick.

"It's just that . . ."

Josh's half-inflated balloon of masculine pride deflated completely. "Just what?"

"It's just that I keep wondering what happened to Sarah Franks."

"You're the one who wanted to wait until we got to Missouri to check the hall of records," he reminded her. "You're the one who wanted to see the marriage lines with your own two eyes."

"Yes." She sighed. "I know." She made a helpless little gesture with her hands. "But just the fact that they married won't tell me whether or not they were happy."

"Look." Josh flailed his mind for a happy solution as he dived the nose of the Porsche into a parking space the car that had been occupying it was only half out of. "I'll . . . I'll hire a genealogist. He can find some of their descendants, and we'll go visit them and ask them if Sarah and Caleb were happy."

Josh wasn't even sure there were a Sarah and Caleb. He wasn't sure that the fantastic story Sara had told him—about being back in Good Hope, Missouri, in the body of a girl named Sarah Franks the whole time she'd been in a coma—was true. He just knew that he loved Sara Blake more than he'd ever thought himself capable of loving anyone, and that if *she* thought it were true, he was at least going to *pretend* to believe it—with every fiber of his being.

Sara cupped his face with her hands and looked deeply into

his eyes. "You are so very dear, Josh." Her voice trembled with the intensity of her feelings. "Thank you for loving me."

He leaned over and kissed her, humbled to know how much his love meant to her. His love. Not his looks, nor his influence, nor his wealth. His love.

Gratitude for having found and won Sara Blake flooded him. He sent up a small prayer that today they'd find something to bring her smile back again. She'd been so quiet lately, he'd been worried that maybe she felt she was making a mistake.

Now that he'd been reassured on that point, he wanted her to find something really special in one of the shops to commemorate what he knew was going to prove to be the most important day of his life. He'd attempt to buy her the moon, if that was what she wanted.

He untangled his six-foot-two frame from the car and walked around to Sara's door. When she came up out of the low sports car, he swept her into his arms and crushed her for an instant before letting her go. "I love you, Sara."

"I love you too, Josh. With all my heart."

But she didn't smile, and he missed the joyous sparkle that usually lit her eyes. Even though his relief and joy that he wasn't the cause of Sara's gloom were boundless, he still wasn't pleased.

He was beginning to feel a little resentful. He resented the pall Sarah Franks and Caleb Wells were casting on the most important event of his life.

By the time they entered the third antique-cum-junk shop, Josh was getting a little grim. Sara seemed almost gloomy, and he was deeply troubled.

Sara looked sideways at him, and saw the way his jaw was set. She wished she could make him smile again.

It was her fault that he was upset, she knew, but she couldn't seem to help it. No matter how hard she tried, she couldn't stop worrying about whether or not Sarah and Caleb had married, and whether or not they had been happy.

She wished she could, because she didn't relish walking up the aisle under her own personal little cloud, but until they located someone who could tell her how things had turned out, she knew she wouldn't be content.

In her mind she cried out, *"Oh, Sarah, I wish you could tell me how everything turned out for you. Wondering so hard is taking the gloss off my wedding day."*

Suddenly she felt, as if in answer to her plea, the almost-forgotten tingle. Sara gasped, then stood statue-still as it strengthened.

"Sara. Honey. Are you all right?" Josh loomed over her protectively, his voice full of concern.

The tingle grew stronger, electrifying her. Sara turned toward its source, zeroing in on it. The humming in her ears kept her from hearing him when Josh growled, "Sara, dammit, what is it?"

Suddenly the whole shop became vague and dim. The humming in her ears strengthened to a dull roar. Anticipation zinged through her.

Everything around Sara paled and blended mistily into a fog. Only one thing stood out sharply—a tiny Victorian table with a little stack of small leather cases on it.

Sara went to it as if she were a sliver of iron and the table a lodestone. She stood looking down at the lovely cases. They looked almost like slim volumes of poetry, leatherbound.

One of the cases stood out from all the rest. To Sara's eyes, that one seemed to glow with an inner light all its own.

The embossed leather was slightly worn on the corners, the edges a little fuzzed by the passage of time, but the pattern was still clearly raised on the flat surfaces, and the brass hinges and latch seemed to glitter and shine. Sara knew that they really didn't, of course. They were as old and time-tarnished as the brass on all the rest of the cases in the stack. It was a signal to her that existed only in her mind, she knew.

Her hand reached for that one daguerreotype unerringly.

Josh was right behind her as she lifted the clasp with trembling fingers. Poised to open the case, she leaned back into Josh's embrace and touched her cheek to his shirtfront. As his arms tightened around her, she opened the case to see the picture inside.

Faded to shades of silver, it was the picture of a man, his wife, and five children. One, a baby, was in the arms of the tall, smiling woman. The man was smiling, too, and there was a grin on the face of every child. Even the baby seemed to be smiling.

Sara began to weep gently. Josh crushed her in his embrace.

"Oh, Josh. It's her. It's Sarah. And Caleb. And they look so happy." She raised her face to him, her eyes swimming with joyous tears. "It's all right. They were happy."

Josh held her tighter.

Sara snuggled closer. "Oh, Josh. I can't tell you what a weight this takes off my heart. I couldn't bear not knowing what had become of them, when I was so happy." She blinked away her tears. "Will you buy it for me?"

"What do you think?"

Sara clasped the daguerreotype to her bosom and smiled radiantly up at him. She was herself again. Relief and joy surged through him.

"Well, please hurry and do it, darling," Sara told him briskly. "I have to get back. I have a zillion things to get done. I'm getting married tomorrow, you know."